FRACAS IN THE FOOTHILLS

ELLIOT PAUL

FRACAS IN THE FOOTHILLS

Elliot Paul

COACHWHIP PUBLICATIONS

Greenville, Ohio

Fracas in the Foothills, by Elliot Paul
© 2015 Coachwhip Publications

First published 1940.
Elliot Paul (1891-1958)
No claims made on public domain material.

Front cover: Background © Flypaper Textures; Bull skull
      © Stef Hill

CoachwhipBooks.com

ISBN 1-61646-296-5
ISBN-13 978-1-61646-296-3

CONTENTS

Part Three: The Sheep and Cattle War

Part One

The Broadening Influences of Travel

1

In Which a Redman Takes a Reasonable Precaution

THE LAST DAYS OF FEBRUARY are comparatively dreary in Montparnasse. The café *terrasses* are still enclosed with glass and heated by gleaming braziers. Rug peddlers are hidden in the Arab quarter, whiling away the days by smoking, playing cards or poring over the Koran. The plane trees are stripped of leaves, a few of which, yellowed and damp, lie in the gutters. Only the most faithful of the taxis linger in front of the Dôme, the Rotonde, the Select or the Coupole in the hope of finding stray customers. To the resident of the quarter, however, the famous intersection of the boulevards Montparnasse and Raspail is never without allure. The neighborhood restaurants, when the chefs are not pressed by the rush of tourist traffic, offer excellent fare. The wines are fragrant and wonderful in any season. And those hardy Montparnassians who can brave the Paris winter rains are likely to have an inner life strong and rich enough to carry them over from one gay period to another.

Homer Evans had just returned from his annual pilgrimage to Morocco, where he delighted in spending long semi-tropical nights in a certain café near Xauen, listening to an Arab orchestra and a native singer trace endless variations on the haunting old melodies of the African sands. He was tanned, somewhat thinner than when he had departed from Paris, but his philosophic calm, always remarkable, seemed to have been intensified by his sojourn among the enigmatic desert folk whose language he spoke fluently and whose manner of thought he seemed so well to understand. At

four o'clock in the afternoon, well before twilight, he made his way
softly from his apartment in the *rue* Campagne Premiére to the
Café du Dôme where, after weeks of separation, he was to meet
Miriam Leonard for the afternoon *apéritif*. Later he planned to
take her to the Hôtel des Hirondelles, where, unknown to the Paris
police, a famous Arabian *danseuse*, who had crossed from Ceuta
on the boat with him, was to perform that evening in a secret chamber the dance known as *D'la dits* which not many non-Mohammed-
ans have been privileged to witness and which, once seen, is said
to exert a mellowing influence on the beholder which lingers until
after the sixth succeeding feast of *Raspa'zaz*. That was the way
Evans liked to greet Miriam after a prolonged absence, to take her
into strange surroundings from which they could emerge but
gradually and, in the process, could renew their acquaintance in
some fundamental way.

On arriving at the Dôme, Evans noticed that his watch had
stopped. No doubt he had neglected to wind it while on the desert,
where he preferred to tell time by the stars. Consequently he had
half an hour to spare before Miriam would put in an appearance.
On the table in his hallway he had left unopened an accumulated
stack of mail and the daily newspapers he had missed, and he had
asked his bewildered landlady not to give him the list of urgent
telephone calls she had noted down. He wanted time to adjust himself to Europe again, for he had been oppressed, of late, with the
feeling that an ominous change was stealing over the continent,
that the tranquil years which had followed the World War were
drawing to a close. Several months had passed since he had been
called upon to solve the notorious tarantula murders and in the
course of that time he had remained adamant to all appeals, both
public and private, designed to draw him out of his solitude and
interrupt his studies and leisurely contemplation.

His favorite waiter greeted him tactfully but cordially as he took
his place, just left of the center and far enough from the brazier so
as not to be bothered by its fumes. The waiter knew that when
Monsieur Evans entered the *terrasse* with that faraway look in his
eyes, and reached for the chair as if he were in the dark, it was

better not to engage him in conversation. There were a few regular clients in their places, reading the afternoon papers, and a few passers by on the damp sidewalks. After the glare of the African sunshine, the dim light of Montparnasse in February seemed unreal. So did the damp pedestrians, grotesquely attired in dismal colors and huddling into coats and wraps for protection against the chill air. How awkward and uneasy, compared with the robed and sandaled Arabs! In what jerky rhythms Europeans scurried along.

One man, however, arrested Evans' full attention, in spite of the detached state of his mind. The newcomer was tall and rangy, and was wearing a buckskin coat and colored muffler. As he approached, before Homer could make out his features or his straight jet-black hair, the stranger's walk, a natural easy stride, set him far apart from his metropolitan surroundings. He was surely alien to Paris. Furthermore, he was in no way a peasant. His bearing was proud and aristocratic, his manner suggestive of latent self-reliance and power.

"An American Indian, by Jove," said Homer, his curiosity aroused. "And unless I am mistaken, he has lost his way."

The Indian, indeed, seemed to be doubtful about his bearings. Not that he appeared anxious or undignified, but obviously he was looking for somebody or something. At the famous intersection of the boulevards, he stood erect and motionless, looking first to the north, then east, south and west. He saw the glow of the brazier and noticed that several men were sitting around it, then unhurriedly he made his way across the *terrasse*. He presented a fine figure standing there by the curb at the entrance to the Dôme, with his pantherlike poise, his swarthy out-of-door complexion, his sharp, distinguished profile and piercing dark eyes.

"A native of the plains," said Homer to himself. "And surely not from one of the Southern tribes. He's too tall, and the colors on his scarf are Algonquian. Probably of the Piegans, or some related nation. A fine upstanding tribe."

The reader will recall that Evans, soon after he was graduated from the University, did considerable research work in the Western States of America on behalf of the little-known Society for the

Preservation of Indian Culture, and in the course of those studies, which resulted brilliantly although Homer insisted on remaining anonymous, he had picked up a fair working knowledge of several of the Indian tongues.

As the redskin came nearer, Evans noticed that his moccasins were dyed a dull black.

"Ah, that settles it," Homer said. "The rare color distilled from meadowsweet, and one of the few that is permanent on elkskin. Our friend is of the Blackfeet, and no mistake. And the son of a chief, to boot."

The object of Homer's tactful scrutiny entered the *terrasse*, fished out a phrase book and tried to make an inquiry of a waiter. The latter shook his head regretfully.

"I speak only French, worse luck," the waiter said.

Evans rose courteously. "*Kit kse mat taim mo!*" (I greet you), he said in the Algonquian tongue.

The Indian faced him gravely, but his dark eyes glowed with pleased surprise. "*Nit okh si tuk ki*" (I am pleased), he replied.

"Will you join me for a smoke?" asked Homer. "Perhaps I can be of service. I have hunted hereabouts many seasons."

"*Eeeeeee*" (Thank you), said the Indian, and extended his hand. "I am Rain-No-More, of the Blackfeet," he said simply. "And if you are acquainted in this city you can help me, indeed. This is my first journey across the great blue water."

"First let us smoke and collect our thoughts," Evans said. "You will think it strange, but I have heard much about you. However, let us not be hurried, like fretful squaws. Be seated, I beg of you."

As the Indian sat down and Homer followed, the waiter arrived with Homer's drink of rum. For a moment, Evans was nonplussed. He knew what effect firewater was likely to have on Indians, and still he did not want to appear inhospitable. As if Rain-No-More had read Homer's thoughts, the redman smiled.

"Do not be afraid," he said in perfect English. "I spent two years in a white man's college just to learn to drink. My father, Shot-on-Both-Sides, a wise chief, explained to me how much our people had lost because of inability to cope with white man's liquor. So he sent me all the way to Berkeley, California, commanding me not to return to the tribe until I could outdrink any student in my class. At first the task was hard. I passed much time in jail, and my father was obliged to spend several of his bank accounts to pay for property and domestic animals I destroyed. However, after two years, I put to bed, single-handed, the assistant professor of English, the college drinking champion, after a bout that lasted about a quarter of a moon, and then I felt justified in quitting the University and rejoining my father, who had need of me."

Evans smiled his most winning smile and said to the waiter: "Another large rum." To Rain-No-More, he added: "We shall be friends. *Nit okh si tuk ki*" (That's fine).

For answer, Rain-No-More reached into the pocket of his buckskin jacket, drew forth a pipe marked with tribal decorations, filled it with tobacco, lighted it and handed it to Homer.

"*O tsis e*" (Smoke), he said.

"*Eeeeeee*" (Many thanks), said Homer, and accepted the token.

As they sat on the *terrasse* side by side, a fine rain, almost a drizzle, began to fall, clouding the glass partitions. The two men sipped their rum contentedly for perhaps five minutes; then the Indian was first to speak.

"You said, friend Evans, that you had heard of me? Were you in earnest, or in kindness trying to put me at ease in a strange country?" asked Rain-No-More.

"A mutual friend has often mentioned good hunting with you on the lower stretches of the Yellowstone," Evans answered. "But first, tell me what I can do for you here. I had the impression that you were looking for someone. Perhaps I was wrong."

"I am, indeed," Rain-No-More said. "I made the journey all across America and the ocean, which proved to be much vaster than I had imagined, in order to communicate with the daughter of an old trusted friend, a Miss Miriam Leonard. . . ."

"But she is the mutual acquaintance I just mentioned. How fortunate," Evans said. "In fact, she will be here within ten minutes."

"Ah," sighed the Indian, with relief. "Then we can drink until she comes." With that he beckoned the waiter and, in graphic sign language which was readily understood, ordered a couple more glasses of rum. There ensued a few more minutes of contented silence, during which they watched the passers-by and puffed the tribal pipe in turn. Then Rain-No-More said:

"Friend Evans, I see that your words, however surprising, may be fully relied upon. You'll forgive me for a moment of doubt, but I have been so bewildered at times by white men's palaver that when you told me the girl I had traveled five thousand miles to see would appear, in this lodge, without delay, I could not give your assurance full credence. While I have been passing through huge cities and traversing water days on end, the chances have seemed so remote that I should accomplish the errand my father entrusted to me, that your words sounded too much like empty medicine. Now I know better," the Indian said. For his sharp eyes had caught sight of Miriam, far down the boulevard Montparnasse, a good two blocks before Homer, whose eyesight was far better than the average, had been able to recognize her.

The meeting between the childhood playmates was moving, indeed, and somewhat startling to the clients of the Dôme. As Miriam was about to enter the *terrasse*, both Homer and Rain-No-More rose in their places. Miriam paused, she dropped her handbag as her hands flew upward in a gesture of astonishment, her dark blue eyes seemed to grow larger.

"Elk Calf!" she said, and hurried forward, upsetting two chairs and a *café crême*. "Elk Calf! Can I believe my eyes?"

"Bird Cherry," said Rain-No-More, using the nickname he had given her when she was a wild long-legged child in the Montana coulees. "The Chief, my father, sends greetings . . ."

Suddenly Miriam turned white and clasped her hands. "But Dad? My father? Nothing awful has happened?"

The Indian raised his hand with a comforting gesture.

"Your father is robust and well," he said. "At the time of the harvest festival he walked all the way from the ranch to our lodge on the reservation, a matter of eighty-four miles, to be present at the celebration. He is kind enough to remember, on all occasions, that he is an adopted member of our tribe. But he doesn't know I have made this journey. That is why I did not bring you his greetings."

"Homer Evans! However did you find him?" Miriam asked, and blushed deeply, for in the excitement of seeing, unexpectedly, her childhood friend she had let it slip her mind that Evans was just back from Morocco and that she had been looking forward to their reunion many uneventful days.

"Rain-No-More found me. His instinct led him straight to the Dôme," said Homer, smiling. Then he added: "It's good to see you, dear."

The Indian was immediately aware of a slightly awkward situation. "Perhaps I should return tomorrow," he began.

Both Miriam and Homer made haste to reassure him. "On the contrary," Homer said. "I know you have traveled many days to give an important message to Miss Leonard. I'll leave you alone until dinner time; then I shall have a suggestion to make. I remember, when last I was on Poplar River, that some of my acquaintances, members of the Crow Water society, gave me an unforgettable sausage made of the loin meat of elk and white-tailed deer. . . ."

"*Ep tse sin nas yeat*," said Rain-No-More. "How I should like some now! The food on the boat consisted mainly of vegetables and other frivolous provisions. I long for meat."

"Tonight you shall have it, in plenty," Evans said, and, rising, was about to leave the *terrasse*.

Rain-No-More restrained him gently. "I hope you will stay, to hear what I have to say," he said. "Bird Cherry, who perhaps I should learn to call 'Miss Leonard,' will need your counsel, and so shall I."

"I know there's something wrong with Father," Miriam said anxiously. "For a long time I've sensed some kind of disaster. His letters have been strained and unnatural. Please tell me, Rain-No-More. Why did your father send you here?"

"The story is a long one," Rain-No-More began.

"We'll be patient," said Miriam. "Only do let's get started."

"Since you left the valley," said Rain-No-More, "the sheepmen, headed by Larkspur Gilligan, got the Northern Pacific to build a branch line from Glendive to Circle, just north of Mountain Sheep Bluffs. By that means, Gilligan and his crowd are able to ship direct to Minneapolis and Omaha from the Piney Buttes range."

"I'm glad they don't have to drive them up Redwater Creek any more," said Miriam. "The sound of them, days and nights on end, meeeeh . . . meeeeh . . . meeeeh . . . was enough to drive anybody crazy."

Rain-No-More raised his hand for silence. "There have been other results, not so pleasing, of the railroad's enterprise," the Indian said. "Gilligan now is able to get rid of all his sheep at a good profit, and could sell many more if he had them. The range west of Redwater has become too small for him."

"Just let him dare to cross the deadline," said Miriam, her eyes flashing. "My dad would let daylight through the first sheepman who set foot on the east bank of Redwater Creek."

"Gilligan knows that, but he's greedy for more money. Just what he could do with it, I can't understand. He has plenty for himself and his friends, but avarice is the white man's plague. But, to get on with my story, one day in early winter, when the sheep were on the winter range, miles away in Idaho, I rode to Circle to get some tobacco. No one knows me there, so I hung around the store a while, and Gilligan came in with a short dark man from back East. He called him Donniker Louey. . . ."

"Donniker Louey!" repeated Evans in astonishment.

Miriam and the Indian turned to him expectantly.

"Do you know him?" asked Miriam.

"I only know that he's a trigger man for one of the toughest gang leaders in Chicago. Tom Jackson, when he was on the *Tribune*, was nearly bumped off by Louey because he wrote a story Louey's boss didn't like. . . . Now what would Donniker Louey be doing in Circle, Montana?" Evans asked.

"I am sure that was the name," said Rain-No-More. "The man was short and dark, like an Italian, with part of one ear missing. He wore a bright blue suit with an orange necktie and smoked long twisted cigars. I couldn't make out half he said, for he spoke the dialect of the Great Lakes region, but I heard Gilligan mention Redwater Creek, Three Buttes and the cattle range east of the deadline. Several times he spoke your father's name, and once the short Italian said: 'Don't worry, boss. I'll take care of this Leonard guy.'"

In her agitation, Miriam had grasped Evans' hand and was holding it tightly. "Larkspur Gilligan's the biggest crook in Montana," she explained to Homer. "More than once he's tried to poison our cattle, and one year he tried to hire a bunch of Cheyennes to run 'em off the range."

Rain-No-More nodded acquiescence and continued: "I should not have thought the incident in the store at Circle was important if six weeks later I hadn't been riding along Redwater Creek and hadn't seen the Italian named Louey bouncing along on a tame old work horse not far from where Cottonwood Creek flows into the Redwater. Of course, I saw him a mile before he could see me, so I hid my pony in a coulee and watched the man. I thought he was headed for Cottonwood Creek, so I went to the head of the creek bed and waited. You remember the place, Miriam? It's not ten miles from your ranch house at Three Buttes, the Opera Lodge.

"The Italian hitched his old plug to a clump of sage and started off on foot, keeping out of sight. I wasn't many yards behind him. Then I saw your father riding toward us, on the sorrel, Star. You remember the sorrel? You broke her yourself."

"Oh, yes. But Father . . ."

"Well," Rain-No-More said, "your father rode along at a trot, headed for Cottonwood Creek, where the Italian and I were hiding. But you know how your father is. A meadowlark can't hop within range of his eyes without him seeing it. This Italian from the East stuck his head above the sagebrush, where he was stretched out, automatic in hand. Your father saw something move. So he halted and circled around, to find out what it was. Then he took his rifle from behind the saddle and took a pot shot that didn't miss Louey six inches. The Italian hot-footed it down the coulee.

"When I got back to the lodge I told my father, the Chief, what had happened and what I had heard in the store at Circle. That was why he sent me over here to find you. He had heard the sheepmen were looking for trouble and thought you ought to know," Rain-No-More said, and reached for the tribal pipe which Evans had retained while the Indian had been speaking.

Miriam, thoroughly alarmed, was on her feet, clutching at the shoulder of Rain-No-More's buckskin jacket. "But Rain-No-More! How could you be so careless? That gangster will get my father some other time. He'll be more cautious in the future. Oh, Homer! What shall I do?"

The handsome young Indian smiled. "I think Jim Leonard will have no more trouble with that Donniker Louey," he said. "I took precautions." And with that he reached into one of his breast pockets and drew forth a dried scalp which he laid on the table before them.

2
To Part Is to Die a Little, So What the Hell

LESS THAN AN HOUR after the encounter described in the previous chapter, Miriam was sitting on the edge of the bed in her room in the Hotel Vavin, staring disconsolately at the wet window pane. Outside, the single plane tree in the courtyard swayed fretfully in the storm, for the wind had risen and was driving the cold rain obliquely across the world capital of art and letters and was moaning in a way designed to ruffle even the steadiest nerves. Miriam turned her gaze from the plane tree she had learned to love to the harpsichord in the corner, a present from Homer. Involuntarily she began to cry.

From the moment Rain-No-More had told her of her father's danger, there had been no doubt in her mind that she must hasten to his side without delay. In fact, an open suitcase was sprawled in front of her on the floor. But Paris, in the course of the past three years, had introduced its narcotic virus into her blood. She had reveled in its sights and breathed its odors. All its doors, because of Evans, had been open to her, its most intimate secrets divulged. Still, she was aware that Paris, superb as it was, was not the reason for her black despondency. She was cutting herself off from Homer Evans, after their years of rare and intimate companionship. That she had the will power to carry out the maneuver, which had become necessary because of her father's predicament, Miriam did not question. But what would remain of her spirit and her zest for life was a far graver problem, and one she tried to face as the rain beat down. That very evening was to have been a happy time

of reunion, but as matters stood she could not face it. She had
begged to be excused, on the ground that she must pack her trunk
and her valises, and had left Homer to entertain Rain-No-More
and give the Indian a quick view of a kind of life that was strange
and incomprehensible to him. The *Ile-de-France* was sailing at
noon the next day, the boat train would leave the Gare St. Lazare
at eight-fifteen in the morning. Her dismay deepened as she tried
to picture herself on board, with Paris and Evans receding in the
distance, the coast of France sliding slowly away, out of reach, a
page turning relentlessly in the book of her young life. To relieve
her feelings, she began grasping at garments and throwing them
helter-skelter into the suitcase, while tears pattered down, unre-
strained, and spotted the freshly ironed laundry.

"Steady, my girl," she seemed to hear her father say. That carried her thoughts across the miles of sea and land to her home on
the range. Well she remembered the mutterings and threats of the
cattlemen when, eight years before, Larkspur Gilligan, by conniv-
ing with unscrupulous politicians, had caused the country west of
the Redwater to be opened as a summer range for sheep. Gilligan
had received his nickname because it was common talk that he had
planted the deadly larkspur, which kills cattle in the spring, but
ceases to be dangerous before the sheep are brought up to the summer range. The weed had taken hold in the coulees of Redwater
Creek, Coyote Creek and along Big Dry Creek in the shadow of
the Piney Buttes. Once the larkspur had begun to flourish on that
watershed, Gilligan had used the fact as an argument why cattle
should be excluded and the sheepmen permitted to use the range
as a grazing land.

When first the news came through that Gilligan had got what
he wanted from government officials, Jim Leonard had said there
would be bloodshed. Nevertheless he had abided by the law. His
cattle had ranged from Redwater east to the Yellowstone and north
as far as the Missouri, and no clashes had occurred. Now, according to Rain-No-More's story, it was evident that Gilligan intended
to invade the country east of the deadline and drive cattle from
the entire valley of the Lower Yellowstone. That meant war, no less.

Miriam knew her father, his fiery temper as well as his stern control. He had been pushed as far by Gilligan as he would go. He had submitted, out of respect for law and order, to unjust and foolish regulations. If Gilligan persisted, the showdown was at hand. And, it went without saying, she must stand at her father's side and fight.

While Miriam was pursuing her inner conflict and trying to fit recalcitrant articles into the limited space her baggage afforded, the *terrasse* of the Café du Dôme had livened up a bit. Rain-No-More, who had neglected to remove the scalp from the table, had taken an interest in Homer's recital of the history of rum and the picturesque incidents attendant on the trade in the early days of the American Colonies. In the midst of the story, however, Evans had been interrupted by a roar and a slap on the back, the breeze of which caused the brazier to sputter and glow.

"Shiver my timbers," said a hearty voice. Looking up, Evans was overjoyed to see, standing jovially behind him, Hjalmar Jansen, the big Norwegian-American painter who, because of the insistence of several of his female friends, had been obliged to quit the Quarter for a long sea voyage just as the tarantula murder case was coming to a close in the preceding spring.

"Sit down," said Homer cordially. "But first meet my friend Rain-No-More, of the Blackfeet. He has just crossed the ocean, too."

"Glad to meet you, sir," Hjalmar said, and collared a passing waiter. "More rum," he bellowed. "I see you're right, Homer, as usual. Whiskey when the sun shines, rum when it's damp. That's the way to keep your health and strength. By the way, are you boys hungry?"

"I long for meat," said Rain-No-More.

Hjalmar had picked up the scalp of Donniker Louey and was examining it with a chuckle. He had never handled one before. "Say, Chief," he said. "How's chances for this to make me a tobacco pouch?"

"I dislike refusing anything to a friend of Mr. Evans," said Rain-No-More, "but I think I should keep it for a while. The man I was obliged to kill, as Evans knows, was about to shoot from ambush an old friend of my tribe. Under the circumstances, if the body is found, which is possible although unlikely, an enemy will try to pin the murder on my friend. As long as I keep the scalp, I can, if necessary, prove that I am the guilty party."

"Damn sporting of you," said Jansen, glancing at his new acquaintance appreciatively.

Evans, meanwhile, had picked up the scalp and was looking at it through his pocket reading glass. When he had finished his scrutiny he turned to Rain-No-More. "How far back do the records of your tribe go, about scalping, I mean?"

"About three hundred years," said Rain-No-More. "To tell you exactly, I'd have to consult my father. We learned it from the Great Lakes Indians, after we had started riding horses."

"The practice was first introduced in Connecticut," Evans said. "The white men there hired Indians to slaughter white enemies for them. At first the Indians were obliged to cut off the heads and bring them in, in order to collect. Later the scalp was deemed sufficient, and of course was less bulky and more convenient."

"My father will be most interested," said Rain-No-More. "He dotes on history."

The conversation was just about to shift to the subject of restaurants where meat was plentiful when an astonished gasp behind him caused Jansen almost to choke on his rum.

"In the name of Heaven, what is that gruesome object with human hair?" asked a familiar voice, and they all saw Chief of Detectives Frémont, whose gaze was riveted to the scalp on the table.

Evans, always equal to embarrassing situations, introduced Frémont to the Indian and explained that the scalp was a tribal relic from North America and did not mean extra work for the Paris police department.

"I trust it did not belong to a Frenchman," Frémont said, sighing. "In that case . . ."

"It was taken from an Italian," said Evans, "and one who is much better off without it, I assure you."

"Ah, America," Frémont said, and sighed again. "It was about America that I wished to speak with you, my friend. I trust your companions will pardon me."

"*O ko kit e ki sok o*" (I long for meat), murmured Rain-No-More to Homer, who immediately proposed that they all dine together, at the Brasserie Schmitz in the avenue Mott-Piquet, where the food is good and plentiful and the surroundings conducive to comfort and relaxation. Rain-No-More was invited to ride with the Chief of Detectives, since he liked the sound of the siren on the cheese-colored roadster. Evans and Hjalmar followed in a taxi.

"I hope Frémont's got another case with lots of rough stuff," Hjalmar said. "This weather makes a man wish for action."

To his surprise, the big Norwegian noticed that Evans was not listening. He was sitting well back on the cushions, his hands resting lightly on his knees, oblivious to conversation within or the downpour without, completely lost in thought. Hjalmar, who was anxious not to do any heavy thinking, either about the past or the future, until the weather cleared, fidgeted in silence until the ride was over, then touched Homer on the sleeve. "Here we are," he said.

"Oh, quite," said Evans, arousing himself.

After selecting a quiet corner table, Homer went straight to the kitchen, where the chef greeted him enthusiastically. Evans explained that he had as a guest an American redskin who cared little for vegetables, and within five minutes Rain-No-More, Hjalmar, Frémont and Evans had before them a platter about the size of an archery target, piled high with Strasbourg ham, *andouilletes de Vire*, sausages from Lyon, Belfort, Perpignan and Bordeaux, *paté de foie gras* from Nancy with Perigord truffles, smoked sturgeon from the Volga, *sobresada* from the Balearic Isles, *pepperoni* from Genoa, smoked mutton and reindeer meat from Sweden and other tidbits to carry them along until the roast of beef should be *au point*. Whenever a seidel was empty, which was often, the waiter promptly brought another filled with foaming beer.

The clientele of the Brassèrie Schmitz is from the neighborhood, with a sprinkling of non-coms and soldiers from the Ecole Militaire near by, and several taxi drivers who know where to get the most for their money. Tourists seldom, if ever, find the *brassèrie*, but if they do they have plenty, on returning, to tell the folks back home. The rain coursing down the spacious windows did not discourage the customers *chez* Schmitz. In fact, it seemed to spur them on to better efforts, until all the regular waiters and a couple of the patron's nephews were gliding to and fro. Little was attempted in the way of conversation until after the cold cuts, the roast, the turkey and the cheese had been disposed of. Then Evans ordered filtered coffee and a special *marc de Bourgogne* that caused Rain-No-More's stiff black hair to rise and fall quite perceptibly as he took his first swallow. Frémont, usually most abstemious, for once was drinking with abandon.

"Oblivion," he muttered, as he reached for the *marc*.

Evans, who, in spite of his preoccupation, had missed nothing of Frémont's strange behavior, gave him an opening to unburden his mind.

"America," he began.

"Ah, America," said Frémont, rolling his eyes in despair. "Not only is it baffling, in all its manifestations, but I, personally, have been ordered to go there."

"I'm not surprised," Evans said.

Frémont nearly bounced out of his chair. "Not surprised! Not surprised, did you say? Myself, I'm dumbfounded! The prefect of police, undoubtedly the prince of all the fatheads in France, summoned me to his office today. He was gaily dressed, with a flower in his buttonhole. He was smiling so benignly that I knew I was done for. 'Frémont,' he said, in that oily voice of his, 'you have earned a rest. You have conducted your department brilliantly and brought glory to all of us.' I stood there, sweating, and waited for the worst. I did not have long to wait. 'The minister and I have decided,' the prefect went on, to send you to America for a prolonged tour of study, say six months, with a possible extension. You are to take with you, for the good of the service, Sergeants Schlumberger and Bonnet . . .'"

"The situation is quite clear," Evans said. "Your superiors want you out of the way for a while. Not only that, but they want the brightest officers in your department to be absent and distant also.

I have suspected for some time that a scandal of tremendous dimensions was afoot. The Minister of Justice has lost eighteen pounds, and came out sixteenth in the annual national domino tournament he almost invariably wins."

Frémont did not appear to be comforted. "I, too, have suspected there was something in the wind, but, as you know, I've never meddled in politics. I'm a police officer, painstaking and conscientious, that's all. Now I've got to visit all your large cities, New York, Chicago, San Francisco, others I never even heard of, and learn how criminals are stalked abroad. A fine kind of fool I'll make of myself, trotting from police station to police station with my hat in my hand. And Hydrangea! I can't leave her here. Because of her color, I can't let her travel with me in your eccentric land."

"Leave her in Harlem," suggested Hjalmar. "She'll wait for you there."

"That's what I'm most afraid of," Frémont said. "If ever she gets to Harlem again, she'll stay there. . . . I am ruined, that's all. My life has been scrambled like an egg. And all because, in the past three years, I have been given credit for solving the difficult cases Monsieur Evans has unraveled for me." Frémont turned to Homer, his broad honest face eloquent with appeal. "I beg of you, Monsieur, let me go to the prefect and confess I am a dunderhead, let me convince him that my apparently brilliant record is a sham, and entirely due to your talents and modesty. Let him demote me, send me back to pounding the pavements on an ordinary beat. At least I should be patrolling in Paris, and not scuttling from pillar to post in foreign lands, with the woman of my heart cavorting among millions of her dusky race and being estranged from me. My house of cards is collapsing. Unless you will hearken to the voices of reason and friendship, I am undone."

Rain-No-More, who had listened attentively and tried his best to grasp Frémont's problem, extended to the latter the tribal pipe of peace. "This squaw of whom you speak," he said. "Is she really so unruly in your absence? My father, Shot-on-Both-Sides, acquired two such women in a raid on the Shoshones, and, although he grew inordinately fond of them, both eventually escaped and got back to their tribe. There are squaws who take to new environments, and others who are incurably homesick. If you have hit upon one of the latter, best forget her, my friend."

The Chief of Detectives began to sway and moan, then to crunch liqueur glasses. "This is the end," he said. "Exile to be followed by dismissal! The loss of all that's dear to me! Contentment, farewell!"

"What the hell," said Hjalmar. "A little trip won't hurt you, if the government pays the bills. And as for women, you don't know how lucky you are. It's all right when they're trying to get away. It's when they can't live without you that they start to get in your hair."

"Alas, you foreigners are bereft of the finer feelings," wailed Frémont and signaled to the waiter to replenish his glass. In another half hour, the Chief of Detectives fell into a troubled sleep on the table, so Hjalmar bundled him into a taxi and rode with him to the *place* de la Contrescarpe, where he put him to bed in the Hotel Murphy et du Danube Bleu.

While the meal and the ensuing conversation were taking place, the rain had ceased, so that the pavements outside were gleaming with the reflections of street lamps and neon signs. Evans, sensing that his companion was eager for a little exercise, suggested to Rain-No-More that they walk across the city to settle their meal and get some fresh air in their lungs before visiting the night spots of Montmartre. The wind howled as they crossed the deserted Champ de Mars but when they reached the sheltered narrow streets on the way to the Invalides, Evans tried to draw the Indian out concerning the impending cattle- and sheepmen's war.

"Are there other ranches besides Leonard's on the cattle range east of Redwater?" Homer inquired. "When I was out in the Yellowstone country I didn't get back into the foothills in that region. I was fascinated by the badlands on the east side of the river, so I didn't cross over."

"There are a few dry farmers on the flats near the Dakota border," Rain-No-More said, "but you know what farmers are. They fence in a few acres of homestead and squat there. Our medicine man, Trout-tail III, says it's a wager with the Great White Father in Washington, who bets three hundred and sixty acres that none of his children from the Eastern tribes can stay in that country two years without starving to death."

"Who has Leonard got to help him, if Gilligan and his gang try to run him out of the valley?" Evans asked.

"His cowpunchers and the Blackfeet tribe. But Gilligan is thick with the politicians. He'll arrange to have a gang of crooked deputies to keep us on the reservation if there's a fight," said Rain-No-More. They were passing the Invalides. The Indian stopped to cut a straight stick from one of the shrubs in the *place* and, almost in the shadow of Napoleon's tomb, he scratched a map in the damp earth and pointed to it as he explained the situation. Evans listened eagerly, weighing every word.

The range where Miriam's father grazed his stock was almost rectangular in form, running about one hundred and fifty miles north and south and one hundred east and west. There were no roads, except the stage road near the river, and no fences except those around the claims in that same section. The Yellowstone formed its eastern boundary, the Missouri skirted it on the north. Mondak, on the Great Northern Railroad at the confluence of the two great rivers, was the shipping point, about fifty miles from Leonard's ranch. The Great Northern officials, Rain-No-More explained, favored the cattlemen in every way, since the profits for transporting the steers fell to them. On the other hand, the Northern Pacific crowd, influential in the State Legislature, was anxious to help the sheepmen.

The two continued walking, after Homer had got the lay of the battleground firmly fixed in his mind. It seemed, at first glance, as if Leonard, with his cowboys, might be able to defend himself, but Evans' mind kept reverting to the late Donniker Louey. The end of the prohibition era, Homer knew, had released a horde of gangsters from the comparatively wholesome occupation of smuggling whiskey and beer. Dozens of the toughest men in Chicago, or in the world, for that matter, were footloose and on the make. Gilligan took at least two trips east every year. What was more natural than

that in Chicago he should make the acquaintance of some gang
leader, get to talking in a bar, and make a deal for the invasion of
the cattle range? Long ago, Montana had lost nearly all of her cattle.
In fact, Jim Leonard's isolated corner of the State, unspoiled because it was inaccessible, was the last stronghold of that noble industry.

In the *place* St. Michel Evans and Rain-No-More sat down on
the *terrasse* Au Depart, a spot that is redolent with history, and
Evans sighed as he glanced over his shoulder and saw the towers
of Notre Dame setting themselves against the flying clouds. To the
right was the grim Conciergierie, the maimed Tour St. Jacques,
from which Napoleon had removed the church, the slender spire
of the Sainte Chapelle, and, beyond, the teeming *place* du Châtelet.
A pained, almost agonized expression crossed Homer's face as he
turned to look at the fountain and the world-renowned Boul' Mich'
at his left. Rain-No-More, observing that his companion was un-
dergoing some kind of struggle, sat silently, impressed by the his-
toric sights because they were new and strange to him. What inscrutable folk were the white men, he was thinking. With woods
and fields all around them, they piled up enormous cities that stood
while nations prospered and decayed. Instead of seeking their food
where it abounded, they had it brought miles in trucks. They sold
their health for money and their freedom for a false security.

"Two more rums," the Indian said, in French, phrase book in
hand, and was pleased that the waiter understood him.

The Indian's words aroused Evans from his reverie. "Forgive
me," he said. "I'm forgetting my privilege as a host." And from that
moment until five in the morning he was gay and scintillating. From
the slopes of Montmartre, where Evans was greeted everywhere
with cordiality, the two new friends traversed the great central
markets where pyramids of cabbage, carrots, parsnips and cauli-
flower stood twelve feet high in rows extending hundreds of yards.

"*Tais kut te*," grunted Rain-No-More, for the Blackfeet called
vegetables "useless food." Such fare would not sustain them on the
trail or the warpath.

"*Po kit e ki sok o*" (Plenty meat), said Evans, and led him to the vast sheds where carcasses of beef and mutton hung in tens of thousands. There Rain-No-More was truly impressed. A year's meat for all his people in a single building! His face remained impassive but his dark eyes glowed. In years to come he would have much to tell his tribesmen around the fragrant campfires. The question was: would they believe him? But Evans had stranger sights in store for him.

At two o'clock in the morning in Paris, the police make the round of the bridges, alleys and the most wretched cafés in the quarters where tramps seek shelter and the miserable army of the disinherited is aroused from sodden slumber and forced to trek across the *place* in front of Notre Dame and go into the central market area. The theory is that some of the derelicts will be able to pick up a few crushed turnips or cabbage leaves to keep them alive and others will earn a few sous by carrying loads on their backs from the trucks to the wholesale stores. Rain-No-More, at Evans' side, stood facing the great cathedral and watched hundreds of the lowest of the low shuffle past with listless gait and defenseless faces, with occasional policemen in uniform to herd them along.

"I shall leave this land tomorrow," the Indian said simply. "I shall return to the plains where braves share their meat and squaws sew garments for all."

Evans nodded, but in order to top off the evening on a happier plane he took Rain-No-More to the Bal Tabarin, where they arrived in time for the Can-Can. The Indian responded to the mood of the dance and went to his hotel singing the provocative tune at the top of his voice, with words from old Blackfeet legends.

Three hours later a strangely assorted group assembled in the gare St. Lazare. At seven, Homer, refreshed by nearly two hours of sleep, called for Miriam at the Hotel Vavin and found her sitting, pale but resolute, among her bags. Moritz, her faithful Boxer, his forehead wrinkled into a most apprehensive frown, was at her side.

"I've asked the proprietor to have the harpsichord moved into your apartment, until I can send for it from America," said Miriam, her voice sounding thin as a wisp of disappearing smoke.

"It will be safe there," Evans said, and rang for Stenka, the maid, whose dismal wailing could be heard all along the hallway. The big Serbian girl, since Miriam had rescued her from Godo the Whack in the course of the tarantula murder case, had thought of nothing but serving Miriam. The thought that her mistress was about to go across the ocean, perhaps never to return, filled Stenka's candid heart with woe. Excusing himself to Miriam, Evans stepped into the corridor and spoke a few words softly to the Serbian. Stenka's wails rose in pitch, then suddenly took on a joyful note and she ran down the hall and out of sight.

"I'll take down the bags," Evans said, and reached for the suitcases. Moritz, the dog, with a sigh and a doleful shake of his head, fell into step behind. Once before in his life he had seen French Line tags stuck on baggage and he knew what it meant—a prolonged journey cooped up on a rolling strange-smelling conveyance, with yapping Pekingese in cages near by. He hoped at least there would be a police dog or a Doberman aboard, but it was not his responsibility, so he trotted along and hopped easily to his place in the taxi.

At the station a surprising number of people, considering the season, were signaling porters and heading for the boat train. Among them were Chief of Detectives Frémont and Sergeants Schlumberger and Bonnet, all in civilian clothes with boiled shirts and stiff collars. The trio, each one looking more miserable than the other, had been grouped in front of their baggage by the newsreel cameramen and were blinking and sweating as the cameras clicked. Hydrangea, most fetching in a going-away outfit of jade green trimmed with silver fox, was watching the procedure from a distance with sparkling eyes. Thoughts of her beloved Harlem were buzzing around her head like bees on a frigola bush, to such a point that she had chucked her package of seasickness remedy into a trash receptacle. When she saw that Miriam was also going to sail on the *Ile-de-France*, the chic ex-Blackbird's spirits rose even higher.

"Look well on one who, after years of service, is being hounded from the land of his birth," Frémont said, shaking hands limply with Evans. "I shall be set upon by urchins all up and down your

Fifth Avenue. And meanwhile, criminals will romp. The prefect will lose track of three-quarters of them. After dark, the citizens will quail behind barricaded doors, if they are wise. Ah, well! It was kind of you to cable Monsieur Hugo Weiss to meet me at the pier and guide me to a respectable hotel. But if the journalists publish my picture, in the state I shall be in on arriving in New York, American crooks will conclude that if such a one guards public morals in France, Paris is a desperado's paradise. No doubt they'll come over in droves."

"You'll find much in America to interest you," said Evans.

Miriam, winking hard to keep back her tears, beckoned a porter and started for the train, just as Rain-No-More, carrying his wardrobe trunk on one shoulder, arrived on foot from the Hotel Opal in the *place* de la Madeleine.

"*Kit kse mat taim mo,*" he said, looking fresh and fit.

"Hello," roared Hjalmar Jansen, emerging from a taxi.

The porters found the places in the train and stowed away the baggage. Along the quai, vendors of food and drink, magazines, pillows and souvenirs plied their trade while tearful friends and relatives embraced the voyagers again and again and shouted hysterical advice. Miriam was seated near the middle of a coach, with Rain-No-More beside her and Hydrangea in front. Frémont, Schlumberger and Bonnet were across the aisle. Hjalmar was grinning as he tried to cheer the Chief of Detectives on the subject of life at sea. Homer, after having arranged with the conductor to have Moritz ride with the other passengers instead of being tied up in a baggage car, stood close to Miriam's chair. How well she behaved, this brave American girl, he was thinking. No dramatics, no harrowing demonstration. She simply sat there, hands clenched tightly, looking neither left nor right, and praying for the train to start moving.

"All aboard," the conductor said, and piped his little whistle. Hjalmar got up from the arm of a chair.

"Good-bye, Homer," said Miriam. Then she faltered, for Evans was making no move toward the doorway. A moment later her eyes grew wide; she caught her breath and came as near fainting, in the good old Victorian way, as she ever did in her life, for Homer, smiling ruefully, cast a farewell glance at the gare St. Lazare and said:

"I made up my mind last night to toddle along, if you don't mind. I've never met your estimable father, you know. And this Gilligan person interests me. In fact, my luggage is aboard and I've brought Stenka along to look after you. She's in third class, where she'll be more at ease, but we'll pick her up at Le Havre."

Hjalmar Jansen let out a roar. "I'm blasted if I don't go with you," he said and fished in his pockets for money.

The Boxer, sensing how the mood of the gathering had suddenly soared, indulged in one joyful bark, then turned his eyes toward Miriam for forgiveness, as almost imperceptibly the train started gliding toward Le Havre.

3
Of Life on the Ocean Wave, and Particularly in February

BY THE TIME THE GONG RANG as a warning to dress for dinner, the group of friends the reader knows were disposed, for better or for worse, in the well-appointed cabins, decks and salons of the *Ile-de-France*. They had boarded the liner without fuss or flurry, and had stood at the rail as the hawsers were cast off and the ship got under weigh. The weather had cleared and the sun shone thinly on the roofs and towers of Le Havre as they rounded the breakwater. It was just at that point that the liner felt the first sea swell and performed a sort of curtsey in acknowledgment.

"France and other things, farewell!" groaned Frémont and stumbled down the companionway in a direction he mistakenly supposed would bring him to his cabin. After pointless meanderings, he was retrieved by a steward and guided to his bunk, which by that time was dipping and cavorting merrily. He was joined without delay by Sergeant Schlumberger, whose wide experience in police work had never brought him on deep water before and, according to his statement as he struggled to pull off his enormous white shirt, it never would again. Bonnet, on the contrary, hailing as he did from Brittany, was a sailor from birth and walked the deck with glee, extending his legs to keep pace with Rain-No-More, who was trying to explain, as they put the miles behind them, why Indians ate meat for breakfast and preferred to sleep on the ground.

Miriam spent most of the afternoon in her cabin, helping Stenka arrange her clothes and toilet articles. The big Serbian girl, who stood six feet one in her stockings, when she had them, was in a sort of trance. Not having been to school and being of an uncurious nature, she had never acquired any facts about oceans, although she had dimly heard of them. During lulls in unpacking, she glanced out of the portholes, saw miles of rushing waves bent apparently on the vessel's destruction, and began to murmur Serbian prayers. But when she looked at Miriam and saw her beloved mistress smiling and tripping gaily from corner to corner, overflowing with relief and joy, Stenka decided that she had fallen in with some enchanted folk who either didn't care what happened or enjoyed some mysterious immunity from harm. She resolved to string along with them as best she could. When the *Ile-de-France* touched Southampton, the honest maid thought the trip was over and started throwing articles wildly into valises until forcibly restrained.

Homer Evans and Hjalmar were seated at a comfortable table in the smoking room, and were sampling the famous champagne cocktails which set the French Line apart from merely commercial steamship companies. Between sips, the big Norwegian was scribbling a hasty letter to Horsecollar Phoebe at Rouen, explaining that his projected visit there would have to be postponed on account of an emergency that was taking him suddenly to the west of North America. Evans was studying the passenger list. A gaily uniformed *mouche*, or bellboy, passed, and Homer called to him.

"Please ask Monsieur Rain-No-More if he can come here at his convenience," Homer said.

The boy was off so quickly that Hjalmar blinked and made several scattered blots of ink on his letter. Although he had a master mariner's ticket, he had seldom traveled on board ship as a passenger, and found the luxurious surroundings and prompt service disconcerting.

Rain-No-More appeared so noiselessly at Homer's side that Hjalmar was startled again and had to throw away his epistle and start all over again. Champagne was not good for his nerves, he concluded, and he switched to straight whiskey.

"It's a strange coincidence," Homer said to the Indian, "but a passenger named Gilligan got on at Southampton and, according to the purser, his home is in Montana. Terence Gilligan is his name."

"Bad medicine," grunted Rain-No-More. "He's Larkspur Gilligan's son."

"Does he know you?" asked Evans.

"To him, one Indian looks just like another," said Rain-No-More.

Evans handed the Indian the passenger list and pointed to another name: Umberto Santosuosso.

"An Italian," said Rain-No-More. "I've only known one Italian and him I didn't like."

"Sit down a moment, and have a cocktail," Evans said. "There may be more in this than meets the casual eye." After the waiter had brought a round and Hjalmar had given up letter writing in favor of the wireless, Homer started to explain.

"Umberto Santosuosso, if I am not mistaken, is the son of Antonio Santosuosso, known to his intimates as Baldy Santo," he said.

"He's the mug who tried to take Tom Jackson for a ride in Chicago. He's boss of a beer-running mob," Hjalmar said. "Bum beer at that."

"Not only leader of a gang, but the gang of which Donniker Louey was a charter member," Evans continued. "And furthermore, Umberto, son of Baldy, came aboard at Southampton arm-in-arm with Terence, of the Gilligan clan. The pair will bear watching."

"Maybe we ought to dump 'em overboard, for luck," said Hjalmar, and Rain-No-More nodded gravely in assent.

"Better wait and see if they are generous with information, in or out of their cups. Neither one of them looks discreet. It's lucky they don't know us," Homer said.

Rain-No-More scowled. "Young Gilligan knows Miriam," he said, narrowing his eyes.

"In that case we must warn her," Homer said.

Just at that moment the first gong sounded, letting it be known that dinner was only a brief half hour away. The steward who beat the instrument must have had suppressed desires, for he seemed to take a fiendish joy in pummeling the bronze until it gave forth sounds expressive of all shades of feeling between anxiety and Milton's "O dark, dark, dark, amid the blaze of noon."

Hydrangea, increasingly elated because the miles between herself and Harlem were being ticked off gaily by the nautical log,

peeled off her jade-green costume and started fishing in her wardrobe for a suitable evening gown. Dimly she remembered her days
of seasickness when she had crossed the Atlantic, eastbound, with
the Blackbirds, and that recollection caused her to sigh with sympathy for Frémont, to whom the voyage already seemed like a
troubled geologic era during which he was being written into the
rocks. Stenka, in Miriam's cabin across the corridor, mistook the
gong for a signal to abandon ship and started struggling with a life
belt, which she tried to slip on from down under like a pair of pants.
Miriam tried to reassure her, but the wind chose that particular
moment to rise and waves began dashing up over the porthole, so
that the *Ile-de-France* started pitching and rolling in a way that
would have made a Montana broncho ashamed of himself. Stenka,
still wrestling with the cork jacket, wrung her large but shapely
hands.

"Once, when I was six years old, I stole the priest's snuffbox,"
she moaned, imploringly. "They say God remembers everything.
Is that really true?"

"Well, yes and no," said Miriam.

A tap sounded lightly on the door, and in response to her invitation, Evans stepped inside. Succinctly he told her about Terence
Gilligan's presence on the liner and asked her to join him in the
smoking room for a consultation as soon as she was dressed. For
the first evening aboard, she chose a silver lamé evening gown that
had all the simplicity of a Grecian robe, with a lapis lazuli brooch
and dark-blue buckles on her slippers. Homer was seated with
Rain-No-More and Hjalmar Jansen as she entered the doorway
near the bar, and even the impassive Indian let out a grunt of surprised approval. The barman dropped a shaker containing the
makings for six Martinis. But the most unexpected response came
from a table several times removed from Homer's. A tall queenly
woman rose in her place, as did the distinguished Frenchman with
decorations all across the lapels of his evening clothes, who was
seated beside her.

"Miriam, my dear. Is it possible you are here?" said a finely
modulated voice, and a second later Miriam was embracing

Eugénie de Sault, formerly the Marchioness de la Rose d'Antan and since the Louvre murder mystery, Madame Hyacinthe Toudoux. Her husband, the renowned doctor, shook hands with unfeigned enthusiasm.

"The Minister of Justice did me the honor to appoint me as delegate from France to the international conference of toxicologists in Chicago," the medical examiner said, as Homer and Hjalmar joined them. Being oblivious to political events, the good doctor was not aware that Chief of Detectives Frémont had also been railroaded from France. Toudoux was overjoyed to hear that his colleague was on board. A sprightly general conversation followed, enlivened no end by the famous champagne cocktails, so that Homer had no opportunity for his talk with Miriam before Terence Gilligan and young Santosuosso, the latter somewhat self-conscious because of his London-tailored tuxedo, came into the smoking room. The pair glanced speculatively around the room, then went straight to the bar. Homer gave a sigh of relief. For Gilligan had looked straight at Miriam and had failed to recognize her. In truth, in her silver evening gown, by Maggy Rouff, and matured by her long association with Evans, she looked quite different from the girl who had attended high school with Gilligan in Glendive, Montana. Dr. Toudoux was deep in conversation with Rain-No-More, discussing the medicinal properties of bog asphodel, Dyer's greenwood, woodruff and other wild herbs of the prairie. Hjalmar was explaining latitude and longitude to Sergeant Bonnet and Hydrangea, who had entered alone and was welcomed warmly by the company. Rain-No-More was glancing covertly toward the pair at the bar and reflecting that the night would be dark and the decks deserted later on.

Miriam, always thoughtful of others, remembered that Stenka was alone in the cabin, and terrified. Since Madame Toudoux was Junoesque in stature, it occurred to Miriam that the doctor's wife might lend a gown to the Serbian girl, who had come aboard with no clothes except the humble ones she had been wearing. So when the group assembled at the Captain's table, Stenka, impressive in a low-cut creation of Poiret, was seated tremulously at Hjalmar

Jansen's left, while Hydrangea was paired with Rain-No-More. Evans, after consultation with the wine steward, chose a Montrachet *blanc* and a red Château Lafitte, asked the waiter to bring a triple portion of Lyonnaise duck for Rain-No-More, and the meal progressed in a memorable way to such a point that even Stenka laid aside her misgivings and decided to enjoy the voyage to the full. The Captain, pleased that he was to make the crossing in such varied and agreeable company, trotted out his special brandy, known as "Philosopher's Delight," and although the *Ile-de-France* did everything but turn somersaults the group of friends, beloved of the reader, were snug and happy as fleas in an Aubusson carpet.

Homer Evans was the life of the gathering. With each member of the party he conversed on congenial subjects, even evoking from Stenka the incident of the priest's purloined snuffbox, but in a spirit unmistakably gay. Between times, however, he was thinking of Terence Gilligan. It was inevitable, he concluded, that the young man would see Miriam's name on the passenger list and eventually would realize who she was. So after dinner, and before the horse races in the salon began, he advised her to throw Gilligan off the track by telling him that she was going to New York to round out her study of the piano. Hjalmar and the Indian, advised of the strategy, looked disappointed but were willing to trust Homer's judgment. In fact, before the evening was over, young Gilligan and his Italian companion were included in the party and danced with Miriam, Stenka and Hydrangea while Frémont and Schlumberger writhed and suffered below with a stoicism increasingly hard to maintain. Eugénie and Hyacinthe Toudoux, meanwhile, enjoyed a remarkable foursome of contract bridge, with Homer Evans and Rain-No-More, who had learned the game in Berkeley in order to recoup some of the expenses to which his course in imbibology had put his father, Shot-on-Both-Sides. It was already evident that Hjalmar was hitting it off with the Serbian girl in no uncertain way, to the discomfiture of Santosuosso, who, although a head shorter than Stenka, was dizzy with admiration of her Slavic charms.

"I was painting London red when the old man sent for me," Terence Gilligan confided to Miriam, who was all attention.

"Perhaps he needs you on the range," she said.

"He's afraid I'll quit that God-forsaken country," Gilligan said. "And he thinks I ought to earn a living. I can't see the sense of that. He's made a pile of dough, and someone has got to spend it. Why not I?"

Stifling an impulse to defend her homeland, so remote and untrammeled, Miriam pretended to agree. "I haven't been out there since the branch railroad was built to Circle," she said.

"Dad's a smooth one," said Gilligan, with a self-satisfied air. "He's cleaning up more money every year. Too bad your governor sticks to cattle, or he could get in on the graft."

The ship gave a lurch, piling up the dancers on the starboard side, and somehow Hjalmar landed square on top of the Italian, who came out of the scrimmage much the worse for wear. The gangster was about to protest, but just then Jansen was obliging the orchestra by lifting the piano back into place, single-handed, so Santosuosso decided to bide his time.

The inevitable break in the precarious relationship with the pair of outsiders occurred with suddenness and dispatch on the following afternoon. A few amateurs were passing the time shooting clay pigeons on the promenade deck, but with such shots as Miriam, Homer Evans, Rain-No-More and the son of Baldy Santo, whose first toy had been a sawed-off shotgun, the contest degenerated into a mild form of physical exercise, the brunt being borne by the sailor who worked the trap. While Santosuosso had the pump gun in his hand, a playful porpoise, the first to make its appearance on the voyage, leaped from the waves, surveyed the *Ile-de-France* with a pale blue eye, and began playing around the bow. The Italian, with a malicious grin, fired from the hip and peppered the porpoise with shot, so that he lashed the water in pain and disappeared. Miriam turned white with fury.

"What a cowardly trick!" she said. A clay pigeon was spiraling in the air, against a background of swiftly moving clouds. Whipping out her automatic from her handbag, she fired once and shattered the whirling disc into smithereens, then stamped her foot and went down to her cabin.

"Gee, that broad's got a temper," said the Italian. He found himself face to face with an Indian whose eyes were boring into his more deeply than the shot in the porpoise's hide.

"I beg your pardon," said Rain-No-More. "In future you will refer to that young lady as Miss Leonard, if it becomes necessary for you to speak her name at all."

"Just skip it," said Santosuosso nervously, and walked away. The Indian turned to Gilligan, who had flushed with resentment. "Any questions?" Rain-No-More asked curtly. Gilligan dropped his eyes and followed his disgruntled companion below.

4
Stormy Weather on the Range

FOR THREE DAYS A FITFUL WIND had been driving the snow, like sharp white powder, across the bleak stretches of the Lower Yellowstone. The tops of the foothills, blown bare, were like islands in a sea of white, and deep drifts choked the coulees. In disconsolate detachments, the tough short-horned cattle, whose hair had grown shaggy to protect them from the bitter cold, were moving slowly toward the river, their backs hunched to the tempest. Some of the weaker ones had dropped out, lain down resignedly and patiently had died.

In the ranch house at Three Buttes, known as Opera Lodge and built of logs, Jim Leonard, whose silver-white hair made his shrewd blue eyes look darker than they were, was tying and untying knots in a length of stiff hemp rope and glancing uneasily, now and then, at the frost-covered windows. On a bench near by were two of his cowboys, Hank and Laramee Bob, watching idly the skillful play of Leonard's calloused fingers. A discarded copy of *Western Story Magazine* lay on the floor at their feet, and in the broad fireplace two eight-foot cottonwood logs were crackling and emitting pale lemon-colored flames while shadows danced grotesquely on the wall.

"Should we take a ride down Cottonwood Creek, to save a few steers?" Hank asked.

Jim Leonard shook his head. "It isn't worth the risk," he said. Hard pressed as he was, on account of the stormy season and the decline of cattle-raising, generally, his first thought was always for the safety of his men.

Wing Lee, the No. 1 boy, came silently in from the kitchen with a steaming pitcher of grog.

"Plenty hell outside. Cold air, warm belly," he said.

"Jake," said Laramee Bob.

Two other cowboys, Slipnoose Pete and one with iron-rimmed spectacles called the Professor because he could thump out tunes on the piano and twang the jew's-harp, were shoveling a path through the six-foot drifts to the bunkhouse, the barn and stable, and another smaller building with a crescent carved out of the door.

"Don't you ever hanker to go back teaching school?" asked Pete. "I'm getting blind as a bat from the glare of the snow."

"You've talked about nothing but weather since last Christmas," was the Professor's rejoinder. "Why don't you try to improve your mind?"

Pete, straightening up in preparation for a choice bit of repartee, saw some horsemen struggling through the snow on the trail beside Bison Coulee, which extended from Three Buttes to the Missouri.

"Damn my hide," he said. "Some ornery buzzards don't know when to stay home where it's dry and warm."

The Professor shielded his eyes with a buckskin mitten and spat tobacco juice into the snow pile he had made. "Now wouldn't that rattle a man?" he said.

The two cowboys started for the lodge and entered so precipitously that Wing Lee, bearing his empty tray, was almost overturned.

"What for no makee path to can?" he asked indignantly.

"We got company," said Pete. "Five fella ride up coulee."

"Five time fella bloody fool," was the Chinaman's comment.

Jim Leonard, Hank and Laramee Bob rose slowly to their feet, only half believing what their colleagues said, for the cowpunchers did little else in winter time than play tricks on one another. Leonard brushed off the steam from a small section of the windowpane spared by the frost and nodded in surprise.

"That looks like Larkspur Gilligan," he said, and narrowed his eyes.

"That's who it is," said Hank, "and he's got that mangy pair of sheepherders with him."

"Shucks," said the Professor disgustedly, and spat into the fireplace.

Ten minutes later, there was a knock on the ranch house door. "Come in," said Leonard. He detested Gilligan and loathed sheepherders on principle, but the door of Opera Lodge had never been closed to wayfarers in a storm.

With much stamping and slapping of numbed hands, Larkspur Gilligan, his two sheepherders and two strangers came into the room. One of them was introduced as the new sheriff of Dawson County, the other was the storekeeper from Circle. Gilligan was obviously nervous. He warmed himself elaborately at the fire and avoided Jim Leonard's piercing eyes. The Chinese No. 1 boy came in with a broom and swept the snow from the floor, ignoring contemptuously the sheepherders, who had to step this way and that to get out of his way. When the tall stranger was introduced as the sheriff, however, Wing Lee stopped sweeping and vanished like a mirage. He relished no contact whatever with the law.

"We may as well get down to business," Gilligan said at last.

"Since when do we do business with sheepherders?" asked Hank, looking him straight in the eye and setting himself to rise. Leonard motioned for him to be silent.

"You'd better stay the night," said Leonard. "You can't get back to Piney Buttes, that's a cinch."

Gilligan disregarded the invitation. "We want to talk to you, Jim, alone," he said.

"We don't have any secrets on this ranch," Leonard said. "What you have to say, you can say in front of the boys."

"It's serious," Gilligan said, and the sheriff, as if prompted, nodded. He had been elected in November, on the ticket backed by the N. P. railroad, taking the place of Tumbleweed O'Flaherty, Leonard's old and trusted friend, and there had been much talk among the cattlemen as to how the votes were counted.

"Crap or get off the pot," drawled Hank, and spat within an inch of Larkspur Gilligan's riding boot.

"See here, Leonard," said Hockaday, the young sheriff, trying to speak more gruffly than was natural to him. "We came here all the way from Glendive . . ."

"Not today, you didn't," interrupted the rancher.

"Well, as a matter of fact, we started yesterday. Took the stage to Mondak and caught a handcar with section hands going as far as Muddy Creek on the Great Northern," the sheriff said.

Leonard scowled and glanced at Hank, who grunted and nodded. The lanky foreman had told his boss, not six weeks before, that Johnny Highpockets, Gilligan's lawyer from Glendive, had been smelling around the division superintendent's office in Mondak, getting acquainted with the new superintendent for the Great Northern. Wherever they found traces of Gilligan or his cronies, they had learned to expect trouble. Already, evidently, the Gilligan crew had become friendly enough with the super to ride on handcars, which was strictly forbidden.

"Is a sheriff supposed to go wandering out of the State?" asked the Professor, who read law books in the long winter evenings. "What if the county should start running wild?"

"We couldn't get here by way of Leonard Creek, from the Yellowstone side," the sheriff said, less and less at ease. "The drifts there are eight feet deep."

"You might have waited till next spring," suggested Laramee Bob.

Gilligan, whose anger was rising because of the interruptions and the sheriff's hesitation, objected again to the presence of the cowpunchers. All of them were armed, not with automatics they considered newfangled, but with Smith & Wesson six-shooters. Above the door at the entrance, Jim Leonard's Winchester 40-40 was resting on two spikes. He kept it there in case, in season, some Canadian white geese flew over low or a marauding coyote was careless enough to let his silhouette stand out a moment too long on the crest of one of the surrounding foothills. If it came to a showdown, Gilligan's crowd, handicapped by the presence of the sheepherders, would be sure to get the worst of any shooting affray. The sheepman was counting on Jim Leonard's well-known respect for law.

Suddenly Jim Leonard walked up to Gilligan and faced him squarely. "Gilligan, your office boy," indicating the sheriff, "is tongue-tied. Why don't you speak your little piece yourself?"

Slipnoose Pete, at that point, ambled over and placed his back against the door. The sheepherders, itching and squirming because of the heat from the fireplace, drew closer together on the bench and looked at Gilligan apprehensively. One of them, a Shoshone half-breed called Stumpbroke, had testified the year before against a few of the Blackfeet who had wandered off the reservation and for that reason he was especially nervous when called upon to go into the northeastern corner of the sheep range, across the Missouri from the Blackfeet's land. His partner, irreverently nicknamed Jill, was a moon-faced lad from somewhere down the Mississippi who had been run out of Pocatello, Idaho, for reasons he never mentioned but which were common talk among the cattlemen. Not long after 1900, a law had been passed requiring sheepmen to send out herders in pairs, for in nine cases out of ten one man who spent weeks or even months alone with twenty thousand bleating woollies began talking to himself and imagining some of the most attractive of his charges were human. According to the cattlemen, the new arrangement had not resulted in any noticeable improvement in the situation, unless one was given to splitting hairs.

Larkspur Gilligan, challenged directly by Jim Leonard, took over the role of spokesman. "It's thisaway," he said. "About a month ago a friend of mine named Louey rode over to this range from Circle, bound for Three Buttes, to talk business with you, Leonard. He's never been heard from since. Two days afterward his horse came back to Piney Buttes, still saddled and with sagebrush hanging from the lines, where he'd been tied. There were no signs that Louey had been dragged. What have you got to say?"

"I never saw the man or heard of him," said Leonard.

"Sorry, Leonard, but that isn't what my boys tell me," Gilligan said.

"Do you or any of your boys want to call me a liar?" asked Leonard, and all the cowboys rose.

"Now, keep your shirt on, Jim," said Gilligan, adopting another tone. "If you're innocent, you can sure clear this thing up. What I was aimin' to say was that my two herders, Stumpbroke and Jill, here, were near the head of Cottonwood Creek the day Louey started out, and they saw him ride by."

Hank strode into the middle of the circle. "What business had this lousy pair of sheepherders on the east side of Redwater? That's what I'd like to know. If I'd 'a' caught 'em, they wouldn't have seen nobody but God."

The sheriff spoke up. "This is a free country, Hank," he said.

"Not since they started pinning badges on a coot like you," said Hank.

"There's nothing to kick up a row about. My boys crossed the creek to look after some strays," said Gilligan.

"The head of Cottonwood Creek is close to forty miles from the deadline. What were them strays, antelopes?" asked Hank.

"Let me handle this," said Leonard, and the foreman subsided. "Go on, Gilligan. What else did the herders see?"

Gilligan turned to Stumpbroke. "Stand up," he said, "and tell 'em all what you saw."

The sheepherder stood up, avoiding Leonard's eyes. "I saw Jim Leonard riding across the mesa near the head of the creek. He was on a sorrel. All of a sudden he stopped short, circled and shot at something with his rifle."

"Where was Louey then?" asked Gilligan.

"I'd lost sight of Louey, but he was up the creek, just the same. On foot. His horse was down the gully, tied to a clump of sage-brush," Stumpbroke said. His partner, Jill, confirmed what Stumpbroke said.

"Do your duty," said Gilligan to the sheriff.

"You'll have to come along with me," the sheriff said.

Hank and the other cowpunchers began to roar with laughter.

"Listen to the tin-horn politician," the foreman said. "Say, kid," he added, walking up to the sheriff and taking a firm hold on his shirt, "you got as much chance of getting Jim Leonard out of this house as a cub bear has to read music. You can bunk here tonight, on account of the storm, but at daylight you start back where you came from, and take this crummy bunch of fourflushers with you. Understand?"

"He's got a warrant, signed and sworn," said Gilligan. "The grand jury's decided that he'll have to stand trial, that's all."

"Let me see the warrant," said Leonard.

The sheriff handed over an official paper, bearing the signature of Judge Patterson, who had been lawyer for Gilligan's bank in Glendive before he was appointed to the bench. The rancher read the document calmly. "It seems to be in order," he said. Then he turned to Johnny O'Brien, the storekeeper from Circle, who up to that time had not uttered a word.

"Johnny," Jim Leonard began, "I didn't expect much else from the rest of this gang, but I'm surprised at you, to be mixed up in a frame-up against one of your neighbors." He was about to go on when he saw O'Brien wink one eye, almost imperceptibly. Leonard, who had been standing between the storekeeper and the others, desisted. O'Brien had had some friendly motive for coming along, of that the rancher was certain, and it cheered Leonard to find that he had a friend in the opposite camp.

"Will you go peaceably? It's the law, you know, Jim," said Gilligan.

"You'll have to find the body," the Professor spoke up. "I'll give you chapter and verse for that in the statutes of Montana. You got to produce the *corpus delicti*, and that's flat."

"The sheriff and a posse will have a look along Cottonwood Creek when the snow melts in the spring," said Gilligan.

"Why didn't you wait till then to raise this hullabaloo?" demanded Laramee Bob. "Jim's been here forty years. He wouldn't run away."

"Just a formality. It isn't my doing. The grand jury acted. But don't forget that Louey was my friend," Gilligan said.

"So much the worse for him," said Pete.

"Are you going to come peaceably?" repeated Gilligan to Leonard.

"Do you want to start now, at this time of day?" asked the rancher.

"We couldn't make it, even as far as the Missouri," said O'Brien, the storekeeper. "We'll have to stay the night." Again he partially closed one eye, for the benefit of Hank, who caught on and started making arrangements for extra blankets to be taken to the bunkhouse. He hollered for Wing Lee, and getting no response found the kitchen was empty. A little later Slipnoose Pete and Laramee Bob, who went down to the barn to water the saddle horses and throw them down some hay from the loft, found the No. 1 boy and his Chinese flunkey, Wing Sam, hiding in the granary Protesting, the two Chinese were dragged back to the kitchen and, after being reassured that the sheriff had no interest in them, they started preparing an enormous meal. It had been a tradition at Three Buttes that the grub was good and the help ate with the boss in the ranch house.

Before the large metal triangle that hung outside the kitchen door was beaten with a short length of lead pipe, to announce the evening meal, Johnny O'Brien was closeted with the foreman, Hank, in a secluded empty stall. Fearing that they might be interrupted, the storekeeper cut his story short.

"You know I make my living off the sheepmen," O'Brien began. "They hang around the store in wintertime . . ."

"How come those two herders aren't down in Idaho on the winter range, where they belong?" asked Hank.

"That's not the only thing that smells fishy," said O'Brien. "First of all, you know as well as I do that Jim Leonard wouldn't kill no Italian just for fun, and if he had to kill one he wouldn't hide the body. Now Gilligan and this Donniker Louey did quite a bit of drinking in my back room and they talked a lot, too. I pretended to pay no attention, but I got an earful just the same. That Louey started out for Three Buttes to gun for Jim Leonard, or I'll lose my guess. I saw him when they boosted him up on that old white horse, and he was heeled for bear. And you can't tell me those herders were forty miles off their range in search of stray stinkers. Of course, Gilligan has all the politicians eating out of his hand and the judge has built a brand-new house, which he couldn't have done on his salary. They want Jim Leonard out of the way for a while.

"Now I'm giving you just one tip that may lead somewhere, and again it may not. You know Rain-No-More, the son of the Blackfeet chief," O'Brien said.

"A good Indian," said Hank, and the storekeeper nodded.

"Well, he heard Louey and Gilligan talking, a few days before the Wop disappeared." Very slowly, the storekeeper lowered his left eyelid.

"I'll hit for the Blackfeet lodge tomorrow morning," said Hank. "And much obliged."

"Whatever I can do for Jim, I'm glad to do," said O'Brien. "Only don't let on. Gilligan thinks I'm crooked, too, otherwise he'd take my store away, or burn it down."

5

On Peering into Gift Horses, from Any Angle at All

THE FIRST FOUR DAYS AT SEA passed quickly and pleasantly, except for
the incident of the porpoise, after which young Gilligan and
Santosuosso kept pretty much to themselves, drinking from morning until night and watching Rain-No-More sullenly whenever the
Indian crossed their line of vision. The latter had become fascinated by white men's shipboard pastimes, to such a point that he
became the undisputed champion of the boat at ping-pong, shuffle-
board, deck tennis and ring the cane. Hjalmar put on boxing bouts
almost nightly with a competent heavyweight from the forecastle
and only once forgot himself and knocked his opponent clean over
the ropes and into a dress buyer's lap, which opened the way for a
pleasant clandestine romance between the sailor and the talented
business woman from the Bronx. Eugénie and Hyacinthe Toudoux,
whose devotion to each other warmed the hearts of all those on
board who had them, spent the days walking arm in arm or reading in deck chairs, side by side, hands clasped beneath their
steamer rug. After dinner, there was always a game of bridge with
Evans and Rain-No-More, the quality of which was in indirect pro-
portion to the infinitesimal stakes computed in sous.

Two days out of New York, however, the weather reversed its
tactics. The sun shone brightly, the swell subsided as the storm
was left behind. Porpoises and sea birds disported themselves on
all sides of the gallant white ship and Moritz, having convinced
the dog steward of his complete reliability, was given the run of
the upper deck, where he raced and wrestled judiciously with a

shaggy Newfoundland whose amiability was never ruffled, although he was no match for the Boxer in a free-for-all.

Not long before lunch time, when the orchestra was struggling with selections from *Carmen*, the group of friends who made it a practice to meet for a cocktail before meals were astonished to see, appearing like a wraith in the smoking-room doorway, a much-chastened Frémont. He had lost his ruddy complexion and approximately fourteen pounds, avoirdupois. He shuddered apprehensively when the liner's timbers creaked or the refreshing sea breeze caused a door to slam. His legs were a trifle unsteady, but he was on them, at least, and for the first time since leaving dry land could think of food without disgust. His response to the hearty greetings he received was somewhat reproachful, since his fellow travelers, aside from Schlumberger, had found the voyage delightful, notwithstanding the heavy weather. Hjalmar, to reassure the Chief of Detectives, led him out into the corridor and showed him the chart with the little tricolor flags which showed each day's run and the noontide position of the *Ile-de-France*. Frémont was so relieved that he actually smiled, for down below decks he had not been able to believe that the liner was making headway against the wind and waves, and had feared they all were still about as far from New York as they had been when the boat set out from Le Havre.

"Would it be possible to return to France by way of Alaska and Siberia, where most of the distance could be accomplished by rail, or even in a cart?" he asked, after having been fortified with his first champagne cocktail.

"Now you've got your sea legs, you'll like ships," Hjalmar said. "Even vessels like this one, which is fitted up more like a hotel. Just wait till you feel yourself gliding along with all sails spread, and a spanking breeze behind you."

"I beg of you not to joke about serious things," Frémont said. "More than once, in the past several days, I have been on the point of death, so near extinction, in fact, that not even Hydrangea could cheer me. . . . Where is she, by the way?" The Chief was not exactly comforted when told that his sweetheart was on deck with the

Indian, and had discussed the possibility of getting into her bathing suit for a swim, if the weather's clemency continued. Not having been shown around the liner, Frémont knew nothing of the swimming pool and thought his dusky sweetheart had contemplated diving over the side, to be rescued, if at all, by the redman who scalped Italians so highhandedly. But he thawed when the ex-Blackbird came in and was so obviously delighted to see him safe and comparatively sound.

AT HOMER'S SUGGESTION, Miriam had, the day before, dispatched a cablegram to her father, announcing her impending arrival. The men on the ranch, when she was away, slackened up perceptibly in their housekeeping. As soon as word was received that she was *en route*, they would scrub Opera Lodge from attic to cellar, shine up their boots and buckles, wash carefully behind the ears and make up the beds and bunks from scratch, which they seldom did without outside incentive. Wing Lee and Wing Sam would start making frosted cakes and pies. And her bedroom, from which in good weather the hazy colors of the distant badlands across the river might be seen, would be unlocked and thoroughly dusted. All day she had hoped to receive a reply, in fact, had been so disappointed when the morning brought no answer that her fears for her father's safety were redoubled, and Homer had been hard put to reassure her.

Just before the first gong rang, a red-uniformed boy approached the table with a blue envelope in his hand. Her heart jumped wildly. Excusing herself, she hurried down to her cabin in order to be alone when she opened the message. Lunch time arrived and she failed to reappear. Stenka's place was also vacant in the dining room. Homer remarked also that neither young Gilligan nor Santosuosso had showed up for the meal, although usually they were among the first to go into the dining salon.

The Captain had not put in an appearance, so Homer apologized to Madame Toudoux, who with her usual grace and tact had assumed the role of hostess, and went below. He tapped softly on the door of Miriam's cabin, then heard wild sobbing within.

Opening the door, he saw Stenka convulsed with grief and Miriam, her face white and strained, still staring at the cablegram. Despairingly she handed it to Homer who read:

> MIRIAM LEONARD
> ILE-DE-FRANCE
> BOSS IN GLENDIVE CHARGED WITH MURDER
> FIFTY THOUSAND CASH BAIL DIRTY FRAMEUP
> HURRY HOME
>   HANK

Although the news had stunned Miriam, it set off Evans' active brain like a rocket.

"Pull yourself together, dear," he said brusquely. "I'll have your father free within two hours." And sitting down at her writing desk he ripped off a radiogram blank and wrote a message to Hugo Weiss, the genial multi-millionaire and philanthropist whom Evans and Miriam had rescued from kidnappers three years before.

Thus it was that Honest Jim Leonard, staring through the small barred window in his cell in the Glendive jail, saw his friend, the former sheriff, Tumbleweed O'Flaherty, pushing a wheelbarrow down the main street of the town and turning in at the court house. The barrow contained one hundred and twenty-three pounds of gold, in coins of various denominations, and reluctantly Judge Patterson, who had fixed the bail at what he had supposed to be a prohibitive amount, considering the state of the cattle business, had been forced to give way. Fifteen minutes later Jim Leonard was being cheered by his many friends in the bar of the Hotel Jordan, across from the railroad station, and the young sheriff, Warren Hockaday, was saddling a horse to ride out to Circle to discuss the mysterious development with Larkspur Gilligan.

The bewildered rancher, whose temper had been mounting toward the danger point while he had paced the cell for hours, pausing only to throw a few chunks of wood into the Sibley stove, was more surprised than the judge and the sheriff by the miraculous appearance of $50,000 in gold for his bail. As soon as he could get away from his well-wishers at the Hotel Jordan for a moment, he went into conference with Tumbleweed O'Flaherty, who could do little to clear up the mystery. According to Tumbleweed, he had been informed *sub rosa* by a cashier at the Glendive Stockmen's Bank and Trust Company that strict orders had come through from the East to place fifty thousand dollars in gold to Leonard's credit. The directors, all under Gilligan's thumb, had intended to keep the matter quiet, not even informing the prisoner of his good fortune, until a consultation could be had with Gilligan. O'Flaherty, however, having been tipped off by the clerk, and possessing an old power of attorney from Leonard, formerly used in paying for shipments of supplies via the N.P., the deposed sheriff had confronted the directors and demanded the cash. The bankers had not dared refuse to turn it over. That was all O'Flaherty could say.

Before the afternoon was over, Hank and the Professor, numb with cold, came into Glendive on the stage. Having received the radiogram from Miriam, the foreman had postponed his projected visit to the Blackfeet and had started out on skis with the Professor, hitting toward the stage road along the Yellowstone by way of Leonard Creek. They had figured that the stage would be held up overnight, half way between Mondak and Glendive, and their calculations had proved to be sound. Leonard was overjoyed to hear that his daughter was on her way home from Paris, but, after checking up with all his friends in Dawson County and phoning all the cattlemen on the Yellowstone range, he had been forced to the conclusion, since Miriam was the only person outside Montana who had been informed of his predicament, that she had been instrumental in raising the colossal sum for his bail. That worried Jim Leonard no end. He had always had slight misgivings about his daughter's long stay in a foreign land, and especially in the city known to itinerant preachers as the modern Babylon.

How was it possible for her to dig up on an hour's notice more money than he had made raising cattle in the last five years? Once in a while, out of sheer boredom, he had read stories in the various pulp magazines his buckaroos enjoyed, and he remembered dimly several cases in which pure-hearted young women had exposed themselves to worse than death in order to get their parents out of hock. That, in practically every instance, the heroines of the stories had escaped intact until a preacher or J.P. had made everything according to Hoyle did not comfort the anxious rancher to any noticeable extent.

In fact, Jim spent the remainder of the day, not in planning revenge against Larkspur Gilligan but resolving, if necessary, to scour the East and even Europe to catch up with any tenderfoot who might have taken advantage of his daughter's solicitude for her father's safety. Of course, he did not confide his misgivings to Hank or Tumbleweed, neither of whom could understand why a man who had just got out of the clink should be more morose than he had been under lock and key. They were further disturbed to see Leonard, who had never gone in for reading much besides the *Cattlemen's Companion*, strip the news stand at the Jordan of every magazine on display and devote the evening to perusing them and throwing them, one by one and with increasing violence, into the red-hot pot-bellied stove.

"I haven't killed a man yet, except in self-defense and anger, but, by God, that isn't saying that I might not do it," he was heard to mutter, at one stage of the game. Hank, Tumbleweed and the Professor shook their heads sadly and headed back to the bar.

"You don't think just one night locked up could have unsettled the Boss's mind?" asked Hank, apprehensively, as he tipped up the bottle of Old Crow they had decided to split.

"Shucks," said Tumbleweed, to comfort him. "Jim's just a bit off his feed, that's all. He's slept outdoors so much that having the door locked got on his nerves. Some kind of phobia, the schoolteacher calls it. Says it accounts for the existence of cowpunchers and bums."

"I'd rather be a bum than teach school," Hank said.

"You'd do better at it, and that's a fact," Tumbleweed rejoined.

Disconcerted by the talk about schools, the Professor, who had taught a few terms in Minneapolis before he could get a stake to buy an outfit to go west, poured himself a drink of Old Crow right to the brim of the glass. "I'm sure anxious to hear Miriam play some of them French tunes," he said. "She must have gone a long way since I helped her figure out the lessons from that correspondence school in Omaha."

THE OBJECT OF THE PARENTAL and friendly solicitude mentioned above was lying wide-eyed in her stateroom on the *Ile-de-France*, listening to the swish of water as the hose was played on the deck just above, and waiting for morning to come, in the hope that the day would bring news direct from her father. She had the message from Weiss to Homer, stating that the matter of the bail had been attended to, but to be out on bail, she knew, was not to be acquitted. And with the judge, the jury and a countryful of Gilligan's witnesses all controlled by the sheepmen, what chance would her father have to go free? Only one, and that meant that her childhood chum and hunting companion, Rain-No-More, must be hanged by the neck until dead. At Homer's insistence, not a word about Leonard's arrest had been divulged to Rain-No-More. Both of them knew that the Indian would give himself up the moment he landed, producing the scalp as evidence of his guilt, if he knew the rancher had been accused of the deed he had found it necessary to commit. Trained in the simple direct ways of thinking characteristic of the Northwestern tribes, it had never occurred to Rain-No-More that he should leave a gangster, bent on murdering his friend, in any position to carry out his intentions. And the Indians had little faith in the white man's law.

Evans felt sure, and so did Miriam, that Jim Leonard would not consent to having Rain-No-More sacrificed if any other way of clearing up the situation could be devised.

Round and round in Miriam's troubled mind, fears and apprehensions pursued one another, until she threw off the bed clothes, dressed herself without arousing Stenka, and started for the promenade deck to wait for the dawn. As she was about to turn a corner in the dimly lighted corridor, however, some instinct prompted her to go cautiously. So she paused, close to the wall, and glanced around without exposing herself to view.

What she saw caused her to draw in her breath sharply, and reach for her automatic. For Santosuosso was emerging from a cabin, not his own, which he locked from the outside with a key before hastening to the foot of the deserted stairway, where he was joined by Terence Gilligan. Miriam waited until she thought the pair had had ample time to return to their own deck, the one below. Then she proceeded along the corridor and noted the number of the cabin from which the Italian had come. It was the one occupied by Rain-No-More. Softly Miriam tapped on the door, using a signal familiar to the Indian, one, in fact, that in terms of revolver shots had served to help them locate each other in the brush by the river, after a day's hunting was over. There was no reply. She tried again, louder. Again, no answer.

Miriam was about to return to her cabin to arouse Homer by telephone, when she remembered that since the nights had become clear, Rain-No-More had told her that he preferred sleeping in a lifeboat in the open air, covered by a tribal blanket. Softly she made her way to the boat deck and glanced into each lifeboat and *canot*. Lightly as she trod, her footsteps were enough to arouse Rain-No-More, who was fully awake and smiling when she discovered him in No. 27, amidships.

"Wakeful, Bird Cherry?" he asked.

Quickly she explained what she had seen, and the Indian vaulted lightly from the lifeboat to the deck. "Wait here," he whispered as he strode away. In five minutes he was back, his handsome face impassive, except for his eyes that glowed with anger.

"It has been stolen," he said, gravely.

"What? Oh, not the scalp?" asked Miriam.

"Exactly," said Rain-No-More. "My money, which was lying in plain sight on the table, is intact. Nothing else is missing. I shall go find this Italian and . . ." He made a sort of paring motion with his bowie knife, which made Miriam shudder.

"Please do nothing until we talk with Homer. There must be some reason why the scalp and nothing else was stolen, and why Mr. Santosuosso has a key to your room. Have you lost your own?"

For answer, Rain-No-More took his key from a pocket of his buckskin jacket, verified the number and handed it to Miriam for inspection.

A moment later the telephone rang softly in Homer's cabin, which was farther forward than Miriam's. In an astonishingly short time he appeared on the boat deck, fully dressed. Miriam told him what had happened, and at once he also urged Rain-No-More to bide his time before accusing Santosuosso.

"When the radiogram was delivered to Miriam yesterday noon," Evans said, "Terence Gilligan and his friend were standing at the bar. The bellboy, to whom all American names are alike, handed the envelope to Gilligan, who had been tipping him lavishly, and asked him who and where was the addressee." Suddenly Homer snapped his fingers, as if struck with an idea, and one not too pleasant. "Have you got the radiograms from Hank and Hugo Weiss?" he asked. Miriam hurried below and returned white with dismay.

"They are missing, too," she said. "I left them in the drawer of my bed-table. Both of them are gone."

"Do you lock your cabin door?" asked Evans.

"Always," said Miriam. "I had the messages in my purse until bedtime. Then I laid them on the table, and I saw them there when I was dressing to come out on deck this morning. It was then I put them in the drawer."

"If you are sure of those facts," Evans said, "then the radiograms must have been stolen since you have been above decks, within the last half hour, as a matter of fact. We know that Gilligan and his buddy have been snooping around the ship, armed with a pass key. The question is: what has aroused their curiosity, and how deeply is it rooted in their youthful minds? Are they merely playing pranks? I think not, but I propose to find out. Will you undertake to help me?"

Both agreed without reservation.

"Your first assignment will not be a pleasant one," said Homer. "I want you to contact Gilligan and Santosuosso, as soon after breakfast as possible, make it appear that the incident of the porpoise is forgotten and forgiven. That will throw them off their guard. Particularly, I would like to have you engage them in a deck-tennis match, which you must contrive to keep as even in score as possible, so that it will go the full five sets."

The Indian groaned. "I could easily beat them both together, without conceding a game," he said.

"Swallow your competitive pride, in the interest of science, this one time," Evans said. "I want to be sure they are away from their staterooms."

"*Nit stoo si kooy ye*" (Well, all right then), said Rain-No-More.

"By the way," asked Evans of Miriam. "Are you carrying your gun?"

She reached into her handbag, then stamped her foot with annoyance and surprise. "Why . . . That's gone, too," she stammered.

With a smile, Evans took her automatic from his pocket and handed it back to her. "Forgive me, dear. I had to have a little practice, just in case I needed to pick a pocket, later on. You will remember that Kaufman the Great, the sleight-of-hand artist, one of the few remaining who is worthy of the name, taught me how easy it was to snatch articles from unsuspecting persons. It's been a long time since I had occasion to test my skill."

"I'm just another dumb girl," said Miriam, still smarting with discomfiture. "To think that you could take my gun away, without my knowing it."

"You might tie a little bell to the trigger guard," suggested Evans, who knew from experience that he could restore Miriam's good humor more easily with a sly jibe than with commiseration.

Until breakfast time, Rain-No-More and Miriam walked the decks and enjoyed what the Goddess Aurora was able to do with a smooth and silent sea. Evans, on the other hand, as sensitive as he was to colors, stared into space from the rail, excluding all else from his mind but the problems on the order of the day. Only once he chuckled with satisfaction.

The reader will remember that in the course of the case of the Mysterious Mickey Finn, Evans got himself appointed Agent Plenipotentiary of the United States Government in France, with powers to right wrongs, relieve distress, expedite justice and, in the words of the imposing document he carried, "to do any and all things necessary or expedient, as he shall deem best, in matters pertinent to crimes, felonies or misdemeanors, and/or attempts at crimes, felonies, misdemeanors or breaches of confidence tending to affect the interests or prestige of the United States of America, threaten the national defense, etc., etc." This all-embracing certificate, signed and sealed with colored wax and ribbons by the American Ambassador and stamped and countersigned by the French Minister of Justice, the Minister of Foreign Affairs, the Prefect of Police of Paris and the Director of the Sûreté Génerale, was in one of Evans' suitcases, carefully pressed between two volumes of a rare edition of Rabelais, illustrated by Gustave Doré.

Any reader familiar with French officialdom can readily understand that merely the seals and ribbons, without the imposing text or the endorsement of the renowned Chief of Detectives Frémont and the medical examiner and distinguished scientist, Dr. Hyacinthe Toudoux, were enough to impress the Captain of the *Ile-de-France* to the extent that he was willing to give Evans the keys to the ship, access to all records and complete *carte blanche*. First, Homer asked the Captain to call to his cabin the purser. The latter arrived promptly, and extremely nervous. Foreigners were always losing expensive jewelry and complaining of theft, which meant a long secret search of the liner from bow to stern, and particularly inconvenience and resentment in the crew's quarters. Evans assured him at once that the matter in question was not of that nature. He simply asked the purser to inform him, confidentially, if and when one of the cabin stewards reported the loss of a pass key.

From the Captain's quarters, Evans went to the sports deck, forward, where he found in his snug cabin the radio engineer. Showing the latter the seals and ribbons on his credentials, and the note from the Captain urging all officers and sailors of the French Line to give the bearer all possible information, regardless of precedents or rules, Homer asked to see the files of incoming and outgoing radio messages covering the entire voyage. Within ten minutes he had come upon the following:

TERENCE GILLIGAN
ILE-DE-FRANCE
HAVE UNO INVESTIGATE NEW YORK WHO PUT
UP FIFTY GRAND BAIL FOR JIM LEONARD STOP
BELIEVE SOME FRIEND OF DAUGHTER IN-
VOLVED STOP SHE IS ON ILE-DE-FRANCE STOP
PICK UP WHAT YOU CAN FROM HER AND HELP
FORMER N.P. DICK TRAIL HER FROM MOMENT
SHE LANDS STOP DICK WILL MEET YOU AT
DOCK DONT GIVE SHOW AWAY
DAD

"Ah," said Evans to himself. "The finding of the scalp, then, was accidental. Our unworthy Santo, referred to rather transparently as Uno by Larkspur Gilligan, must have seen Rain-No-More go up to the boat deck for a snooze in the open air, and must have watched Miriam go up there later. He was searching for possible messages and clues to the fifty grand, which he knows now came from Hugo Weiss. Having had a crack at Rain-No-More's cabin, and that of Miriam—of course, he assumed correctly that Stenka would sleep like a log—our amateur seeker after truth will rifle my cabin next. Just now, my room steward is bustling in and out, and Santo, I observe, is playing deck tennis in a sports shirt of a particularly obnoxious color. The attempt will be made at lunch time, when I am safely at table."

Smiling with satisfaction, Homer walked to the port rail and for a moment allowed the beauty of the sparkling Atlantic, calm and fragrant under the warm sunshine, to renovate his consciousness. Sea birds were more numerous and bolder. Sienna and amber-colored seaweed drifted past in the counter-current of the beneficent Gulf Stream. If Evans thought of the gaiety of Montparnasse, the quiet of his deserted apartment, or the Old World sanctuaries and relics of former civilizations, no nostalgia was discernible on his sensitive countenance. For the lands along the Yellowstone were as old or older than the caves of the Neanderthal man, and if the races who had inhabited them had not built

cathedrals, at least they had kept the country's resources intact
and the mysterious and vast landscape unspoiled before the coming of the Europeans. Memories of volcanic badlands—pale brick-
red, hazy violet, ochre, colors of ancient earth and ashes—were
superimposed on the background of the glassy sea.

In place of dress buyers, minor diplomats, dilettantes, remit-
tance men, rich widows, professors, movie stars and his own companions, who made up the passenger list of the *Ile-de-France*, he
visualized the Mound Builders at work on their stupendous monuments, great herds of buffalos grazing on the plains, the Indians
on the warpath, or engaged in their peaceful pursuits. He strained
his ears for the sound of coyotes wailing to the moon. He remembered the smell of sage and saddle leather; horses, cattle, deer and
antelope; the neatness of the foothills and the mesas, tier on tier;
the rivers and the mountains; seasons that were definitely seasons;
constellations sharp and quartz-like in the cold, near and pulsing
in the heat of summer. Regretfully he refocused his attention on
the scalp of the late Donniker Louey, who had lived by the rod and
died by the blade, as it were, but he could not feel sorry that the
said memento had been lifted and was partly instrumental in calling him from a smoldering and decaying Europe back to the land
of his birth.

Another brief consultation with the purser made it certain that
in searching the cabins of Santosuosso and Gilligan, Evans would
not be disturbed by the room stewards, who were given tasks in
other corridors. But all Homer's thoroughness and patience net-
ted him precisely nothing. The scalp was simply not there. Surprised and disappointed, Homer went over both cabins a second
time, more carefully, if possible. Again he drew a blank. He went
up to the sports deck, where Rain-No-More was stoically winning
and losing points, almost alternately, in pursuance of his instructions. Unobserved, he went through the pockets of the coats and
sweaters belonging to Santosuosso and Gilligan as well. They were
both so elated at being able to hold their own at deck tennis against
the Indian they disliked and despised that they noticed nothing
They had already accomplished the errand for the elder Gilligan,

they believed, and that raised their spirits, too, and diminished their alertness.

Baffled for the moment, Evans mounted to the deck between the smokestacks, where Moritz was playing with the Newfoundland, and a couple of Scotties were waddling, protestingly, on the end of leashes. The Boxer was so glad to see Homer and so pleased because he could at last smell land that he reverted to his puppy tricks just once, and put his large front paws on Homer's trousers. Evans, to remind him that there are such things as discipline and restraint, touched one of Moritz's hind feet with his shoe. Then he snapped on the breast harness and led him below, to his cabin, carefully keeping out of sight of the tennis enthusiasts.

Hydrangea, in a leaf-green bathing suit by Lanvin, was diving discreetly into the swimming pool and sunning herself on the tile rim, with Chief Frémont in a deck chair near by, cautioning her uneasily. Hjalmar was teaching Stenka to swim, and, in truth, they made a handsome pair, six feet two and six feet one, respectively, with light brown hair and skin as white as marble. Had Manet been present, he would have used his "Olympia" for a brush rag and tried again, with his principals in bathing suits and the ocean for a background instead of a boudoir wall. Rubens, on the other hand, would have barged into the pool, palette, clothes and all.

Evans, with Moritz at his heel, paused for a whispered consultation with Frémont, who rose reluctantly and followed him, after exacting a promise from Hydrangea that she would get dry and dressed without delay. On the way, they sought out Dr. Hyacinthe Toudoux, who said good-bye to his Eugénie with such fervor that one might have thought he was going to quit the *Ile-de-France*. The doctor joined the small procession.

In Homer's commodious cabin a strange scene unrolled itself, as the French would say, and Evans, noting the perplexity of his two companions, did nothing to guide them out of the fog. First he took from his pocket a soiled silk shirt that resembled in color, if anything, borscht and cream stirred together. That the garment belonged to Santosuosso and had been pinched from the Italian's cabin a little earlier that morning was not divulged. Unsnapping the leash, Homer asked Moritz to sit down and listen attentively, which the Boxer did. His sensitive nerves had told him he was somehow on trial, and in advance he was determined not to let Homer down.

Extending the shirt, crumpled in his hand, Evans held it near the dog's damp black nose. The latter sneezed.

"Excuse me. Too close," said Evans, and placed the garment on the floor. Moritz caught on, and sniffed the shirt, looking upward and wrinkling his forehead in anticipation of further instructions. Then Homer asked Frémont and Toudoux to leave the cabin for a moment and return, one by one, unlocking the door as stealthily as possible.

"You're sure the dog won't misunderstand?" Frémont asked, still weak from his bout of seasickness. He had seen Moritz in action before and did not feel equal to taking him on, even to please the eccentric Evans.

"I shall stay here with him," Homer said.

A moment later the Boxer's stiff short hair bristled as light footsteps were heard in the corridor and the latch of the door began to move, almost imperceptibly. "Quiet, old boy," whispered Evans, and made the usual tranquilizing signal with his thumb and forefinger. When the door came open, millimeter by millimeter, however, Moritz left his place at the bedside and started toward the doorway. "No," said Homer, and the Boxer returned, bewildered. Four times the maneuver was repeated, until Moritz did not even blink when either of Evans' confederates made their entrance.

The next step nonplussed the two French officials even more than the initial ones. They were asked to tiptoe to the door and drop the borscht-colored and crumpled shirt at the threshold. When Frémont did so, Evans, with his hand close to the Boxer's muzzle, slapped the palm of his hand with his fingers. Head down and growling savagely, Moritz charged toward the door. After a few more rehearsals, Homer smiled.

"I think he has the idea," he said.

"He has the advantage of me," said Frémont, somewhat reproachfully, and he was seconded by Dr. Hyacinthe Toudoux.

"Shall we try him out with a stranger?" asked Evans.

"If you do not value the stranger," Frémont said.

They left Moritz locked in the cabin and in the next corridor Homer found his room steward. "Would you mind going to my cabin for the book that is on the bed-table?" he asked.

"Not at all, Monsieur," the steward said, but before he could get started Frémont detained him.

"Are you a war veteran?" the Chief of Detectives asked.

"Naturally, Monsieur," the steward replied.

"Father of a family?" inquired Toudoux.

The face of the steward at once betrayed suspicion and alarm, since he had established, for his convenience and to the detriment of no one concerned, a small-sized family at each end of the run. Evans reassured the man promptly and sent him on his errand. In two minutes he was back with the book, smiling happily.

"What a gentle dog you have there, Monsieur Evans," the steward said. "And with such a deceptive appearance of ferocity."

Evans had fished out a hundred-franc note and was unfolding it carefully. "Will you do me another favor?" he asked. "Perhaps I ought to tell you that these gentlemen are the Chief of Detectives and the Medical Examiner of Paris, respectively."

The nearest porthole was open and Homer was obliged to restrain the steward from diving through it like a terrier through a hoop. When he explained that he only wanted him to stay away from the vicinity of Cabin 614 during the noon meal hour, the man's face was eloquent with relief.

In the smoking room, just before the *apéritif* hour, Evans was in earnest conversation with Frémont and Toudoux.

"Chief," he said, "you have been sent to America to study methods of tracking down criminals, have you not?"

"Unfortunately," said Frémont, and sighed. "Where or how I shall begin such a wild-goose chase, I have not been able to decide."

"You are free to go where you wish, and conduct your research in any way you see fit?"

"That makes it harder," said Frémont. "The prefect won't even take the responsibility of indicating a suitable itinerary."

"Then why not come west, with me?" Evans asked. "I can tell you gentlemen in confidence that a situation has come to my attention which bids fair to become one of the notorious criminal cases of the decade. It involves, not only personal relationships and various degrees of murder, but huge business interests and one of America's last lingering frontiers. Needless to say, you can be of inestimable service."

In the course of their three years' association, Evans had never seen Frémont so deeply moved. The Chief was, in fact, burbling with gratitude and clinging firmly to Homer's coat sleeve, as if he were afraid to let go for fear that Evans would change his mind and leave him on his own again.

"You have saved me so many times on land," Frémont said, "that nothing remained, I suppose, except for you to rescue me from disgrace and ridicule at sea."

In his corner, Dr. Hyacinthe Toudoux was squirming impatiently.

"Would you, perchance, have need of a biologist, toxicologist, chemist, or even a first-aid attendant?" he asked, dusting of the decorations on his coat lapel. "My leave of absence is of six months' duration, the congress at Chicago will last but a single afternoon. Besides, I promised Eugenie to show her the Natural Bridge, Niagara Falls and all the National parks. Those points of interest cannot be far distant from the department you call Montana."

"The Natural Bridge, the first spot you mentioned, is not farther from Montana than the Land of the Midnight Sun is from the Paris prefecture," Evans said, smiling. "But I shall be honored and relieved if you will lend a hand, and can promise you an unforgettable tour of Yellowstone Park, once the hurly-burly's done."

"I am a young man again. Life stretches before me," the doctor said, and leaving his place at the table he began skipping and cavorting across the smoking room, humming inexpertly a tune the effect of which was about half way between "Sumer Is Icumen in" and "Dansez la Carmagnole."

Meanwhile, confined in Homer's cabin, which he had practically memorized from deck to ceiling, Moritz, the dog, was doing a bit of creditable cerebration on his own account. He had seized the fact that he had been placed there to work on an intruder, and not any John Doe intruder, but one who had recently lost a shirt. Moritz reasoned thus: if he growled and raised a scandal the moment the key touched the lock, the party of the second part would be warned in time and would make his getaway, while Moritz pined behind locked doors. On the other hand, if a dog should take his place behind the door, as it opened, and be patient until the wrongo got well inside the cabin, the possibilities of the situation would increase by leaps and bounds.

It was the second course of action on which Moritz decided as the gong was given the first strokes of an unusually thorough trundling by the steward with repressed desires.

6

For the Reading of Which the Reader
Should Be Wrapped Warmly

IT IS TO BE HOPED THAT THE READER, in being transported suddenly from the sunswept decks and well-heated cabins of the *Ile-de-France* in the mild Gulf Stream to the lodge of Shot-on-Both-Sides, Chief of the Blackfeet, on the frigid northern shore of the ice-bound Missouri, will not catch pneumonia. Nevertheless and notwithstanding, it is on or near the last-named reservation that the opening events of this chapter take place.

A steady night wind, following an afternoon thaw, had formed a hard crust on the snow. So, with a pair of skis each, Hank and the Professor had set out from Glendive, to follow up the lead given them secretly by Johnny O'Brien, the storekeeper at Circle, to the effect that the Blackfeet Chief, and particularly his son, Rain-No-More, might shed some light on the disappearance of Donniker Louey. The strange behavior of Jim Leonard, their boss, had abated somewhat in the early morning and he had started for Mondak, on the stage, intending if possible to hike from the intersection of Leonard Creek to Three Buttes and make preparations to receive his daughter and learn the worst. Tumbleweed O'Flaherty accompanied the rancher, and together they hoped to figure out some line of defense against the murder charge.

Hank and the Professor got a ride in the caboose of a freight train from Glendive to Circle, saving them nearly a hundred miles, and from Circle, after another consultation with O'Brien, they headed for Redwater Creek, the deadline drawn by the cattle- and sheepmen when the government officials, at Gilligan's instigation, had insisted on opening the Western range to the woollies. The crust, softened slightly by the sun, which that day shone on cowpunchers as well as passengers on ocean liners, was ideal for skiing, and the two men glided easily along. Once they had reached the head of the creek, the journey to the Missouri was downhill all the way, and by nightfall they had made Coyote Creek, where they camped in the lee of a sheepherder's shack, refusing to risk getting lousy inside. On a sled they had taken turns in dragging were blankets, tarpaulins, a bottle of Old Crow, two back numbers of *Snappy Stories*, a corkscrew, a can opener, bacon, flour, sugar, coffee and a coffee pot, beans, Bull Durham, papers, souvenir handkerchiefs for the Chief, a tin box filled with matches, and pages 306 to 353 of the Montgomery Ward catalogue of the previous year. Also, thanks to the Professor, there were a couple of pies which the waitress at the Hotel Jordan had given him. The waitress, like the clerk, the cook, the bartender and the rest of the staff of the Hotel Jordan, was decidedly pro-cattle in the struggle that had developed on the Lower Yellowstone and which involved every man, woman and child in the country in one way or another. It was impossible not to take sides, although some people, for business or personal reasons, hid their feelings, while others spoke them openly, prepared to back their opinions in frontier fashion, any place or any day.

Around the campfire that night the two buckaroos discussed the disappearance of Donniker Louey and, like the immortal Persian poet, they "came out by the same door that in they went."

"Heck," said Hank, "I can see how a tenderfoot could get himself lost in the foothills. I can't tell them apart myself, hardly, in broad daylight. But that Eyetalian was roosting plumb on a creek. And a creek's bound to lead somewhere."

"Like as not he tried to hit it for home across country. A man can't figure what those scissorbills'll do."

"And what business did he have with the boss? You noticed Gilligan never said what the business was," Hank continued.

"Too bad for that old white horse," said the Professor. "He had to walk all the way across the sheep range with his head cocked to one side, so's not to stumble over the lines."

"Must of been a damn fool horse to go home to Gilligan," Hank said.

"Instinct," the Professor said. "That's what's always got me in wrong. Here I am out in the foothills, backed up against a sheepherders' shanty where I could use the well-known brass monkey for a footwarmer, when I ought to be raising kids in Minneapolis and singing in the choir."

"I've been in Minneapolis twice," Hank said, "but neither time I didn't get any farther uptown than the hotel bar across from the N.P. depot."

"Pass the hootch," said the Professor. "And to hell with Minneapolis."

Hank handed over the Old Crow, then walked a little farther up the gully, where he broke a couple of limbs from a dead cottonwood tree and, returning, tossed them on the fire. Across the creek, a coyote raised his whimpering song, ending in a fusillade of yaps and barks so that it was hard to tell whether there was one or a dozen. A new moon, rising, silvered the vast expanses of snow and mellowed the brown of the foothills swept bare. Of timber there was none, except in the gulches out of sight. Only drifts and lava rock, crumbling sandstone cliffs and low clumps of sagebrush, and the earth frozen two feet deep. Warmed by the whiskey and the crackling fire, and pleased because the wind had gone down, the cowpunchers sat on their heels in immense frigid solitude. It was barely six o'clock, but they had planned to turn in early, in order to get started before dawn and make the reservation by mid-morning. The Professor unrolled his tarp, shook out the blankets and his slicker, and began fixing up his bed. Hank whittled off some kindling wood and placed it inside the door of the shack where it would be ready for the morning. Already the coffee in the pot was frozen solid, as were the leavings of the beans. Suddenly the foreman stepped back into the shadow, and in the act drew his gun.

"Shhh," he cautioned softly, when the Professor was about to ask what was loose. The foreman pointed toward the rim of the hills across Redwater Creek. Someone was approaching, still distant, with a peculiar gait that was neither like skating nor running.

"Snowshoes, by God. It's an Indian," Hank whispered.

"Now what would an Indian be doing over here at this time of night?" asked the Professor. "If you ask me, I'd say this whole God-blasted country has gone loco."

"Now you've scared him," said Hank, for the Indian disappeared from view. The cowpunchers waited a while, then continued their preparations for bed by breaking the crust of a drift and scooping out a hole in which to place their tarps. Before they had got very far with their necessary chore, however, they were startled by a voice.

"*Kit kse mat taim mo*" (Hello), the voice said.

"We're from Leonard's ranch. Come on and get warm," yelled Hank in response. He knew about six words of Blackfeet lingo, and was relieved that the nightfarer was of that friendly and reliable tribe. Both cowboys were astonished when the Indian strode gravely into the circle of light around the fire. He did not betray, either by his words or his demeanor, that he found it strange to come upon a couple of buckaroos camping out on the sheep range in the dead of winter, at least eighty miles from the nearest white habitation. Chief Shot-on-Both-Sides had fought the whites and, when overpowered but not conquered, had tried to live in peace with them. Their ways were strange and productive of headaches if one examined them in the light of reason. That was his slant on the situation.

"Well, doggone my hide if it isn't the Chief, himself," Hank said, extending his hand.

"*Stoo ye*," said the Indian, which meant "cold."

"Good evening," the Professor said, and made signs toward the remnants of the food.

Shot-on-Both-Sides, also by means of signs, indicated that his belly was full. He had set out from his lodge after dinner. The bottle of Old Crow was fortunately out of sight, so the Chief was spared the pain of refusing a swig of its dangerous contents. He knew his limit, from painful experience, and admitted to himself that it was zero. He did accept with pleasure some Bull Durham and, after waiting politely for both Hank and the Professor to take a few puffs, he smoked his tribal pipe, squatting easily on his heels and watching the glowing embers thoughtfully. A decent interval ensued, for both the cowboys knew a little of Indian ways. Then Hank let fall the remark that he was glad to see the Chief. Shot-on-Both-Sides nodded solemnly. The Professor then went further along the same line. He said, slowly and distinctly, that they were bound for the Chief's own lodge, on a pressing errand. The Chief pointed due south, described a circle with his finger to indicate the name of that town, then swept his arm eastward until it was right in line with Glendive, and made train noises the while. He was on the way to Glendive, via Circle, and hoped to catch the early morning train.

"Jim Leonard, the boss. Heap trouble," the foreman said.

That thawed the reserve of the Indian, who never volunteered unnecessary information. He had heard, by means of the amazing tribal grapevine that seemed to operate like the radio, that Leonard had been arrested, but did not understand what for. By means of signs, some Indian words and a choice selection of English, the foreman tried to explain the situation, and he had not got far before Shot-on-Both-Sides got the drift. It had not occurred to him up to that moment that his friend Jim Leonard's clash with the law was connected in any way with what Rain-No-More had disclosed weeks before about the incident on Cottonwood Creek. The Chief had started on his two-hundred-mile journey across country merely to verify the report that Leonard was in jail and offer his resources to free his friend. Having learned that Leonard was out, on bail, and had started back to Three Buttes, Shot-on-Both-Sides decided to wait on Coyote Creek until the cowboys had slept, then go back with them to the reservation. The offer of blankets and space in the snowbank, the Indian refused politely.

"I shall sit around the fire," he said. "I wish to think, and can sleep some other time." He said it in his own language, but the cowpunchers understood and turned in. The moon floated steadily across the sky. Shooting stars described desperate arcs, then flared out. Coyotes, attracted by the fire, came nearer and watched from the darkness, and the Chief caught occasional glimpses of their glowing amber eyes. The sheep range to the west was deserted; the cattle to the east had taken shelter many miles away.

At four o'clock in the morning, Hank, the foreman, stirred, shook the fine snow from the flap of his tarp and stuck his head out of the snowbank.

"Come on, Professor. Signs of life," he said. "You don't want to stay in bed all day and wear out the bedclothes."

"The hell I don't," the Professor said, but he yawned and sat up, just the same.

JUST SHORTLY AFTER THAT MOMENT, allowing for the difference in time, the passengers on the *Ile-de-France* began to assemble in the dining salon for lunch. At the Captain's table there was unusual good cheer because Sergeant Schlumberger, blinking in the sunlight, made his first appearance and was greeted with words of encouragement. The honest Alsatian's clothes did not seem to fit. He closed his eyes and shuddered now and then when waiters passed too near with trays of herring or steam ragouts. He glanced reproachfully at an American traveling salesman who was smoking the last end of his cigar while waiting for filet of sole. But Schlumberger's face had lost its greenish tinge and was in the old parchment stage, with little russet and purple veins at the cheekbones and around his nose, to indicate that he had not neglected himself before going to sea.

At the table for two, ordinarily occupied by Gilligan and Santosuosso, the former was sitting alone, and it seemed to Homer, who was observing his actions carefully, that he was definitely uneasy. He merely toyed with the *hors d'œuvres*, in spite of the exercise involved in the tennis match, which should have sharpened his appetite. It chanced that while he was eating French fried potatoes the ship's whistle let out a blast to salute a passing liner.

Involuntarily Gilligan tossed a golden sliver of *pomme frite* all the way into the lap of a missionary who was browsing over an old *Christian Endeavor World* three tables away.

Let us leave the diners to their excellent meal and peep for an instant into the corridor leading past Cabin No. 614. It chanced that the dog steward, a fine upstanding Norman lad, had left his charges to their own devices in the kennels and was on his way aft to the crew's dining quarters. When he was not more than ten yards from Evans' stateroom, he was startled by an assortment of animal noises not surpassed by anything he had heard while he had previously worked in the circus. A split second later, there emerged from No. 614, the door of which was ajar, what looked like a human pinwheel with a faun-colored rim. Having grown accustomed in the circus to all kinds of emergencies, the steward contrived to catch Moritz by the scruff of the neck and shout soothing phrases into his closely cropped ears, at the same time wrenching the victim loose with his other hand.

Young Santosuosso, for it was he, was close to collapse from fright. Like so many products of the crowded slums, he understood animals not at all and had an atavistic dread of them. The dog had bitten him, not too deeply and only in the softer parts away from vital spots, for Moritz had felt sure that Homer didn't want the intruder killed outright but merely was anxious for him to be taught a lesson. So after a number of introductory bites, the Boxer had started shaking his foe, taking hold first by the back of the collar, then later by the seat of the pants.

Once the dog steward had restored a semblance of order, he advised the injured man to rush to the doctor for first-aid treatment. That was the last thing the Italian wished to do, and the Norman at once became suspicious, and at the same time aware that he was overdue for his lunch. Moritz, seeing that the steward was in a quandary, took hold lightly on Santosuosso's trousers and tugged toward the open stateroom. The Norman caught on, and agreed. He shoved the limp passenger back into No. 614, closed the door, and looked over him carefully. Painful but not dangerous, was his verdict concerning the Italian's wounds. The steward looked at Moritz, to make sure there would be no more rough stuff, and the Boxer, to show that he understood, assumed that prone position known to trainers as *"platz."*

"Don't leave us alone. He'll murder me," the Italian pleaded.

"Your name isn't Evans, that's plain," the steward said. "I'm going to leave you here until Mr. Evans gets back from lunch. The dog won't hurt you, unless you provoke him." And with that the Norman backed away and closed the door.

Gilligan, in the dining salon, grew increasingly nervous. Once or twice he started to leave his place, but always Evans' eyes were upon him and he didn't dare move. Homer, when the meal was over, had a whispered consultation with Frémont, and the two men went below. They found, to their surprise and satisfaction, that Santosuosso was cowering in a corner and Moritz was in the alert position between him and the door.

"Good afternoon," said Evans, smiling ominously. "I want to introduce you to the Chief of Detectives of Paris, who has authority in all parts of France and on French liners, which are technically a part of the Third Republic."

"I'm not talking," Santosuosso said grimly. Jail or no jail, or even if he was to be thrown overboard, he felt easier now that he had human company to protect him from the dog.

"Not necessary, I assure you," Evans said. "I'm not going to be vindictive because you tried to search my room. My life is an open book, more or less. There's just one thing I want from you, my misguided young friend. You may keep the cablegrams you filched from Miss Leonard's cabin. We both had read them, anyway. What I shall require you to produce, if you do not wish to be placed in irons and taken back to France for trial as a common thief, is another object you removed without authority from the cabin of Monsieur Rain-No-More. That has a sentimental value and cannot easily be replaced."

"I haven't got it," said Santosuosso, slightly thawed by the prospect of getting off more easily than he had expected.

"Then tell me where it is," Evans persisted.

"I chucked it overboard," the Italian said.

Evans sighed. "You make things very difficult," he said. Then he turned to Moritz. "Moritz," he continued, "would you like another workout, or would that be asking too much?"

For answer the dog rose to his feet and got set. His strong muscles bulged as he lowered his head. The effect on Santosuosso was heartrending indeed. The young man dissolved in terror, his eyes distended, his hands clasped as if in prayer. In eloquent Chicago English and with a smattering of his parental tongue he swore by all the saints that the scalp was in the briny.

"I got jittery," he pleaded. "When I saw it had been stripped off a white man, I got superstitious, so help me Christ, I did. I didn't want the thing around. I can't understand how I happened to pinch it in the first place."

Homer turned to Frémont, who nodded. "I think he's telling the truth, for once," the Chief of Detectives said.

Sighing again, Evans jerked his head toward the doorway, and the Italian streaked through, and was not seen by Evans or his friends, except at a distance, during the remainder of the voyage.

THAT AFTERNOON, which was morning on the snowswept range, two men, widely separated in distance, race, temperament and cultural heritage, were deep in thought on related matters. One was Chief Shot-on-Both-Sides, who on snowshoes kept pace easily with the cowboys on skis, as they glided northward down the Redwater toward the Missouri and the reservation. The other was Homer Evans.

The old Indian, whose face was impassive, was weighted down, not by his years, which troubled him scarcely at all, but by impending tragedy. When Rain-No-More had told him what had happened to Donniker Louey on Cottonwood Creek, before snowfall, the Chief had nodded his approval. Certainly no self-respecting Blackfeet brave would leave an assassin roaming the foothills with the intention of killing from ambush an old and trusted friend. Even more certainly, no son of a chief would let a friend pay the penalty of death in his stead. Those two incontrovertible truths formed the basis for the Indian chieftain's sorrow. Eventually, the three men came to the broad frozen Missouri and crossed to the northern side, and within a half hour they were seated in the Chief's tepee, being served a second breakfast by the Chief's two daughters, Unreal Bear and Tinted Cloud, both of whom had attended white men's school. After stationing a trusted sentry to insure privacy, the Chief listened to a full recital of the events leading up to Leonard's arrest, and the miraculous appearance of a wheelbarrow load of gold. The daughters acted as interpreters, switching skillfully from Blackfeet to English, with a quaint Southern accent, since their teacher had come from South Carolina. Then, to gain time, the Chief informed the cowpunchers that Rain-No-More was far away, across the ocean, and would tell them what he could when he returned.

All day, after Hank and the Professor had started for Three Buttes, Shot-on-Both-Sides sat in his lodge without replenishing the fire, or allowing the squaws to enter. Late that evening, he sent for his second son, Longtime-Pipe.

"Son," he said, "it may be necessary for you, in the future, to guide the destinies of our tribe."

Longtime-Pipe, an easygoing young Indian adept at white men's golf, was filled with dismay. But of course he could not question his father, or ask why life-long plans had been suddenly changed. It had always been assumed that Rain-No-More would be elected chief, because of his aptitude for leadership and his thorough education. However, while the squaws wept in secret, young Longtime-Pipe set forth for Berkeley, California, to master paleface's firewater as part of the special training Shot-on-Both-Sides required of a possible successor.

COINCIDENTLY, RAIN-NO-MORE, aboard the *Ile-de-France*, was sitting stoically in Evans' cabin, with Homer and Miriam, and all of them were heavy-hearted. Rain-No-More had been informed of Leonard's arrest, and he well knew the political situation in Eastern Montana. His first thought had been to produce the scalp and give himself up. But the loss of the evidence had complicated what otherwise would have been, for him, a simple problem. Because he had not wanted to involve any of his innocent tribesmen in connection with the gangster's death, Rain-No-More had disposed of the body in the Missouri, in such a way that no trace could be found, even if the river bed was dredged for miles, which was impossible. Larkspur Gilligan did not want merely to convict an Indian. He wanted Jim Leonard out of the way. How could Rain-No-More prove he was guilty, if the sheriff would not take his word for it, which was not within the realm of probability? Surely young Santosuosso, if produced as a witness, would be primed in advance by Gilligan and deny having seen a scalp in Rain-No-More's possession.

"We've got to sit tight," Evans said. "I can't believe Gilligan thinks he can get away with convicting Mr. Leonard without producing the body or any evidence except the flimsy story of the two sheepherders, who did not state they had seen a crime committed, but merely that they had seen Mr. Leonard halt, circle and fire his rifle."

"Let me shoot it out with Gilligan," Miriam said, her eyes flashing.

"Perhaps we can think of something with a bit more finesse. Who knows?" asked Homer. "This is not a simple case of murder. In fact, we all know it's not murder at all. In the place of Rain-No-More I should have done exactly as he did, except for the touch about the scalp. That was ingenious, but it would not have occurred to me. Probably, also, I should have announced what I had done and taken my chances with the law, which of course would be folly for Rain-No-More. What troubles me most is the larger aspect of the situation. Gilligan wants the range east of Redwater and will go to any lengths to get it. He has been making careful preparations many months, perhaps years. If he has enlisted in his services the lawless element from Cicero and Chicago, with Baldy Santo at its head, the conflict will take on heroic proportions. Now we have in our ranks Hjalmar, Frémont, Dr. Toudoux, aside from those present, and, of course, Sergeants Schlumberger and Bonnet. Hugo Weiss will furnish money in any quantity, and money forms the sinews of war, as has been so aptly said by some wise man or other. Perhaps, also, Hugo will loan us his two excellent subordinates and horsemen, Lvov Kvek and Grigori Lidin, from the recent army of the late Tsar. Tom Jackson will act as scribe. Besides, we have Mr. Leonard, himself, his staff of buckaroos, and one of the noblest tribes of aborigines extant. For good measure, we have right and justice on our side. I refer of course to abstract justice, and not the kind hatched up by Gilligan. On the whole, we're not badly off."

7
Of the Influence of Sex on Ways of Getting Rid of Money

As THE ILE-DE-FRANCE APPROACHED the American shore, the passengers on board who had never seen that continent could not conceal their eagerness and curiosity. Eugenie Toudoux, née de Sault, leaned wistfully against the rail, well forward on the starboard side, between her husband and Rain-No-More. Even before the lookout in the crow's nest cried out "Land," the sharp eyes of the Indian saw a hazy streak in the distance and pointed it out to his companions. Chief of Detectives Frémont and Sergeant Schlumberger, both well on the way toward recovery, could not restrain themselves from gamboling and chirping with glee as the cliffs, trees and buildings of Staten Island became discernible.

In the forecastle, where he was hobnobbing with the crew, Hjalmar Jansen was bellowing a ribald chanty to the accompaniment of a harmonica played by Sergeant Bonnet.

> *We anchored of Algeria,*
> *The weather it grew drearier,*
> *And all the whores*
> *Along those shores*
> *Got wearier and wearier.*

Miriam and Homer stood side by side, saying little or nothing. There is something about a return to one's native land, after years abroad, that stirs memories and anticipations and discourages conversation. Both of them were anxious to get through the formalities of landing and to reach the scene of action, which still was three thousand miles away. Also, Miriam's reticence was due in part to a radiogram that had been slipped beneath her door that morning before she was dressed. "All will be forgiven" was one of the more cryptic of the phrases, and the message was signed simply "Dad." It had suddenly occurred to her that certain details of her life in Paris would be difficult to explain in terms her father would understand.

The pilot scrambled aboard, at Quarantine the immigration officers took possession of the salon and the smoking room, while passengers stood uneasily in long lines and looked at their papers again and again to make sure they were in order. Homer accompanied the French-speaking members of the group and acted as interpreter, but he had arranged with the Captain to have Gilligan and Santosuosso detained until after the others had gone ashore. Santosuosso, huddling in a corner of the salon, was a picture of apprehension. When, after standing in line, he reached the desk where the passenger list was being checked, the curt officer told him to wait. The Italian was afraid he would be arrested, and young Gilligan began to bluster, which got him precisely nowhere.

"It's that guy Evans who has the drag," Santosuosso said. "I only hope he gets near enough Chicago so the old man can take him and his damn dog for a ride." Moritz, so irreverently referred to, had been released from the kennel and was behaving his best, at Miriam's side.

When the skyscrapers of lower Manhattan came into view, resplendent in the morning sunshine, Frémont's face looked definitely reproachful.

"It's clear that Americans will stop at nothing," he sighed. "Ah, well! Perhaps we French are wrong and old-fashioned to cling to moderation. Five stories, six stories, yes, if they do not obscure public monuments or architectural treasures. But building wantonly, up and up." The Chief of Detectives shook his head. As a matter of fact, Rain-No-More was thinking much the same thoughts, except that his preoccupation concerned hunting facilities and not Gothic cathedrals.

Perhaps the most excited member of the party was Hydrangea. She was pointing out objects of interest to Stenka, the Serbian maid, who had stopped trying to hook up New York and its skyline with reality and was crossing herself with practically no interruption. Once or twice when she lost sight of Miriam, Stenka became frantic and charged from deck to deck, overturning passengers, stewards, trunks and even officials, who thought a blonde tornado had passed by. That Miriam had entrusted her valises, filled with lovely clothes, to perfect strangers, was considered by Stenka to be the height of folly.

Slowly and with queenly majesty, the *Ile-de-France* left behind the Statue of Liberty, skirted the Battery and started up the Hudson, passing pier after pier. Neatly it was swung around and sidled up to No. 88. The gangplank had scarcely touched the floor when Hugo Weiss, in faultless morning clothes, was escorted aboard by an official of the French Line. He was followed by two tall handsome Russians in equally impeccable attire and swinging gold-headed canes. The first Russian, Lvov Kvek, embraced Homer Evans, weeping with joy and uttering fervent greetings in practically all the modern languages. Grigori Lidin, in less happy days the doorman at the Plaza Athènée, clasped Hjalmar in a bear hug and they started waltzing. Hugo Weiss greeted Miriam, beaming with heartfelt pleasure.

"Ah, Miriam," he said, when she tried to thank him for his service to her father. "How seldom it is that one can be glad of having wads of money! Not only my life I owe to you and Homer Evans, but a quality of friendship that nearly always is denied the ultra-rich. The adventure we had three years ago I would not exchange for the directorship of fifty corporations, and now we shall have another. I feel it in my bones. No! Don't object! I'm going west with you and see this thing through. All arrangements have been made. The wheels of industry and finance will continue to turn in my absence, although that is in strict confidence. Ah, there's Chief Frémont and Dr. Toudoux!"

In short, the hearts of all concerned were warmed and, arm in arm, the gay companions trooped into the customs shed where, because of Weiss, the little orange stickers were being plastered on the baggage as fast as the trunks and valises reached the bottom of the chute. The members of the group had been so engrossed in their welcome that a modest couple standing on the sidelines and smiling wistfully were almost overlooked. It was Hjalmar who first spied them and announced his discovery with a roar.

Side by side, so close together that her sleeve was touching his coatsleeve gently, were Beatrice and Anton Diluvio. The former was carrying a small but exquisite bouquet of dwarf moss-rosebuds for Miriam. The violinist was imploring Evans to let him lend a hand in the case before him, so eloquently that Homer, whose heart was ever vulnerable, could not say no. That the pair who had been brought together for eternity in the hay-strewn hold of the *Presque Sans Souci* were happy was so evident that to mention the fact is almost indelicate.

"I shall cancel the rest of my concert tour," Diluvio said.

Beatrice looked up at him and smiled. "As you wish, dear, but let me go, too. I can cook, you know, and ride."

"Of course you shall go," said Hugo Weiss gallantly. "In fact, I am placing my special cars at Mr. Evans' disposal and we'll all go west in style. When do we start? This evening? So much the better." His secretary, who was always in the offing, lit out for a booth to make the necessary telephone calls, and by the time the company was seated for lunch the two luxurious Pullmans, Pelleas and Melisande, were being polished and dusted within an inch of their lives. Telegraphs had clicked and stuttered from coast to coast, over the intricate network of railroads, and the cars were being routed from New York to Glendive, Montana, with a stopover in Chicago.

The former N.P. detective, known to his intimates as Nutcracker Ike, was in conference with young Santosuosso and Gilligan behind a couple of packing cases. The dick didn't like the look of things at all. Had his array of opponents included only one man in frock coat and striped trousers, that would have been enough to make him nervous. That there were three disconcerted him completely, but he edged over near enough to Weiss to overhear the conversation.

"I have it," said Hugo Weiss, slapping Hjalmar on the back. "The portrait! I promised to sit for you, my boy, and I shall do it. You can paint it on the train. I'll have a special studio car attached to the rear of Melisande and you can paint as the miles roll by."

Frémont could contain himself no longer. With longing eyes he glanced at the gangplank still leaning against the *Ile-de- France.*

"Do I understand that in process of being rushed across this vast country, at a speed of God knows how many kilometers per hour, and at a cost that will approximate the national debt of one of the smaller nations, you are about to indulge in oil painting?" Seeing confirmation on the faces of his friends, the Chief of Detectives turned to Schlumberger and sadly shook his head. "We are lost," he said simply.

"I had a grandfather who saw little soldiers marching in and out beneath his doorsill . . ." the Alsatian began.

"You have done the old gentleman an injustice," said Frémont. "He was born in the wrong country, that is all."

Meanwhile Beatrice Diluvio, *née* Baxter and according to Massachusetts statistics at present listed as Mrs. Andrew Flood, was engaged in a friendly argument with Hugo Weiss. In the course of the tarantula murders she had inherited half a billion dollars and she thought Weiss ought to loosen up and let her share the expenses of the punitive expedition to the badlands.

"I don't like to ask indulgence on account of my sex . . ." she began.

"Sweetheart," murmured Anton Diluvio.

"But, you will admit," Beatrice continued, "that a woman can't dispose of millions as easily as a man can. I can't direct corporations. Actually, I've never understood exactly what a corporation is. And I can't pretend to be a judge of old or modern paintings. About all I can fall back on are hospitals, and I've fairly littered New England with those."

"All right. I'll be a sport," said Weiss. "We'll go fifty fifty. But it must be understood with Evans that he's to spare no expense."

The three members of the Paris police force began to quake and show signs of alarm. "If this excursion into the wilds of America continues as it has begun," said Bonnet, the least excitable of the trio, "we shall become pushovers for psychiatrists, if any such have the temerity to operate here."

"I shall lock up André Maurois for criminal understatement in his published works about America, also Celine, the Abbé Dimnet and Bernard Fäy," Frémont said. "They must have had fraudulent intent."

So it happened that at six o'clock that evening a string of special cars was attached to the Overland, Limited, in the following order:

> The Pelleas
> The Melisande
> Chez Schmitz (A special diner with Alsatian cooking)
> Café du Dôme (A drinking car)
> Montparnasse (Hjalmar's studio)
> The Castor And Pollux (A ladies' and gents' hair-
> dressing parlor)
> The Saint Cecilia (equipped with a grand piano so
> Diluvio could practice)

Hydrangea, who had listened to the plans for the trip, could not pass it up, notwithstanding her longing for Harlem, and when she told Frémont that she had decided to stay at his side, the Chief of Detective's joy overcame his apprehensions, so that as the Overland pulled out of Grand Central Station there was not a passenger in the special section whose heart was not blithe and gay. Only Weiss' far-reaching influence prevented the unusual expedition from being publicized in the press.

Of course, in one of the ordinary Pullmans far up toward the locomotive, Terry Gilligan and Santosuosso were seated in a section, face to face. They were worried about many aspects of the situation, but shadowing Miriam had turned out to be about as difficult as keeping track of the calliope in a circus parade. It was so easy, in fact, that young Santosuosso was focusing his twisted mind on how to get even with the Indian and Moritz, the dog. The latter had been comfortably installed outside Miriam's sleeping compartment in the Melisande and, having had his pound of raw beefsteak with a few dog biscuits broken up in it, to make it last longer, the Boxer was getting in some good sound sleep, with one eye slightly open.

The four astounded Frenchmen, headed by Frémont and Dr. Hyacinthe Toudoux, with Schlumberger and Bonnet bringing up the rear, passed the first hour on the Overland inspecting the unusual train. Each item of appointment that had been rigged up for the passengers' comfort and convenience caused their eyes to pop out a little farther from their sockets. When, in the Pelleas, they found a telephone exchange more modern and even larger than the one in the Paris prefecture, they hit for the Dôme car and ordered stiff Pernods all around. Dr. Toudoux started fumbling with his notes for the address he was to deliver to the assembled toxicologists on new uses for snake oil, but the doctor found it difficult to collect his thoughts. Miriam, at a near-by table with Eugenie, was still pondering her father's "All will be forgiven."

In a soundproof booth in the telephone exchange, Evans was in earnest conversation with Tom Jackson, who had worked as reporter for several big newspapers in the United States and even done a few stretches on the New York *Herald* in Paris, as a respite from Prohibition conditions, and now was working in Chicago.

After explaining as much of the situation as was necessary, Homer asked Jackson how he stood with Baldy Santo, leader of the gang of needle-beer distributors who had terrorized Chicago while the dry law was in force.

"He's off me," Jackson said. "Last year he tried to take me for a ride."

"Can you find out where he is, and what he's doing?" Evans asked.

"Sure," said Jackson. "I'll call you back later this evening. The boys down at headquarters ought to be able to tell me right off the bat. If not, I'll try the G-men at the F.B.I., and some of the other gangsters. Toodle-oo."

"Just a minute," Evans said. "I forgot to ask you to quit your job and get ready to ride west with us tomorrow. We'll have our special cars hooked on to the Golden Gate Express. Leaves at six-ten, if I'm not mistaken."

"And how am I going to eat?" the reporter asked.

"Weiss has decided to buy you a newspaper of your own," said Homer. "You're going to take over the Glendive *X-Ray*, at least for the time being."

"Are you kidding?" asked Jackson.

"Perish the thought," replied Evans, and hung up the receiver, smiling. He was not smiling, however, when just after midnight Tom called back and made his report.

"I can't understand it," the reporter said. "I thought I knew this burg, but I'm just another little Lord Fauntleroy. None of my sources can find hide or hair of Baldy Santo, and that isn't all. Every member of his gang, except a few palookas, who are no good anyway, has disappeared. Not one of 'em's in Chicago or Cicero or anywhere else. They've evaporated, dusted, skidooed."

"Damnation," said Evans. "We didn't get started a moment too soon."

8

In Which Whiskers Are Soundly Painted
and Spots Marked "X" Surveyed

IN OLDEN TIMES, before the Greeks got into a rut and started devoting themselves almost exclusively to the restaurant business, the Goddess Aurora, whose rosy fingers tint the dawn, was usually good for a stanza or two at the beginning of a chapter, while the poet was warming up. But in stories in which Hjalmar Jansen, Lvov Kvek and Grigori Lidin are concerned, and particularly when they are enjoying a reunion, Aurora, if she figures in the picture at all, horns in near the end of the festivities. The fleecy clouds of what is known as a "mackerel sky" were taking on a sort of postcard pink and the sun was casting its first beaming rays along the cindered New York Central roadbed when the big Norwegian, with ex-Colonel Kvek and Grigori on either side, murmuring something about a breath of air, started from the Dôme car for the observation platform. There they found Diluvio, stretched out full length on the floor and covered with the tribal blanket, tightly woven in blue, red and gray, of Rain-No-More. The latter, undoubtedly the most clear-headed of the five, was squatting on his heels and watching the violinist, to be sure he would not roll over fitfully and fall off the train, which was making seventy miles an hour.

Hugo Weiss, the genial host, had asked indulgence on account of his age and had gone to bed an hour before, and Evans, who had been too preoccupied all evening for conscientious drinking, had excused himself at the same time.

Thus it was that early risers and light sleepers in the towns beyond the outskirts of Chicago were treated to verse and chorus of "Let Me Call You Sweetheart" sung so lustily that the fireman of the Overland was hard put to make his whistle heard above the din. The two colored waiters in the Dôme, called respectively Washington and Cromwell, were removing broken glass with a snow shovel and preparing fragrant breakfast coffee in the polished silver-plated coffee machine. A boy came in, balancing a tray on which were crisp warm *croissants*.

Hjalmar Jansen had drunk elbow to elbow with his cronies hours on end, but he had not lost his sense of responsibility, which operated only where painting was concerned. The portrait of Hugo Weiss, which was to make him famous and, incidentally, bring him in enough money to buy himself a schooner, was to be started at eight o'clock, rain or shine. The result was a triumph of mind over matter. Hjalmar, leaning over the aft rail and trying not to look at the blurred ribbon of railroad ties unzipping below, suffered buckets of ice water to be poured over his head by Rain-No-More. Grigori and Kvek, depressed by the sight of so much water, climbed up to the top of the car, where they strolled back and forth, averring that aloft they got a much better slant at the scenery.

It was thus that the revelers were discovered by Frémont and Dr. Hyacinthe Toudoux, who had risen early in order not to miss the panorama of America that seemed so strange to them. The former, groaning, snatched a cup of coffee and a roll, ate it with his back to the observation platform, then hurried forward to his stateroom again. The medical examiner, whose works on the resuscitation of drunks were standard throughout the civilized world, began taking rapid notes, after asking permission to record the pulse and respiration of all five of the men and count the empty bottles, which had been placed by the waiters in two clothes hampers, filling them to the brim.

By eight o'clock, a semblance of order had been restored. Right on the dot, Hugo Weiss appeared in the studio car, in a fresh black frock coat, pin-striped trousers, and wearing a cornflower in his buttonhole. The multi-millionaire nodded with approval when he saw that Jansen had already put on his smock, set up his easel, arranged the posing platform and was in the act of squeezing oil paint from tubes onto his enormous palette.

"Good work, my boy. A creditable comeback. I always choose my executives on the basis of their ability to resist alcohol, and I'm seldom deceived," Weiss said.

Had not the Saint Cecilia been soundproof, they could have heard from the music car the preliminary drone of Diluvio's priceless Guarnerius, known as "The Sinner Without Malice." The violinist, refreshed by his nap in the open and spurred on by the example of Hjalmar, had pulled himself together and was having a go at the difficult Mendelssohn Concerto, so near the open window that a station agent, gaping at the Overland as it passed at reduced speed, fell over backward ducking Anton's flying bow.

The ladies, all except Miriam, had breakfast in bed, but soon they were assembled on the sun porch of the Melisande in fetching negligee or street clothes.

The dingy suburbs grew thicker and more populous. The train entered the city limits of Chicago and soon the special section was uncoupled in the railroad yards and shunted to a convenient sidetrack, where armed guards kept prowlers and urchins at a distance. Evans, who was determined to get news of Baldy Santo, decided to shadow the son, and for that purpose ventured out alone. Miriam, at his request, had marshaled the non-working members of the company for a tour in a rubberneck wagon.

Reading from front to back of the commodious blue bus, the members of the sightseeing party were seated as follows:

Dr. and Mme. Toudoux	Frémont and Sgt. Schlumberger
Miriam	Beatrice Diluvio
Rain-No-More	Sgt. Bonnet
Grigori Lidin	Hydrangea
Stenka	

Up front, beside the driver's seat, stood the guide, and near by, with an extra megaphone, was ex-Colonel Kvek, who repeated in

French and Serbian the guide's remarks about the points of interest they passed. The skyscrapers, like terraced mountains, looked
massive compared with the needle-like structures of New York. As
soon as the guide was informed that some of the distinguished foreign visitors were interested in crime he directed the chauffeur to
drive first to some of the spots that had been marked "X" in the
newspapers all over the world. Among them were:

> The scene of the Haymarket bomb explosion.
> The site of the prison where the anarchists had been
>   hanged in 1888.
> The Holy Name Cathedral in State Street, where
>   Little Hymie Weiss and his pals were machine-
>   gunned on their way to mass.
> The flower shop of Dion O'Banion, where the first
>   handshake murder was committed, followed by
>   a $100,000 funeral with twenty-six truckloads
>   of flowers.
> The Negro quarter over by the Union Stockyards, the
>   scene of the bloody race riots of 1923.
> The corner in Cicero where Assistant State's Attor-
>   ney McSwiggin was bumped off.
> The garage in North Clark Street where the St.
>   Valentine's Massacre was accomplished by gang-
>   sters wearing police uniforms. Death toll, seven.

"Enough," groaned Frémont, whose head was reeling. "Am I to
understand that only in the case of the unfortunate anarchists a
conviction was secured, and that turned out to be fraudulent?"

"What can one expect, when neither citizens nor bandits are
required to carry identity cards?" Sergeant Schlumberger said.

It was only a short distance from the notorious garage to the
Lake Shore Drive, and there the verdant parks and palatial resi-
dences revealed another aspect of the Windy City's life. The party
was shown the world's most modern zoo, where Hydrangea tried

to make arrangements to buy the baby giant panda. For the benefit of the women, a brief tour was made through the world's largest merchandising building, with its own police and fire department.

In the stockyards, the men saw squealing pigs head into buzz saws on conveyor belts, and emerge a few moments later as pork roasts, ribs and sausages. Droves of cattle were malleted, slit and dismantled before their eyes, in lakes of blood. On the other hand, in the art museum the women had all the best of it, and admired the Grecos, Tintorettos, Picassos, Van Goghs, etc., while their escorts snatched a quick one in a neighboring bar.

They were shown where the lantern was kicked over and started the Chicago fire; the preparations for the Eucharistic Congress; the World's Fair; the ball fields of the White Sox and the Cubs, respectively; in short, the sights. The blasé chap with the megaphone had never had a more attentive batch of clients.

Frémont, almost numb with astonishment and awe, had a twinge of conscience and asked to see the police headquarters, so the bus pulled up in front of that imposing structure and was promptly shooed away because of parking regulations. The Chief of Detectives was just as well satisfied. He had intended to force himself to enter and ask about methods, but lost his nerve at the last moment. Whatever he learned in America, he had already concluded, would be of no use to him or posterity in France.

In the crowded La Salle Street Station, Homer Evans had had no difficulty in picking up young Terry Gilligan and Santosuosso without being observed, and was more than gratified when he saw the former being greeted, not without affection, by a tall lanky Westerner with heavy black eyebrows and handlebar mustaches to match.

"Larkspur Gilligan, himself," said Evans, as he slipped into a taxi and handed the driver a ten-dollar bill with instructions to follow the cab in which the trio above-mentioned were ensconced. "Larkspur, by Jove. Ah, well. Another testimonial to the wisdom of Lefty Gomez, the southpaw philosopher, whose immortal lines 'I'd rather have luck than be right' (*Mieux la chance que l'adresse*) will eventually be posted up in school rooms and public libraries. Larkspur must have the wind up or he would not have hot-footed it east to meet his son. We must keep watch over Hugo Weiss. Don't want to lose him again, as we did three years ago. Not by a long shot."

Knowing that the multi-millionaire was posing for Hjalmar at that moment, Evans dismissed from his mind the possibility of his being kidnapped. It would take at least half the bad men of Montana to pry a model out of the Norwegian's clutches, in the throes of a morning's work. For Hjalmar painted as fervently as he played, or very nearly.

From where he sat, Homer felt sure that Santosuosso was peering through the back window of Gilligan's taxi to see if they were being followed. However, the traffic was fairly heavy and when it thinned out and Homer saw which way his quarry was heading he had one of those flashes of intuition, or perhaps a rapid association of ideas, that aided him so frequently in his investigations and set him apart from unimaginative men. Quickly he asked the chauffeur to turn into a side street and drive at top speed to the Stockmen's Hotel, offering another ten dollars as a bonus if they got there well in advance of the other taxi. The driver, whom Homer had sized up carefully before entering the cab, lived up to expectations. Taking hair-trigger chances, he steered in and out of traffic, cut corners, beat the gun on lights, and Evans was safely hidden in the lobby, behind a copy of the *Tribune*, when Larkspur Gilligan, with Terry and Santosuosso came in. The two boys did not register, but followed Larkspur straight into the bar, which otherwise was deserted at that hour.

A telephone booth was near by, and from it Evans called Tom Jackson who had been instructed to hold himself in readiness for action. Five minutes later the reporter entered the lobby and took a seat near Homer, without betraying that they were acquainted. Without moving his lips, Evans instructed Jackson to go into the bar, pretending to be moderately drunk, and pick up what he could in the way of information. Tom did as he was told, but the moment he lurched within hearing distance, the trio lowered their voices until their talk was inaudible. The reporter ordered whiskey and closed his eyes, as if dozing, with his elbows on the table. Minutes passed and Tom was getting discouraged and was considering bailing out for fresh advice, when a slim well-dressed Englishman pushed open the swinging doors from the street entrance, adjusted a monocle, surveyed the barroom with distaste, and approached the bar.

"I'll have a Scotch and soda, if the Scotch is not too foul," he said.

Now Tom Jackson was a rough-and-ready young man who made no pretense of maintaining an Olympian attitude. He had his prejudices, and one of the strongest of them was a dislike of Englishmen, generally, and a particular loathing for those who affected the single-glass or spats. The chap at the bar had both. In spite of himself, Tom began to glare through half-closed lids at the newcomer, almost neglecting in the process the proper objects of his attention. He was rewarded by seeing young Santosuosso sidle over toward the Britisher and, after glancing furtively at Jackson and concluding that the latter was dead to the world, take from a side pocket what appeared to be a scalp and slip it into the pocket of the Englishman's tweed lounging jacket.

"Come up to No. 34. We can't talk here," the Italian said.

After another round of drinks, Larkspur Gilligan, his son and Santosuosso left the bar, crossed the lobby and took the elevator. Jackson was nonplussed. He always expected fantastic things to happen whenever Evans was involved in a case, but after all, scalp-passing by Italians to Englishmen in Chicago barrooms was a bit over the borderline, it seemed to Tom. Should he consult Evans, and thus lose sight of the Englishman, who obviously was a confederate of Gilligan, or should he stick where he was? The Englishman solved the problem for him. After waiting a decent interval he drained his Scotch and soda, removed four bits from a change purse and placed the coin reluctantly on the bar. The bartender, who evidently saw eye to eye with Jackson concerning monocles, jammed down the keys of the cash register with unnecessary vigor and rolled the change across the bar, so that a dime hopped off and fell into the sawdust on the floor.

"Oh, I say," objected the Englishman, but he stopped and fished out the coin. Then he went into the lobby and rang for the elevator, presumably to join the others upstairs.

Tom paid for his whiskey and reported to Homer what had happened.

"The devil," said Homer to himself. "That young thug hoodwinked me, also Frémont, after all. He must have given the scalp for safe-keeping to the same steward who loaned him the pass key, no doubt for a price. The loss of a pass key was never reported. I thought all along that was strange."

But Evans was not the one to brood over past mistakes, at the expense of future accomplishments. "Tom," he said, "we've got to get that scalp. I need it badly."

"A new fad you've taken up?" asked the reporter.

"Unfortunately," continued Homer, ignoring the question. "My face and figure are well known to young Gilligan and his anti-social pal. Don't you know a pickpocket who would undertake an easy job for a liberal honorarium? Weiss is anxious to have the cost of this inquiry mount up, so I pay well above the standard rates for services."

"I did Galilee Zach a good turn once," said Jackson.

"Phone him. Ask him to come at once," Evans said. "I've got to get out of sight before Gilligan spots me. Wait here with the dip until the Englishman comes down. Then show Galilee Zach this bill ($100) which will be his when he gives you the scalp. Wrap it well and bring it to me in the car named Pelleas, in our special train. And, by the way, you're all set to go west at six-twelve?"

"My better judgment is against it, but I'll be ready," Jackson said. "So long."

Meanwhile, in the studio car, Hjalmar had been making heroic progress. His wealthy but amiable model had posed patiently, refreshed every hour or so by what he called an old-fashioned cocktail although it contained no fruit, only a few grains of sugar and less than ten percent, by volume, of H_2O. He did not look at the painting, knowing that a sitter should refrain from comment on unfinished work. If he had, the multimillionaire would have been astonished, or at least intrigued. For Hjalmar's *bête noire*, or Jonah, had always been whiskers. Sometimes he had turned them out to look like putty, again they had resembled chickweed, but seldom could his finished product be mistaken by insects or art critics for actual human hair. Consequently, the big painter had resolved to get the hardest part of his task over first.

Before lunch time, Tom Jackson, having secured the scalp according to schedule, made his way past the guards into the railroad yards and peered through his glasses at the bizarre array of special coaches. Stumbling by accident first into the studio car, which was deserted, the reporter saw on a large white canvas, otherwise utterly bare, a set of disembodied whiskers neatly trimmed in the style known in sartorial circles as "Vandyke." The sight did not assuage his qualms about the adventure on which he was embarking. Depositing his suitcase in the Pelleas, he worked his way aft to the Dôme car, where he found Evans and handed him gingerly a package wrapped in Neon red cellophane. The reporter's sigh of relief was so deep that it brought both waiters to the table in double-quick time.

"I begin to see light," Evans said, as he gave his order to Cromwell. "The faint glow that, let us hope, precedes the dawn is softening the horizon."

"That Englishman must be tied up with Baldy Santo's mob," said Jackson, "although no one in town ever got wise to him before. He looks more like the tail end of the Oxford Movement than a gangster."

"Exactly," Evans said. "We shall meet him again, if I'm not mistaken. But this afternoon, we all can relax. I want to drop in at the toxicologists' convention, to hear our friend Toudoux on snake oil. Also I would like to buy a few phonograph records to while away the long winter evenings on the ranch, for I foresee a possible period of inactivity before major operations open up in the spring. Let's see, I shall choose a few by Purcell, Monteverde, Monteclair, William Byrd, Rameau . . . and some American bits by

Pinetop Smith, Hersal Thomas, Earl Hines, Albert Ammons, Count Basie, a rather unusual blues shouter named Kid Lindbergh . . ."

"Now you're talking," Jackson said.

The chef of the Alsatian dining car, whose name was Corrigan, outdid himself at noon that day. Since there was a tang of frost in the air and so many of his clients had been out of doors all morning, Corrigan put out a menu a bit on the substantial side. Following black *boudin* against a background of mashed potatoes and sauerkraut, washed down with Mercurey, '21, there were pickled partridge with currant preserves, blue-grained cheese from Hartmanswillerkopf, peach strudel, coffee and liqueurs. Sergeant Schlumberger, of Strasbourg, fairly purred and was set back a bit when, in trying to felicitate the chef, he found they had no common language. Had the results been posted up, however, Lvov Kvek would have been listed as winner, Hjalmar Jansen placed, and Diluvio and Stenka were tied for third.

The meal put Dr. Hyacinthe Toudoux in such a good humor that later, in Odd Fellows' Hall, he was the life of the toxicologists' convention and received a vote of thanks for his paper on the medicinal properties of the oil of the American prairie rattler (*Crotalus confluentis*). Evans and Miriam sat with Mme. Toudoux throughout the performance and Eugénie was filled with modest pride. Since her unjustified incarceration in the madhouse, the former Marquise de la Rose d'Antan had been in terror whenever strange doctors put in an appearance, but at last her fear had been overcome and she shook hands with the learned members of the society without a tremor as they lined up to bid her husband *bon voyage*. Tom Jackson attended, although he knew nothing about poisons. He simply wanted to enjoy listening to papers and speeches without the necessity of collaring the speakers afterward for a résumé of what they had said, in terms the readers of the *Tribune* could understand. By force of long habit, notwithstanding, the reporter grabbed an afternoon edition from a newsboy as the group left the hall and turned a pale shade of green. A public clock near by said four forty-five, which left nearly an hour and a

half before six twelve, and Jackson wished fervently that he were
aboard the C. M. & St. P. express, or on some rapidly moving conveyance headed out of Chicago. For a two-column cut on page one
contained a flattering picture of the Englishman Tom had caused
to be rolled that morning and the headlines read:

BRITISH SUBJECT SLAIN

A closer perusal of the sub-heads and lead paragraph set forth
that Montmorency Lewson-Phipps, nephew of the prominent
dudelsack collector, Amery Buttorford Lewson-Phipps, R.A., V.C.,
of Phipps-Wickey, Dorsetshire, had been shot to death by unidentified gangsters as he emerged from a cut-price drug store with a
bottle of Pluto Water clutched in one hand. A soda jerker who had
sold the Pluto to the deceased told the police that a short dark man
had accosted the Englishman and asked curtly: "Have you got it?"
On receiving a negative reply, the short dark party had retired to
the sidewalk and, with another man, still shorter and darker, evidently an acquaintance, had riddled the deceased from sawed-off
shotguns, slightly wounding three bystanders, one of whom was
a nine-year-old girl on her way to be confirmed. Because of the
insistence of the British Consul, who had threatened to call a man-
of-war into Lake Michigan unless satisfaction was forthcoming, the
Mayor had ordered the police to investigate. The owner of a large
Chicago daily, who had ambitions to represent the United States
at the Court of St. James's, had offered a reward of $20,000 for
information leading to the arrest and conviction of the gangsters
who had committed the breach of hospitality.

"Any news?" Evans asked, observing the reporter's uneasiness.

"Glub," said Jackson, swallowing hard. Homer, sensing something grave, persuaded the Toudouxs to have a final go at Marshall
Field's before entraining, and asked Miriam to accompany them.
"The Union Station, West Jackson Boulevard. Don't be late," he
cautioned. Reluctantly, Miriam led the doctor and his wife away.

It was the work of an instant for Evans to read the story of Lewson-
Phipps demise, and its possibilities of disaster did not escape him.

"What about Galilee Zach? Will he squeal?" Homer asked.

"He'd send his mother to the chair for twenty cents, let alone $20,000," Tom Jackson said. "I knew we'd get in wrong if we monkeyed with scalps. I felt it in my bones."

"Does Galilee know we're pulling out tonight?" Evans asked.

"He'll describe me, and tell the cops I work for the *Tribune*. The cops'll barge into the city room, and the editor will say I quit on a moment's notice last night, for no reason I could explain. Won't that look good? I throw up a good job, give a dip $100 to frisk an Englishman of a dried scalp. A little later the Englishman gets plugged, and all the tall hats in Chicago come off their pegs and start moving around. I'm cooked, old man. No matter where I go, I'll be extradited. I suppose by now, the guy who lost the skin from his onion has been found in Humboldt Park, propped up against a police box."

"That, at least, won't happen," Evans said. "Let's slip into a tavern and think this over. It's Gilligan's work, of course, carried out by some intimates and social equals of Santosuosso. Luckily you have a wonderful alibi."

"The alibi sounds fishier than any of the rest of it. What would I be doing, passing my last afternoon in Chi with a lot of toxicologists? I didn't take any notes; I didn't even listen. No one knew me there except you and the Toudouxs. You can't appear, and both of them are foreigners. What I'd better do is hit for the Canadian border," the reporter said.

"Call Zach," said Evans, briefly.

"Have a heart," Jackson said. "He'd turn me in right here."

"Perhaps I can dissuade him, but if you're skeptical, beat it to the Union Station. Find Hjalmar, ask him to black you up and get you a white coat and a porter's cap. Then keep busy, dusting and pottering in the studio car. I'll interview Galilee Zach and see if he won't listen to the siren song of reason."

Sighing dolefully, Tom Jackson found a telephone booth, nodded that he had contacted the pickpocket, then lit out with a speed most unusual for a reporter. The last time he had given Evans a hand, he had found himself involved in a free-for-all in a loony bin. As he dove into a taxi, keeping in the shadow as much as possible, Tom wished he were back in the madhouse. Nevertheless, he carried out his instructions to the letter. Homer glanced at his watch, and saw that he had only half an hour to make the train. Within five minutes, to Evans' relief, a dapper young man came into the tavern and glanced around. He was very good-looking, in a girlish sort of way, with large dark eyes and long lashes, and his fingers were carefully manicured. In fact, Evans was quite sure the nails had been stained a faint shade of pink.

"I hope I'm not mistaken," Homer said to himself as he gave the newcomer the eye. The young man proved to be Zach, all right, but a moment's conversation revealed to Evans that the dainty young dip had not read the afternoon papers. He had been too busy spending the $100 for lotions, assorted toilet preparations and clothes. With his usual adaptability, Evans accepted the new situation. He told Zach that he had another little job that would net him $200.

"Not another nasty old scalp, I hope," Zach said with distaste. "I hate to mention it, but the one I pinched this morning actually had dandruff."

Homer reassured the dip, but told him it would be necessary for him to board a train. "I'll let you off in Cicero . . ."

"Not Cicero, where all those rowdy gun molls are. Make it Berwyn," Zach said.

"All right. Come along," said Evans.

Tom Jackson, his face transformed by powdered charcoal, was in the act of moving Hjalmar's easel, on which the canvas now displayed a frock coat and formal tie, an appropriate distance below the whiskers. He was dismayed to see Evans and the pickpocket, arm in arm, approaching the Pelleas. What he did not see was that Homer, on entering that coach, left Zach in his stateroom and held a quick consultation with Dr. Hyacinthe Toudoux.

"Ah, by all means. The Mickey or Michel Finn," the doctor said, and took from his vest pocket a small phial.

"Won't you have a drink?" Homer asked of Zach, who was enchanted with the atmosphere of tasteful luxury. He had noted that

Evans, whom he already had grown to admire almost to the point of worship, used an Eau de Cologne discreetly scented with Molyneux No. 5. As he accepted the offer of a drink, Zach resolved to buy a large bottle the moment he got his two C's for whatever it was he had to do.

Five minutes later, the dip was stretched on the floor of the film-developing compartment, dead to the world, and four minutes after that the Golden Gate Express slid out of Union Station and started clicking off the miles along the roadbed of the C. M. & St. P.

As if for the benefit of the visitors who were seeing the U. S. A. for the first time, under such favorable auspices, Luna, pale goddess of the moon, put on one of her most entrancing numbers. Her soft rays caressed gently the Pelleas, the Melisande and the auxiliary coaches, as the goddess reflected dreamily that the Mann Act was about to be subjected to no ordinary drubbing, unless she misread the company's prevailing mood. It was not long before the train was speeding along the east bank of the Mississippi, Father of Waters, and Luna fairly surpassed herself in silvering the heavily wooded slopes, the mosaic of farm lands and pastures, acres of which already had been furrowed by the plow.

"Incredible," murmured Frémont, and the medical examiner, the Alsatian and the Breton nodded reverently. "Myself, I am an unadventurous man, ironically in a dangerous profession. I have often wondered if men have been wise in removing themselves from pastoral surroundings in favor of smoky cities, and in exchanging the dangers of wild beasts for the perils that stalk the alleys and pavements. Oddly enough, while I was recovering from the gunshot wounds I received in the Rosary investigation, I learned from the books in the hospital library that many literary men have had similar misgivings, although I was familiar with many of their *dossiers* and was aware that most of them had not been out of sight of the Tour Eiffel since childhood, except to do their military service,"

"Everything in this amazing country is on a heroic scale. Buildings go up, not ten stories, but a hundred. Gangsters massacre not two or three, but seven or more. Hummocks are hills, and hills are mountains. Ten million men are out of work, not merely a thousand. Jewish bandits attempt to go to mass. Catholic assassins hide in synagogues. Floral offerings are disposed of by the truckload, and are real, not artificial. In short, we are deeply indebted to Monsieur Evans for an unforgettable chance to see the world, to shake off the chains of our chauvinism, the curse of modern France," said Dr. Toudoux.

"*Ach, Gott*, what farming land," the Alsatian said prayerfully.

"And lakes, almost end to end, for navigation. Observe that expanse of river to our left, and to think that our accursed politicians sold great chunks of it for a song. By the way, is this Louisiana, this beauteous department?" asked Bonnet.

"Too far north. We are now in Wisconsin," Evans said, smiling.

When his friends were happy, he was happy, too. He wanted everyone to feel the surge and flow of life, to taste its possibilities. And he could not stifle the pride he felt in his country. Indeed, Europe seemed remote, actually alien, even backward to him then. Was he catching the fever that drove so many of his countrymen to pointless activity? Miriam, at his side, and sharing his thoughts, was trembling. Eugénie de Sault, remembering only a fleeting instant the walls of the asylum that had shut her in five interminable years, brushed a tear from her cheek. Hydrangea, shuddering briefly, said a goose had crossed her grave, then recovered her gay spirits with the mercurial aptitude of her race. Stenka was breathing deeply and seemed more statuesque than ever as she stopped thinking entirely, to enjoy the fragrance of earth and trees and the great rolling river. Hugo Weiss had forgotten that money existed, Beatrice and Anton Diluvio that there were other passengers on the train. The Russians began singing, as if exile and privation were merely courses in musical appreciation, as indeed, they are. Hjalmar, elated at having passed the whisker ordeal successfully and having followed it up with a dark coatsleeve that would have done credit to Derain, gave the handbrake on the platform such a boisterous twirl that it flew off its moorings and caromed down the track. In the Dôme car, Washington and Cromwell were taking full advantage of an easy evening. Rain-No-More, lost in thought, was squatting motionless on the roof of the Pelleas, where he had climbed for meditation. His ancestors had roamed almost to the lake region, in pursuit of stray Iroquois who had imperialistic notions and had tried to extend their influence to the plains. Whether the Blackfeet tribe survived or not depended more on Rain-No-More than anyone else. His brother, Longtime-Pipe, would never be a leader. But no tribal or other considerations would induce Rain-No-More to let Jim Leonard swing. How to prove his own guilt without tangible evidence was the Indian's problem and he found no solution as the miles streamed backward down the track.

Had a vote been taken, it would have been hard to decide which the company found more beautiful, Wisconsin by moonlight or Minnesota in the light of the morning sun. The Express glided smoothly through La Crosse, East Winona and Trevino, wormed its way through St. Paul and finally came to rest in Minneapolis. Before the terminal was reached, however, the handsome young dip named Zach had been revived, refreshed and installed by Homer in a spare bed in the sleeping quarters of the Castor and Pollux. That Zach had passed out and missed getting off at Berwyn did not seem to trouble him at all. Homer and Jackson had assured him that his shady profession would not be disclosed to his traveling companions. In turn Zach had sworn that he would go in for no free-lance work, but only follow Evans' instructions. To sum up, the occupants of the special cars were like one big happy family, all for one and one for all.

In Minneapolis, nonetheless, Evans made a quick visit to a dealer in firearms and ammunition, with a letter of credit from Weiss that would have equipped the Mexican army, and before the special coaches were shunted over to the N. P. tracks, four dozen cases of rifles, automatic revolvers, sub-machine guns, ammunition, night sticks, hand grenades, tear-gas guns and bombs, and some baseball bats of straight-grained ash were loaded into the music car and the studio, without discommoding the violinist or the painter in the least.

"A stitch in time, you know, my boy," said Hugo Weiss delightedly, when he saw the arsenal come aboard. The multimillionaire smiled even more broadly and rubbed his hands when Evans told him he had ordered a battery of six-inch cannon to be shipped via the Great Northern to Muddy Creek, the nearest railroad point to Three Buttes.

"The distances are enormous on the Yellowstone range," said Homer, in explanation.

"That's the ticket! Foresight! Prudence tempered with audacity! I told you, my boy, that I seldom was mistaken in choosing men for executive positions," Weiss said, and, linking his arm with Homer's, marched him straight to the Dôme.

9
Marooned in the Openest of All Possible Spaces

BECAUSE HE HAD BEEN SO TOUCHED by the profound emotions of his foreign companions when they had entered New York Harbor and had their first glimpse of that astonishing metropolis, and later when they had devoured with their eyes the Illinois countryside, reveled in Chicago, and followed the course of the vast Mississippi, exclaiming with astonishment at every turn, Homer Evans decided to stay over one night in Minneapolis in order that they might cross the prairies and the badlands by daylight aboard the North Coast Limited. Miriam readily agreed, herself almost famished for the first sharp tang of the sage and the sight of a bunch of shaggy horses, kicking up their heels and running playfully from the train.

Evans' thoughtfulness was well rewarded. For while the French contingent had been somewhat prepared for American cities by views they had seen on postal cards, and were familiar with forests and farming land, although on a smaller scale than in Wisconsin and Minnesota, nothing in their experience had prepared them for the flat country, where the plains are spread before the eye like a dun-colored sea, and the beholder gets his first notion of terrestrial immensity. From Fargo on through North Dakota, scarcely any member of the party, except Hjalmar and Diluvio, who painted and fiddled dutifully, could keep their seats.

Miriam, again in her element, kept winking back the tears. Hydrangea, who had concluded they were approaching the rim of the world, added Baptist prayers to the Greek Orthodox entreaties of Stenka. Eugénie de Sault stretched her arms rapturously to the cloudless sky, as if asylum walls were tumbling, and Beatrice Baxter, or Mrs. Andrew Flood (Diluvio), felt also a surge of release from the prison of her former loneliness. For once she was glad she had half a billion dollars, and not a mere million or two.

The North Coast Limited, with its exotic string of special cars in tow, traversed broad tablelands, with farms the size of Swiss cantons, mounted tiers of foothills, then set out on long tangents at a higher level. The sage was everywhere, and at intervals were herds of horses and cattle. Marking the course of the creeks were clumps of cottonwood trees. Rain-No-More again retired to the roof of the coach, perhaps in order to hide his own emotion. Frémont, the Toudoux, Schlumberger and Bonnet could not take time out to eat their lunch, but munched sandwiches without tasting them, while Homer told them of the part their countrymen had played in developing the Western country.

They had never heard of Louis Barrette, who had led the Cedar Creek gold rush, or of those fur-trading pioneers, the Finleys, François and Jacques, the last of whom gave his name, in an Americanized form, to Jocko River. Tales followed of the exploits of Joe Mallette, who brought freight across the prairies where wheels had never made their tracks, of René La Brie and his arrowheads, Pierre Menard, trapper, of the Vigilante trail. They looked almost reproachful when Homer recounted how Pere Wibaux had, with his cowboys, terrorized Chicago and turned in a record bill of costs to the court for the lawsuit he won.

"May the devil take the English, whose chicanery robbed our adventurers of the fruits of their toil and their daring," Frémont said. "Unless I am careful, when and if I get back home, I shall be unfairly severe with such British as do wrong in my jurisdiction."

"My poor grandfather saw little soldiers . . ." Schlumberger began.

"Mine lugged soil in straw baskets to grow peas on his rocky cliffs in Brittany," Bonnet said.

"When I think of the number of prairie rattlers this colossal department could accommodate, I grow dizzy," said Dr. Hyacinthe Toudoux.

"You work far too hard," his wife said, gazing at him with touching solicitude. "Here, in the great outdoors, we shall escape from the toils of science for a while."

"As you wish, my dear," said the doctor, and sighed.

The Russians, who, having inhabited the Caucasus, had never seen the Siberian steppes, began to long for them just the same and roared nostalgic songs nonetheless harmonious because of the vodka. Then, when near Bismarck, the North Coast Limited plowed into an area deeply blanketed with snow, they switched to songs about wolves and bears, and moujiks dozing on top of stoves and wondering if, after all, God couldn't forget, as well as remember, if it pleased Him.

"To think, Grigori Hippolitovitch, that soon we shall be astride horses again, with a chance to exercise our true profession," said Lvov Kvek.

"I shall embrace my mount with a thousand fervent kisses," Grigori replied. "I shall embrace our enemies, before cleaving them from skull to crotch. . . . By the way, Lvov Vassilievitch, exactly who are our enemies and what is the row about? Have you ascertained?"

"What a question for a military man!" Kvek said, reproachfully. "We follow Evans' orders, and in the past, I assure you, that has led me into some never-to-be-forgotten mêlées. Remember your Tennyson, Captain. Yours not to reason why."

"We must drink to Alfred Georgovitch and demolish the glasses," Grigori said.

It must not be assumed by the reader that while the characters just described were reacting so forcibly to the call of the great open spaces Larkspur Gilligan and his cohorts had been idle in the smoking compartment of a Pullman far up toward the locomotive. The unscrupulous sheepman and his companions were without baggage, having had to abandon it and leap from the evening train the day before when they discovered the special section was not attached to the westbound No. 1. But neither Larkspur nor his son Terry cared a tinker's catoot for scenery, having lamped little else all their lives. For equally valid reasons, Santosuosso and Nutcracker Ike didn't like it either. If now and then they could fill two pair or a four-card flush, the Grand Canyon or even the Taj Mahal could go to hell, as far as they were concerned.

The elder Gilligan had prepared his offensive in Minneapolis, where he had bribed a clerk to omit from the papers handed the conductor of the Limited any mention of the Pelleas, the Melisande or any of the special coaches. Next he had fixed the engineer and the brakemen. So that when the train entered the desolate volcanic country near the Montana border, where badlands stretched at least a hundred miles in all directions, the special section was uncoupled and ever so gradually, then quite rapidly, was left behind.

This was discovered simultaneously by Tom Jackson and Rain-No-More, the difference being that only the latter could do much of anything about it, for the reporter, impelled by his instinct for news, had gone forward in the train and was three cars away when the coaches containing his friends and allies began drifting to the rear. The Indian, however, observing the widening gap from the roof of the Pelleas, descended the iron ladder and gave the alarm with such a resounding whoop that Hjalmar, in the Montparnasse, smeared one of the ears clean off Weiss's portrait.

"Adrift, by yee," was the Norwegian's brief comment.

"Ah, well. We'll have to flag No. 1, when she comes along about midnight," said Weiss. "Let's have an old-fashioned. You mustn't overwork, my boy."

Homer Evans did not take such a casual view of the situation. They were in the most deserted stretch of country between Minneapolis and the coast, or practically anywhere else in the world. If Gilligan had left them there, it was not merely to delay them twelve hours. Of that Evans was certain. As the ill-fated coaches slowed down, Homer's mind speeded up. First, he observed they were on a slight upgrade and that the momentum of the section would carry them almost to the summit. Beckoning to Rain-No-More to follow him, Evans, with surprising strength, ripped off the iron ladder from the rear of the Dôme car and leaped to the roadbed as soon as the coaches came to rest. The remnants of the twisted ladder he wedged quickly behind the rear wheels of the observation car, so that no pressure of wind would start the section sliding backward down the grade.

He did not know that the North Coast Limited, out of sight in the volcanic hills, had slowed down to let off the Gilligans, father and son, and their two confederates, Santosuosso and Nutcracker Ike, not half a mile from one of the amazing areas of pasture land concealed by helter-skelter heaps of faintly colored ashes, lava rock and petrified ruins of prehistoric trees. Neither did Evans know that, without the knowledge of or permission from government authorities, a gang of outlaw Shoshones were camped in that vicinity and that the same Indians, led by a deposed disgruntled chief named Tall-Horse-in-Flytime, had done odd jobs of rustling and rebranding for Gilligan over a period of years.

In the Dôme car, a quick consultation was called, attended by the men and Miriam, but as soon as Evans had called the meeting to order he let out an ejaculation.

"How stupid of me!" he said. "I had forgotten the telephone."

Excusing himself from the café car he went back to the Pelleas, which had been deserted for some time before the uncoupling incident, and what he saw there brought him up short with dismay. The operator, a New York Central clerk about whom nothing else was known, lay sprawled on the floor in a widening pool of blood, his throat cut and his scalp removed. Instantly Evans leaped over the corpse to test the wireless apparatus and found it had been demolished. The lethal instrument, a knife with the Blackfeet's tribal colors on the handle, lay in a corner.

When Homer returned to the Dôme car, the gravity of his expression brought the company to its feet almost in unison. Succinctly he told them what had happened. Miriam was sent to the Melisande, where the other women were gathered, to deter them from witnessing the shocking spectacle. Dr. Hyacinthe Toudoux, followed closely by Frémont and the sergeants, scrambled in haste to the scene of the crime.

"The cause of death is plain," the medical examiner said.

"And the time?" asked Evans.

"Between twenty and thirty minutes," said Dr. Toudoux.

Frémont glanced anxiously through a window, and what he saw outside was not much more reassuring than the ghastly sight within. Sometime in long past ages, the earth's crust in that neighborhood had been shattered by heat and pressure from the planet's molten core. No one since had undertaken to clear away the debris. The Paris Chief of Detectives, who never before had been out of sight of a friendly roof or church spire, was at a loss as to how to proceed. The most impressive dragnet he ever had spread in Paris would seem futile and ridiculous in the vastness and great silence of the badlands.

"I shall post an offer of a reward of $100,000, although I suppose Madame Diluvio will insist on furnishing half of it," said Hugo Weiss.

"Excuse me, sir, but where shall you place the posters?" asked Sergeant Bonnet.

Rain-No-More took Evans aside for a whispered consultation, strapped on a cartridge belt with an automatic in the holster, then noiselessly strode from the car and disappeared into the hills.

"Luckily the snow is heavily crusted," Evans said, as he watched the Indian until he was out of sight.

"At least we have food . . ." began Schlumberger.

"And liquor," Hjalmar added. "But I'm afraid there won't be any major-league rough stuff in this Godforsaken place." Then clearly he saw Evans lower the lid of one eye.

"Please bring back Miriam. Then meet me in the studio," Evans said. "And I must caution you about alarming the women unnecessarily. We may have trouble and we may not, but it is more than likely that we shall. I am informed by Rain-No-More that we are near the stamping ground of a detachment of treacherous Shoshones who have done dirty work for Gilligan several times before. I shall ask Colonel Kvek to inspect rifles, small arms and ammunition and see that each man is properly equipped. Rain-No-More will act as scout and intelligence officer. Frémont will take command of the French squad, to consist of Toudoux, Schlumberger and Bonnet. Kvek will command the international contingent, with Captain Lidin, Hjalmar and . . . Let me see . . ."

Both Hugo Weiss and Galilee Zach stepped two paces forward. The face of the little pickpocket was so pale that his long fringe of dark eyelashes looked like mascara. As he stood at attention, Evans could see that his knees were knocking, but he spoke up just the same.

"I'll fight those awful Indians, so there now," he said, stamping his foot, and Evans, pleased by his show of spirit, gave Zach the vacant place on the squad.

"But, damn it," objected Weiss.

"There will be plenty for all of us to do. I want you, Weiss, to take stock of the commissary and report as soon as possible. We may have to ration out the food and must know just where we stand."

"No. 1 will come through in twelve hours," the multi-millionaire said, almost regretfully.

"I am not clairvoyant," Evans said, "but I am an amateur psychologist. I do not think as bright a man as Larkspur Gilligan would bribe half the staff of a transcontinental railroad, as he must have done, and cause murder to be committed, merely to delay us half a day in these incredible badlands. Were there the least possibility that you would not be outstripped by the Indians on snowshoes and hopelessly outnumbered, I would send out a squad to patrol the tracks."

"Do me the honor," said Frémont, advancing.

"Excuse me, sir," interposed Lvov Kvek. "You, who have a family and a government, should concede me the privilege."

"Gentlemen," said Evans, indulgently, "if we are to form a military organization, we must proceed in a military way. We shall elect a leader in due form, if you wish."

"Unnecessary," said Frémont. "If anyone can get us out of this pickle of the era, you are the man."

This was seconded by acclamation.

"Very well," Evans said. "I shall expect you not only to obey my orders, but not to scramble for a share of the glory. I repeat, there will be work and laurels enough for all. We are none too numerous."

"Agreed," said Frémont, and the others nodded.

Diluvio, the only man absent, except Tom Jackson, at that moment came to the end of the Paganini variations, which he had never tossed off with more verve. He was mildly surprised to discover that the train was not in motion, and entered the Dôme car, Guarnerius in hand.

"Is something wrong?" he asked.

10
A Moot Point Concerning Women in Warfare

WHEN THE NORTH COAST LIMITED pulled into Glendive, right on time, the only passenger to get off was Tom Jackson, sans money, baggage, overcoat or hat. There was, however, a curious handful of natives on the platform. The long train, lights faintly glimmering, resumed its westward journey after the conductor had checked his orders with the station agent.

"Everything jake?" asked the agent.

"Slick as a whistle," the conductor replied.

"Let's highball," yelled the rear brakeman, swinging his lantern.

It would not be accurate to say that Jackson did not attract considerable attention. The inhabitants of Glendive, gateway of the Lower Yellowstone country, had seen tenderfeet arrive in all sorts of costumes and conditions, but the newcomer seemed to be set apart from the ordinary run of Easterners. Most of them had too many, and too colorful clothes. Tom was without hat or overcoat in the dead of winter. The clerk of the Hotel Jordan, who usually moseyed over to watch the trains come in, was certain that no one had made a reservation and, with the instinct hotel clerks have, he felt sure that Jackson had no funds. Warren Hockaday, the new sheriff, strode up and down the platform in polished riding boots and with clinking spurs, surprised that Larkspur Gilligan and his party were not in evidence. He did not associate the mild-looking bespectacled ex-reporter with the cattlemen's allies. However, he was new in authority and responsible for the county's safety, so he paused in front of Jackson, nodded non-committally, and said: "Howdy, stranger. Where you from?"

Tom, seeing the star on Hockaday's shirt front, felt somewhat relieved. "You the sheriff?" he asked, ignoring the request for auto-biographical details.

"That's me," the sheriff said.

"You ought to start a posse, or a locomotive, back to the bad-lands," Tom said sincerely. "A party of my friends, in special cars, got left behind. The coaches came uncoupled. That's why I haven't got a coat or a suitcase. I was up ahead when it happened."

The sheriff began to understand why Gilligan had not showed up. "You don't say?" he asked, assuming his best poker face. "Come into the depot, and we'll have a talk with the agent. He just checked the conductor's orders."

Relieved, Tom Jackson followed Hockaday into the station, not only pleased that he had got a rescue in process of organization so promptly, but on account of the red-hot, pot-bellied stoves that were going full blast in both the ladies' and gents' waiting rooms. The N.P., Tom was gratified to note, did not pinch pennies in the matter of fuel. The reporter was so intent on warming himself af-ter his few moments on the chilly platform that he did not see the sheriff give the station agent the high sign.

"This young feller from the East has got an idea that some cars broke loose from the Limited, back in the badlands," Hockaday began.

"Nope," the agent said, briefly, and spat into the fire.

"You're wrong," said Jackson. "I saw them. There were two spe-cial sleepers, a barber shop, studio, music car and French saloon."

"Drunk," the sheriff said calmly.

"Plastered to the gills," the station agent rejoined.

The reporter began to vibrate and stutter, then to bang his fist on the telegraph desk so violently that an instrument, clicking madly, hopped an inkwell and tipped its contents over several bills of lading in quadruplicate.

"I'm as sober as a judge," he insisted. "Those cars and all the passengers are back there, at least one hundred and fifty miles . . ."

"Too bad. A young feller, too," the agent said, retrieving his records and dabbing at them absent-mindedly with a rocking blotter.

"He'd better not try any rough stuff, had he?" the sheriff asked, his hand on his holster. "We don't hold much with formalities out here."

"He looks like he might be a reasonable sort of duck, when he's himself. Give him a chance," the station agent said.

The sheriff placed a firm hand on Jackson's shoulder, while the agent, with a paperweight grasped firmly, sidled nearer on the other side. "Look here," the sheriff said, "we don't aim to be mean, especially on the first day a stranger gets to town. You better come down to my place, and that's what you'd better do. I'll make you comfortable. Later we can talk this over calm like and maybe you'll change your mind about them floating opera houses and Frenchified saloons."

Before Tom could reply, the agent took down a huge bearskin coat from a hook and placed it over Jackson's shoulders, at the same time jamming a fur cap well down over the reporter's eyes.

"Go ahead with Warren, pardner," the agent said. "And just to make you feel good, I'll telegraph back all the way to Bismarck to make sure there are no stray specials left behind in the hills." To add substance to his reassurance, the agent began ticking furiously on a telegraph instrument that was not hooked up.

"Where is your place?" Jackson asked the sheriff suspiciously.

"Down the road a piece. Come on," the latter said.

A few minutes later Tom Jackson was pounding on the walls and rattling the bars of the same crude jail in which, a few days previously, Jim Leonard had spent one night and part of a day. The building was apart from the town, on a sagebrush flat, and was surrounded by a high board fence, several lengths of which had been blown down in the recent storm. In the corner of the cell, resting in a shallow box of sand, was a stove pipe that flared out at the bottom and had a rusty door. The reporter's teeth began chattering, in spite of his rage, for the cheap thermometer on the outer wall registered only as far as thirty below zero and no mercury whatever was in sight. A coyote, emboldened by the cold and his hunger, sat down behind a clump of sage two hundred yards away and howled its woes to heaven.

"The wolves, by God," said Jackson. He had heard that wolves were shy about fires, and noticing for the first time a pile of shavings and some stove wood in a box, he studied the Sibley stove a moment, then started a blaze. He was astonished at how quickly the cell lost its chill and took on a rosier atmosphere. The sheriff had left a can of beans and some hardtack on a shelf, in case his guest got hungry before morning. These Jackson opened by up-ending his iron cot and punching a hole through the tin with one of the legs. The water bucket, which contained a lump of solid ice, Tom hung on the damper of the stove pipe, which was red almost to the ceiling. When he found, on top of the pile of rough blankets a sack of Bull Durham and some papers, he tried to roll a cigarette. The fourteenth time he got one together and lighted it with a pine shaving. Four other coyotes, encouraged by the first one, stole out of their hills and began to encircle the jail, pausing now and then to mingle plaintive cries.

BACK IN THE BADLANDS, across the Dakota line, Hugo Weiss was checking on materials and supplies, in accordance with Evans' orders, and the multi-millionaire was dismayed to learn how many of the expensive gadgets he had installed for the comfort of his guests in his palatial private cars were not self-sufficient but depended on electric current, steam from the locomotive or other impetus from outside.

There was food enough for two days in the Alsatian car. Corrigan, the chef, insisted on wearing sidearms and had been promised active service in case the train was attacked. The electric stove was worse than useless. Consequently Hjalmar and Stenka had been detailed to gather firewood, which was by no means plentiful, and to build an outdoor oven out of chunks of lava rock. Anton Diluvio, who as a lad in Stowe, Massachusetts, had stalked a deer on occasion, and his wife, who had hunted in Maine, set forth beneath the sharp starlight and had the good luck to see, against the sky on a crag, a mountain ram. They fired simultaneously and each insisted that the other had made the kill. Lvov Kvek and Grigori, brought to the scene by the sound of gunfire, scrambled over the rocks and ravines as if they were goats themselves and returned with the ram, which was skun by Miriam and cut into quarters and cleaned by Corrigan.

Diluvio, who in the course of his profession had learned about the preparation of gut for viol strings, busied himself with the intestines in the hope of turning out a pair of snowshoes. By that time the fire was roaring and four wash boilers were filled with clean snow, to be melted for use in cooking and bathing. Of course, the elaborate johns in the special cars were not usable while the train was standing, as all travelers know. Also, the tubs, sinks, needle baths and showers were devoid of water, and the pipes and radiators, that had kept the cars at an ideal temperature while they were still attached to the locomotive, were stone cold. The supply of bedclothes was adequate for heated coaches, but not for a temperature of thirty-five below.

Miriam, who was busy teaching her companions to shift for themselves under the unforeseen conditions, was pleased with their response. Eugénie de Sault was as considerate and gracious as if she were in a salon in the Faubourg St. Germain. She smiled bravely when Miriam made an impromptu lining of old newspapers for her flimsy but fashionable clothes and wrapped her feet in flannel to protect them against the frost. Hydrangea, who would have been a wow in the tropics, stuck close to Mme. Toudoux and imitated the latter's *sang froid* as best she could. She had read, somewhere, that freezing was an easy death. Stenka, of course, felt quite at home, for the first time since she had quit her Serbian village. She was a match for most of the men in strength and hardihood. Between bouts of hard labor, she frisked and frolicked with Hjalmar in the snow as lustily as ever a D. H. Lawrence heroine blew her top in a wheatfield or on a lawn.

Frémont's squad had been given the first tour of guard duty and had been posted in pairs, above and below the train, to be relieved every three hours by Colonel Kvek's contingent.

Homer Evans seemed to be everywhere, directing operations. First he put away the corpse in the developing room and locked the door. Then he rearranged the billets, inspected the commissary and kitchen, gave instructions to the sentries, checked up on the ordnance. The cars were aligned as follows, and could not be rearranged:

In the rear was the Dôme car, with observation platform. Next was the Alsatian diner, the Saint Cecilia, the Montparnasse, the Pelleas, the Melisande and, on the western flank, the Castor and Pollux.

Evans chose for headquarters the St. Cecilia and there, just after the evening meal, he called a staff meeting attended by Miriam, Hjalmar, and the squad leaders, Frémont and Kvek. Diluvio had been selected as liaison man between squads and headquarters, since his memory had been developed to an amazing degree by his musical studies and he could repeat orders verbatim after a single swift hearing.

"When Rain-No-More comes back, we shall know what the enemy is about," said Evans. "But he may be late in returning and we must be prepared for any contingency. In case the Shoshones, prompted by Gilligan, try to rush the train, the women—of course, I don't mean Miriam, our best sharpshooter—should be taught to take their proper stations away from the windows, as follows: Mrs. Diluvio will remain in the Melisande, Madame Toudoux will repair with Hydrangea to the Pelleas, Stenka will guard the entrance to the arsenal in the Montparnasse."

Miriam nodded. She herself was to be on duty in headquarters at Evans' side.

"The men," Homer continued, "will take emergency stations as follows: Colonel Kvek and Hjalmar will defend the western outpost, in the Castor and Pollux, while Captain Lidin and Private Zach will man the Melisande. On the other flank, Frémont and Bonnet will take up positions in the Dôme, Dr. Toudoux and Schlumberger in the Montparnasse. Miss Leonard and I will sustain the center, in the St. Cecilia. Diluvio and Rain-No-More will act as mobile guard."

A knock sounded sharply on the door.

"Who goes there?" asked Evans.

"*Sit i ka kooin*" (a Blackfeet), was the reply.

"*Poke si put*," said Evans, which means "Come in."

Quickly Evans dismissed the others, all except Miriam, after asking them to hold themselves in readiness to return for instructions when the appropriate call was sounded on the Steinway grand, the tone of which carried magnificently in the frosty air. The face of Rain-No-More was, as usual, impassive.

"The Shoshones are on the warpath," Rain-No-More began. "They have with them not only the four white men who formerly were on the train, but a number of others, who, if I understood correctly their dialect, are from the populous Lake Regions and are unaccustomed to the open trail. Four miles east of here, they started an avalanche on a steep hill, thus destroying fifty yards of roadbed and tracks."

"As I thought," said Evans. "Tonight they will attack our train. The No. 1, if it is not wrecked, will back up to the nearest telegraph station, seventy miles away. No doubt they had blocked the east-bound trains as well, for No. 3, due at six o'clock, has not put in an appearance."

"The Shoshones are led by my old enemy, Tall-Horse-in-Flytime, whose brother I just waylaid." Rain-No-More took out from his belt, concealed beneath his buckskin jacket, a fresh scalp and laid it on the music rack of the Steinway.

"Oh," gasped Miriam, "was that necessary, Elk Calf, my childhood friend?"

"Quite," said the Indian. "The Shoshones, observing my handiwork, may be led to believe that the Blackfeet are on their trail. That will throw such a scare into them that, in order to get them to advance, the whites will have to feed them firewater. The result will be chaos. We can slaughter them at will, as the first Great White Father did the Hessians."

"Are the whites supplied with liquor?" Evans asked.

"Inside and out," replied Rain-No-More.

"How soon, in your judgment, will the Shoshones attack?"

"Two hours, three at the most," said the Indian.

"How many of them are there?"

"*Nis it sip po*" (Fifty).

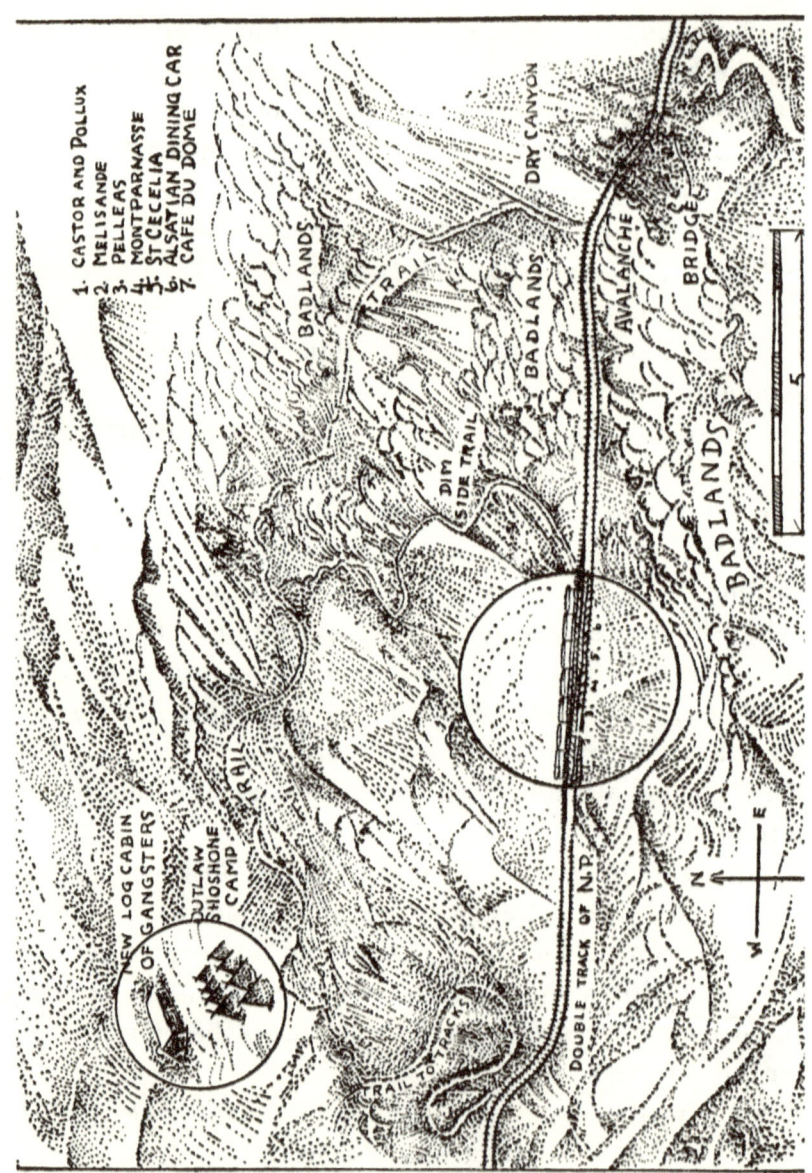

"We are twenty, counting Miriam and Stenka as effectives and the six colored porters as reserves. Fortunately the Castor and Pollux is well supplied with razors, if it comes to a hand-to-hand fight."

Homer went to the piano and with one finger sounded loudly the call to headquarters. Without delay, the other men, excepting those on sentry duty, trooped in and stood at attention, sensing that an emergency was at hand.

"Men," said Evans, "I am reminded, in our present situation, of the late Marshal Foch who dictated a communiqué, in the darkest days of the war, substantially like this: 'Our left wing is outnumbered and is falling back, our center is hard-pressed, the right wing is outflanked and subject to an enfilading fire. We are attacking.'"

"*Vive la France*," shouted Frémont, abetted spontaneously by Bonnet, Schlumberger and Toudoux.

Evans held up his hand, as the Russians were about to give the old Cossack yell and Rain-No-More and Hjalmar, the latter having been instructed by the Indian, got set to let out the Blackfeet tribal warwhoop.

"I have decided, in spite of the fact that we are outnumbered more than two to one, to take the offensive," Homer said. His companions restrained themselves from cheering, but at the cost of several buttons which gave way under the strain of their enthusiasm and pinged against the windows of the car. At that same moment, however, both Frémont and Galilee Zach saw the scalp on the piano. The latter, whose distaste for scalps had mounted until it had reached the proportions of a minor complex, let out a shriek and would have collapsed had not Stenka held him up by the collar. Frémont's face grew severe.

"I trust," he said, "that in future we shall observe the rules of civilized warfare."

Rain-No-More shrugged his shoulders. "Our medicine man, Trout-tail III, has wisely said that warfare is never civilized. It is frequently necessary, occasionally diverting, usually a bore, but, I repeat, it is never civilized. This atrocity was perpetrated with a salutary purpose, namely, to terrify and disorganize the enemy forces, who fight on the side of injustice. Moreover, if scalping is practiced conscientiously, it is impossible for the chiefs to fake the casualty lists, as, I understand they did frequently in the great paleface war to end wars."

Dr. Hyacinthe Toudoux, to whom odd fragments of human bodies were mere bagatelles, made a pertinent suggestion. "May we not thrash out the ethics of this maneuver at some later date, preferably when our loved ones are in a place of safety?" the medical examiner said.

"The rough stuff? When does it begin?" Hjalmar asked.

"I shall not delay you long," Evans said. "The white men from the Lake Regions, with liquor inside and out, are, I strongly suspect, certain members of the Baldy Santo mob, led by Baldy himself. They were not to be found in Chicago, you remember. Undoubtedly Gilligan has hired them to terrorize the cattlemen. It is probable that the white men in the other camp will not be involved in tonight's attack. They would prefer to let the Shoshones do the work and take the blame."

Setting up a blackboard Corrigan had used for chalking up his menus in the kitchen, Homer drew a map, with the help of Rain-No-More, who communicated details to him in the Blackfeet tongue. The enemy camp, which consisted of a new large log cabin for the gangsters, and the tepees of the Shoshones, lay about five miles west-half-north and was separated from the special section of the train by impassable volcanic hills and ravines. A winding back trail eleven miles long led eastward from the camp to the scene of the avalanche. Another side trail led to the N. P. tracks four miles west of the train. By means of that, Larkspur Gilligan and his three companions had reached the camp of the Indians. According to Rain-No-More, there was a very dim trail, almost imperceptible, connecting the back trail with the railroad, not a hundred yards from the train. This perilous pathway cut the back trail about half way between the outlaw camp and the avalanche.

"The Shoshones will take the side trail that exposes us from the north," Evans said. "They will try to take us by surprise, massacre the men and kidnap the women."

At that, both Toudoux and Frémont began to gesticulate and growl, growing alternately white with horror and mauve with rage.

"We must save a last cartridge," Frémont said. "Hjalmar, you have no heart, where women are concerned. It is you who must take that shocking responsibility."

"Those who want to be bumped off will have to raise their right hands," said the Norwegian.

Galilee Zach, still trembling, stepped two paces forward and performed a creditable salute. "I'll shoot 'em," he said. "It wouldn't be so hard for me."

"What is the talk about?" asked Stenka, in French.

"They're planning to shoot us, to save us from the redskins," Miriam replied, "but I'll talk them out of it."

"*Oh, merci, chére mademoiselle,*" said the Serbian girl. "*Vous êtes bonne et adorable, et bougremente intelligente, d'ailleurs.*"

To restore military order, Evans brought them back to attention.

"Perhaps we can avoid the sacrifice of our wives and sweethearts," Evans said. "Listen closely, for the time is short. My plan is as follows: The Shoshones will take the back trail, branch off just north of us and try to rush the train. They will have three miles to go, as the crow flies, and about six, as the trail winds. Rain-No-More says the path is so treacherous and narrow that a coyote might fall and break his neck if he tried to pass over it at night."

"A coyote? *C'est incroyable,*" objected Schlumberger.

"The natives here speak in parables, like our Blessed Saviour, only far less restrainedly," explained Bonnet.

"Frémont and his squad, assisted by Rain-No-More and Corrigan, will start northward along the trail I have mentioned, and meet the Shoshones half way. In fact, they must arrive at a suitable ambush in time to set up a machine gun and wait silently for the Indians to come."

"If I have not the agility of a coyote, at least I can show more courage," Frémont said. "Lead on, scalper of redmen and Italians. Only understand that if corpses are to be mutilated, it must be done when I am not looking. As a reserve officer of the Third French Republic, I must insist on that."

"Quite all right," said Rain-No-More, handing him the tribal pipe, which, however, had gone out while the company had been standing at attention.

Colonel Kvek and Captain Lidin were dizzy with disappointment and chagrin, but Evans turned to them with an understanding smile.

"You, Kvek," he began, and the Russian saluted eagerly. "You, Kvek," repeated Evans, "will take the other side trail to the west, the one which leads to the gangsters' hideout and the Indian tepees. Miss Leonard and I will undertake to guide you and give you a hand."

"In one instant, you have wiped out the memory of years of humiliation," the former Colonel said gratefully.

"Skull to crotch. Zowie. Boom! Bam! Zing!" murmured Lidin, and only his early military training prevented him from doing a Caucasian dance on top of the Steinway piano.

"Captain Lidin," Evans said, "you will have no saber practice this evening. I have a better idea. The gangsters and the Gilligans will be drinking to the success of their allies. The night is still, very fortunately for us. Our duty will be to drench the thugs with tear gas, the effect of which, and especially on drunken men, will last at least eight hours. The Shoshones, having been surprised and sobered by Frémont's machine-gun fire, will return to the camp, those who survive the clash, with blood in their eyes. They will think Gilligan has led them into a trap, because they know too much about his past operations. What they will do, when they find the whites not only too drunk but helpless and half blind with tear gas I shall leave to your individual imaginations."

Hugo Weiss fairly beamed and broke ranks to place his hand on Evans' nearest shoulder. "A wonderful plan, my boy. Napoleonic! Split their forces! Only you go Napoleon one better. You divide a house against itself. That, my boy, was a Hebrew plan. I can point it out in the Talmud, if our scheme works out and I ever see that venerable book again."

In Which Holes Are Kicked in the Wisdom of Ecclesiastes

BY MORNING, EVERYBODY IN GLENDIVE knew that something had gone wrong on the main line of the N.P. The eastbound Limited had been sidetracked, the locomotive reversed on the turntable, and had headed back toward Billings, so that the passengers could be routed on another line. The morning train for Minneapolis had not showed up at all, and nothing had come through westbound. Snowslides in the badlands were not uncommon in that season, and it was assumed, in the absence of accurate information, that the tracks had been blocked by what is known technically as an act of God.

The proprietor of the local newspaper, the Glendive *X-Ray*, was a short spry journeyman printer named Skinner Bruce, who after years in the West still spoke with a Cockney accent. Bruce had been on the platform when Tom Jackson arrived and had seen him led away, in a huge borrowed bearskin coat and fur cap, by the sheriff. Lacking news about the railroad tie-up, Bruce sought out the sheriff early the next day and asked if he could interview the prisoner. Hockaday was reluctant, but Bruce had done him so many election favors that he did not like to refuse.

"The dude's plumb loco," the sheriff said.

"He'll be good for a few sticks of copy, anyway," said the editor.

"He thinks a string of circus cars got loose in the badlands. You wouldn't mention nothin' like that. It would make work for me," Hockaday said.

"Nothing serious. Just a little story about life back east, that's all," the editor promised.

The sheriff decided to take a chance. So the two men saddled up a couple of bronchos and set out across the sagebrush flat.

Tom Jackson, in the chilly night, had had ample time for reflection. He had a generous stack of horsehair blankets, and he had spread the bearskin coat on top of those. Also he had worn all his clothes to bed, and protected his ears with the fur cap. What he had not known, never having roughed it much before, was that intense cold comes up from under. He had placed too many of his blankets on top of himself, and only one underneath. The supply of firewood was so limited that he did not dare keep the Sibley going, for fear of freezing in the morning. The coyotes, goaded by the Goddess Luna and the dearth of grub, had howled and yapped until dawn.

Thinking back over his brief stay in Glendive, Jackson was convinced that the sheriff and the station agent were in cahoots with Gilligan and had no intention of reporting the loss of the special coaches until the information leaked in from other sources, which might well be too late. The reporter decided to play dumb, get out of the cooler, if possible, and telephone Miriam's father. He remembered the name of the ranch house, Opera Lodge, and the location, called Three Buttes. Consequently, when the sheriff opened the door and introduced Skinner Bruce as proprietor of the *X-Ray*, Jackson pretended to be repentant and forgetful.

"I must have been stewed last night," he said.

"There's nothing much else to do on a train," the editor said.

"I'm a newspaper man myself," said Jackson. "How are chances for a job?"

"You don't remember what you told us last night?" asked the sheriff.

"I don't remember a thing since I left Minneapolis," Jackson said. "I was in a bar, and some duffer advised me to go west. I had money enough for a ticket, and a few drinks on the way, but I forgot my overcoat and hat."

"You must have had a beaut," said the editor. He needed a man badly, to do reporting, read copy, write headlines, correct proof and make up the *X-Ray*. The setting up of type, Bruce could do as well as the next man, but the rest of the work was arduous for him. "Have a heart, and let this man out. I'll guarantee he won't be a charge on the county," Bruce said to the sheriff. "In fact, I'll stake him fifty bucks right now, so he can get a shave and some breakfast," the editor added.

"You're sure none of them pipe dreams will come back to you?" asked the sheriff, beginning to believe that his prisoner was amenable to reasons and had a good idea of which side his bread was buttered on.

"That's the way I am. When I draw a blank, I can't recall a thing, not even years afterward," said Jackson. "My old man was like that, too. So were six of my uncles and aunts."

"You can't get mulled on Wednesday or Thursday. That's when we go to press," Bruce said. "What you do outside of working days is none of my business."

"I'm beginning to like this town," Tom Jackson said.

The sheriff offered to let him ride behind the saddle, but Jackson was afraid of horses, the few he had seen at close range. They had seemed to have ideas at variance with his own, and a fiendish way of exploiting his nervousness.

"I'll hoof it," Jackson said, "but thanks just the same." He had in the pocket of the borrowed fur coat two twenty-dollar gold pieces and a smaller one he assumed was a ten, although he had not examined it carefully. Within half an hour he was in the Hotel Jordan and was eating ham and eggs, while the waitress, glad always to see a new face, was giving him the lowdown on practically everything in Eastern Montana. Tom let her run on until he was sure she sided with the cattlemen and detested Gilligan. Then he told her she resembled an old girl of his back East, only that she was more candid and aboveboard. The exchange of confidences resulted, among other things, in a secret telephone call, on the part of the waitress, to Jim Leonard at Three Buttes.

Outside the kitchen door of Opera Lodge the metal triangle clanged. The saddle horses, on edge because of the cold and their lack of recent exercise, kicked, neighed, pranced and shied. Cowpunchers came running from all directions. Wing Lee and Wing

Sam looked at each other uneasily and began to search their respective consciences. Was the Law about to make another onslaught? Had another stranger disappeared?

Hank, the foreman, was the first to reach the huge living room, in which sat Shot-on-Both-Sides, staring gravely into the fire. Sweat was running from his brow.

"Indian build small fire, stand close," the old Chief said. "White man build big fire, stand way back. White man damn fool."

Jim Leonard was still lambasting the triangle, so Hank asked Shot-on-Both-Sides what was eating the boss.

"Eating is over until . . ." the Chief pointed straight upward and then at the sun that was shining thinly at the quarter mark. "Talk box ring. Boss hear um. Put quick talk back in um. Pound medicine triangle like hell."

The Professor came running in, followed by Laramee Bob and Slipnoose Pete. Tumbleweed O'Flaherty, who had been dozing in his bunk upstairs, came down in his shirtsleeves.

"Don't shoot till you see the whites of their eyes, pardners. That's what Brigham said," the old sheriff observed.

Jim Leonard, glancing in through the window, saw that all his men were on hand and hurried inside.

"Gilligan's got Miriam," he said, trying to control his emotion. "She and a bunch of her friends were left behind when the Limited went through the badlands, just across from Beef Slough. Some cars were uncoupled. The sheriff and his gang are wise, and hushed the thing up in Glendive. Pete, you and Bob saddle all the horses, and put a sack of feed behind each saddle. Hank, you tell the Chink about grub and get it into the saddlebags. Let every man take all the ammunition he can. God knows what we can do. We'll have to ride all the way to Glendive, then follow the N.P. tracks. It's a good hundred and fifty miles to town, and more than that back to the place the coaches got loose."

"Can't we cross the Yellowstone at the mouth of Beef Slough? It's frozen solid," Hank said.

"We couldn't get through the badlands. If we could, it would save two days, but we'd never make it," Leonard said.

Chief Shot-on-Both-Sides rose solemnly. "Blackfeet make it," he said.

Jim Leonard, his face pathetic with eagerness, faced his old friend. "You mean there's a trail?"

"A faint trail," the old Indian said. Then he added: "My boy, Rain-No-More, on same train. He take care of Miriam. Maybe take care of Gilligan, too." Vividly the Chief, with two forefingers held on top of his head like a compass, described a circle.

"Hadn't we better split up, so half of us can try the badlands and the others could get there later, by way of Glendive, if the first bunch couldn't find the trail?"

"We make it," said Shot-on-Both-Sides. "Powwow finished."

THE GODDESS AURORA, as the reader has already surmised, had not been in form that morning. At dawn thin meaningless clouds had obscured the sun which penetrated them fitfully from time to time later on. Leaving Frémont and Kvek to defend the train, which was white with frost and snow-blown by the wind from neighboring drifts, Homer, with Hjalmar, Miriam and Rain-No-More, set out stealthily for the side trail leading to the outlaws' camp to find out what had happened the night before.

From his well-chosen ambush half way between the frost-bound section and the back trail, Frémont and his squad, guided by Rain-No-More, had acquitted themselves most honorably. Before midnight, the Shoshones had stolen along the perilous pathway like panthers on padded feet, single file, at a dogtrot, each man stepping carefully in the tracks of the leader, who was not Tall-Horse-in-Flytime but one of his lieutenants named Noisy Snake. Frémont had to do some quick thinking, because his machine-gun emplacement, the only one available, faced along the trail and was useless for broadsides. He had not dared to let the first of the Shoshones pass by. As soon as the leader was within range he had let fly such a shower of lead that Noisy Snake and the two Indians next in line were riddled with bullets, while the others, more than forty in number, doubled back so fast that they stepped in anybody's tracks they could find and left behind them such a well-trodden pathway that

Rain-No-More had caught up with the rear and bagged two of the
hindmost, bringing the score up to five to nothing. The young
Blackfeet was chagrined at having failed to encounter Tall-Horse
and challenge him to single combat.

Tall-Horse-in-Flytime's success as an Indian had been due to
his prudence and cunning more than his valor. The medicine man
of his tribe had told him, once, that he was going to live a long
time, and the Shoshone brave, who liked the old sorcerer, did not
want to make a sucker of him by an untimely shuffling-off. He had
waited at the intersection of the trails while his warriors, under
Noisy Snake, had set out to do the spade work. When they came
running back, with tales of a gun that spit bullets faster than a
woodpecker could drum on a tree, Tall-Horse-in-Flytime made a
quick decision. He had got the small end of the stick from Gilligan
several times before. The Shoshone outlaw began to think more
kindly of the United States Government and concluded that it
would be better to lead what was left of his band back to Idaho,
where they could live less dangerously on the reservation, and leave
Gilligan and his gangsters from Chicago to shift for themselves.
Consequently, by dawn the only Shoshones left in the State of
Montana were a brace of squaws back in the tepees, of both of
whom Tall-Horse was growing weary.

The gas attack on the blockhouse northwest of the train had
been carried out as scheduled by Evans, Miriam and Kvek with his
international squad, and with brilliant success. They had left the
Gilligans and the gangsters gasping, choking and digging fists into
their smarting eyes, but had not stayed to witness the slaughter
they had expected would take place, because of the off chance that
some of the Shoshones might break through Frémont's barricade
and terrorize the women in their absence. A careful reconnaissance
in the morning revealed that the Shoshones had fled the State, leaving their dead on the trail. The gangsters, sick and shaken from
their baptism of tear gas, were in such a sullen mood that Gilligan
and Baldy Santo were having a hard time restraining them from
shooting the abandoned squaws, then starting on foot for Chicago.

Content to leave the enemy in a demoralized condition for the time being, Evans and his scouts returned to headquarters. The snowslide that cut off help from the east had been carefully inspected by Hjalmar, who reported that the tracks, wires and road-bed had been swept into a deep canyon, leaving a gap about fifty yards long. To repair the damage would require several days' work by a large section gang, since dirt would have to be borrowed from the solidly frozen ground to replace the downhill side of the embankment. Work would undoubtedly be started within a day or two, at which time the party could get into communication with Bismarck or even Minneapolis.

Relief from the west was likely to be more prompt, Evans thought, since he believed Tom Jackson had got as far as Glendive and would think of some way to circumvent the officers of the law and employees of the railroad who were in Gilligan's pay. The legal aspects of the situation merited a careful analysis. According to the railroad map, they were in the State of Montana, Dawson County, the stronghold of the Gilligan political machine. It would be difficult to prove that the sheepman had been responsible for the uncoupling of the special section, or that he had instigated the attack on the train by the outlaw Shoshones. Neither could it be established in a hostile court that Gilligan had imported Baldy Santo's gang from Illinois, with felonious intent or malice aforethought. The murder of the telephone clerk would have to be cleared up, another delicate task. The body, minus scalp, was packed in snow, an unnecessary precaution considering the temperature of the all-steel cars, with the thermometer reading thirty below zero at noonday and descending in the night. Five dead Shoshones were lying in the snow on the faint side trail, and since, however wayward, they were wards of the United States Government, some explanation would have to be forthcoming.

In the other camp, Larkspur Gilligan was alone with his thoughts, as the song writers say. He knew he could get away with a great deal, since his patronage meant so much to the railroad, and the office holders were nearly all his own creations. Nevertheless, there was a limit, and Larkspur, reckless by nature, could also be cagey. The section boss at Glendive would eventually be obliged to send out a wrecking crew to inspect the tracks. So on the strength of that assumption, Gilligan decided to start hiking westward along the tracks and himself report the distress of the special section. Without the Indians, his gangsters were outnumbered. They had proved less tractable in the great open spaces than they had been in Chicago's crowded precincts. Gilligan planned to say in Glendive that he had met Baldy Santo in the East, and had been moved by the man's sincere desire to reform himself and his followers.

Most of all, Gilligan wanted to find out more about Hugo Weiss, the Croesus who was backing Jim Leonard and the cattlemen. So without confiding his intentions to Baldy Santo, who would have insisted on going along, Gilligan and his son, Terry, stole out of the gangsters' hideout. On reaching the railroad, they started hiking west as fast as their legs could carry them. It was a long chance, but Gilligan had never been loath to take chances. Besides, he had had one dose of tear gas and preferred to risk freezing to death rather than to repeat the experience.

In and around the Pelleas, the Melisande and their frost-bound auxiliary coaches, the members of the party were fighting, not Indians or gangsters, but the cold. A fine snow had begun to fall and the sullen sky, according to Rain-No-More, held signs of a blizzard. Not far from the train, in the side of a sandstone cliff with thick layers of lava rock, was a natural cave which faced away from the prevailing direction of the wind. This cavern had an opening in the ceiling, which acted as a chimney. So Evans asked all hands to forage for firewood, stack it near the mouth of the cave, and a fire was built inside. Corrigan had several large pans in his kitchen and these were filled with live coals and served to raise the temperature of the cars to a point where it was supportable. Both Miriam and Diluvio shot several grouse, which roosted on the lower branches of the scrub evergreens in the dry canyon to the east. Stenka heated and lugged huge washboilers of water. Hydrangea taught Beatrice Diluvio and Eugénie Toudoux a simple dance routine which served to keep them warm and to occupy their minds.

It was not long before the women became quite proficient, and more than once the toiling men paused, smiling and wiping frost from their eyebrows and whiskers, to watch the Stomp or the Susie Q. The former Marquise de la Rose d'Antan, whose aristocratic family and dissolute first husband had never permitted her to dance, was especially enthusiastic and made the ex-Blackbird promise to give her daily dancing lessons.

"I begin to know what it is to be a pioneer, to feel in my veins the blood of those magnificent Frenchmen, whose names I failed to jot down, but who conquered this inscrutable wilderness," said Dr. Hyacinthe Toudoux, who had been moved almost to tears of joy by the sight of his Eugenie, so raptly engaged in practicing "*La derriere noire*" or Black Bottom.

"For my part," said Frémont, "I am inclining toward a theory I once heard expounded, to the effect that places and not races are the determining factor in human behavior. Which one of us has not, since landing in America, felt the urge to lay aside his native caution? Much as I hesitate to confess it, I must tell you, Doctor, that just now, when Miss Montana was playing that barbaric tune— er, hallelujah, kerplumb, hallelujah—and my beloved Hydrangea was following its measures so gracefully, I, reserve officer of the army of France and Chief of Detectives of Paris, felt the inclination to prance and sashay. Of course, I restrained the mad impulse."

"So did I," the doctor said, "but I am not sure I shall do so in future. Monsieur Evans, you who have encyclopedic knowledge, what is, exactly, a Susie Q? I do not find the term in my pocket *Larousse*."

At that point, Stenka, having lugged enough water for the day, came in out of the driving snow and joined the dancers, contributing a Slavic peasant dance, with a haunting melody, to be performed and sung by women alone, arms outstretched, hands clasped and moving slowly in a circle. Hydrangea caught on instantly; the older women were not long in joining in. Kvek and Lidin, roaring with approval, began pouring out vodka by the tumblerful. Hjalmar, Diluvio, in short, the entire party tossed care to the rising winds and drifting snow. Rain-No-More, in a corner by himself, was rehearsing in a tentative way the steps of the tribal raven dance. Galilee Zach was having a go at Pavlova's "Dying Swan."

It was at just that moment that Chief Shot-on-Both-Sides, of the Blackfeet, advance scout of the rescue party from Three Buttes, peered in through the frosty window of the St. Cecilia and promptly ducked into the brush again to think things over. The old sachem had seen seventy-two winters, but in the course of none of them had he run across anything like the spectacle he had just witnessed.

THE OVERLAND JOURNEY of the rescue party had been accomplished without misfortune. Jim Leonard, Tumbleweed O'Flaherty, Hank, the Professor, Slipnoose Pete and Laramee Bob, leading two extra horses apiece, had followed Shot-on-Both-Sides across the bare spaces on the windward side of Leonard Creek, crossed the stage road at dusk and reached the Yellowstone at midnight. The river ice, two feet in thickness, had been swept clean by the blizzard and they were able to ride south on it to Beef Slough before making camp. At Beef Slough, they had chosen a sheltered location, had thrown up brush corrals for the horses, blanketed, watered and fed the animals and turned in for a few hours' sleep until dawn. The difficult trail, if it could be called a trail, through the badlands, lay ahead of them and only Shot-on-Both-Sides was confident it could be traveled as far as the railroad, which lay forty miles to the southeast.

In the morning, after bacon and coffee in the thinning darkness, the cowpunchers had drawn lots to determine who should stay behind with the horses. Laramee Bob was the unlucky man. The agreement was that he should wait three days, then turn loose all but one of the horses and ride to Glendive for help.

Doggedly, Shot-on-Both-Sides took the lead, with Jim Leonard close behind him, and as the old Indian struggled through sagebrush and ice-coated cactus ten feet high to reach the first crumbled foothill, he reflected that his grand-uncle, the Chief of the Piegans, had blazed that self-same trail, in defiance of tribal superstitions, had entered the unknown area of colored ashes with hot springs that steamed and bubbled through fissures, of snakes and lizards, forests turned to stone, and had found a way to surprise the Shoshones, put them to rout and appropriate their youngest and hardiest squaws. It was thus among the tribes, his own father had taught him. Some had sturdy braves and lazy squaws, others first-class squaws and braves with hearts of coyotes. Only the Blackfeet, the Crows and the Cheyennes had sons and daughters of equal prowess in their respective spheres.

As he broke trail, the old Chief paused now and then, glanced to one side or the other for landmarks he had almost forgotten, sometimes sunk to his waist in drifted snow, again moved forward at a swift dog trot over expanses of hard crust or solid lava. Constantly the precarious hidden pathway mounted. The men, hard as nails and inured to the biting cold, went forward, eyes glued to the footsteps of the man in advance, saying little except when it was necessary to halt. The cattle range across the river was bleak and wild, but nothing compared with the badlands, where Nature seemed to have spent herself in prehistoric rioting.

"This isn't fit country for a turkey buzzard to roost on," the Professor said to Hank.

"It's sure desperate," the foreman replied.

Jim Leonard and Shot-on-Both-Sides were looking anxiously at the sky. Wordlessly they looked into each other's eyes and nodded. They were fine specimens of their respective races, the one with silver hair, the other's still jet black. Both of them knew a storm was coming and what it meant. They might reach the railroad and find their children, but how, in a blizzard, could they get back again?

"Boys," said Leonard grimly, "you better go back to the river."

Hank looked hurt and dropped his eyes. "You can't fire us unless you pay us off. That's the law," he said.

"I can give you chapter and verse," said the Professor.

"I ain't working for you, anyway," said Tumbleweed O'Flaherty. "I'm just along for the exercise."

"Is that the way you feel, Pete?" asked Leonard. "There's no use in my telling you it's going to snow."

"We're wasting time," Pete said.

"*An e tuk it*" (Lead on), Leonard said, and Shot-on-Both-Sides nodded.

For two hours more they struggled through disintegrated granite and thorned cactus, over slippery heaps of lava made treacherous by a thin coating of ice. There was no mid-day thaw, and no easy going until, on an isolated mesa they crossed one of the hidden areas of pastureland.

"Squirrel meadows," grunted Hank, and Jim Leonard nodded. Between drifts, the feathery grass showed brown in spots, and was thickly matted.

The storm held off, and just before noon Shot-on-Both-Sides pointed out a thin column of smoke, then another. The party headed for the first one, and when they were within a few miles of it, the Indian, by means of sign language, asked Leonard and his buckaroos to approach the nearest fire cautiously. Meanwhile the Chief set out to investigate the farther one. It was agreed that the first to find traces of Miriam, Rain-No-More or a cast-off train of cars was to fire a revolver three times.

Jim Leonard, spurred on by his anxiety, redoubled his pace. When he was within five hundred yards of the gangsters' cabin he saw the top of the chimney. Having asked O'Flaherty and the Professor to wait for them in a near-by cavern, the rancher and Hank went forward on their hands and knees. It was not long before they caught a full view of the gangsters' camp, and were surprised to see also numerous Indian tepees, inhabited only by two Shoshone squaws. The mysterious new log cabin was big enough to house a dozen or more men. Leonard crawled ahead, until he could peep into a window of the cabin. There he saw a group of dishevelled strangers, evidently from the East and more than half drunk, playing stud poker on a long board table.

Astonished and disappointed, the rancher crept back to where Hank was waiting in the driving snow. They were trying to decide what to do when they saw a pair of the tenderfeet leave the cabin and walk slowly down a trail leading to the railroad tracks. Leonard pointed to his rope; the foreman nodded and patted his own. Keeping well out of sight, the rancher and Hank stalked the wandering pair and, at a silent signal, let fly with their lariats. One noose dropped cleanly over the head and shoulders of young Santosuosso; the other, thrown by Hank, pinned the arms of Nutcracker Ike and jerked him off his feet. Both victims choked back their protests when they found themselves looking into the neat blue muzzles of Smith & Wesson revolvers that looked about the size of the Red Sea.

"Where are you fellers from?" demanded Jim Leonard grimly.

Into the confused mind of young Santosuosso leaped one of the first phrases he had learned at his father's knee. "I'm not talking without a lawyer," he said.

Hank slapped his shaggy chaps with glee. "The lawyer's just stepped out," he said. "He won't be back till spring."

Jim Leonard looked hard at Nutcracker Ike. "I didn't come here to make trouble. I'm looking for my daughter, that's all," he said. "Speak up. Where is she?"

"I don't know her," grunted Nutcracker Ike.

"And who is that bunch of scissorbills back in the bunkhouse?" asked Hank.

"How about them Indians?" demanded Leonard. "The nearest reservation is more than a hundred miles north of here and that's for Blackfeet, not Shoshones."

The two captives remained silent.

"Well," said Hank, "I can see that we'll have to make an example of one of you, to make the survivor more sociable." The lanky foreman, keeping Santosuosso covered, took the noose off his neck and slung it over a horizontal branch of a dead tree. He tugged and nodded. "Seems solid enough," he said.

"We'd better hang the other one," said Jim Leonard. "He hasn't got as long to live, anyway."

"I favor the runt. He's fresher than the old one, and Saint Peter will be easier on him, on account of his youth," Hank said.

The youth referred to riposted by spitting in the foreman's right eye.

"That settles it," said Hank.

The dead limb was almost horizontal, and about eight feet from the ground. Hank built up a pedestal of snow, and prodded the young gangster with his revolver. Santosuosso stood his ground and refused to move. The foreman, losing patience, brought up a haymaker that laid him out flat in the snow. Before he could rise, Hank bound his arms and ankles and tied a bandanna over his eyes, then picked him up and stood him like a tenpin on the snow pile. Swiftly he adjusted the noose around his neck, and tossed the free end of the rope over the limb, securing it firmly to a near-by stump.

"Are you going to answer civil questions, or shall I kick this snow away?" Hank asked.

The answer was in the form of an invitation that Hank showed no disposition to accept.

"How about you?" asked Leonard of the former railroad dick.

The result might have been tragic for Santosuosso, although beneficial to mankind, had not three shots split the frosted air, half muffled by the whine of the storm.

12
Of Parents and Their Children

HANK GREENLEAF, WHO, although he never talked about it, had been born in Vermont, understood much more than he expressed about human behavior. He knew that young men of Santosuosso's type fear pain much more than death. So when Jim Leonard started to double back on their trail and motioned Hank to follow with the prisoners, the lanky foreman put up his Smith & Wesson and got out his hunting knife, which bore the trademark of Montgomery Ward. By inserting about half an inch of the blade into the young gangster, he persuaded the latter to precede him peaceably. Already the storm had almost obliterated the footsteps, but Leonard and his foreman were able to find the cave and turn over their captives to O'Flaherty. Then they set out after Chief Shot-on-Both-Sides.

The latter, squatting motionless on his heels, with his back to the storm, was not at his best. He had been prepared to find his son and the latter's companions half frozen, famished, ravished by Shoshones, buried in snowslides or clawed by wildcats. The fact that they were dancing in several uncoordinated styles and drinking paleface hootch, in a series of wagons so fantastic that the Chief blinked whenever he recalled them to mind, perplexed the wise old Indian. Rain-No-More, his first born and most promising son, had always been a brave, his father had thought, who could keep his eye fairly well on the ball. He had been sent across the world to bring back Miriam, the daughter of the Chief's old trusted friend. But while he seemed to have brought the girl back, all right, he had done so under circumstances Shot-on-Both-Sides did not relish reporting to the stern father of a handsome unmarried young squaw.

"*Nit okh si tuk ki*" (I am pleased), he said, however, when Jim Leonard and Hank put in an appearance. Like so many conventional greetings it was by no means literally true.

"Is she safe?" asked the silver-haired rancher, unable to conceal his fears.

"*A ki sa,*" replied Shot-on-Both-Sides, which means "Yes, and no." Abandoning all attempts at oral explanation, the old Chief grunted and led the way to the railroad tracks. There the eyes of the rancher and his foreman began to pop, blink, rotate and shuttle from side to side. For Hjalmar and Stenka were doing a robust two-step on the floor of the Saint Cecilia; Kvek and Grigori were dancing a kazotsky on top of the grand piano, and Hydrangea and her two sedate pupils were trucking toward the Dôme, in which Rain-No-More and Hugo Weiss were shooting at electric bulbs with champagne corks, to the huge delight of Moritz the dog.

Only one coincidence saved the day. Miriam, at the keyboard of the sonorous Steinway, had run out of hot jazz tunes and had been forced to fall back on a march she had learned on the ranch from the lessons mailed by the Seek and Ye Shall Find Correspondence School of Omaha. The march, entitled "The Ben Hur Chariot Race," had been her father's favorite since first her girlish fingers had touched the keys. In fact, the old rancher had doted on that particular composition to the point where frequently, in the course of a long winter evening, he had asked her to play it for him no fewer than a dozen times. The measures of that descriptive piece, composed by E. T. Paull, melted suspicion in the old man's heart and brought tears to his eyes, so that, forgetting his former misgivings as to the source of the fifty thousand dollars, the rancher rushed into the Saint Cecilia, scattering dancers here and there in his haste, and clasped Miriam in his arms.

"Daughter, look me in the eye," he said gruffly, a moment later, to hide his emotion. But when her clear gaze met his, he bowed his head with mingled feelings of relief and embarrassment.

Meanwhile, Rain-No-More, perceiving his father standing gravely by the tracks, hastened out to greet him respectfully and report the success of his difficult errand. Hjalmar Jansen, who about the same time had observed Hank, the foreman, did not notice he had not been with the party all along and roared:

"Come in and have a drink."

All in all, in spite of the raging blizzard and the inaccessibility of the region, the ensuing moments were joyous indeed. Hugo Weiss was the cordial and thoughtful host, Homer Evans the tactful master of ceremonies.

"Don't mention it," said the multi-millionaire, when Jim Leonard tried to thank Weiss for forking up the bail. "Don't mention it, I beg of you, sir. If you forfeit it, I shall be rid of that much responsibility."

The rancher's face showed strain from worry.

"I'll stand trial," he said, "but there's no telling what those lawyers'll do. There was a time when there wasn't a lawyer in this country . . ."

"Sorry I missed those days," said Weiss, "but good times are coming. The more I see of this country, the more I'm determined to save it from development. That may cost a pile of money, but I've got plenty, and Mrs. Diluvio, who was a Baxter, has at least half a billion she doesn't need."

Evans, who wished to correct the impression of frivolity his companions had given the Western plainsmen, called his men to attention and sent them back to their respective tasks. Then he invited the rancher, the foreman and the Blackfeet Chief to make an inspection tour of the coaches. They had not progressed far when all three of them began to believe that the tenderfeet, while somewhat eccentric, were not unresourceful in emergencies. Homer did not show them the stiff on ice in the dark room of the Castor and Pollux, or Galilee Zach wielding a powderpuff in the silver-plated washroom. But the pans of coals glowed warmly in each of the cars, and the smell of hot food issued from the kitchen. They found Diluvio in the act of stringing up a creditable pair of snowshoes, saw Hjalmar figuring out his bearings from notes he had taken the

day before while shooting the sun, observed Dr. Toudoux bandag-
ing skillfully a burn on one of the waiter's hands. In fact, Jim
Leonard and Shot-on-Both-Sides concluded that their respective
offspring had the knack of making friends who not only seemed to
have unlimited money, but talents and fertile brains as well. The
rancher began to feel that the cards were no longer stacked against
him; the Blackfeet leader that perhaps, after all, he could make
peace with the whites.

As soon as Homer had placed his guests at ease, he focused his
mind on immediate problems. Rain-No-More was sent back with
Hank to guide Tumbleweed O'Flaherty, Slipnoose Pete and the
Professor from their shelter, and it was agreed that the prisoners,
young Santosuosso and Nutcracker Ike, should be sent back to their
cabin after being warned that any gangster who left the clearing
would be shot on sight. Evans' plan, approved by Jim Leonard, was
not to take the gang to Glendive where the officials would play into
Gilligan's hand but to load them on the first east-bound freight
and ship them back to Minneapolis, unarmed and without funds.

As soon as possible, Homer asked for a private interview with
Shot-on-Both-Sides. For that purpose he led the Chief to his stateroom, where, after sitting uneasily on the edge of one of the up-
holstered chairs, the Indian asked permission to squat on the floor.
There were perhaps five minutes of complete silence while the two
men collected their thoughts. The pipe was passed from hand to
hand; then Homer stood up to speak.

"Heap trouble," Evans began, in the Blackfeet tongue.

"Too much," replied the Chief.

Before continuing, Homer reached into a suitcase and produced
the scalp of Donniker Louey. Not a muscle moved in the face of the
old Chief, but his eyes grew very sad. Evans pointed north toward
Cottonwood Creek, where the gangster's death had occurred, Shot-
on-Both-Sides made a series of gestures painfully descriptive of
hanging, followed by intense mourning and tribal desolation.

"Rain-No-More did well," Evans said.

"A good son," agreed Shot-on-Both-Sides. "But finished. *Kyi!*"

"Not finished," said Homer. "He must not talk."

"He will not let his friend be hanged," the Indian said.

"Jim Leonard will not be hanged," said Evans.

"Gilligan has strong medicine," the Chief said.

"I have more powerful medicine," said Evans.

The old Chief rose to his full height and looked straight into Homer's eyes, so searchingly that Evans felt as if he were transparent and lighted from within.

"*Ap is to tuk kit*" (One can trust you), said Shot-on-Both-Sides. "Rain-No-More will not confess until we try your medicine. If you save a Blackfeet, you become brother of the Blackfeet and a member of the tribe."

"*Nit okh si tuk ki*" (I shall be honored), Evans said, and bowed solemnly as he picked up the scalp and handed it to Shot-on-Both-Sides as a token of confidence.

Around them the badlands, with their weird shapes of hills, crumbled rocks and natural ruins, sank deeper beneath their covering of snow. Brown of windswept meadows, dull red and ochre of sandstone cliffs, black crags and fossils disappeared, were modified and cloaked with white, as were the special cars, the roadbed and everything within range of vision. The men took turns at the outdoor tasks, replenishing the huge central fire in the cave from which coals were obtained, melting snow and ice for water, keeping watch on the tracks, east and west. Cottonwood knots, soaked in olive oil, were lighted as darkness settled quickly around the coaches, and the silence was broken only by the whining of the wind. Miriam, who had been close at her father's side all afternoon, brought him to the Dôme at the aperitif hour and soon the rancher thawed, in good company, and held the Frenchmen spellbound with tales of the range and the trappers' old trails, of herds of buffalo and cattle, old round-ups and rodeos.

"Ah, America, Americans," said Frémont, in awe once again. "How wise you have been to discard all order and reason! Even Nature, which is decorous in France, lures one to extravagant words and deeds on this overwhelming continent. And to think that when I was twenty-two my father, with the best of intentions, struck at me with his cane because I had lost my umbrella."

"My poor grandfather saw little soldiers march in and out beneath his doorsill," said Sergeant Schlumberger.

"I filled a straight flush once and nobody stayed," said Hank.
"Hey, waiter! Give me a slug of that perfumed whiskey if you
haven't got Old Crow."

Corrigan, the chef, outdid himself for dinner. He loved to cook
for hearty eaters, after years of pandering to queasy travelers on
trains, and Evans, having ascertained that the gangsters had several weeks' supply of grub, including cases of spaghetti, links of
Milano and pepperoni, huge Bel Paese and Gorgonzola cheeses,
bottles of olives, cans of antipasto and sardines, had told the cooks
they could dish out a tremendous banquet. Hjalmar had sawed and
whittled out wooden horses and jockeys and colored them with
quick-drying paint so the company could enjoy betting on the races
after dinner. The portrait of Hugo Weiss, now finished, was un-
veiled in showers of beer and champagne. Diluvio entertained with
classical and popular selections. Dancing, both old style and new,
was indulged in freely, and it was close to four o'clock in the morning (Mountain Time), which after all was only 11 A.M. in Paris and
6 A.M. in New York, when the last of the revelers slid into their
bunks, each one of which had been warmed with a pan of embers
by Stenka and Galilee Zach.

For three days the snowstorm tied up transcontinental traffic
all the way from Bismarck to the Great Divide, which gave Evans
time to get acquainted with Miriam's father, and with him to shape
up future plans. As soon as help should arrive from Glendive, and
in spite of Gilligan this could not be delayed much longer, Homer
decided to leave Hjalmar, the Russians and the cowboys to guard
the gangsters and herd them into box cars eastbound when the
freight came through. Rain-No-More was to stay with that detachment to guide them overland to Three Buttes when their duty had
been performed. The special coaches were to be hauled back to
Jamestown, North Dakota, transferred to the branch line to Leeds
and thence westward again over the Great Northern as far as Muddy
Creek, only forty miles north of Three Buttes and Jim Leonard's
ranch. There was a commodious side track at Muddy Creek, on the

edge of the Blackfeet reservation, where those of the party who were not needed at the ranch house could make their headquarters in the special cars. Chief of Detectives Frémont and Hydrangea, Dr. and Mme. Hyacinthe Toudoux, Hugo Weiss and his secretary, Sergeants Schlumberger and Bonnet, Anton Diluvio and Beatrice, Galilee Zach, Corrigan the chef, Cromwell and Washington, the waiters, and the porters and other attendants were assigned quarters in the special cars, with Weiss as host and director of operations.

Evans, accompanied by Jim Leonard and Miriam, Stenka, Tumbleweed O'Flaherty, Shot-on-Both-Sides and Moritz the dog, made preparations to ride with the wrecking crew to Glendive, where they hoped to find Tom Jackson and Laramee Bob. The saddle horses left on the Yellowstone could not be rounded up until good weather set in, so another bunch of bronchos would have to be bought in Glendive for the trip to Three Buttes.

The frozen corpse of the telephone clerk, and those of the brother of Tall-Horse-in-Flytime and the five unidentified Shoshones, were to be turned in to Government authorities at Leeds, North Dakota, on the Great Northern, where the railroad men and local officials favored the cattlemen and were outside the sphere of Larkspur Gilligan's influence. At Shot-on-Both-Sides' suggestion, the two abandoned squaws were taken away from the gangsters for transportation to the Blackfeet reservation, where husbands would be provided for them. If, said Shot-on-Both-Sides, the husbands were not the best men among the Blackfeet, at least they would be an improvement over anything the Shoshones had to offer, and when this proposal was translated into the Shoshone language by Evans, the distracted pair of women stopped wailing, which they had kept up for nearly four days continuously. When they thought they were unobserved, they giggled slyly at the prospect of a change of Indians.

The fourth day after the reunion on the N.P. tracks, the sun broke through the clouds, the thermometer soared almost to zero, and the Glendive contingent were the first to depart, leaving their cheering comrades along the track on both sides. Next morning, an enormous wrecking crew appeared from Bismarck to tackle the snow slide in the canyon, and before a week had elapsed the gangsters were counted roughly, disarmed, marched from their cabin to the tracks, and, with grub and water enough for the journey, locked into empty box cars on the eastbound freight. The temporary trestle over the gulch proved strong enough to sustain the freight train, so the engine came back to hook on the special train and tow it as far as Jamestown Junction.

Then, with Rain-No-More as scout and leader, Hjalmar, Kvek, Grigori and the cowboys hit the trail on foot through the badlands. Both Colonel Kvek and Captain Lidin had been offered a ride to Glendive, but the prospect of finding horses near the Yellowstone camp site, remote as it was, lured them from the cushions. The men they had seen riding in Central Park, New York, they had considered merely as passengers on horses, and the Russians were eager to see if, in the West, men really rode. On their part, the cowboys were quite as curious to see what Cossacks would do with unbroken Western bronchos, or *vice versa.*

Part Two

Death Haunts the Yellowstone

13

A Rapprochement of Several Races

THE REMAINDER OF THAT REMARKABLE WINTER at Opera Lodge stands out in the memory of those who were even remotely concerned, and is especially vivid in the minds of the members of that smaller group from whom tragedy, vague and lurking, was never distant. The spacious ranch house, built of logs and clapboards, with a tight roof the shingles of which had beer shipped all the way from Minneapolis and carried by pack horses up the winding trail along Bison Creek to Three Buttes, had been given its name because on clear days in the summer and fall the badlands, miles distant across the muddy Yellowstone, could be seen from the upper windows— pale colors of forgotten ages, ochre, rose, dull violet and indigo.

The early adventurers, passing that way, had believed that the view was like the setting for an opera, a belief that was far too kind to that incongruous institution. For nothing ever painted on back drops could awaken the feeling of vastness and prodigal upheaval the broad valley and the badlands evoked. Just south of the ranch house and its scattered outbuildings stood the Three Buttes, from one of which gushed two springs, side by side, one icy cold, the other boiling hot. Leonard Creek, a mere trickle that gained volume downstream until it became a roaring torrent in the spring, flowed southeast to the Yellowstone. It was parched and dry in summer. Bison Creek had cut a crooked channel in the opposite direction, due north to the Missouri.

The logs of the lodge, the two large bunkhouses, the barn, the stable and the various corrals had been stained by the weather until

they blended with the drab of the sage and dry grass of the foothills and mesas until they seemed to belong to the country as did
the relics of the Paleozoic age. In the dead of winter, all was white
and brown, valleys drifted level, high areas of sidehill were swept
clean by the wind. On the range, which extended miles and miles
in all directions, as far as the Redwater to the west and Mountain
Sheep Bluffs to the south, Jim Leonard's cattle fought the elements
for their existence, between fall and spring round-ups, drifting with
the blizzards, growing shaggy coats of hair to resist the biting cold.
In summer they browsed tranquilly on the crest and in the gullies,
in bunches of hundreds, sometimes thousands, tough shorthorns
with wild appraising eyes, docile if a man was on horseback, contemptuous of or even hostile to a man on foot.

Of the company the reader knows, men and women from divers
lands and of varied experience, who had gathered on the Lower
Yellowstone from motives of adventure and friendship to help the
harassed rancher make a stand, nine were housed in the main
lodge, as follows: Jim Leonard, the host, who was under indictment; Miriam, whose hunger for the ranch and anxiety for her
father had been so intense that she radiated relief and happiness;
her faithful maid, Stenka; Eugénie and Hyacinthe Toudoux, the
first-named the former Marquise de la Rose d'Antan, the latter
medical examiner of Paris and a famous scientist; Anton Diluvio,
renowned concert violinist and his Boston bride, *née* Beatrice
Baxter; and the multi-millionaire and philanthropist, Hugo Schusschnigger Weiss.

The wealthy financier, having safely brought the special train
from the badlands back through North Dakota to the northeastern
corner of Jim Leonard's range, had quit the private coaches which
now stood on a sidetrack near Muddy Creek, and had been installed
in one of the big upstairs bedrooms of Opera Lodge. Already, after
a few momentous weeks on the ranch, he had sworn he would never
return to Wall Street or the dusty museums of the East, even if his
fortune piled up so high that it wrecked the capitalist system. In
fact, he expressed the hope, in the course of the third evening in

front of the crackling fireplace, that some such cataclysm would occur and that nobody would tell him about it.

Jim Leonard slept, as usual, in a corner room downstairs, with a rifle loaded and handy. He had formed the habit of sleeping on or near the ground, prepared for action, while riding the range or camping with the Blackfeet in past years, for he had come to Montana before he was full grown and long before Montana was a state. Miriam occupied the bedroom that had been hers since her mother had died, while she was still less than five years old. On an Indian rug inside her doorway slept faithful Moritz the dog, who thought the ranch, without traffic or fences or restrictions beyond the dictates of his own good judgment, was heaven. To complete the girl's happiness, Homer Evans had taken the huge attic, just above, and at night, when she was wakeful and he was thinking of the struggle to come, she could hear his footsteps as he paced back and forth, always lightly yet firmly, and she was comforted. Stenka, her maid, had already made herself indispensable around the house and was busy from morning until night, chopping wood for the Chinks, sweeping, shoveling, lugging water and mending clothes. The freedom enjoyed by Anton Diluvio, released from the martyrdom of concert tours and assiduous practice, day after day, was exceeded only by that of Beatrice, his wife, who, because of Anton, had shaken off the cobwebs of Back Bay society and, in her late thirties, had begun to learn that life is not only real and earnest but excellent fun.

But no one, unless it was his charming wife, could have relished the remoteness and almost agonizing appeal of the ancient valley as did Dr. Hyacinthe Toudoux. Already huge packing cases had started arriving from Sears, Roebuck, Montgomery Ward and a number of manufacturers of laboratory equipment, dealers in chemical supplies and books in several languages. A large shed, formerly used for storing dynamite and powder for blasting stumps, had been assigned to him as a laboratory.

"Ah, science!" he exclaimed aloud to himself, which disconcerted some of the cowboys until they got used to him. "Science!

Beloved mistress of my youth and riper years! At last I am alone with you. No more does the clanging of a telephone summon me to peer into corpses, analyze secretions, carve up organs and fill out endless reports in triplicate and quadruplicate. Here in the vastnesses explored by my intrepid countrymen, whose names Monsieur Evans has promised to jot down for me, I shall crown my life's work. I shall entreat my distinguished colleagues of the Academy to journey here, every five years or so, not oftener, and here beneath the skies, as coyotes slink from bush to bush, let them read their immortal papers, with whitened buffalo skulls for paper weights and eroded cliffs for rostrums. Reeking civilization, handed down from Egypt, through Greece and Rome, to France, farewell! You must, like me, begin again, in the clean open air, amid the howls of wild and domestic beasts. In short, may the devil take you, as you took my wasted years, before I met Eugénie."

In bunkhouse No. 1 lived Hank, the foreman, and his cowboys, the Professor, Laramee Bob and Slipnoose Pete. Bunkhouse No. 2 housed Hjalmar Jansen, Lvov Kvek and Grigori Lidin, the two last-named having auctioned off their tall hats, frock coats and gold-headed canes. The lusty Russians wore chaps and spurs, and thus far, had ridden what few horses were available, facing either way and with or without a saddle. Already they thought of the East as a distant catastrophe, like the Russian revolution, which would never occur again.

It must not be assumed by the reader that because the special train was sidetracked forty miles to the north, on the edge of the Blackfeet reservation, that the members of the expedition who had elected to live on it were isolated from the group at Three Buttes. Nothing could be further from the truth. Forty miles in the Yellowstone country is about like half a block in New York or Phila-delphia. It is a comfortable jaunt by saddle horse when the weather is fine, and during storms on the Yellowstone, one stays comfort-ably at home except in cases of emergency. Chief of Detectives Frémont was in charge of the Muddy Creek detachment, aided faithfully by Sergeants Schlumberger and Bonnet. Hydrangea was making conscientious, if rather futile, attempts to teach him

English, although he insisted that since all his neighbors were Indians it would be of more practical value if he learned the Blackfeet tongue.

The Blackfeet had proved to be most friendly and sociable, although at the request of Shot-on-Both-Sides and Rain-No-More the chef kept the firewater under lock and key, with a military guard at all times of day and night, in order to remove temptation from the redmen and prolong the life of the whites. A most striking pair of friendships had grown up between the princesses, Tinted Cloud and Unreal Bear, on the one hand, and Sergeants Schlumberger and Bonnet, on the other. Long hours each day, the couples strolled up and down Muddy Creek or lounged in corners of the Dôme, murmuring and whispering their lessons in English, which, since the girls both spoke with a Southern accent, began to issue forth from the Frenchmen in picturesque admixtures of Alsatian, Breton and South Carolina, with a few Algonquian inflections thrown in. Unable to cope with the Indian names of their gentle companions, Schlumberger and Bonnet had translated them into French as follows: *Nouage si doucement couleuré* and *L'Esprit de petite oursine*, abbreviated as Nono and Bébé.

The Indian girls, in turn, had given nicknames to their pupils, calling Schlumberger *Mi u ko kus nat to se* (Gruff moon) or Mi ko, for short, and Bonnet *Ksix in um ok kan nas we* (White lightning) or Ksix, because he was so quick to laugh and learn. It has been said, with some justice, that in the spring a young man's fancy takes a turn or two. With middle-aged Frenchmen, the urge quite often gets the jump on the season.

Thus it was that an atmosphere of harmony and mutual understanding pervaded the Pelleas and Melisande and extended all through the auxiliary coaches, to the point that Corrigan became friendly with the squaws and Galilee Zach never tired of vying at sports with the braves. In short, relations between the natives and invaders of our great Northwest had never reached such a level of cordiality and mutual trust. Longtime-Pipe, recalled from the University of California, but not until he had acquired a certain proficiency with strong waters, made plans with Cromwell and

Washington for first-class golf links and got permission from the
Great Northern to use the railroad shanty as a club house.

On Saturdays all the forces gathered at the ranch or on the train
for a dinner and dance, to which the Blackfeet were invited. Hydrangea, who was tireless in teaching the Indians the pale- and
blackface dances, was made an honorary member of the squaws'
auxiliary of the exclusive Stick Game Society. It is noteworthy,
however, that her pupils of whatever race seemed to have a marked
preference for the blackface dances, and particularly the Charles-
ton and the Susie Q.

Beneath the cloak of gaiety, however, there was an undercur-
rent of dread at Opera Lodge. Not that Jim Leonard ever relaxed
his genial hospitality or inflicted his worries on his guests. On the
contrary, he astonished Evans with his gruff good humor and amazing integrity. Miriam, in her father's presence, seemed to have shed
her sophistication and to have become a young girl again. She
stayed close to her father's side, as if to make up for the years of
her absence, tried to cheer him with music and to reveal in subtle
ways the qualities of her friends who had volunteered to help him.
She spoke freely of Hjalmar's exploits, the renown of Dr. Toudoux,
the fame of Frémont, the courage of Eugénie Toudoux.

But when it came to Homer Evans, she was tongue-tied, and
for that reason was overjoyed to see the way in which they took to
one another. Accustomed from childhood to play a lone hand, Jim
Leonard began to find that he could confide his inmost thoughts
to Homer, and even lay his doubts and fears like cards face-up on
the table. Evans, on the other hand, was at times humble in the
face of the rugged pioneer, who instead of dabbling with intellectual pleasures had wrested a living from the herds and plains and
made himself a part of the soil of his country. Homer would ski far
into the foothills and spend hours in self-appraisal, returning with
one firm resolution in mind. Anything he had learned in his strange
hit-or-miss fashion, in universities, jungles, salons, laboratories,
or battlefields he would place at the disposal of the rancher he
admired and whose daughter had marked a turning point in his
lonely life. This was to be his most significant case, and Evans did

not think for a moment that the mere extinction of a marauding gangster and the seven incidental deaths which had already occurred gave any indication of the scope of the combat that threatened not only Jim Leonard, but the honorable industry he represented.

On the way from the badlands to Three Buttes they had, of course, stopped in Glendive and tried to get the lay of the land. The hesitancy with which everyone in town spoke about the suspected murder of Donniker Louey, the arrest, the unexpected posting of the bail, or the plans of Larkspur Gilligan, was impressive, to say the least. Tom Jackson, who had become handy man on the Glendive *X-Ray*, avoided public contact with Evans or Jim Leonard, as they did with him, but it was arranged that Tumbleweed O'Flaherty, the former sheriff, who knew the town from A to Z, should act as go-between. With funds advanced by Weiss, a distant cousin of O'Flaherty's, who lived in Spokane, had bought the *X-Ray* from Skinner Bruce for a price the Cockney printer could not refuse and which he did not disclose in full to Gilligan. Secretly, the deed had been transferred to Tom Jackson, who now employed Bruce as linotype man and had convinced him that he had best string along and obey instructions. Bruce, who had never liked Gilligan, was willing and apt, and was able to start a bank account for the first time in his life.

But Jackson, alert as he was, had had little to report to Three Buttes. A convenient code had been arranged, with the help of the waitress at the Hotel Jordan, so that telephone messages could be exchanged at will. There was nothing Tom could say, except that he liked the look of things less and less. Gilligan and his son were sticking close to their sheep ranch. Several big shots from the N.P. offices in Chicago had been in town. Neither the sheriff nor the judge nor any of the lawyers concerned said a word about Leonard's indictment. Jackson had been able, however, to win a certain amount of misplaced confidence from the sheriff, the station agent who had lent him the bearskin coat and Judge Patterson, who had fixed the enormous bail. The latter, who had ambitions to become State Senator and later to try for the Governorship of the State, had sensed that Jackson was not only the controlling factor of the local *X-Ray* but that he understood in no uncertain fashion the mysteries of publicity, which Judge Patterson loved above all else.

Tom became a fixture in the week-end poker games at Patterson's large new residence, was played up to by Mrs. Patterson, a Michigan beauty of the slim, restless type, who had formerly taught school in Billings and who wanted to be first lady of Glendive, of the State, and later the country, if she had her way. Mrs. Judge Patterson, whom Tom now called Myra at her insistence, depended on Tom for instructions about cocktails, bridge, knives and forks, parlor games, and on the nights the judge was in his study, closeted with some henchman, appealed to Tom to sit with her in the dimmest sort of lamplight and listen to things she had never breathed a word of to a soul. As a matter of fact, the reader must not think Myra was unattractive or that she did not have certain just complaints about the judge, or that Jackson's work on the four-page *X-Ray* and his growing friendship with Polly, the waitress, were so engrossing as to leave him no time and thought for other things. Indeed, reader, situations occur frequently in life where business may be combined with pleasure, without detriment to either, in spite of the popular superstitions about mixing those necessary elements. And Judge Patterson, for various reasons, seemed heartily pleased about the agreeable developments, such of them as he had the leisure to observe.

Paradoxically enough, the man who was most deeply troubled by what the law might do about the murder of Donniker Louey was not the man accused and held on bail on account of the killing, but the chap who did the deed, none other than Rain-No-More. He had inherited his father's magnificent patience and the philosophy of his race. Nevertheless he brooded because the whites did not act. His father, Shot-on-Both-Sides, had been so absorbed by the tales he had heard about Paris that the old Chief had expressed a desire, once the case was over, to round out his life's memories with a visit to those amazing hunting grounds on both banks of the Seine. If the trial was postponed or dragged on too long, the end might come too late.

In the absence of his father, Rain-No-More would have to take up the tribal responsibilities, which, considering that the Blackfeet were still technically at war with the Government of the United States and had never recognized its authority, were considerable. He would put a stop, Rain-No-More had decided, to the practice indulged in by certain frivolous squaws, who skipped off the reservation and passed themselves off as Spanish women, and of dissolute braves who migrated to Arizona and New Mexico to earn an easy living from gullible female tourists. He would stock the waters of the land with fish and game, scientifically, re-introduce the tribal sports, games, arts and ceremonies. Since his Paris experience and his long journey with Evans, Rain-No-More had entertained a hope that his tribe would survive, perhaps become great again. The whites had little faith in their own wasteful complicated ways; perhaps the red man could wait, if only he could keep alive and strong and resolute. So Rain-No-More contained big thoughts and moments of strong emotion, only to be jerked back to earth, which just then was slushy because of an early thaw, by the trivial incident involving Donniker Louey.

"*Ai pis tsik un nat si u ke ti tse mim*" (Hell), he muttered, and decided to ride over to the Dôme, a distance of fifty miles, for a drink.

14

Spring's Awakening, Etc.

SET FREE BY THE STRONG SPRING SUNSHINE, a jump ahead of the almanac, the snow on the slopes of the great watersheds began to sag.
Small streams trickled down the gullies, gathered momentum in
the creeks and coulees, until volumes of icy water poured into the
Yellowstone and the Missouri. High on the range, or huddled in
the brush of the river beds, the cattle began to stir. Sharp reports,
like the crackling of infantry fire or the booming of artillery,
sounded up and down the tortuous courses of the frozen waters.
Ice heaved, groaned and split into helter-skelter shapes like fragments of a colossal jigsaw puzzle, as water spilled over it from the
mouths of the Redwater, Big Dry Creek toward the north, and
southward from Indian Coulee and Beef Slough. Far westward, on
the Great Divide, the same immense operation was being repeated
on a continental scale. Bears brushed their eyes with the backs of
their shaggy paws, growled sleepily and lumbered out of their dens.
Buzzards wheeled overhead and coyotes searched the melting drifts
for the carcasses of sheep or steers which had been among the
season's grim casualties. With so many sounds and odors in the
air, the tang of which had changed so perceptibly, it is no wonder,
reader, that Moritz the dog, notwithstanding his dignity and poise,
felt a surge of uneasiness.

At Opera Lodge, around the bunkhouses and corrals, the buckaroos and their new collaborators, Hjalmar, Kvek and Grigori, were
making gleeful preparations for the spring round-up, adjusting
straps, braiding quirts, cleaning boots and saddles and engaging

in that rough good-natured banter that keeps men in control of their tempers, no matter how long they are cooped up together. The sight of those men, all tall and strong, and ready for whatever the awakening season has to offer in the way of danger or solitude, work, fight or frolic was not lost on anyone from the ranch house who chanced to look at them. Hugo Weiss had to hold his head between his hands to keep within bounds the plans which shaped and reshaped themselves in his ever-active mind, plans of solitary empire, of an area of the world retrieved from the ravages of predatory schemers and the ultra-refinements of diseased aesthetes. Not one Botticelli or Leonardo da Vinci should enter that valley as long as he drew breath or checks, he was resolved, and neither should the bleat of sheep be heard where now mooed and bellowed the shorthorns.

Stenka, whose memory was as deep as her vocabulary was shallow, paused often to glance toward the cowpunchers at work or at play, and was spurred to such efforts on the woodpile that now and then she sent the sharp edge of the axe all the way through a cottonwood chunk and buried it so deep in the chopping block that Hjalmar had to pry it loose for her.

But the most avid worker, and the one who coordinated the activities of the rest, was the rancher, Jim Leonard, himself. Buoyed up by hope and the unusual array of friends who had flocked to his aid, and glad as always that the long winter stretch of inaction was coming to an end, the stalwart old man was everywhere, advising as to this or that, weighing one detail against another, planning already to recoup the losses the severe and capricious season had inflicted on his struggling business. In the evenings he listened with awe to Miriam and Diluvio, both of whom had set aside the formal classics for the tunes of the country, which they embellished instinctively with similar rugged melodies from Purcell and William Byrd, Monteclair and Rameau, Glinka, Granados and Schubert, all of whom had gone straight to the soil for their inspiration. And frequently the Professor got out his old fiddle, which he said had been whittled out of the back of a Studebaker wagon, Laramee Bob produced his harmonica and the company cleared the living room for a quadrille or Virginia reel.

On the evening in question, Miriam, flushed with the pleasure of playing without restraint and sharing the enjoyment her father was betraying in his diffident way, did not notice that her staid and loyal Boxer was not at his place, just left of the piano. Homer Evans, however, who missed no detail out of the ordinary, began to wonder about the dog with increasing interest and misgivings. Evans, too, had heard the roaring of the torrents, the cracking of river ice, had seen the cattle moving faster on the slopes, and watched the meadowlarks and curlews, first of the birds to come back on the winds of the spring to the awakening prairies. He was convinced, after a short period of observation, that Moritz's perturbation was not seasonal or physiological. Something was in the air. The enemy was about to strike.

RAIN-NO-MORE, BECAUSE OF THE THAW, was making slow progress in his ride toward the Dôme. He had intended to risk the river ice, but obviously that was impossible, so he skirted the Missouri as best he could, on his tough pinto pony whose natural camouflage of brown and white made him almost invisible while snow was on the ground. As at last he was nearing Muddy Creek where the special train was moored, he felt an urge to pause and approach the coaches with care.

The pinto, responding to a light pressure of Rain-No-More's knee, ceased moving and stood like a statue while his rider peered into the darkness. Having eyes like a cat, the young Indian saw leaning against the Melisande a man who looked neither like a cowboy nor a railroad hand, and surely had no connection with the visitors from the East. Dismounting, Rain-No-More crept nearer. The intruder was trying to look into the women's car through a slit in the curtains. Rain-No-More, hearing a slight sound behind him, sidestepped and wheeled. Another man was approaching from the main-line tracks. The Indian glided behind a pile of railroad ties and saw the second stranger join the first. From the Melisande the furtive pair went down the track to the Mine, where the curtains were open a good six inches. Inside sat Hydrangea and Frémont, Tinted Cloud and Unreal Bear, the two French police sergeants,

Galilee Zach and Corrigan, and on the tables before them were assorted liqueurs in small glasses.

Keeping one eye on the suspicious pair, the Indian glanced around. There were no horses in sight, except his own, but on the main-line tracks he saw a shape that by an intense effort he was able to identify as a handcar. Still, the intruders were not railroad men. Of that he was sure. And the handcar was not a small one, but intended for a number of section hands. Ergo: the intruders had either stolen it or borrowed it, and railroad officials were strictly forbidden to lend one. Also, no railroad man would leave a handcar sitting on the tracks of a main line.

As long as the two men stayed together, Rain-No-More could think of no way to capture them without raising an alarm, but when they separated to inspect the other coaches he stole noiselessly behind No. 1, choked off his wind, roped and gagged him in a jiffy, then stretched him out behind the pile of ties before his partner missed him. To stalk and truss up No. 2, who proved to be young Santosuosso, was the work of a few seconds more. Both of Rain-No-More's prisoners were unable to speak, although they made muffled sounds from time to time, and the Indian, with his racial instinct for the dramatic, uttered not a word. He was thinking quickly, however.

The presence of young Santosuosso and another of the Santo mob at Muddy Creek, when they should have been plying their trade back East, had a history. The gangsters, when loaded into box cars in the badlands by Hank and Hjalmar, were permitted to take with them several dozen cartons of Fatima cigarettes. Old Baldy Santo, chagrined at having been hijacked and deported from the area where he was sure of protection, got his mind to working before the locomotive had gained headway. He thought first of burning a hole through the side of the box car, but since the doors were locked he was not willing to take the chance of being trapped and roasted alive. Noticing that the Fatimas were wrapped in heavy lead foil he set his men to unwrapping them and collecting the lead, which he rolled into a sizeable ball and tied up in a pair of overalls. Using the weapon as a sort of swinging ram, he succeeded, before

the train had reached Jamestown Junction, North Dakota, in breaking several of the boards and making an opening large enough to
permit escape. He had no funds, so he hid his gang in an empty
gondola on a siding until dark, then robbed the local bank, getting
not only twelve thousand dollars in gold but several spare automatics and some ammunition which had been left in the vault for
safe-keeping. Armed, he held up the railroad lunch room as soon
as it was rid of its last legitimate customer, fed his boys, took along
the cook and flunkey, then phoned Gilligan's lawyer in Glendive
and got an address, which turned out to be the local hookshop,
where he and his gang could hide. Gilligan, as soon as he got back
to Glendive from the badlands, arranged to have the fugitives transported to Wibaux, Montana, and entertained there until further
notice.

Thus it was that young Santosuosso, under strict orders but
also harboring thoughts of personal revenge, chanced to be peek-
ing into the Melisande when he felt firm fingers on his windpipe
and a rope that squeezed like a constrictor binding up his limbs.

Coincidently, in the ranch house at Three Buttes, forty miles
distant, Homer Evans was observing the undue restlessness of
Moritz the dog. It was nearing bedtime, for the workers on the
ranch had to hit the hay early in order to roll out at dawn. As soon
as everyone had scattered to his or her respective bed or bunk,
Miriam had noticed that Moritz was not disposed to lie down on
his warm Piegan rug of gray, blue and red. The Boxer was trying in
his patient way to communicate his forebodings to her, an unkind-
ness she knew the dog would never commit without reason. A tap
sounded on the door and, since Moritz showed relief instead of
displeasure, she knew it must be Homer.

"Come in," she whispered, making a cursory survey of her pale
orchid nightgown.

To her surprise, Evans was fully dressed for out of doors. He
cautioned her to be quiet, then asked her to dress warmly and join
him at the kitchen door. Moritz looked up questioningly and Evans
nodded. "Yes, old boy. You're going with us. In fact, you're to be
the brains of this expedition, if we have any," he whispered.

Trembling with excitement, Miriam got into her riding clothes, and before strapping on her automatic, she examined it almost affectionately to be sure it was in order. In France, when she had been obliged to bump off several men and wing numerous others, she had done so, not with hesitation, which would have been fatal, yet never with relish. But to get a potshot at an enemy of her adored father, that was a cartridge of another caliber. She did not want Gilligan and his toadies merely to be punished according to the statutes. She wanted to dish out his and their deserts in person, and was so shocked when a fleeting thought of scalping them in the bargain traversed her mind that she sat down on the bed in dismay.

Downstairs, Jim Leonard and Evans were in deep conversation, the rancher somewhat more subdued than was usual with him. For his sharp ears, trained by a lifetime in the open, had caught the first of Homer's footsteps on the attic stairs, and when Evans had descended, the rancher, shotgun in hand, had been watching him from the foot of the stairs. That Homer was smiling, in spite of the gravity of the situation, was due to the fact that he, also alert to an incredible degree, had seen the old man's parental gesture although he had pretended not to notice. Quickly Evans explained that he wished to investigate the anxiety of Moritz the dog, and wanted Miriam to go with him.

"Won't one of the men do better?" asked Jim Leonard.

"Can you find me one who can shoot as well in starlight and the glimmer of the snow?" asked Evans.

"You got me there," admitted the rancher proudly. "I taught her to hold her first rifle, but now she can give me cards and spades."

"I think you ought to tell Hank to keep watch around the buildings until we get back. No telling who may prowl around. There's no one at the moment, or Moritz would bark, but when he's away you couldn't be sure."

Gently the old rancher extended his hand and touched the boxer on the scruff of the neck. "He's a damn smart dog," Jim said, and Moritz wagged his stump of a tail, left-right, left-right.

Rain-No-More, by the tracks at Muddy Creek, had come to a decision. His nearest counselor was the medicine man of the tribe, Trout-tail III, whose lodge was not eight miles distant, for Trout-tail's predecessors had believed there was mystic virtue in the east, in fact, that good medicine blew from east to west. So the Blackfeet medicine men had always camped near the eastern border of the reservation. Rain-No-More's problem was to transport the two prisoners across country. He knew that Frémont's detachment kept a couple of saddle horses in a lean-to near the freight shed. Quickly the Indian unhitched the horses, and, with difficulty, since the animals were frisky in the chill night air, loaded on young Santo-suosso and his pal, and roped them securely. Retrieving his pinto, he led them through the icy creek and westward in the direction of Trout-tail's lodge. Before departing, however, Rain-No-More, believing that Homer Evans would soon put in an appearance, scratched an arrow in the snow, and at its tip a medicine hat to indicate his destination. Behind the arrow he made three marks, two in advance, side by side and linked together, and one following. That would mean, to the discerning eye, that there were three in the party, all were mounted, and that two were prisoners.

From the wide board porch of Opera Lodge, Evans, with Miriam at his side, glanced at the stars.

"Eleven o'clock," he said, "Mountain Time."

The night was clear and, luckily for Homer, the wind after sunset had blown cold, so the bare slopes were comparatively dry and a thin crust was on the snow. The thaw had done its work with such incredible rapidity that Bison Creek, which had been a mere ribbon, had become a careening freshet, rolling chunks of ice and large fragments of rock along the bottom.

"Where are we going, Homer," asked Miriam, "or shouldn't I be curious?"

"We shall leave that to Moritz," Evans said, and at the mention of his name the Boxer stiffened, let out an almost silent bark, humped his sturdy back and with one of those surprising bursts of speed that contrasted so vividly with his usual staid behavior, Moritz raced like a streak down Bison Creek, a hundred yards or so along the trail, then skidded, wheeled and raced back again.

"Evidently we are going north," said Evans. But just then the Boxer, who was waiting for them by the far end of the stable, forgot his exuberance and started sniffing. Cautiously, nose to the ground, placing his huge feet deliberately, he circled slowly, stopped, looked inquiringly at Evans, then started northward, evidently following a trail of some kind.

"Maybe he smells a coyote or a jack rabbit. He's never been out West before," said Miriam.

"Neither a coyote nor a rabbit rolls from side to side, like a sailor, as he walks. The former lopes or single foots, the latter hops," Evans said. "No, the scent our friend Moritz has hit upon is that of a man, and one who takes long strides and stops to rest too often. A short man in a hurry, I should say, and one who is not in the best of condition."

"There are no short-winded runts on the ranch, or anywhere around this country," Miriam said.

"Precisely," agreed Evans. "Moritz, like me, is attracted by the unusual."

"Oh, are you, Homer?" breathed Miriam, standing close to him. . . . When they looked down the trail again, Moritz was standing still, one paw raised quizzically. The dog did not go on.

"He must have found something he wants me to see. That's the most remarkable feat of intelligence our dog has performed to date. It is true that bears, after two years on this hazardous planet, learn that men follow them by sight and not by what seems to them the more practical way. Therefore, a young bear will cover his scent, when pursued, and leave tracks all over the place, while an older bear will cover his tracks and take chances with the wind. Moritz, when it comes to cerebration, needs no handicap from Bruin, which is a compliment, indeed."

And true to Evans' prediction, when they caught up with the Boxer they saw a footprint half in the snow, half in the frozen mud.

"A leather shoe. Not even overshoes," said Homer. "Now what short unathletic man would be ass enough to venture into the lower Yellowstone region at this season in stylish low Oxfords?"

Miriam, quivering with excitement, let slip an answer. "Baldy Santo," she said, and at once grasped Homer's arm. "I don't know why I said that. The words slipped out."

"By Jove," said Evans. "How blind I have been! In the *X-Ray*, weeks ago, there was the story of a bank robbery in Jamestown. Now that I think of it, the technique was like that of the Santo mob, before they turned comparatively honest and started running beer. An interesting possibility, and one not flattering to me. I should have sent a guard with the gangsters as far as Minneapolis, but of whom could one ask the favor of riding, days on end, in a box car with chaps like those? Ah, well, I daresay they would have come back again, anyway."

"But isn't it better to have something on them, something definite, I mean?" asked Miriam. "Now you can have them arrested in North Dakota."

"Let's find them first," said Homer, and Moritz wagged his tail. "I'll stay here and study exhibit 'A' while you go back to the ranch and saddle a couple of horses. Pick two that are well shod. It's slippery as the devil underfoot."

"I should not be likely to select a pair that had roller skates," said Miriam, with asperity, but quickly she smiled and set out on her errand.

Homer began talking, experimentally, to Moritz and himself. "Now how could Monsieur Oxford approach the ranch, from the windward side, in daylight, and not be seen or smelled?" Evans asked, and the answer was not long in coming. "At mealtime, which here is far too early, about six. I remember that Moritz was having his raw elk meat and hard bread at the same time we were eating. Of course, no guard had been posted. He didn't get fidgety until afterward. About five hours ago, then, Mr. Oxford was standing on this spot, which, I regret, cannot be marked with the definitive 'X' just yet."

Miriam approached with the horses, one the white-faced sorrel mare named Star which Jim Leonard had ridden on the fateful day when, unknown to him, the late Donniker Louey had been lying in wait. The other horse was a rangy dark roan called Jesse with a wicked eye and a talent for marksmanship with all four feet

and from any angle or direction. Jesse had been practically an outlaw before Homer had arrived at Three Buttes. When, on his first
visit to the stable, Evans had stepped into Jesse's narrow stall, Jim
Leonard had turned gray and shouted a warning and Miriam had
nearly fainted. To the astonishment of everyone concerned, and
particularly the cowpunchers who had given up Jesse as a bad job,
the tall roan had behaved as if he were in Sunday school. It was
not so much that Evans had selected Jesse as his favorite mount,
as that Jesse had adopted Homer. When, four days later, the outlaw had followed Evans all across the yard to the steps of the ranch
house, whinnying contentedly, Slipnoose Pete, who had been laid
up three weeks the spring before with a broken collar bone on
Jesse's account, got roaring drunk and had to be forcibly restrained
from riding to Glendive to buy himself a Mother Hubbard and applying for a job, any job except playing the piano, in a certain group
of buildings set apart from the town, surrounded by a high board
fence and marked with red lanterns on each corner.

"If we are careful of our horses and don't cause them to break their
necks on this trail, we can make Muddy Creek by dawn," Evans said.

"How wonderful to be riding here alone at night! I have
dreamed of this, but I never dared tell you. Be honest, Homer. Do
you regret leaving Paris for a while?" asked Miriam.

"I have never regretted leaving anywhere. I have rebuked myself afterward, for staying in certain places too long, but not often,"
he said. "We can talk of this at leisure, if Moritz doesn't lose the
Oxford chap."

So they mounted, and side by side they rode northward, over
the crests of hills, into treacherous declivities, at times with ample
foot room, again, in single file, where the horses stepped like cats
and sweated and trembled with apprehension but always obeyed.

"I should like to live like the animals," Homer quoted.

"Oh, please go on," said Miriam, and beneath the cool Montana sky, as the miles rolled beneath them, Evans recited from
memory page after page of *Leaves of Grass*, while Moritz, nose to
the ground and panting, kept his mind on his work and found it
not too exacting. The Oxford chap, and a companion about whom

the dog had tried to inform Evans without success, because of the spell of Whitman, might have been humdingers at broadjumping in Chicago but a Pekingese could have trailed Herr Oxford as he had hiked downstream. Near the ranch house he had hidden his trail.

THE EIGHT MILES BETWEEN MUDDY CREEK and the lodge of Trout-tail III, the medicine man, were covered by Rain-No-More and his prisoners in about eighty minutes, according to the stars. But on the flat top of a butte, four miles from their destination, Rain-No-More had paused and had built a signal fire, after the manner of his race, with slender sticks in conical form. Consequently the wise old medicine man, informed by the distant glow that scullduggery was afoot, had the stage well set when the son of his Chief arrived. At a sign from Rain-No-More, the medicine man said not a word. He was painted railroad red with black stripes running longitudinally, wearing the sardonic furred Kit-Fox headdress and carrying in his hand, like a torch, an implement wound with snakeskin and rattles.

Approaching the captives ominously he pointed with his medicine stick to a tepee of elkskin stained with tribal and symbolic designs, none of which was comforting in character. The lodge was illuminated dimly with an evil blue light that issued from a weasel's ribs, and the walls were lined with whitened buffalo skulls spotted red and black on the foreheads.

"Cripes, what a joint! We're going to get the works," said young Santo's pal, known as Beetlebuzzer Tony.

Both Indians, as if shocked, hissed for silence, and when young Santo showed signs of disregarding the admonition, Trout-tail III evoked a yell of pain from him by prodding him with the medicine stick which had, concealed by the rattlesnake hide, a sharply pointed rat-tail file* in the tip, an accessory that the medicine man ordered by the dozen from Montgomery Ward. In former days, the tip had been fashioned of antelope bones, but Trout-tail was a modern medicine man who saved himself labor whenever possible.

* Catalogue No. 84 C 1464.

The bonds of the two gangsters were loosened and they were re-bound in a squatting position, supportable but wearing on the nerves. Reaching into a grotesquely painted sack, Trout-tail brought forth a number of objects, including a bouquet of dried newts and lizards, a nettle and cactus back scratcher, and another gadget like a primitive horse syringe which was loaded with crab-apple butter and an irritant distilled from dog's mercury and squirrel manure. Each one of these he examined and discarded in turn, but beneath his skillfully camouflaged mask he was observing the effect of his act on the parties of the second part and already had decided that Santo, *fils*, was a tough egg, while Beetlebuzzer showed signs of being the more tractable patient.

The movements of the medicine man were disconcerting, in that they alternated between extreme unhurriedness and sudden frenzy. In a period of calm, however, he rummaged more deeply in his sack and came up with two packages, one green and red, the other brown, with an animal medicine sign. They were, as the reader has already guessed, Lucky Strikes and Camels, respectively. The packs were sealed, and as the medicine man was opening them, Beetlebuzzer let out a nervous exclamation.

"Gee, I'd walk a mile . . ." he began, and his words were cut off by an anguished yell as he felt the point of the rat-tail file.

However, Trout-tail III held out the two packs to each of the gangsters in turn, Santo accepting a Lucky and Beetlebuzzer the alternate brand. Soon the aroma of those two popular cigarettes mingled and blended with the smoke of the blue incense and the steam from a pot in which some gophers and hoot owls were simmering. Then very softly, in a circle around the lodge, tribal drums began to sound, not in unison, but sweeping in a clockwise direction round and round. Shrill willow flutes joined in as the drummers and dancers moved nearer. The braves, not one uttering a word, wore raven feather headdresses, were painted red, white and black, and each one who was not busy drumming or fifing held symbolic rattles which, the prisoners knew, were equipped with the murderous mail-order rat-tail files.

Fires had been lighted all around the lodge, so that dancing shadows crossed like scissors on the elkskin walls, and raven feathers flapped. After about thirty minutes of deliberate dancing, the drummers and flute players sat in a circle, continuing their maddening beat, and from a carved chest near where the prisoners were tied, Trout-tail began passing out live rattlesnakes. That their fangs had been extracted, the gangsters did not know, but the information may put the reader a bit more at his ease. Young Santosuosso conveyed his comment by spitting in the eye of the nearest snake, which evoked a tribal howl of horror. But the mother of Beetlebuzzer Tony must have been frightened by a snake, if indeed, she had not been one, for Beetlebuzzer began to give evidence of panic that proved more pungent than the combination of Lucky and Camel smoke, blue incense and hoot owl stew.

Rain-No-More rose and left the lodge to get a little air and some sleep. The grilling would not get fairly started until dawn, he knew, and he was sure the medicine man would call him in time, since no one else could question the captives or note down their replies, spoken in what they believed to be English.

Had there been anyone within hearing distance, except the thugs and the participants in the questioning, or intelligence ceremony, he would have heard the drum beats circling all the rest of the night, at a nerve-racking pace about like that of the disc of an electric meter, near the end of the month. Each painted brave, as he passed the door of the tepee, stared at young Santo, then held his nose in a contemptuous gesture when he shifted his gaze to the cringing Beetlebuzzer.

When the starlight began to thin, Trout-tail III retired to his private lodge to take off the hot headdress and ceremonial robes for a while and consider the situation as he puffed a cigarette. The cigarette, it should be said, was not taken from either of the packages previously offered the brace of sweating patients.

Aurora, goddess of the morning, as she was putting the finishing touches on her rose-tinted nails, saw as sorry a pair of young mobsters as could be found on the Western Hemisphere in the center of the circle of tireless Blackfeet, drumming and dancing around the painted tepee. The morning goddess also observed Trout-tail III tapping gently on the flap of his guest lodge in which Rain-No-More slept.

"The patients are in fair condition," the medicine man said, when his guest awoke. "But they are of widely divergent types, so I shall give them different medicine, each according to his need and to each according to his ability to take it. But, my friend, in the lodge of a medicine man the mystification should go one way, and not be reciprocal. Perhaps you will give me a hint, therefore, as to what this powwow is about."

"The two palefaces are hirelings of Gilligan," Rain-No-More said.

Trout-tail III began to groan. "Why didn't you tell me?" he asked. "I could have given them the *ski nas sa am*, the ordeal of ants and alkali, that has not been used in our tribe since the Iroquois massacre."

"Can you make these men talk? I must know the strength, location and intentions of their party. The tough one is son of an outlaw chief, allied with Gilligan against Jim Leonard."

The medicine man smiled. "He will talk whenever you are ready," he said.

"And the other? The one with such deplorable lack of control?"

"He will spew forth words as the Redwater pours forth water in the spring. Or should I make him talk slowly? Do you understand their baffling lingo, when they are under stress and fail to aspirate between syllables?"

"These men speak the dialect of the Great Lakes regions. Nevertheless, I can grasp the meaning of what they say," Rain-No-More assured him. "I should also tell you," he continued, "that one of my friends and white brothers, a man with the strongest medicine I have yet encountered among strangers, may call on us without delay. In fact, I shall be surprised if he is not already in sight, arriving from an easterly direction."

"*Okh si u sa am o pi pete pin a pots im,*" said Trout-tail III, concluding his sentence with a gesture toward the west. Translated, the proverb means: "Good medicine travels from east to west," but since there is no word for "west" in the Blackfeet language, the mystic destination of the sun is indicated only by motions and signs.

"You are sure young Santo will talk?" Rain-No-More persisted.

The wise old medicine man smiled and whispered a few words in Rain-No-More's ear, causing the latter to relax and grin.

"*A kai em e eat sis na taps sin*" (Many [ways] to skin a cat), Rain-No-More said.

"*A a kan o*" (many, indeed), agreed the medicine man.

"Here comes my friend, the white medicine man, with Bird Cherry, daughter of Jim Leonard, also their thinking dog," said Rain-No-More, and he hastened across the flat to greet his guests. Not one of the braves who were dancing and drumming, round and round, moved as much as an eyelash as he passed.

"All animals think," mused Trout-tail III, "but they speak only to those equipped to understand them."

15

In Which a Man Bites a Snake, and a Body Is Found

THE GODDESS AURORA, having touched with her provocative scented fingers the Blackfeet reservation, passed lightly on to the badlands across the distant Yellowstone. She was accustomed to seeing strange doings around the lodge of Trout-tail III, but in the vast volcanic ruins, tinted deeply with natural colors, the goddess of the morning was at her best. There in the solitude evocative of long past ages she could let herself go, and what she did, with snow on which to glisten, dark crags for shadowy contrast, and the old earth steeped in ochre, rose and indigo, was, perhaps, too moving for city folks to dwell upon.

Hank, the foreman, on guard near the stable at Opera Lodge, turned his back to Bison Creek and started counting his money. He was responsive to nature and had been on the ranch many weeks without going to town. The pranks of Aurora, strange as it may seem, got Hank to thinking about a complaisant young woman named Alice in Glendive, and thus he missed seeing, on the crest of a hill six miles toward the Missouri, a group of oncoming riders with Larkspur Gilligan and Sheriff Hockaday at their head. There were twelve of them, all armed and deputized except Stumpbroke and Jill, the sheepherders, and Tom Jackson, the reporter, who had come ostensibly to cover the scoop for the Glendive *X-Ray*. All along the line Tom had tried to slip away from Gilligan and warn Jim Leonard by telephone, but the sheepman, who suspected that Tom was capable of playing both ends against the middle, had not let him out of his sight.

Homer Evans and Miriam, having been led to Muddy Creek by Moritz, had there abandoned the trail of the party who wore Oxfords and his more cautious companion, in spite of the loyal remonstrance of the dog, and after reading Rain-No-More's message scratched in the snow, had made their way to the lodge of Trout-tail III.

However, by the time the posse with the sheriff and Gilligan mounted the next rise and was exposed to view, Aurora had become more reasonable, and Hank had been able to stifle his cravings and get back on the job. He pulled out his Smith & Wesson and fired three times, a prearranged signal, and although he did not aim at Gilligan, the bullets whistled close enough to give the sheepman food for thought. The posse ducked into a gully as Jim Leonard, the cowpunchers, Hjalmar, Kvek and Grigori tumbled out of bed and into their clothes with no lost motions. The Lees, Wing and Sam, started running across country in their pajamas.

Around Opera Lodge, as a precaution against prairie fires, was a rectangular swath of plowed land, and it was there that Jim Leonard, with his men behind him, took his stand.

"I've had enough from you, Gilligan," the rancher said, as the sheepman approached on horseback. "The first of your gang who steps over that plowed land gets daylight let through him, and that's all I've got to say."

"Now, Jim, don't be unreasonable," Gilligan said pacifically. "I've come to help you clear yourself."

"Let me drag that young punk with the badge off his horse and rearrange his puss," said Hjalmar. "I never liked it the way it is."

Lvov Kvek interposed politely. "At least we might toss a coin for the privilege," he said, fishing out a twenty-dollar gold piece and flipping it into the air. It came to rest tails up, and the former colonel sighed. Since a certain evening he had spent in Des Moines with the precocious young daughter of K. Parker Seldon he had had no luck at cards or dice.

The men who had ridden to the ranch with Gilligan were lined up hesitantly on the edge of the fire swath and none seemed disposed to advance. On the inside rim stood Leonard and his helpers, all r'arin' to go. Hockaday, the sheriff, appealed to Tom Jackson.

"Ride over and talk sense to them," the sheriff said. "You represent the press."

"Come on, Tom," said Hjalmar, and Jim Leonard nodded.

"They've got a warrant to search for the body on Cottonwood Creek," the reporter said. "Where's Homer? He could handle this bunch of palookas."

"Homer rode down Bison Creek in the night, God knows what for. Didn't you see him at Muddy Creek?" asked Hjalmar.

"No," said Jackson.

"We come on a lawful errand," the sheriff yelled.

The rancher and Hank held a whispered consultation and motioned the posse to advance, but all the cowpunchers kept their hands near their holsters as Gilligan and his men rode up to them.

"If the body's not found, the charges against you will be dropped," said Gilligan to Jim Leonard. "That's fair enough, isn't it?"

The rancher scowled grimly. He wished Evans was on hand to advise him, but after a moment's reflection he decided to let the search go on.

"It's only a matter of form," the sheriff said.

Jim Leonard was examining the members of the posse. Most of them were from Glendive and depended in some way on Gilligan for their livelihood. One small swarthy specimen, however, wore city clothes and held on to his saddle horn, shifting his position as often as possible, as if his crotch and his legs were rubbed raw. As a matter of fact, they were.

"Who's the tenderfoot? Has he got a badge?" asked Hank.

"He's the father of the deceased, and he's come all the way from Chicago to identify his son, if we find him," said Gilligan.

The Italian nodded and touched his black felt hat. He had not raised his boy to be a gangster, but had hoped that Louey would settle down and help him run his fruit stand.

Jim Leonard, touched by the look of sorrow on the old man's brow, went up to him and held out his hand. The Italian began to cry, and it was not long before the rancher was brushing tears from his own eyes, the cowboys were turning away to hide their emotion, and the Russians were embracing and sobbing unrestrainedly.

"Rope a horse and round up the cooks," Jim Leonard said gruffly. "Even sheepmen get hungry, and I've never turned a man from my door."

Slipnoose Pete and Laramee Bob, relieved to escape from the touching scene, cut out a couple of bronchos from the bunch in the corral and started after Wing Lee and Wing Sam, who were hiding in the sagebrush near the hot and cold springs on the west butte five hundred yards away.

"All a boy 'e bell no catchum bleakfast," said Pete.

"Topside cop 'e catchum China boy. Bung um one piece jail," said Wing Lee, his teeth chattering.

"No bung um China boy. Look see belong one piece dead fella," said Laramee Bob.

At the mention of the corpse, both Chinese started running again and would have escaped had not the cowpunchers lassoed them and led them back to the kitchen, protesting and squealing. Once at work, however, Wing Lee had the presence of mind to sprinkle one pot of rolled oats with calomel, which he also poured liberally into the pitcher of condensed milk. With twenty thousand cattle many of which were cows on the range, no ranch hand could ever be induced to milk a dogie. They got their years' supply from Sears Roebuck in cans.

IN THE LODGE OF TROUT-TAIL III, about fifty miles to the north, an unexpected development was upsetting the medicine man's careful plans. Evans, after greeting the wise old conjurer respectfully, had taken a look at the prisoners, young Santo and Beetlebuzzer, and, in spite of the stench in the medicine tepee had detected an odor he had easily identified. On returning to where Miriam was standing, Evans smiled.

"Our medicine man, I notice, uses *marijuana* (*cannabis Indica*) in order to soften up his clients. With Beetlebuzzer the soothing weed has worked mercifully and admirably, but no one informed

Trout-tail that young Santo had been smoking reefers practically from birth and is sent, but by no means spent," Evans said.

"I hope I won't have to listen to a lot of screaming," said Miriam. "Those flutes and drums fascinate me, but they set my nerves on edge, too."

"That's what they are for," said Homer.

Moritz the dog was seated on his haunches, following the progress of the dancers, round and round. The Boxer had learned to like the redmen and their ways, because wherever they were to be found the air was redolent with strange and interesting smells.

The circle of dancers, smeared with red, black and white, with raven feathers in their hair, had been withdrawn some distance from the tepee in which Santo and Beetlebuzzer were sitting, with no company except a few loose snakes. One of the serpents, however, was not a tame rattler but an outside bull snake who had crawled in to search for easy prey. For bull snakes earn their place in the sun by subduing deadly rattlers by constriction and eating them afterward. The bull snake in question had just left his winter shelter, in response to the rays of the blushing Aurora and had an appetite sharpened by several weeks of fasting. Nevertheless, he was curious about Beetlebuzzer and, winding himself around the shuddering gangster he mounted first his leg, then his torso and curled around his neck. At that point, young Santo had an inspiration. He knew his pal was about to crack and squeal as soon as the Indians returned, so, leaning forward painfully he took the bull snake's tail in his teeth and bit it. The snake, outraged and angry, hissed and tightened his coils around the helpless gangster's neck, and the tighter he squeezed Beetlebuzzer's windpipe the harder Santo bit. The victim turned mauve, then purple, his eyes began to pop, his tongue sagged out three inches. Before the medicine man returned from his conference with Evans, his only promising patient was stone dead.

"I haven't lost a case before in years," said Trout-tail III shamefacedly.

"There's no time to waste," said Evans, eyeing young Santo sternly. "If Miriam will retire to the guest lodge, and take Moritz with her, I should like to try my medicine on this young upstart. You don't mind a consultation?"

Trout-tail III bowed courteously. "My dear colleague, I am honored," he said.

Rain-No-More smiled. "May I watch?" he asked.

"I deserve no credit," Evans said. "I happen to know this patient's weakness, that's all. He has a horror of scalps. So I'm going to relieve him of his own."

"It's always the simple home remedies that escape our attention," said Trout-tail, graciously concealing his chagrin.

"Homer Evans," said Miriam, her eyes blazing indignantly. "You wouldn't . . ."

"Take the young squaw away," said Evans, and four of the braves bore Miriam, kicking and expostulating furiously, to the distant guest lodge. Moritz, bewildered by the clash of interests between his master and his mistress, considered the situation a brief moment, then followed Miriam and touched her hand with his damp muzzle to comfort her. Faintly on the morning air came to her ears a piercing scream and blasphemous entreaty, then a tribal warwhoop by the braves in unison. At the same instant she saw Evans beckoning and running, and Rain-No-More and Trout-tail III catching tough young ponies and mounting them. Forgetting her resentment, Miriam streaked toward the horses, too, and soon was astride the spirited Star, who, in spite of having carried her fifty miles over a treacherous trail was willing to start home again and give the best she had. Evans, however, could take no chances on losing time.

"We'll leave our horses here and ride back on ponies," he said, and the braves caught two more pintos and shifted the saddles while Homer explained the need for haste.

"Gilligan's on the way to Three Buttes with a posse," said Evans. "He thinks he's going to find Louey's body on Cottonwood Creek."

Rain-No-More said nothing, but inwardly he smiled.

At the head of Cottonwood Creek, ten miles west of the ranch house, a grim group was gathered. The gully was exposed to the morning sun so that the snow had disappeared in large patches and the ground was moist. Gilligan and the sheriff, each with a shovel, were walking back and forth and it did not escape the alert eyes of Hank, the foreman, that the sheepman was unobtrusively sighting on a peak in the distant badlands and getting himself in line between it and another butte miles away on the reservation.

"Ah," said the sheepman, at last. "What's this?"

Jim Leonard came up gruffly; then his face turned crimson with rage and surprise. There was an oblong patch of ground, six feet by three, where sod had been lifted and replaced, and not recently but weeks or months before.

"A grave," said Dr. Hyacinthe Toudoux, uncovering in a perfunctory way.

It was Hjalmar Jansen, however, who got right into action. Grabbing the sheriff's shirt tail, the painter pulled it out and before Hockaday could draw his gun his face was covered and his arms securely pinned by his own flannel shirt. Diluvio, quick to grasp an idea, gave Gilligan the leg and was sitting on him before the most practiced orator could have said "Jack Robinson."

"Not one of you will touch a thing around here until Homer Evans comes," said Hjalmar. "And that's flat."

"Ah, Jansen, little pigeon of the woodlands, how you take the words from my mouth," said Colonel Kvek, collaring the shrinking fruit dealer from Chicago, who began to ask aid of the Virgin and a long list of saints. Tom Jackson got out his Leica and asked the other members of the posse and the cowboys to step back while he took shots of the spot which gave promise of winning its letter as soon as Evans put in an appearance.

"I'm innocent," protested Jim Leonard, and Diluvio shifted his position to sit heavily on Gilligan's evil grin.

Meanwhile, Homer Evans, Miriam, Rain-No-More and Trouttail III were streaking up Bison Creek toward Three Buttes on their tough pinto ponies. The trail was soft and dangerous because of the strong spring sun and landslides which had swept the sidehills clean and choked the raging creek. Moritz tried to keep up for a while, then lagged behind until the riders were lost to his sight.

From the crest of a hill several miles away they saw smoke rising in the usual way from the chimney of the ranch house, but when they passed the stable at a lope they learned that all the men except Wing Lee and Wing Sam were away.

"Topside cop an' plenty luffnecks go for catchim dead fella," Wing Lee explained.

"As I thought," said Evans, to Miriam. Then, of Wing Lee, he asked: "Gilligan 'e go?"

The Chinks nodded. It was apparent that they were much relieved because Evans was back again.

"Boss 'e go?"

"Boss plenty hot. Make talky talk, baim-by 'e go. You ting luffnecks catchim one-piece dead fella?"

"More than likely," Evans said.

"Father belong im dead fella go with topside cop. Luffnecks, bull-a-ma-cowboys, boss all plenty cly. Me no savvy what for boss 'e sorry too much," Wing Lee said.

"Ai ting ai go Glendive, maybe Minneap'lis," Wing Sam said. "Ai no likee see dead fella, luffnecks, cops, two fellas plenty stink 'e herd um sheep."

"But Homer," said Miriam. "They won't find a dead man, or will they?"

"If not, I shall be surprised," Evans said. "But let's go and see. And Wing Sam, don't go to Glendive. We shall all be hungry presently."

At that moment Trout-tail III, who had been helping Rain-No-More catch fresh bronchos in the corral, appeared in the kitchen doorway. The medicine man had not stopped to remove the red and black paint or his weird regalia, and the sight of him proved too much for the jittery Chinese. Side by side they dived through the open window, squealing, and ran into the brush again.

An hour later, the sharp eyes of Hank the foreman saw four riders approaching the head of Cottonwood Creek at breakneck speed.

"Here they come," he said, pointing, and everyone sighed with relief.

"Who's that with them?" asked the Professor, squinting. "Looks like a couple of Indians."

Hjalmar untied the knots in the sheriff's flannel shirt and nodded to Diluvio to let Gilligan stand up and stretch himself. Kvek and the old Italian from Chicago had become firm friends, since the Russian spoke Italian perfectly and had been pleased to have a chance to brush up on the language.

Evans, who was the first to reach the party, dismounted from his broncho while the horse was still skidding to a standstill.

"These friends of yours have been resisting officers of the law. I'm going to run them in," the sheriff said.

Homer smiled. "You'll have enough to do, without wasting your time on trivial offenses," he said. "And understand this right away. You, too, Gilligan! If you take anyone, dead or alive, away from this range it will be because we want you to. I'm going to give you plenty of rope and let you hang yourselves, figuratively speaking. In fact, I shouldn't be surprised if you both looked up a limb before we're through with you."

"We got a warrant," said Gilligan.

"I see you brought shovels, too. Suppose you start digging, since you came so well prepared. But don't imagine I haven't noticed how conveniently this grave is situated to make work easy for a searching party. I thought better of you, Gilligan, than to see you fudge in the spot where the body is to be found between the highest butte in the badlands and the only one in sight to the north," Homer said. He appeared to be looking straight at Gilligan, who flushed with mortification, but Evans was observing the behavior of the sheepherders, Jill and Stumpbroke, and was pleased to see them wince.

Gilligan and the sheriff untied short-handled shovels from behind their saddles and handed them to the sheepherders, who started to dig. The sod was removed and carefully laid aside, and as the hole deepened the pile of fresh earth grew. When they had reached a depth of three feet, Stumpbroke grunted and hopped nervously out of the grave. He had uncovered a human foot in a tan leather Oxford. The old Italian, tears streaming down his face and muttering prayers, threw himself into the hole and got down on his knees, sobbing. "Louey, my only little boy. May God be merciful," he said.

"But you haven't seen his face," said Miriam, touched by the old man's grief as her father had been. Dr. Toudoux was standing by, solemnly, hat in hand, and slowly all the men uncovered.

"Don't cry. You can't be sure just yet," persisted Miriam.

The old Italian raised his tear-stained face, as if grateful for her sympathy. "It his-a shoe. I bought 'em. Box'a calf Oxford, $3.95, Italian store, North Chicago."

Jim Leonard stepped up to the side of the grave and placed a hand on the old man's shoulder. "I didn't kill your boy," he said. "I never even saw him."

"You admit that you fired a shot," said Gilligan.

"Not at anything in particular. I thought I saw something moving, that's all," the rancher said.

Evans interposed with a question. "You had a rifle. Was it by any chance that one I saw last night within reach of your bed? The Remington 30-40."

"There ain't no such thing as a Remington 30-40," the sheriff said.

"Perhaps I was mistaken. Maybe it was a 40-40 Winchester," Evans said.

Miriam's face showed bewilderment. It was not like Evans to blunder. The sheriff nodded. "That's more like it," he said. "Now let's go on with the work."

"Permit me," said Evans, taking a shovel from Stumpbroke and stepping into the grave.

"Is this regular?" asked Gilligan.

"Let the dude find out what it's like to swing a muck stick," the sheriff said.

Skillfully Evans removed the dirt from above and around the body and when the face was uncovered the Italian threw himself flat on the ground and lay there half-conscious, moaning "Louey. My poor-a kid. My poor-a littla boy." Tom Jackson's Leica was clicking at full speed as he aimed it into the grave, then back to the prostrate father, the defendant, the creek bed, the tell-tale shoes

which had set back the old fruit dealer $3.95, the posse, the shov-
els and particularly the vividly painted medicine man. Now that
he was the owner of a paper, he did not stint himself when it came
to illustrations. As a matter of fact, he had pepped up the *X*-Ray
until it was read all the way from Butte to Fargo, had increased its
size from four to eight pages, three of which were paying ads, and
had secured the services of Myra, wife of Judge Patterson, as editor of the society columns and the women's page.

The county coroner, Doc Lougee, began pottering around inef-
fectively until Evans introduced Dr. Hyacinthe Toudoux, as the
famous medical examiner of Paris, and asked the sheriff's permission to let Toudoux handle the post mortem. Hockaday, believing
that expert testimony from a well-known doctor would bolster up
his case, nodded acquiescence.

"The deceased died instantly, without pain . . ." he began.

"Ah, *Dio grazia. Maria grazia,*" cried the Italian. The Russians,
weeping wildly, began to tear their hair and knock the sheepherders' heads together. Miriam rushed to her father and buried her
face on his shoulder.

"Oh, Dad," she said. "I won't let them take you away. I won't. I
won't."

"The law'll have to take its course," said Hockaday.

Dr. Toudoux continued his examination. "Death occurred about
four months ago, between four and five, caused by a bullet fired
from a rifle at a range of less than one hundred yards, about eighty,
I should say. The projectile pierced the heart wall, was deflected
from a rib and is lodged somewhere near the kidneys, if I am not
mistaken."

"Was the deceased lying flat on his stomach in the sagebrush
when he was shot?" asked Evans.

Gilligan again looked uncomfortable.

"He was erect when hit by the bullet," said Dr. Toudoux.

"Are you sure?" asked the sheriff.

"I am not accustomed to pronouncing my opinions loosely," the
doctor said. "The deceased was erect and the bullet was fired by a
man also standing and on the same level."

"What caliber was the bullet?" the sheriff asked.

"I will tell you later, after I have extracted it," said Dr. Toudoux.

"It was fired from a Winchester 40-40," said Evans laconically.

Both Gilligan and the sheriff sneered. "Can you qualify as an arms expert in a court of law?" the latter asked.

Homer smiled. "As a matter of fact, I can," he said. "If you will take the trouble to look up Commonwealth vs. Ledbetter, Mass. Superior Court, pages 204 to 276 of the testimony, you will find that the presiding judge was generous enough to thank me for clearing up a number of rather tricky points. In that case, the murderer used an artificially heated Luger, expanded to carry an off-size bullet."

"Where is your Winchester 40-40? I'll have to take it along," the sheriff asked Jim Leonard.

"It's right here in my hand, but you're welcome to it," the rancher said. "The day I rode out here and fired it, I didn't once get off my horse, and you heard the doctor say the shot was fired by a man on foot."

"Maybe the horse was kneeling down," said Gilligan.

"I'm going to ask Judge Patterson to rescind the bail," the sheriff said.

"I'm not going to run away," Jim Leonard said.

"It wouldn't be healthy to try," the sheriff retorted.

"Shall I work on his puss?" asked Hjalmar of Evans.

"I have other plans," Homer said.

Meanwhile, Rain-No-More and Trout-tail III were deep in consultation. Alternately they peered into the open grave, then over toward the Missouri. Observing their preoccupation, Evans stooped down to arouse the whimpering father.

"Tell me," he said in fluent Italian. "Did your son always have such a good head of hair?"

"Every day, once, twice, three times, he comba da hair, put on vaseline, bay rum, $1.75. He was mucha proud. Mucha ladies' man. I pay $40 to get him out of woman scrape before he was twelva years old," said the Italian.

"Is your name Luigi, too?" Homer asked.

"No, you don't. The American language is good enough for us out here. If you speak any more Wop, I'll run you in," said the sheriff, suddenly growing suspicious.

"That would be an interesting charge. Dawson county vs. Evans et al. For speaking Italian," Evans said, but he shifted to English and asked the fruit man again if his name was Louis or Luigi.

"My name'sa Mike," the Italian said.

"Maybe your father's name, or one of your brother's names was Luigi, or was the boy born on St. Louis' day, or in St. Louis, perhaps?" Evans persisted.

"Say, what's all this about. Is it getting us anywhere?" asked Gilligan.

"Just idle curiosity," said Evans.

"Sure. The boy he have an Uncle Luigi. I name-a him Louis for him," the Italian said.

"Let's go back to the ranch," said Hank. "I want some grub. I'm not used to finding stiffs around the coulees, and it upsets me. Gets me to thinking about going to town to blow my winter's wages."

"A good bat sure soothes a man," the Professor said.

16

Science Makes, Perhaps Not Strange Bedfellows but Unusual Pals

THE SHERIFF LEFT TWO OF HIS DEPUTIES on guard, while others set out for the ranch for a wagon to cart the remains to the railroad. But when Jim Leonard and his party started for home, Evans lingered behind and asked Miriam and Dr. Hyacinthe Toudoux to join him. Instead of heading east toward Opera Lodge, Homer rode slowly down Cottonwood Creek, which had doubled its volume that morning and by evening would be washing rocks, stumps and the carcasses of cattle into the Redwater.

"Ingenious fellow, Gilligan," he said, as Miriam's broncho sidled over to his and caused their knees to rub.

"It's a frame-up," Miriam said indignantly. "But how can we clear Father without involving Rain-No-More?"

"That is the least of my troubles," Evans said. Then suddenly he slid off his horse "Exactly as I expected," he said, pointing to a clump of weeds with broad leaves deeply cleft and tight buds that showed a streak of blue.

"*Delphinium exaltatum*," said Dr. Hyacinthe Toudoux.

"None other. The deadly larkspur," agreed Homer.

"Why, I don't understand," said Miriam, aghast. "I've never seen larkspur on our range before. I've heard dad say that Gilligan planted it on his side of the deadline, but there shouldn't be any growing here."

A painted figure suddenly appeared beside them, as if it had sprung from the ground. "Excuse me. I didn't mean to startle you," said Trout-tail III, "but I also was interested in the flora of this watershed. I noticed this morning, as we rode up Bison Creek, that there was larkspur there."

"We must go back to the ranch at once and consult with your father and Hank," Homer said to Miriam. "I think this explains why the two sheepherders chanced to be so far off their range, and maybe why young Gilligan is absent today. By the way, when does Gilligan bring his sheep back from Idaho?"

"Not before the last of May," Trout-tail said. "The larkspur is not harmful in that season. Only in early spring."

"Damnation," said Evans. "And the only antidote is potassium permanganate. We haven't any, and can't get a supply for several days. Leonard will lose hundreds of cattle, if, as I suspect, the creeks on the Yellowstone side have been planted with *delphinium* too."

"If you will pardon me for making a suggestion," Trout-tail III began, "I think I can be of service. Several years ago, when tribal funds were low because of the panic of 1907, I made a thorough study of larkspur poisoning, to save our horses. Permanganate was expensive, so I found that the oil of the prairie rattler . . ."

"*Crotalis confluentus*," gasped Dr. Toudoux.

Trout-tail nodded. "We call it *sow kee kom o sit*," he said.

"A snake by any other name . . ." murmured Evans.

"My dear colleague," said Dr. Toudoux, "your discovery is of immense scientific importance. With your permission I shall lay your results before the Academy of Science at the Sorbonne. Or better, as chairman of the board of directors, I shall invite you personally to appear, with or without your paint and feathers. Do you use the oil of this lowly but beneficent serpent straight or diluted, may I inquire?"

Trout-tail III smiled. "For the benefit of my tribesmen, who are keenly sensitive to the dramatic or suggestive, I sprinkle in a few powdered hairs from the tails of white spotted horses. But the other medicinal ingredient is a vegetable compound invented and distributed by a paleface squaw, called Lydia, I believe. One drop of this inexpensive and miraculous liquid will render two gallons of snake oil efficacious not only against larkspur poisoning but the dry heaves and spring halt as well."

"I shall invite Mme. Lydia to appear with you at the Sorbonne. We shall create a sensation. The world of science will rock and resound," said Dr. Hyacinthe Toudoux.

Evans leaped astride his broncho, which gave evidence of his surprise in both voluntary and involuntary ways and started bucking, backward, forward and sidewise, spine arched, front legs stiff, eyes gleaming. Homer scarcely paid attention, but motioned Trouttail III to jump up behind him. Afraid he might have to carry the whole party if he did not behave, the broncho snorted and subsided. Miriam, who could make better time because her horse bore the lightest load, streaked ahead to prepare the buckaroos for action. Dr. Hyacinthe Toudoux lagged behind, reflecting that, as the only married man in the outfit, he owed it to his family to take better care of himself than the others were disposed to do.

Since early morning, Moritz the dog had been plodding patiently toward Three Buttes from the Indian reservation. He kept up a steady trot, pausing now and then to sniff or to frown regretfully at a fleeing jack rabbit that seemed to know just when a conscientious dog was busy and could not make detours. The Boxer, having covered the ground before, was able to avail himself of numerous short-cuts, but in crossing a small coulee, a tributary of Bison Creek, Moritz stopped short, one large paw in the air, and strained his ears and nostrils. He had caught a whiff which resembled, in a sturdier way, the faint scent of the chap with Oxfords who had lured him from the ranch house the night before.

Now it was seldom in his career that Moritz had been entirely on his own. In former crises there had been someone to guide him, with varying degrees of judgment and discretion. The Boxer, warm and panting from his arduous run, sat down in the midst of a clump of sage where he was well concealed and started thinking. What to do? He was about half way between the ranch house and Muddy Creek, roughly twenty miles from a human habitation. First, he decided to have a look at Oxfords, and for that purpose moved down the coulee stealthily, from bush to bush, until he spotted his man, who proved to be young Terry Gilligan. The latter seemed to be engaged in pulling up weeds furiously and chucking them into the swift waters of the coulee.

The dog sat down again, and the efforts he made at cerebration caused the frown on his forehead to deepen and his eyes to grow sad. Terry Gilligan, whom he knew to be an enemy, had strapped around his middle a cartridge belt and near his right hip a holster which bulged. That, from Moritz's point of view, was bad. He could not bite through the belt in time to detach the gun and disarm the young man, and neither could he buck hot bullets. If he went to Opera Lodge for help, and was able to make anyone understand, the puller-up of weeds might escape in the meantime. A dull throbbing began to pulse around Moritz's temples and he brushed his hot forehead with the back of one paw. Then, in a flash, his course of action became clear to him. That young Gilligan was up to some deviltry, Moritz did not doubt for a moment, and it was also certain that, having performed his errand, he would not be likely to go up the creek toward the ranch house, but would make his getaway downstream. At Muddy Creek, across from where Bison Creek emptied into the Missouri, stood the line of special cars in which were friendly, if obtuse, fellow travelers. In a jiffy, the sleek Boxer was off and away, but he had traveled far since midnight and seen and smelled some harrowing things, so it was a thoroughly exhausted dog who staggered up the steps of the Dôme car two hours later and scratched insistently on the door.

"Come in," yelled Cromwell, the waiter, thinking the visitor was a Blackfeet brave. The scratching continued and the waiter threw open the door. "Well, I'll be jiggered," he said. "Come right in. Boy, but you're tired." And the waiter reached to a shelf for a huge elk bone.

Moritz, however, tempted as he was by the prospect of food and water, made straight for Chief of Detectives Frémont, who was sitting with Hydrangea playing dominoes.

"Welcome, beast from Boston," Frémont said. "Is Monsieur Evans with you?"

The Boxer shook his head.

"He's come all alone to see us," said Hydrangea.

Moritz sat down, and again his head began to throb. Just how should he begin? First he crouched in an alert position and started off toward Bison Creek, but no one followed him, although Cromwell, thinking he wanted to play, tossed a golf ball after him. That, the dog ignored in a slightly exasperated way.

"Now that's funny. He's thirsty and tired and alone, and he doesn't want to eat, drink, rest or play," said Cromwell.

It was at that point that the princesses Tinted Cloud and Unreal Bear got into action. The former called to Moritz, the other sat square in front of him, on his own level on the floor, to observe and listen attentively. Again Moritz, more hopeful this time, made a jump toward Bison Creek and waited.

"Gruff Moon! White Lightning! Stir yourselves at once. Follow the dog and your devoted Nono and Bébé as fast as you can. How unfortunate that someone has stolen our horses," said Unreal Bear, strapping on her hunting knife and six-shooter with one hand as she rearranged her black braids with the other.

Sergeants Schlumberger and Bonnet, pleased at the prospect of a frolic in the hills, got up to go. Frémont, alarmed, was about to follow them, but Hydrangea detained him with a flood of entreaties. He should not leave the train unprotected, she said, and Tinted Cloud agreed.

"*Soo ops a ke kon it sin na taps sin ni*" (Squaws will locate trouble), she said.

Moritz, given new strength and courage by his luck in finding apt collaborators, lapped up a small dish of water, swallowed a few chunks of elk meat, which he had grown to like better than beef, and led the two princesses and the eager sergeants across the creaking footbridge and over to Bison Creek. There he sat down and confronted the princesses. Each time they tried to follow him closely he sat down again, and the third time Unreal Bear caught on.

"The wise dog wants to go ahead of us. He thinks someone may be coming," said Unreal Bear.

That proposition proved to be entirely agreeable to the Frenchmen, who, if the truth must be told, had not grasped the gravity of the situation and had other things on their minds than cross-country hiking *per se.*

The Boxer's plan proved to be a sound one, for they had not proceeded more than seven or eight miles before he caught the Oxford scent on the breeze and saw Terry Gilligan at work with some tall weeds on Bison Creek proper. Quickly he hurried back to where Tinted Cloud and Schlumberger were examining some stemless prairie violets and blood red snow plant which had bloomed in profusion up and down the gully. Tinted Cloud had placed a chain of violets in her raven hair and, laughingly, had stuck a couple of buzzard feathers behind Schlumberger's ears.

"Behave, Gruff Moon! See, here comes the thinking dog. You have work to do," said Tinted Cloud, and in an adjoining coulee Unreal Bear was putting up a similar argument.

When Moritz started cautiously up the canyon again, the Indian girls followed swiftly on their hands and knees, and the sergeants, with a rueful glance at their pin-striped and neatly pressed trousers, did likewise, grunting and puffing until Tinted Cloud turned around and motioned them to be more quiet. Unreal Bear was the first to sight Young Gilligan, and coincidentally Tinted Cloud snatched a large floating weed as it was rushing by in the waters of the creek and stifled an exclamation. "Larkspur," she said to herself. "Now why should an enemy rid the Leonard range of larkspur?"

From early childhood she had been accustomed to leave complicated questions like that to the tribal medicine man, Trout-tail III, who loved the princesses as if they were his own daughters, of which he had sixteen, although no one else knew it. They had resulted from certain ceremonies, for the relief of childless squaws whom Trout-tail had rendered tactful by the judicious use of loco weed, or *marijuana.*

Tinted Cloud made up her mind that they must capture Gilligan and take him to the medicine lodge for grilling. A whispered consultation was held by the lithe and sprightly sisters and soon they were crawling on what would have been their bellies had not their life in the open made them too firm and slender. They approached the unsuspecting Terry from behind. At a prearranged signal they dove at the young man, one pinning his arms, the other his legs, while Moritz, who had slipped up beside them, took the holster in his jaws and held on, swinging like the damsel in the bell scene from "The Heart of Maryland." Within five minutes, Schlumberger and Bonnet had reached the scene of action and took young Gilligan in hand. As the sergeants and the girls started downstream with their captive, bound for the reservation, Moritz sighed a grateful farewell and trotted wearily to Opera Lodge.

17
Of the Sinful Proclivities of Man and the Universality of Music

MIRIAM'S ENTRY INTO THE DINING ROOM of Opera Lodge was not a conventional one, but it had the desired effect. She threw herself from the back of her galloping bronc as he brushed past an open window, and leaped inside, her eyes blazing and a gun in each hand.

"Hands up, every one of you who doesn't belong here," she said. "And don't make any false moves. That means you, especially, Gilligan." Her guns spoke, right and left, and with audible tinkling both Gilligan's spur wheels flew off and pinged against the wall . . . "And you, you cheap young crook," she said to Hockaday, "if I didn't want the pleasure of seeing you hanged, I'd drill you right here and now."

"Steady, my girl," cautioned Jim Leonard. "He represents the law, you know."

"He represents a lot of tinhorn politicians, but he isn't going to for long," said Miriam, just as Homer Evans and Trout-tail III, the latter still vividly painted, leaped into the room. Meanwhile, Hank and the cowpunchers had got the members of the posse well covered and the latter were reaching for the ceiling as avidly as children stretch their hands toward the top branches of their Christmas trees. Wing Lee and Wing Sam, who had been roped to the kitchen range for safe-keeping, nearly pulled it out from under the stovepipe in their frantic efforts to leave those parts.

Miriam stepped aside as Homer took over and confronted the searching party.

"Take their guns and ammunition, all their weapons," Evans said to Hank.

"But, Mr. Evans . . ." protested the rancher, who was happiest when things were proceeding according to written rules.

"I'll explain briefly that someone, undoubtedly Gilligan, has caused larkspur to be planted on all the creeks on this range, and that the weeds are about to bloom. You know what that means, with half-starved cattle in search for something green."

"You can't pin a thing on me," the sheepman grunted. Miriam, who was across the room from him, took a side shot at the top of his fountain pen, which hopped from his pocket and scattered ink on his shirt and his face.

"Save Gilligan for later, please," said Homer, and reluctantly Miriam put up her automatics, to the intense relief of all outsiders present.

The members of the posse, with Gilligan and the sheriff at their head, were marched out to the corral, leaving their meal unfinished, and, unarmed, were chased across the fire strip and down toward the Missouri, after Evans had told them their sentries with the corpse and evidence would be permitted to follow them. All hands on the ranch were summoned, and Evans, Hank and Jim Leonard, after poring over a map of the range hastily scrawled by Homer, divided the forces into detachments and assigned an area to each. Trout-tail III and Dr. Hyacinthe Toudoux were dispatched to the hills to garner rattlesnakes; Stenka was sent on horseback down the creek to the train with a note asking that several bottles, in fact the entire supply of Lydia Pinkham's compound in the general store at Mondak be rushed to the ranch without delay. Rain-No-More, who was to scour the area adjacent to the reservation, rode his best pinto hell for leather to summon the braves to assist in rooting out the dangerous weed. Jim Leonard and Hank were to explore the southwest quarter of the range, between the deadline and Mountain Sheep Bluffs; the Professor, no mean amateur botanist, rode off northeast to patrol the huge triangle between the forks of the Yellowstone and the Missouri; Evans, Diluvio, Hjalmar and Miriam chose the watershed of Indian Coulee, Beef Slough and

Leonard Creek, on the Yellowstone side. Hugo Weiss, beaming with
excitement, was left in charge at Three Buttes, where the Indian
remedy was to be brewed by the doctors and rushed to all points of
the watershed by the cowpunchers, as soon as it was ready.

The plan of action, rapidly sketched out and agreed upon, was
being carried out at top speed within thirty minutes after the rude
breaking up of the mid-day meal. Ten minutes later, Miriam and
Homer were riding side by side. Diluvio and Hjalmar veered off
west but always kept in sight. It was the first time Miriam and
Homer had been alone since the glorious ride in the moonlight the
night before. This time they were mounted on a pair of bay geldings, named Red and Whitefoot, respectively, and as the horses
walked rapidly on, to get warmed up for the arduous run ahead of
them, Miriam hesitated, then spoke softly.

"Homer . . . Tell me," she pleaded. "You didn't really scalp that
boy?"

"He thought I did, which served the purpose," Evans said, and
she sighed with relief.

"Forgive me. I should never doubt you," she said.

"By the use of adhesive and a phial of warm blood I was able to
give him the appropriate sensation, and, of course, the medicine
lodge contains no mirror and his hands were tied. It's amazing that
a youth with so much stamina should have an Achilles' heel, as it
were, on top of his head."

"I think I can understand his feelings," said Miriam, shuddering.

But Evans was not listening. A groan escaped him and he narrowed his eyes angrily as he sighted, far eastward toward the head
of Beef Slough, a bunch of cattle, about eighteen or twenty, half of
which were lying on the ground. A quick knee pressure set the
horses on the run and within a few minutes both Homer and Miriam
had dismounted. There was nothing they could do to relieve the
stricken animals. Six of the steers, eyes rolling, sides distended,
were drooling and moaning, all four legs tucked under them, the
froth on their muzzles stained green. Near by was a patch of larkspur, from which leaves and buds had been wrenched and eaten.

"I wish I had shot Gilligan," said Miriam, tears stinging her eyes.

"I'm beginning to wish you had myself," said Evans grimly. He was pulling up the rest of the deadly *delphinium* and taking it to a near-by pile of loose lava rock, in which he buried it.

Hjalmar, two miles westward, was studying the drawing of the plant, *delphinium exaltatum*, in a leaf of his sketchbook, while Diluvio was whistling the Scherzo from Beethoven's E-Flat concerto for violin and piano, the beauty of which was attested by his broncho who pricked up his shaggy ears. At the crest of a steep-cut bank, the horses squatted on their haunches and slid downward, bringing up amidst the whitened skeletons of forty or fifty unfortunate beasts.

"Shiver my timbers," roared Hjalmar. "This is tough country and no mistake."

"Good old Liszt," said Diluvio. "La *da*, la *da*, la *dadada*, la *da* deedle-*oo* de la *boom* dee *dee*. You remember. The Dance of Death. And the Berlioz Requiem, where the dead quit their graves and the second fiddlers tap with the wood of their bows. A bit corny, I'll admit, but there's something in it."

"I could paint this God-forsaken country, but who'd believe it?" said Hjalmar.

"Besides, there was Remington," the violinist said.

"He spread the paint too thick, like cooking," Hjalmar said. "The guy I'd like to have met was the one who did Custer's Last Stand on the side of a covered wagon. There's a composition for you!"

"Let me take a look at that sketch. I've forgotten what the weed looks like that we're after."

Two shots resounded, and they saw Evans beckoning.

"Trust old Homer to score first," said Hjalmar, and steered his broncho to the east in a wide circle, as if it were a motor boat. Evans showed them the disastrous weed, the places where it had been growing and the poisoned cattle who were doomed, and sent them to the head of Indian Coulee with instructions to run all the cattle out on the plains before they searched for the larkspur.

All over the huge cattle range, Leonard's riders were finding the same situation, except on Bison Creek where young Gilligan had got in his work. The steers and dogies, famished after the long winter of winds and snows, when almost everything they could subsist upon had been covered, snatched eagerly at the first green plant they saw, and to the extra large toll of the storms was added a long list of new casualties from *delphinium.*

Jim Leonard, who had been in straits before, was sick with disappointment. His shipment to Omaha would be half its usual size and his credit already had been strained to keep the ranch supplied and the cowpunchers paid. That was Gilligan's game, Leonard knew: to get him in a hole financially, then offer him a price for his water rights, without which the whole range was useless. Once the cattle had been driven from the lower valley, the sheepman could pull wires to have the Blackfeet chased from their ancestral hunting grounds and confined with the Nez Percé on the rocky slopes near Glacier Lake. Then sheep would munch the valley clean, swarm north over the Missouri as far as the Canadian border and the hour of the shorthorns would have struck.

Jim Leonard, like most ranchers, had little time for his animals, individually, but collectively he loved them and was proud of them. When the herd of tough shorthorns was gathered for counting and branding, spring and fall, the rancher would stay awake at the campfire, listening to the cattle as they fed, the songs of the cowpunchers whose voices kept them from stampeding, the whine of the coyotes on watch for wayward calves. He knew little about the glories of Greece and Rome; the Conciergerie and Notre Dame were simply buildings on postal cards, as far as Jim Leonard was concerned. He preferred the pictorial calendar sent out each year by President Suspenders to the Adam and Eve of Titian or Ribera's John the Baptist. The Ben Hur Chariot Race meant more to him than Handel's Largo, which because of its discouraging tempo he frequently mistook for My Country 'Tis of Thee. But the plains on which he had lived combated the elements and raised his stock at a hard-earned profit, while devoid of formal art, had felt "ragged claws scuttling across the floors of silent seas" in the Archaean age, when the lower Yellowstone valley had been part of the Pacific's shifting bottom; had known the luxuriant giant shrubs and trees of the Paleozoic period; their muck had spawned apocalyptic reptiles of appalling bulk; the plains had felt the upward surge of the Rockies just westward; and through them had been thrust by smoking lava their thousands of foothills, ovoid, rhomboid, semi-spherical, distorted pyramids and truncated cones. Four great ice sheets had leveled those prairies, filled old valleys, tossed aside rivers, scooped out lakes, but the last of the glaciers had halted at the Missouri, not far from where now stands the lodge of Shot-on-Both-Sides, and since then the valley has abounded in beasts, both wild and tame.

Were the scenes of such upheavals to be desecrated by the blatting of sheep and the furtive tread of sheepherders, while cattle were banished from the land? Jim Leonard did not understand all that had happened in Eastern Montana, but he had found fossils of inkfish and horseshoe crabs in the cliffs of the highest buttes, had noticed the difference between lava flows, the most recent on the lower levels, the oldest on top. History, for him, had not been made, messed up and left mankind exhausted. It had roots in the present and hopes in the future, for his country was unspoiled. Ten thousand years the Indians had used it, without marring it or wasting its resources. Before them, the race of Mound Builders had performed feats of engineering and community labor and left it intact. The whites had exterminated the buffaloes, but had replaced them with cattle. Now the herds of shorthorns were threatened in their turn. Some States had exchanged them for acres of sugar beets and psalm-singing farmers, others for miles of wheat and blasphemous itinerant harvest hands. The lower Yellowstone was the last refuge of the cattle industry, and its principal rancher was Jim Leonard, beset on all sides and now deprived of a fifth of his herd.

Perhaps the happiest man in the Leonard camp that day was Dr. Hyacinthe Toudoux. It is true that he had been an associate of the late Dr. Eugene Kelly in combating the plague of typhus in Serbia in 1917; that in his bureau drawer at home reposed a decoration from the Government of Norway for his work in repulsing the lemmings a decade earlier; and that, but for him and his serum against the *ts'ow e'e* fly's sting, scarcely a white man would still be alive in the African colonies. But the widespread epidemic of larkspur poisoning, while it meant staggering losses to his host, would give Toudoux a chance to make a bad matter not quite so bad, which is as far as a doctor can hope to go. His first thought, when given charge of the rattlesnake expedition, was to go to the badlands across the Yellowstone, but when he communicated this to Trout-tail III, through a couple of interpreters, the old medicine man reminded him that the Yellowstone was filled with moving slush and ice and that the nearest bridge was at Mondak, if it had not been washed away, as usually happened in the case of early thaws. So Trout-tail had led the way to the footbridge at Muddy Creek, and thence to Poplar River where an area had been set aside by tribal ordinance in order that the ceremonial and medicinal supply of snakes should not be depleted. In passing the special train, the pair of savants, the one in morning clothes, the other in red and black paint, were hailed by Chief of Detectives Frémont, who had a prisoner on his hands and did not know exactly what to do with him. Unreal Bear and Tinted Cloud quickly explained, however, and Trout-tail ordered Young Gilligan taken to the detention tepee near his lodge and thrown into chains with Young Santosuosso, who still believed he had been scalped.

When Dr. Toudoux told Frémont of the trouble on the range, the latter insisted on accompanying the doctors on their snake hunt, in spite of the tears and prayerful entreaties of Hydrangea. Also, since Frémont had been sent all the way from France to learn about American methods of dealing with criminals, he was determined to be present when Young Gilligan was grilled by Trout-tail III and to take full notes concerning the means employed to extract information and the results, if any, that were obtained. For the Chief of Detectives knew that if he returned to Paris empty-handed, his prefect would use that as a pretext to get rid of him. He already had missed the scene at the opening of the grave and did not propose to be caught napping again.

That night around the campfire on Beef Slough, while supper was being prepared by Miriam and Diluvio, and Hjalmar was picketing the horses in a sheltered gulch near-by, Homer Evans was deep in thought. They had shot a large grouse apiece, which, with bacon and sourdough biscuits, washed down with black coffee, made a satisfying meal. And since, in the course of his two years in the Arctic with the great but modest Stefansson, Evans had learned to make Eskimo houses of snow, the members of his detachment were to sleep well that night, although the rest period would be brief.

Already they had run several thousand cattle from the slopes of the creeks out of danger to the bleak table lands and Hjalmar had volunteered to ride around the herd all night and sing them chanties which, since the shorthorns could not understand the words, might prove to be reassuring. Diluvio, keen on the outdoor adventure, turned in early in order to relieve Hjalmar when the starlight began to thin.

"Miriam, my dear," began Evans, as they sat close to the glowing embers, sipping brandy from the proper kind of glass, since Homer could not relish good liquor in inferior containers. "Miriam, darling, you have given me a new lease on life. Imagine our friends, this moment, wasting their time and substance on the *terrasse* of the Dôme while we are camped beneath the stars, man and woman, breathing the air of the prairies in common with wild neighbors in the atmosphere of spring. You have made me understand that, although the contemplative side of one's nature must not be neglected (the American disease, I may say), full play should be given at intervals to one's zest for action."

"Ah, that, above all," murmured Miriam, her eyes shining.

"Nonetheless," said Evans hastily, "we must consider, while our memories are still fresh, the touching performance at the graveside this morning."

"That poor honest old Italian. He's a victim of those unscrupulous gangsters, who have taken away his only son. Oh, why didn't I shoot Gilligan, and argue with officials afterward? It would have been worth the risk if it had saved the life of one poor beast who has died today. Any snake can be ruthless, but it takes a real man to be considerate of others. And kindness, not violence, is the highest achievement."

"I see you know your Sermon on the Mount," said Homer, but he touched her hand to show her he was by no means joking. "I honor your sympathy for the tearful fruit vendor known as Mike, but let us examine the man in the light of pure reason, and put aside our throbbing sympathies for the nonce. That is harder for you than for me."

"That's not true, Homer Evans, no matter what you pretend," the girl said hotly.

"Ah, well. Let us both make the effort, however great the strain," Homer said. "As always, I am fascinated by the unusual. Now it is not unusual for a doting father to weep at the sight of his only begotten son in his grave. It is extraordinary, however, that a humble and illiterate fruit merchant, born in Sicily and transplanted at an early age to Chicago, should be able to buy ten-dollar Oxfords for $3.95 and that they should be of the identical make and color of certain Oxfords worn by one Terence Gilligan and the unsavory Santosuossos, or should it be Santosuossi, *pére et fils.*"

"Oh," said Miriam, taken aback.

"Also it is unusual for a proud Italian father named Mike to name his first born son and heir Luigi. Furthermore, it is not the general rule for fruit dealers to have a left thumb toughly calloused and marked by beeswaxed threads. On top of all that, the *corpus delicti*, as the Professor likes to call Donniker Louey, turned up with a scalp intact, when Shot-on-Both-Sides has one purporting to be his in the equivalent of the tribal safe north of the Missouri. The grave, as I pointed out, is tied in between two obvious landmarks, which proves . . ."

"That the corpse is not Louey's," said Miriam.

"Not exactly that. But it proves that the gravediggers, Nos. 1 and 2, were not very bright: ergo, that Larkspur Gilligan was not of their number. Now who would have been obtuse enough to commit an idiocy like that?"

"The sheepherders," Miriam said.

"Good," said Evans. "Now we have established that either Rain-No-More removed some prowler other than Donniker Louey, which is unlikely; or that some other corpse has been planted on Cotton-wood Creek."

"But Mike, the father. Surely he knows his own son," persisted Miriam.

"He is mistaken about his profession, why not about his off-spring? Our tearful exhibit from Chicago is a cobbler and recently has practiced his trade. He gets marvelous bargains in shoes and selects the same kind worn by several members of the Baldy Santo gang, who very possibly stole them in large lots. But our problem in connection with the late Louey is a complex one. We must clear your father without involving Rain-No-More, who very properly has been decorated with a notch on his coup stick for the deed he performed. Shall we prove in court that the corpse is not Louey, or merely that your father did not send its soul soaring upward be-fore its time? Not only must we think of that, and make a wise decision, but we must find out what is the essence of Larkspur Gilligan's plan. He has nothing personal against your father, but has large designs not only on the cattle range your father's short-horns occupy but the ancestral home of the Blackfeet as well. Tom Jackson informs me that he has secured official permission from the Government, through a few Senators indebted deeply to the N.P., to graze sheep on the west side of the Redwater as far as the confluence of the Yellowstone and Missouri. Furthermore, he is awaiting a decision which will remove the Blackfeet from their res-ervation to another farther west and throw open the land from the Missouri north as far as Canada to the sheepmen, all of whom are Gilligan under other names. Gilligan first thought that by planting larkspur on all the creeks of the cattle range, at a time when your father would be short of funds, he might induce your father to sell out for a handsome price and go to California to end his days."

"God forbid," said Miriam.

"I assume that when Gilligan met Baldy Santo and found how cheaply a citizen of this Republic could be got out of one's way, he decided to have Donniker Louey bump off your parent as the course of least resistance. Being resourceful, when Donniker Louey failed to return, Larkspur tried a frame-up. Then suddenly Jim Leonard, who was known to have his back against the wall financially, turns up with a wheel-barrow filled with gold, deposits a staggering amount for bail and produces a trainload of assorted friends and allies. Does that deter Gilligan? The answer is 'No.' He strengthens his hold on the local political machine, imports hordes of unemployed gangsters and, armed with Government papers, intends to establish a *fait accompli*. Once his sheep, due back from Idaho by rail in May, cross your father's range, the land will be useless for cattle, as you know, for years to come."

"One thing troubles me more than all the rest," said Miriam. "The bullet from the Winchester 40-40. The only rifle of that make and caliber I've ever seen out here is the one Dad owns and carries. Men who can't see and shoot as far pack a lighter gun."

"Toudoux said the deceased, the chap found today near the head of Cottonwood Creek, died between five and six months ago, but he was careful not to say how. The bullet, fired by a man on the same level while the body was erect, pierced the heart, struck a back rib and lodged itself near the kidneys. That much we can accept, nothing more. Knowing the corpse was not that of Donniker Louey, I assumed (a) that it was planted on your father's range as false evidence; (b) that as thorough a frame-up would involve the use of a weapon easily identified as belonging to your father, At the grave, I pretended to have mistaken the rifle in your father's bedroom for a non-existent Remington 30-40, and the sheriff obligingly revealed that he knew your esteemed parent owned a Winchester 40-40. Thus I was able to be sure that the sheriff was involved in the frame-up and was not merely the dupe of Larkspur Gilligan. Both of them knew in advance that they should find a body, and that the said body would have been pierced by a bullet shot from a Winchester 40-40."

"Where did they get the body?" asked Miriam.

"We shall have to find out," Evans said. "But our main problem is to protect the range from invasion."

"Not one sheep shall cross the deadline alive," said Miriam.

"I'm inclined to agree," Homer said, "but, first, we must sleep. Tomorrow may prove more strenuous than today has been."

So arm in arm, they scattered the embers, extinguished them with hissing snow, and went to the igloo for some well-earned repose. The stars pulsed in clusters, constellations shifting, while a waning moon cast its dim reflection on the muddy raging streams. A lone Blackfeet Indian, who had been dispatched from the Piney Butte area to suggest to Evans the maneuver he already had adopted, namely, to round up the shorthorns on the mesas and keep them out of the ravines, listened raptly to the voice of Hjalmar as he bellowed to the restless steers a tune he had learned on the Liverpool docks, with words, slightly altered, by Rabelais:

> *"Oh, Thou Whom water turnedst to wine*
> *Transform my bum, by power divine,*
> *Into a lantern that will light*
> *My dogies in the darkest night."*

The song reminded the stray Indian of a tribal melody his grandfather had crooned as his mother had borne him on her back:

> *"Kyi in uk o tsi u sok ko ma pe*
> *Kvis too ye e eat sis*
> *Ne na sknoo nuk kit . . ."*

> [*Bye, Baby bunting*
> *Daddy's gone a-hunting . . .*]

So the Blackfeet brave joined in Hjalmar's song, which gave the painter quite a start, and soon the two men were riding side by side around the lowing herd, swapping stories which, while neither one understood the speech of the other, helped pass the long watches of the night.

18
Touching on Science, Parental Love and Pride, Also Democracy

THE NEW DEVELOPMENTS IN CONNECTION with the murder of Donniker Louey attracted national attention, because of the Santo gang's notoriety and the picturesque details broadcast by Tom Jackson, who had friends throughout the newspaper world. Rotogravure supplements, from the Hearst-fuddled slopes of California to the Howard-blighted pines of Maine, carried three-column cuts of Trout-tail III, in what was called "war paint," making medicine signs by the open grave; of Jim Leonard surrounded by shorthorns and buckaroos; of the weeping immigrant father holding a tell-tale shoe aloft; of Hockaday, the young sheriff, and his deputies, in chaps and spurs; and a photograph made on the French Line pier in New York, showing the famous Chief of Detectives Frémont, Dr. Hyacinthe Toudoux and the two French criminologists, Schlumberger and Bonnet, gazing in astonishment at a grapefruit and a package of Zazz, a prepared breakfast food which, the distinguished Frenchman had just been told, had been shot out of machine guns in airplanes.

When the posse had been run off the Leonard ranch by Miriam, Tom Jackson, to keep up appearances of objectivity, had ridden away with Gilligan and his pals. But before that Evans had found a way to communicate with him and had asked him not to raise any suspicion concerning the identity of the body found on Cottonwood Creek. Therefore the story of the discovery of the *corpus delicti*, without which the State could not proceed against Leonard with hope of conviction, appeared in a very different light in the

Glendive *X-Ray* than it did as reviewed by Homer around the Beef Slough campfire. In the *X-Ray* account of the proceedings, Jackson set forth that Dr. Hyacinthe Toudoux, medical examiner of Paris, France, was assisting Dr. S. Lougee, the local coroner, in the post mortem and that a well-known arms expert, who preferred to remain anonymous, had admitted that the bullet which had pierced the dead man's heart had been fired from a rifle similar to that owned and carried by Jim Leonard. Judge Patterson issued a statement that he was consulting with the State Attorney General about a possible rescinding of the bail and promised his constituents that the trial should be held without delay. Myra Patterson published an interview with Mike Bevilacqua, the bereaved father, on the difficulty of raising motherless boys in the slums of the East and advising widowers to re-marry, for the sake of the kiddies, however disinclined they might feel.

The adventures of the posse on the cattle range was the lead story in the *X-Ray*, but on the corresponding columns of the front page, left-hand side, was an article not less sensational as far as the local population was concerned.

LOWER YELLOWSTONE VALLEY
UNFIT FOR CATTLE
PREVALENCE OF DEADLY LARKSPUR
ON BOTH WATERSHEDS IS
ADMITTED BY CHIEF
CATTLEMEN

The article went on to say that the wisdom of using the land between the two principal rivers, west of Redwater Creek, as a winter range for cattle, had long been questioned by local and federal authorities. Weather conditions were arduous, so that losses from storms and drifts had been great. Now, added to that, was the danger of larkspur poisoning. Several statesmen had been interviewed and were quoted as saying that the cattlemen, if forced to evacuate, should be generously recompensed by Congress, but pointed out the additional prosperity that would come to Eastern Montana should the sheep industry be permitted its normal expansion. The same statesmen showed concern for the Blackfeet Indians, who, they said, had been herded and confined on the arid and bleak wastes north of the Missouri too long, while other reservations more attractive were thinly populated.

Miriam, who rode to the stage road in the morning in time to intercept the stage coach, could hardly contain herself for indignation when she held out to Evans and the others on the Slough the copy of the special murder edition. Had Evans not restrained her, she would have ridden to Glendive, shot up the *X-Ray* office and set fire to the plant.

"When an adversary is crawling out on a limb, why offer discouragement?" Evans said. His words were interrupted by the appearance on the summit of a horse and rider.

"Stenka, by yee," said Jansen, highly pleased. "And she doesn't spare the horse."

Indeed, the animal was covered with lather and nearly spent. The big Serbian girl, without a word, dismounted and started tugging at the thongs that bound two large skin sacks to the saddlebags.

"The medicine," she said in French, and Evans instantly got into action. All morning the party had been pulling up and burying the noxious weeds, chasing stray cattle out of the coulees and cutting out from the herd any shorthorns which showed symptoms of larkspur poisoning. Some of the latter died, others were in desperate condition, still others were more lightly afflicted. Miriam, now mounted on the clever and agile Star, which seemed to understand the game as well as her mistress did, roped and threw the cattle that showed most promise of recovery. Hjalmar, the muscles standing out on his brawny arms and shoulders, pried open their jaws, and Diluvio, buckskin sack in hand, poured in a large swallow of the Indian medicine.

"I shall send a Christmas card each year to the heirs of Lydia Pinkham," Evans said, when the first of his patients gave evidence of definite improvement.

On the three creeks emptying into the Yellowstone and patrolled by Evans, two hundred head had died, and two hundred more cattle were beyond recovery, he had thought. But once he had finished treating the lighter cases, he approached one of the suffering beasts who had rolled over, groaning, on its side.

"Hjalmar, give me a hand," he said, and with the help of the big Norwegian he got the steer's mouth open. Diluvio poured a double dose of the snake and vegetable compound down the agonized throat, and they waited. Miriam, torn by the sight of the animal's convulsions, turned away and slashed at tumbleweeds with her braided quirt. But when she heard a cry from Evans she wheeled swiftly around, and Stenka began to sing and to pray. For the steer, a moment before on the point of death, rolled, kicked and, aided by the ready shoulder of the roaring Hjalmar, struggled to his feet, his eyes blinking, his tail switching spasmodically at imaginary flies.

From that moment on, there was not time for anyone to speak or to make a wasted motion. From beast to beast the rescue party worked, and with most happy results. Three hundred doomed shorthorns were to roam the plains again.

Just as the work was coming to an end, a weary figure trotted across the sagebrush flat and stretched himself, panting, at Miriam's side. Moritz the dog, left behind, had come many miles across strange country to look at Miriam reproachfully and sigh.

"We have won another skirmish," said Evans, after reassuring the exhausted Boxer. "I begin to suspect why a man in Oxfords, probably Young Gilligan, was roaming Bison Creek last night. Gilligan the elder had planned to distract the attention of the ranch hands by finding the body at the appropriate moment, so that the cattle might all get a good dose of larkspur before the presence of the weed was discovered on the range. When the stuff was planted, last fall, it was not known that we should have a special train at Muddy Creek and that traffic up and down the neglected Bison Creek trail would be practically continuous. Hence a Gilligan cohort was dispatched right after the thaw to remove the larkspur from the creek on which it would be promptly discovered."

Leaving Hjalmar and Stenka to drive the herd slowly toward Three Buttes, giving the animals time to graze by the way on table lands only, Homer sent the others riding in all directions to spread the news of the efficacy of Trout-tail's specific on the severest cases of poisoning.

Hugo Weiss, the multi-millionaire and famous financier, meanwhile, was in his shirt-sleeves at the kitchen range in Opera Lodge, a huge frying pan in each hand. For hours he had been frying out rattlesnakes and learning Pidgin English in order more freely to communicate with his assistants, Wing Lee and Wing Sam. The first batch of snakes had arrived in two gunnysacks borne on a stick between the shoulders of two Blackfeet runners, and one of the Indians had presented instructions scribbled by Dr. Hyacinthe Toudoux. To make the Chinese understand just what was to be done was no easy assignment, and the renowned banker's mental qualities had seldom, in the course of a long and successful career, been put to such a test. According to Toudoux, each rattler should first be pinned with a forked stick fitted close behind its head, over which a Mason jar should then be slid. With its head in the jar, the snake should be given a wad of absorbent cotton on which to bite, until the poison in its glands had been transferred to the cotton. Then the head should be cut off clean and the body skun and fried over a hot wood fire until the oil had been rendered. The oil, then, was to be cleared by the use of *croutons* or bits of toast, and allowed to cool and settle. When a gallon of oil was cool, one teaspoonful of the vegetable compound was to be added and the resulting prescription rushed to the field workers on the range.

At first Hugo Weiss had to do practically all the work, since the Chinese could not be made to take the procedure with appropriate seriousness. They had eaten snakes in the old country and had handled them alive, but not rattlers.

"Holdem snake with one-piece flok, now head 'e go in bokis," the financier explained.

"Lattlesnake 'e catchum China boy, make um onepiece dead fella," said Wing Sam. "Ai ting ai go Glendive, maybe Minneap'lis, maybe New York."

Weiss excused himself, went to his room and returned with two hatfuls of twenty-dollar gold pieces which he placed in two equal piles on a kitchen shelf.

"Me, ai bet dough for go China that snake no catchum China boy. Now China boy claiful, can do," Weiss said, and had to restrain Wing Sam from grabbing up a handful of rattlers without forked sticks, Mason jars or even cotton gloves on his hands. The Chinese, cheered by the prospects of returning to their native land with sacks of gold, learned quickly the bizarre routine and soon the remedy was being rushed to all points of the compass. Fresh consignments of rattlers arrived hourly, wood was piled into the range, pungent smoke filled the kitchen and streamed from the windows, and through it all the toiling millionaire sang a spirited song, which he translated into Pidgin English for the benefit of his loyal collaborators. The idea of sending worthy Chinese back to China could be expanded until it relieved him of substantial sums, he believed, and the thought made him gay. His song was as follows:

> *Allasame China, Flisco, evely place,*
> *Fella 'e no catchum cash, catchum plenty hell*
> *Topside fella 'e catch um cash, can do.*
> *Scheme 'e plenty bum.*

or: *It's the same the whole world over,*
> *It's the poor who get the blame,*
> *The rich get all the pleasure.*
> *Now ain't it a bleedin' shame?*

Across the Missouri, on the Poplar River snake preserve, Frémont, Dr. Hyacinthe Toudoux and Trout-tail III were finishing the first part of the labors. Enough snakes had been sacked and shipped to provide medicine for the sick cattle on all the range, venom enough for Dr. Toudoux to use in his experiments for years to come, and snake skins enough to make belts for all the tourists in Arizona. The old medicine man had instructed a number of braves to make the long journey to the badlands via Mondak and replenish at their leisure the supply necessary to tribal safety and well-being. It was the season when the hibernating rattlers were coming out of their holes by the hundreds.

Before Trout-tail III conducted his guests to his lodge thirty miles to the eastward, they were joined by Chief Shot-on-Both-Sides who was eager for an official report on the scene at the graveside. Rain-No-More, meanwhile, was busy with his hard-riding shock troops, pulling up *delphinium*, treating poisoned cattle and starting the general spring round-up which normally would have begun two weeks or more later. If, occasionally, the young Blackfeet let themselves imagine that the herds were buffaloes and the weapons on their saddles not rifles but good ash bows and arrows tipped with flint, that did not interfere with their efficient work, and Jim Leonard, to whom were sent reports from all corners of the range, began to shake off his despondency. The odds were still against him, but he had a fighting chance.

"I don't mind telling you, Hank," the rancher said to his foreman, "there was times when I was almighty skittish about leaving Miriam all by herself in Paris, France. But now, when I've seen what her friends are like, and how the city life hasn't spoiled her, I begin to be kind of glad she's seen the world a bit and had advantages you and me never had."

"She's run with a mighty fine bunch, no doubt about that," said Hank. "We'd be in one hell of a fix without 'em."

"One thing's a-settin' on my mind," the old rancher said. "All this is costin' a heap of money, and I don't know how I'll pay it back."

"Shucks, Jim," said Hank, "that rich guy's just like the rest of us, likes to let himself go from time to time. Why, fifty thousand bucks to a man like him is just like four bits to you and me, when we toss it on the bar. Your smart little girl got him out of a scrape in France. Now he wants to do his part, that's all. That seems natural to me."

"I've always held my end up somehow," said Jim Leonard.

"You've borrowed my winter's wages from me, more than once, and paid 'em back again. Why high-hat this Eastern fellow, just because he's weighted down with money? That ain't democratic, Jim, an' you know it. Maybe the pile was wished on him in a will or something."

"Well, if you put it that way," said the rancher, and mounted his broncho again.

In the detention tepee at the medicine lodge, young Santo-suosso and Terry Gilligan were squatting on their heels. Their hands were bound, their legs were numb because of the unaccustomed position, but their conversation did not indicate that their spirits had been chastened to any great extent.

"To think that I let that wise guy Evans crack me up, and on a stall, at that," said young Santo. "So help me, I felt him cut around the edges of my scalp, in a circle right on top of my head, then peel off the skin, hair and all, while the blood ran down my puss and nearly blinded me. The next time I'll not open my trap if they skin me alive."

"That wouldn't be beyond 'em," said Terry. "We got to get word some way to my old man."

"Mine must be having a fit. He doesn't know where I am," said Santo.

"Beats hell how much they think of us," Terry said. "Hard to figure out why. We haven't done nothing but touch 'em for dough and get 'em in Dutch all our lives."

"Now that's a fact," said Santo, "but why not, if they're suckers enough to stand for it? Believe me, if I had a kid and he tried to get away with anything, I'd fan him silly."

"They say you figure it different, if a kid's your own. It would make you feel kind of foolish, at that, to have some broad hand you over a nipper and say it was yours."

"Knock on wood," said Santo, but his hands were still tied.

A long single file of Blackfeet, drums and medicine sticks in hand, trotted toward the tepee.

"Cripes. It's going to begin. That's the way these bloody Indians start giving a guy the works. They turn loose a flock of skin beaters first, and when they get hot, along comes the wood-wind section. No use kidding ourselves, it softens up a guy. After a half hour or so, you say to yourself, now why can't they change the tune, but they never do. I guess they're too dumb to learn more than one number."

"I could use a cigarette," said Terry.

"Go easy, unless you're used to smokin' tea. So help me, they made Beetlebuzzer and me woozy with reefers. That's part of their act. It's a good thing that snake choked Beetlebuzzer or he'd have spilled the works. He was going to crack, and no mistake."

"I wish they'd get started," said Terry. "This waiting around gives me the heebie-jeebies."

"Just wait till my old man gets to workin' on them tents with his armored cars. He'll make Cicero look like a picnic ground."

"If he finds out where we are," said young Gilligan.

"There's always that," Santosuosso said, and spat. "But I won't fall for no blind scalpin' act again. You'll keep that under your hat, won't you, Terry?"

"Even if I blow my top, I won't give you away," the heir of Gilligan said.

The two young men above mentioned, who were awaiting with more fortitude than patience the impending examination by the Blackfeet intelligence officer, Trout-tail III, had underestimated, if anything, the anxiety of their respective fathers. Gilligan, Senior, was at the time in Judge Patterson's new and elaborate living room in Glendive, conferring with Sheriff Hockaday, the N.P. divisional public relations counsel named simply Brown and a member of the Republican State Committee who had been sent down from Butte to advise the leaders of the local political machine. They were all too agitated to risk playing poker in such shrewd company; the phonograph records Myra had purchased from Sears, Roebuck were all on the classical or standard side and in no way soothing; and none of them dared drink too much whiskey for fear of a burst of indiscreet frankness. At intervals Larkspur, who was obviously the No. 1 conspirator, would snatch at the phone, turn the small crank frenetically and demand the *X-Ray*.

"Any news from the lower valley?" he would ask.

"Not a peep," Tom Jackson would reply.

"Do you think he's holding out on us?" the Republican from Butte would ask.

"He'd better not," said Gilligan.

"Let's have a look at him," suggested the public relations counsel.

It was agreed that Jackson should be summoned, and that if he seemed to be trustworthy he should first be oiled up with a good fat contract for political advertising and then sent out to the Leonard ranch to pick up what he could about the condition of the cattle and the plans for the spring round-up. Tom, after a few bracers at the Jordan bar, put in an appearance and was success-ful in passing muster. He told them that he had followed Gilligan's instructions, that another extra was in readiness, with front-page space reserved for the larkspur catastrophe, but that the silence from the cattle range had been unbroken since the posse had rid-den away. He did report, however, that there had been a sharp re-action in Wall Street and in the commodities market in Chicago because of the disappearance without trace of Hugo Schusschnigger Weiss. Stocks of the numerous important concerns in which Weiss was influential had taken a nosedive and it was reported that sev-eral brokerage firms had gone to the wall. The suicide toll already was mounting and aspirin had doubled in price. The rumor had spread like wildfire that Weiss had fled the country to escape the consequence of a gigantic collapse of the financial empire he had built up.

For the first time in weeks, in fact since the advent of Homer Evans and his colleagues to Montana, Larkspur Gilligan smiled.

"What a story!" said Jackson. "I could get photographs of Weiss hale and hearty, and scoop the world. Every paper in the country would carry it."

The assembled conspirators nearly bit their tongues and stepped on one another's toes to dissuade him, and offer counter propositions.

"If Weiss really goes broke, there's nothing to stop us," said Gilligan. "You keep mum, Jackson, and we'll make it worth your while."

With feigned regret, Tom said that he would string along. The upshot was that Jackson was sent to Three Buttes to get what evi-dence he could that the cattle range was unfit for its traditional use, sound out Jim Leonard on his asking price for water rights, ascertain if Weiss knew about the panic his absence from the business world was causing, and, most important of all to Gilligan, although a matter of indifference to the others, to trace young Terry.

The elder Gilligan's anxiety on account of his offspring was so touching that Jackson felt a twinge of sympathy for the man. Larkspur lived simply; his tastes were inexpensive. He seemed not to crave culture, fame or even power for its own sake. His driving desire was to build a huge fortune for his son and heir, in the hope that Terry would rise to the large responsibility entailed and become a man. What Gilligan had seen of Miriam in action had made the sheepman green with envy, for he loved the plains and believed they should produce a sturdy unbeatable race. The sheepman had never been jealous of Jim Leonard because of his cattle business, which was on the wane, or his fortune which never had been considerable. But now he coveted his daughter and was determined she should be the mother of the future Gilligan clan. As he looked back on the scenes at the ranch and the graveside, the astute old sheepman remembered that there seemed to be some kind of understanding between Miriam and the Nemesis called Evans, who was the brains of the Leonard outfit. So getting rid of Evans had become a principal item in Larkspur's ambitious program. Another item scarcely less vital was to get on the good side of Miriam. That the two projects had conflicting elements did not deter the ruthless old man. No use leaving a commercial and political empire to Terry without the right sort of wife to guide him, of that the elder Gilligan had become convinced.

Another harassed father was pacing the aisle of what had once been a passenger coach on the Great Northern System, later had been sold and used as a lunchroom at Mondak, and at the time this story takes place was temporary headquarters for a contingent of the Baldy Santo gang, the members of which were wanted in several States for such a long list of crimes that space is lacking to enumerate them here. Let it suffice to remind the reader that the last job had to do with the robbery of a bank in Jamestown

Junction. More than twenty-four hours earlier, Baldy Santo, a small benevolent-looking Sicilian with noncommittal black eyes and delicate hands, had sent his son Tony and his nephew, Beetlebuzzer, on a scouting expedition. Neither one of them had returned.

Baldy had been informed that the special train of coaches he had seen in the badlands, and whose inhabitants he had grown to dislike almost to the point of loathing, was on a sidetrack near Muddy Creek. As has been mentioned before, the Chicago gang chief had found it much more difficult to keep his mobsters in hand in the open spaces than it had been in Cicero or South Chicago. The grub available in Mondak, where they had been parked after Wibaux had grown too hot for them, was meager and what there was of it betrayed a Scandinavian Protestant influence particularly distasteful to Italians. Also the liquor was not what the mob had been used to. Baldy had worked out a plan to keep his men busy and at the same time replenish the larder and get revenge on the enemies who had railroaded him out of his hideout and locked him up in box cars bound for Minneapolis. It was not the discomfort Baldy had minded, but the indignity he had suffered and the loss of prestige with his men.

Consequently, he had sent his son Tony and young Beetlebuzzer to reconnoiter. If they reported favorably, Baldy intended to hijack the Alsatian dining car and the Dôme with its load of good liquor, to drive the occupants out into the foothills without arms, food or matches, and lastly to crowbar the special coaches out to the main line tracks just around a sharp curve and just before the westbound express came tearing through.

After waiting and worrying all night and all day, he decided to carry out his design and search for Tony and his nephew at the same time, and for this purpose broke up the stud game and called his gangsters to order.

19
In Which the Life Impulse Gets a Close Decision

TOM JACKSON, WHEN HE RODE UP the Leonard Creek trail, was met on the western butte, where the hot and cold springs gushed from the hillside, by Moritz the dog, who had taken upon himself the duty of giving the once over to any wayfarer who approached the ranch house. From his point of vantage on the crest of the divide, Tom could see busy preparations for the round-up on every side. Far behind him, between Three Buttes and the badlands, two large herds of cattle were already converging toward the main corral. The larger had been gathered together by the Professor, with Kvek and Grigori to help him, and came from the table lands near the fork of the rivers, where ravines were few and the larkspur had not taken much hold. The second was piloted by Hjalmar and Stenka, and as they rode along, and the steers and dogies munched, the big Norwegian was explaining to the Serbian girl why, according to the great François, miles in the country are so much longer than miles in the city.*

Around the barn and the corrals, chuck wagons were being loaded and driven away. Cases of air-tights—canned cow, Mexican strawberries, black strap, etc.—along with sowbelly, sides of elk meat, and sacks of sugar, salt and flour, were being checked out of the warehouse and distributed. Harness jingled, cowpunchers rode here and there, ropes looped and swung through the air. Branding irons, all shaped in the Lazy Jay, were being cleaned and repaired.

* Rabelais, Book II, "How Pantagruel Departed from Paris."

The first disconcerting sight Tom saw was a pen with a low board fence in which were basking dozens of rattlesnakes, while the entire barn was covered with drying rattlesnake hides.

Hank, seeing the reporter's bewilderment, said that since the cattle business was on the bum, the Leonard ranch was being converted into a snake farm, and asked him to put the story in the paper. In the huge living room, Hugo Weiss, whose fate was the riddle of the financial world, was playing cribbage with Eugénie Toudoux. Beatrice Diluvio, *née* Baxter, was busily mending socks and shirts.

In his attic room, far removed from the bustle and activity, sat Homer Evans, staring across the broad plains at the colors and shapes of the badlands miles away. The danger from larkspur having been averted, with comparatively little loss of stock, Evans had withdrawn himself for meditation on the larger aspects of the struggle before him. As loathe as he had been in the past to accept responsibility or to use to the full his extraordinary gifts, in Opera Lodge he was vibrant with satisfaction—not overconfident, but more determined than he had ever been before in his eventful life. The immediate past, he knew, was the most remote from the present, and for that reason its virtues were more obscure and its relics hardest to preserve. Future generations would bemoan the cattle range, if it passed the way of the buffalo. Could it be defended against the thoughtless folk then living?

Again and again Evans had subjected Gilligan's plans and accomplishments to cold analysis. If justice was not on the sheepman's side, contemporary trends seemed to be allied with him. As far as brute force was concerned, Homer did not fear a test of strength, with his friends from Montparnasse, the rough and ready buckaroos, and the Blackfeet braves to back Jim Leonard. Of money, the sinews of war, there was an abundance, apparently, behind both camps.

Ingenuity was not lacking in Larkspur Gilligan's fertile brain. But the real strength of the sheepman's position was its legality on broad lines and contempt for scruples, either legal or moral, when it came to details. Also its political roots.

Homer knew that it is absurd to assume that all men are alike. There are those who will do anything for money, while others draw a line. There are men insensitive to human suffering, while others feel every blow that lands on the back of a struggling donkey, and experience nausea from a casual glimpse of the tragic face of an unhappy child. The men and women in the Leonard camp were not like gangsters, and in war would be correspondingly less ruthless. He could not ask or expect them to be ignoble or indecent, nor did he desire to do so. Instead he must meet trickery with agility of mind, and combat legal chicanery with legal checkmate. How should he proceed?

First there was the trial of Jim Leonard. Evans already thought he had enough at his fingertips to get an acquittal and complete vindication, but the trial would be held, and at the most inconvenient time. Gilligan had tried to disorganize the round-up, and had very nearly succeeded, by planting larkspur all over the range. Homer was confident that the sheepman would arrange to have Jim tried, and his principal helpers summoned as witnesses, at precisely the time when sheep were being shipped back from the winter range in Idaho. It was likely that Gilligan had obtained some kind of legal permission from Washington to use the cattle range, not an authorization that would be likely to stand, if passed upon by a high court, but one that would hold good several years, perhaps, while the case was juggled back and forth on crowded court calendars. Of course, if sheep grazed on the Lower Yellowstone one season, the cattle would starve before a decision could return to them their proper feeding grounds.

"I must get the jump on Gilligan, legally," Evans said to himself, and paced the floor. A tap sounded on his door and he felt a twinge of annoyance at first, for he had given instructions that he was not to be disturbed except in case of emergency. But the tap was Miriam's and he concluded that an emergency was at hand.

"Come in," he said, and Miriam entered, followed by Tom Jackson. Homer was listening intensely to Jackson's report of developments in Glendive when the triangle clanged and roared, announcing the mid-day meal.

HIGH NOON AT THE MEDICINE LODGE on the reservation to the north afforded a widely different spectacle. Terry Gilligan and Tony Santo were still squatting in the tepee, trying to shut out from their ears the insistent drumming which swept in a circle around the tent and making an effort not to look at the details in the disconcerting designs that had been painted on the walls. Silently a Blackfeet brave entered and, after rummaging in the medicine sack, produced a pack each of Luckies and Camels. Young Santo, inured to the effects of *marijuana*, accepted a cigarette. Terry Gilligan gritted his teeth and refused. He was resolved to take no chances.

Outside, Chief of Detectives Frémont of Paris was sitting on a stump, notebook in hand.

"The disadvantage of the use of music in reducing the prisoners' resistance," he was scribbling hastily, "seems to lie in the fact that the presiding officers are affected equally with the suspects, or, as in my case at present, much more severely. Many times I have found myself on the point of screaming and rushing the redskin native drummers and the players of the even more hideous flageolets. The same objection applies to the odors employed by the American police of the Western departments. Myself, I am stifled, my brain will not function at its best, and, as far as I can see, the prisoners are not noticeably discomfited, or at least, not more than those I have seen confined in the cells of the Paris commissariats. In short, I cannot recommend the use of music or vile stenches by the Third Republic as means of extracting information from recalcitrant violators of our laws and statutes. In fact," Frémont added aloud, "should any such methods be introduced I should have to resign, no matter how badly I need my monthly pay."

On second thought, because of the off-chance that the prefect might take a tip from his researches in America in order to make conditions unbearable in the office, Frémont tore up his notes and went to the main lodge, which was windward, for a brandy and soda.

Not only Frémont, but Chief Shot-on-Both-Sides had taken a good look at the prisoners through peepholes skillfully camouflaged by the painted designs. On returning to Trout-tail's private tepee the wise Chief said:

"*Kakh tum o sa a kin ik sin ni*" (That pair will never crack), "Not even after the torture of the ants and alkali, which, since I was instrumental in reforming our criminal procedure, I could never consent to apply."

"What then shall we do?" asked Trout-tail, relieved. He had never tried out the ant ordeal himself, and was not sure he could stand it.

The old Chief got out the tribal pipe, filled and lighted it, and handed it to Trout-tail. Ten minutes they sat without uttering a word, while Frémont, on pins and needles, smoked half a package of Pall Malls, lighting one from the other and puffing furiously. He was too polite to break the silence, however. Finally Shot-on-Both-Sides gave voice to his decision.

"Detail four men to take the prisoners to the badlands and hold them as hostages there. By day they must be concealed, even from the buzzards, and the marches must be made at night. Unless I am mistaken, the pale-face Evans will be able in their absence to get more information from the fathers than we could from the sons. I know a parent's heart. *Kyi*" (Finished), the old Chief said.

Frémont made a grab for his notebook again. "American police methods," he wrote hastily, "are not, in general, suitable for use in France. Kidnapping of the offspring of criminals, for instance, in order to put pressure on wayward parents, would be likely to cause embarrassing questions to be raised in the Chamber and might be used by the political opponents of the Premier to precipitate a fall of the Government, which seldom benefits the public at large and frequently is expensive and wasteful. An Anglo-Saxon poet has written, 'Oh, East is East and West is West.' With equal accuracy, one might paraphrase those enigmatic lines. I am more and more convinced that Europe is Europe and America is America, at least North America is North America, and little or nothing can be done to ameliorate the situation."

Had Frémont known at that moment what was threatening the train of which he was in charge, his blood would have run cold. For Baldy Santo and his gang had quit their hideout in the railroad yards of Mondak and were pumping handcars along the level tangents of the Great Northern tracks toward Muddy Creek. And Baldy's motto for years had been: "Stop at nothing."

"The big shot's jumpy. I never seen him like that before," said Bird's-eye Cohen, who because of his short stature was having a hard time keeping his chin away from the pump-bar as it described its rhythmic arc through the air.

"He was intendin' to make a mission before Easter, but he couldn't find no church around," said Paperhanger Stuntz, letting go of the handle to straighten the kinks in his back.

It was true that Baldy, ordinarily self-possessed, was nervous. He stood in the front handcar, peering across the flats this way and that in the hope of finding his son. Instead he saw an expanse of sagebrush and grass with occasional patches of snow and, near the Missouri, clumps of cottonwoods on which the buds showed faintly green. Because the westbound Limited was due just after sundown he had elected to do the job of hijacking and destruction by daylight, but he had seen Homer Evans and the stern-faced cow-punchers in the badlands and did not relish tangling with them in a country where the cover was none too good for jack-rabbits, let alone his collection of thugs, who were accustomed to working in armored cars or shooting from second-story windows.

When the gang was within a mile of Muddy Creek, Baldy ordered them to stop the handcars, lift them off the track, then to follow him on their hands and knees, from sagebrush to sagebrush, until they were near enough the special coaches to observe what was happening inside. What they saw gave them courage, of which the gangsters had plenty when things were going their way. Hydrangea, in a gaily colored sweater and short skirt, was working away at a dance routine, beneath the admiring eyes of the princesses, Unreal Bear and Tinted Cloud, in the studio car. Galilee Zach, always obliging, was tapping out a dance tune as best he could with one well- groomed finger.

"Isn't that banana who's kneading the ivories a gon from Chi?" whispered the Paperhanger hoarsely. His knees were soaked through with moisture from the damp ground and he was by no means happy. His last recollection of a grown man on all fours was a newspaper cut he had seen of Daddy Browning, and he did not relish the association.

"He's a bronc named Zach, who worked in Marshall Field's. What brings him out to Bridgeport? Bullhorrors?"

"Zipper that mug," hissed Baldy Santo.

Baldy had his eyes on the Dôme car, in which Sergeants Schlumberger and Bonnet were playing *belotte* with Cromwell and Washington, the waiters. Corrigan was in the diner, next door, engaged in grilling *pieds de cerf* in the Alsatian style.

"We got to work quick, before the other bozos come home," said Baldy. "Crawl as near as you can, then, when they see you, rush the train. Never mind the broads, get that bunch of card players first. Paperhanger, you and Bird's-eye take care of the cook."

"I'd rather go for the beetles and the punk," Paperhanger muttered to himself, and got a look from the mild-appearing Santo that caused his teeth to chatter.

The mobsters, numbering nine, worked their way a few yards nearer their quarry. Suddenly Hydrangea stopped to rest and coach Zach at the piano. Unreal Bear saw a meadowlark hopping merrily by the side of the track and went to the window to watch the bird, whose bright yellow breast looked as if it had come freshly from the cleaners. Tinted Cloud was at her sister's side and saw a furtive movement in the brush, one hundred yards away. In a second she saw another, and another. The princess did not lose her head, but without moving her lips she warned her sister, and soon the girls had spotted the nine gangsters. What to do about them was another matter. All the girls had left their guns in the Melisande when they had changed into gym clothes, and to reach the Melisande meant exposing themselves between cars, since the covered passageways had been removed for better ventilation.

The gangsters had seen the girls at the window and were lying low, in the hope that they would not be observed, which gave the princesses a moment in which to make plans. Since they could not warn the men in the Dôme car, or get to their weapons, they decided to make a quick bolt, with the train between them and the prowlers, mount their horses which were hitched in the shed and ride hard for help from the reservation. Baldy Santo, who had been watching the pair, suddenly was aware that they had vanished, and a second later his automatic spoke as he fired again and again at the fleeing girls. At that, the mobsters got down to business according to instructions. Schlumberger and Bonnet, both armed, started shooting through the windows, while shattered glass tinkled all around them. One gangster fell, then another, then a third, but the attackers had divided their forces, so that while the French sergeants stood off one party, another led by Baldy got behind them and crashed in a door of the coach. Bonnet, winged in the elbow, felt his arm tingle and his gun slip from his hand.

"*Je suis foutu, mon vieux.* Use me for a shield and save yourself, for the sake of the women," the sergeant said.

Schlumberger, turning, found himself looking into a submachine gun and a sawed-off shotgun.

"Stick 'em up," said Baldy. "I don't want to bump you off till I've found my son."

Two gangsters tackled the battling Alsatian from another direction. One was sideswiped by Bonnet with his one good arm. Then the two Frenchmen became the center of a whirling mass of arms, legs and clubbed automatics.

"My father was right," mumbled Schlumberger, as the butt of a gun came down on his well-thatched head and caused an explosion like a flashlight bulb. "I should not have joined the police. It is no career for the son of a business man."

Corrigan, in the diner, was putting up a game fight against Bird's-eye and Paperhanger, but the floor was slippery and he soon went down. The Paperhanger promptly gonked him with a rolling pin, and when the chef awoke, he still was wearing his own shirt, socks and B.V.D.'s, while his opponents had his cap, his pants and his apron, the strings of which they had used to tie him up like a turkey ready for the pan.

Hydrangea, at the sound of firing, had yelled for Frémont, then fainted away. But when the gangsters broke into the studio car, the shuddering Zach seemed transformed into a wildcat. Ignoring shotguns, machine guns and automatics, he threw himself on the first comers, scratching and biting until blood streaked their faces and one of them was missing the lobe of an ear. In an effort to shoot the frenzied dip, one gangster got another in the ankle.

"Lay off with them rods," shouted Baldy Santo. "Can't you orangoutangs rub out one punk without artillery?"

The answer, evidently, was no, for Zach fought his way to the platform. Then, bewildered, but still remembering Hydrangea, he tore back into the car again, tears of rage in his eyes, clawing this way and that.

"He's a game little party, for a nance. I'm going to give him a break," Santo said. "Go get me a horse, if there's one left. We got to work quick since those squaws got away."

Zach, still fighting, tripped over the piano bench. A gangster pinned his arms. Another sat on his face and stripped off his trousers. The pickpocket screamed and sobbed and kicked with both legs, stirring up such a commotion that Hydrangea regained consciousness. The Blackbird tried to faint again, but couldn't, when she saw what was going on around her.

Bird's-eye Cohen and Stuntz came up from the shed, leading two balky bronchos, the only ones remaining. Still trying to resist, Galilee Zach was placed backward on the meanest-looking horse, and his ankles were tied beneath the animal's belly.

"How about the eight ball? Shall she keep him company?" asked Paperhanger Stuntz. Baldy nodded. He didn't want one woman, particularly a good-looking one, causing friction in his mob. So the swooning Hydrangea was slung on the other mount, and both horses were slapped soundly on the rump, at which they kicked up their heels and started out across the sagebrush flat, jolting and bruising their helpless riders, who had to cling fast to their tails to keep from sliding under.

The five male prisoners who were left, Schlumberger, Bonnet, Cromwell, Washington and Corrigan, all shaken up and wounded, were loaded on a handcar and taken back toward Mondak, to be relieved of pants and shoes, dumped off and run into the foothills in the most desolate stretch of country along the way. Meanwhile, working feverishly with crowbars, Baldy and the rest of his crew got the special cars moving down the sidetrack, one by one, over the switch and on the main line tracks just west of the curve where an approaching engineer could not see them until it was too late to stop the Limited.

The fortune of Hugo Weiss would soon have been reduced by a sizeable figure had not Rain-No-More and two of his braves, who were rounding up stray dogies and their calves across the river, seen the special train moving slowly along the sidetrack. Rain-No-More, riding hard, got near enough to see that all was not well, then raced for the narrow footbridge, his braves close behind him. The pintos strained their wiry limbs until blood tinged their nostrils, but the detour was so long that before the Blackfeet reached the scene of the melee on Muddy Creek the Santo gang had made a clean getaway, with their wounded and a load of booze from the Dôme. Leaping into the dining car, Rain-No-More found a towel stained with blood that had flowed from the scalp of Corrigan, after it had been bashed with his own rolling pin. From the platform, red rag in hand, Rain-No-More sprang to the back of his pony and streaked down the tracks, cinders flying, while more than once the sure-footed animal tripped over ties and nearly went down with his rider.

The Limited was approaching on the tangent just ahead, at full speed and with its whistle blowing madly. Rain-No-More pulled up his pony in the middle of the track and faced the oncoming train, waving the crimson towel above his head, from which two raven feathers hung.

"Good Christ," said the engineer, jamming back the lever, "that Indian's gone loco."

The fireman did what he could with the brakes, then shut his eyes. Sparks flew from the brake shoes, the spinning car-wheels locked and skidded, passengers shrieked and held fast to whatever they could grab, a scent like burning brimstone filled the air. Rain-No-More's pony, bewildered and trembling, stood flat-footed as if charmed by the onrushing engine snorting smoke and fire, and as the young Blackfeet sat there, waving, the old tribal warwhoop issued shrilly from his throat.

Force! Violence! Momentum! Warcries, battles, deaths, injustices seemed rolled into one in the hurtling mass before him. For an instant his mind flickered. Should he spur his horse forward and dash himself against the speeding monster, symbol of the white race advancing roughshod over his ancestral plains? All men who live their life boldly have a lurking hunger for death. They taste, in tense moments, the urge to challenge the infinite, to cease to exist, "not with a whimper but a bang." But just in time to feel the hot breath of the engine rush past, Rain-No-More dug his heel into the pony's side and the beast, from habit, sidestepped quickly.

One hundred yards beyond, the Limited came to a stop, and indignant officials and passengers began streaking down the tracks.

"Get that damned Indian," the conductor yelled, and some of the passengers reached down to the roadbed for sticks and stones. Rain-No-More scornfully held his ground.

"If you will look around the next curve, you will perhaps be ready to apologize," he said to the conductor in English.

One of the brakemen had had the presence of mind to run ahead of where the Limited was standing, and before the conductor could say another word he saw the man signaling madly. The crowd forgot its murderous intent and streamed in the other direction, and it was not long before the conductor came back, shamefacedly, and stuck out his hand.

"Much obliged," he said. "I spoke out of turn."

"Quite all right," said Rain-No-More, not haughtily but with dignity.

One of the passengers was going from car to car, hat in hand, and bills were showered in, ranging mostly from five to twenty dollars. As Rain-No-More was about to ride toward the medicine lodge to report what had happened, the big genial man in blue serge, pockets bulging with money, came up to him.

"We've made up a little pot for you," the passenger said. "You sure saved us from a smash-up."

"You are trespassing on my tribesmen's land," the Indian said, "and furthermore, we of the Blackfeet have no need for gold except for squaws' ornaments, of which we have plenty just now. I appreciate your gesture, having lived among the whites long enough to understand a few of their foolish ways. But there will come a day when these long steel tracks will be as far back in the memory of man as" (he pointed to a distant cliff) "that last flow of lava. The plains will remain, and, let us hope, will have reverted to their natural usage. Sir, good day."

20

A Field for Missionary Work

IT HAD DAWNED ON HUGO WEISS, who was by no means a self-centered person, that his host, Jim Leonard, was embarrassed in his presence. So with his characteristic directness, the financier resolved to get at the root of the trouble and, even if it took his whole force of engineers and experts to do it, to find a solution. His first step was to consult Evans, whom he found closeted with Tom Jackson. They had done justice to a hearty meal. Although the multimillionaire employed thousands of men in all sorts of capacities, he was careful to select those who could toss off a good repast at any hour of the day or night without squawking about their energy or their innards. To be useful in large affairs, a man should have vitality to spare and be willing to use it prodigally, he had always contended.

Before Weiss had a chance to submit his problem to Homer, Tom Jackson told him about the furor his disappearance was causing back East, and on several continents.

"Ah, boys will be boys," the financier said, and sighed good-naturedly. "They've beared the market, to make a clean-up when I reappear. A transparent maneuver, it would seem, but it always works. You know, I explain to my assistants how difficult it is to struggle along with such a colossal fortune. I make them understand that I want to spend, not save, get rid of my surplus assets, not accumulate more. But the moment they get excited, some baleful instinct gets the best of them and the first thing I know they

have engineered some deal that brings in millions and are patheti-
cally expectant of praise. However, give me the details, in round
figures if you can. No use kicking against the pricks, as the Talmud says, or is it the New Testament?"

Now Jackson, after working on the Paris *Herald* and other cautious sheets, had spread himself when told by Weiss to spare no
expense to make the *X-Ray* a model paper. Tom had subscribed to
the A.P., the U.P., the I.N.S., in fact, all news services, syndicates
and picture services worthy the name, and quite a few that were
not. He dumped on the table a gunnysack of clippings he had collected on the Weiss disappearance and the ensuing panic, and succinctly summarized their contents.

"By Jove," said the multi-millionaire, "I have it! Just the thing!"

Like many busy men, with huge deals buzzing constantly in
their heads, he made the mistake of assuming, now and then, that
his thoughts were audible to all whom they might concern. Evans
smiled and asked him to elucidate.

"I know Jim Leonard has that fifty thousand dollars on his
mind, and is worrying for fear it will be lost and that he won't be
able to pay it back. Also the running expenses of this adventure,
which I wouldn't swap for all my bank accounts combined, are troubling him. Now is the chance for him to make a clean-up. I'll buy
his cattle on the hoof. As a matter of fact, I can get a huge discount
in shipping them to Omaha. Leonard can take the money—I'll give
him a check today—and buy Jar and Bottle stock, and a few other
choice securities in the open market. The brokers are breaking their
necks, and incidentally their clients, trying to sell them.

"When I go back to New York, although I swear I shall stay only
a few days, Leonard can dump his stocks at a colossal profit, re-
stock this range with the best cattle in the land, buy out Gilligan,
if the sheepman's had enough by that time, and have a surplus left
to foot the bills for this whole affair, and to go into partnership
with me, dollar for dollar, in a scheme to keep this country what it
should be. No roads, no fences, not a sheep within five hundred
miles. No farms, no irrigation, no sugar beets, no certified public
accountants, no churches and damn few schools. We'll insulate the

whole valley against radio, breed buffalo on the reservation. We'll wangle a deal so Shot-on-Both-Sides and Rain-No-More can own every foot of the ground they walk on, and tell the politicians to go to blazes."

"Capital!" said Evans. "I'll bring Jim in here and see if we can make the plan clear to him."

"And to think I sweat my knockers off for seven hundred francs ($11.00 plus or minus) a week, years on end," said Jackson.

"Don't be ashamed of honest work, my boy," said Weiss.

"Who said anything about that?" asked Jackson.

By the time Evans got back, with the rancher in tow, Hugo Weiss was striding back and forth, hands clasped behind him, while plans for and visions of an isolated empire, secure from the follies of the machine age, raced through his head. After long silences, during which he would be dictating imaginary letters to absent secretaries, he would slap his knee and shout "Yours truly" aloud. Again he would submit details for Tom Jackson's approval. Jim Leonard, when he came in, was ill at ease. And as point after point was unfolded of the financial manipulation by which he was to get rich, his perturbation did not diminish. Selling his cattle for cash, he could understand, although he was indignant to learn how easy it was for influential bankers to get low rates from the railroad. It seemed that years before he had bought a block of stock in a mine called Old Glory, and that the securities, neatly printed in two colors, had finally been used to paper a privy which long since had been blown down by the wind. Besides, Jim suspected that Weiss had no use for the shorthorns he offered to purchase, and was merely piling up favors.

"Are you in the meat-packing business?" the rancher asked the magnate.

"I'm in practically every business within the law, and a few on the borderline," Weiss said.

"But these stocks you want me to buy are going down, according to the paper," said the rancher.

"Precisely. That's the time to buy, when others are selling cheap," Weiss said. "You can get the stocks on margin, so you won't have to put up more than ten per cent of the cash. That will jack up the profits about nine hundred percent."

In the end, it took Miriam to persuade her father to place himself in the banker's hands, and Evans added his endorsement of the scheme.

"Let's see," said Weiss, reaching for his checkbook and fountain pen. "You've got about ten thousand head, and the price will be about $35 apiece. That's $350,000. With that you can buy $3,500,000 worth of stock. We can figure, conservatively, on a fifteen percent rise, when I show up on the street again. With what the Government takes for taxes and the brokerage fees deducted you can count on a profit of $450,000, maybe half a million. Besides, we can probably get Gilligan to sell the same stocks short, so he'll lose about as much as you make. You see, Jim, on Wall Street we get them coming and going."

Jim Leonard seldom drank before sundown, unless he was in town, but at the mention of $450,000 he reached for the Old Crow and drank a third of the bottle without coming up for air.

"Can the other boys get in on this?" he asked, his misgivings lulled by the potent rye.

On being answered in the affirmative, he went downstairs and clanged the triangle and soon the cowpunchers were lined up at the kitchen table, wages in hand, buying Jar and Bottle stock on margin while they mused regretfully on the neglected bars and honkytonks of Glendive, Billings, Butte and Minneapolis. Hank, whose stake was about $180, when promised a windfall of $15,000, started filling out long order blanks to be dispatched to Sears, Roebuck and Montgomery Ward, the largest item being a silver-studded saddle in the style of the famous Santa Fe and $500 worth each of cotton and woolen socks, so he never would have to do any more laundry. Wing Lee, when approached on the matter, started running full speed across the flat, so distractedly that he bumped plumb into an unbroken broncho and was lifted ten feet into the air. Madame Toudoux, with true French conservatism, sunk her sizeable pile in Singer Sewing Machine Common, that being the

only stock in the list that she had heard of before. The orgy of specu-
lation continued throughout the afternoon, so that the wires were
hot between Three Buttes and Glendive, from which point the orders
were relayed to Chicago and New York in a secret code that so mis-
led the station agent, who was also the only telegraph operator,
that he informed Gilligan that Weiss was dumping his holdings
and caused the sheepman and his political allies to dig up all the
cash they could and sell short.

"Daughter," said Jim Leonard gravely to Miriam, "if this deal
don't pan out, I'm done for."

"Go on with you," said Miriam, patting his shoulder. "I can still
give music lessons and support you."

The rancher sighed and shook his head.

WHILE IN OPERA LODGE the company was busy making fortunes on
paper, other and starker problems confronted the scattered members of the Muddy Creek detachment. Hydrangea and Zach were
being carried by their stubborn bronchos farther and farther into
the flats of North Dakota, a dreary stretch of country that had
tempted no homesteader or rancher in all the years it could have
been had for the asking. Sage and a low-growing thorny cactus were
the only vegetation; what little water there was was alkaline and
bitter; and nothing flourished but prairie dogs, coyotes and curlews. The horses had got tired of running and were grazing as best
they could, heading toward their home range which was several
hundred miles eastward. When the bronchos got near enough to
one another, Zach tried to think of some comforting words to say
to his desolate companion in misfortune, but twilight fell before
any suitable phrases came to his mind. His legs had been rubbed
raw and the sharp backbone of his mount was slowly splitting him
in two, he believed, and his flair for logic forced him to conclude,
that something similar, though not identical, was happening to
Hydrangea, although he was delicate enough not to mention it.

Eventually, the broncho on which Zach was tied, facing rear-
ward, got fed up with carrying his burden and lay down on his side,

with the intention of rolling. Zach, one leg pinned, found that his wrists, tightly bound, were near a rock with sharp flinty edges, and by working frantically the pickpocket was able to sever the buckskin thongs and free himself. In a moment he untied and lifted down the ex-Blackbird, more dead than alive. The bronchos, who had got used to their riders by that time, approached, ears erect, and sniffing, to inspect them now that they were afoot. Zach uprooted a sagebrush and chased them away. The bronchos were nearing the horizon and were the only objects worth mentioning in sight, when it occurred to the city-bred dip that he had got himself into the class with Snodgrass, whose famous error, the reader will remember, cost his team the world's series.

On the other side of the distant Missouri, a disconsolate party was stumbling through the foothills, hopelessly lost. The members were Sergeants Schlumberger and Bonnet, Corrigan the chef, the waiters, Cromwell and Washington, and the gangsters known as Bird's-eye Cohen and Paperhanger Stuntz. The two last-named had been, in a manner of speaking, hoist by their own petard. Acting on instructions from Baldy Santo, the thugs had selected a particularly vile stretch of country along the Great Northern tracks and there had stopped the handcar and escorted their prisoners, whose trousers had been confiscated, into the near-by hills. But neither Bird's-eye nor Paperhanger had ever been in the foothills before and had not realized how much alike they were. After abandoning their charges in what they believed was a safe and secluded spot, the gorillas had tried to get back to the railroad, had walked in widening circles in the wrong general direction, and it was not more than an hour before they got back to where they had left the others, who, although bound, fell upon the exhausted gangsters and gave them such a going over with their knees and elbows that they yelled for mercy and, under duress, untied the ropes that bound the sergeants, who immediately tied up the gangsters in turn.

While the gesture gave the Frenchmen some satisfaction, it did not otherwise improve their situation, which was worse than deplorable. All around them were hills, and then hills. They were insufficiently clothed, bruised and wounded, without food or water

and devoid of knowledge as to how to take care of themselves in
the great outdoors. Corrigan, by instinct, had lighted a fire.
Cromwell and Washington, having disarmed Bird's-eye and Paperhanger, were out after game, but the only rabbit they got within
range was blown into so many pieces by the Thompson sub-
machine gun that not even the left hind foot could be retrieved.
Bonnet and Schlumberger were engaged in an ethical argument,
as to whether they would be justified, when worst came to worst,
in slaughtering and eating the gangsters, who, having been in company with so many Italians, could understand a little French and
were deeply shocked.

But no one in Montana or North Dakota was in the state of
agitation that possessed Chief of Detectives Frémont when the
Indian princesses came riding like mad into Trout-tail's camp and
informed the Chief, their father, what they had seen at Muddy
Creek. The thought of Hydrangea at the mercy of a band of criminals for whom the Ten Commandments were mere springboards
caused Frémont to bellow and throw himself about like a bear in a
swarm of hornets.

"Heart of my heart, my dusky queen of all that is soft and gentle,
what suicidal impulse caused me to abandon you in this wilderness?" he said, tearing out his shirttail and great handfuls of hair.
Chief Shot-on-Both-Sides, to whom the spectacle of a Latin in the
throes of grief was an unprecedented experience, concluded that
his guest had nibbled loco weed, and sent a brave on the hotfoot
for a bottle of the white squaw Lydia's remedy, which had proven
helpful in cases involving the accidental swallowing of *cannabis
indica*. When the good Chief learned that Frémont's despair had
been caused by the loss of a squaw, Shot-on-Both-Sides held out
the peace pipe and offered his guest any six women on the reservation, excepting only Tinted Cloud and Unreal Bear who had whispered to their father their yearning for Schlumberger and Bonnet,
respectively. Frémont, however, refused to be comforted, and soon
the war drums were sounding, while the make-up men were splash-
ing war paint on all comers, and knives, war clubs and old-fashioned Springfield rifles were being passed out in the ordnance tent.

Dr. Hyacinthe Toudoux was conferring with Trout-tail III about first-aid precautions and making rapid notes concerning the salves, antiseptics and counter-irritants the medicine man brewed from simple roots and herbs. Single file, with Shot-on-Both-Sides in the lead and Frémont a close second, the Blackfeet and their guests lit out on the warpath and had not covered many miles before they were met by Rain-No-More, who saluted his father in the Indian fashion and made his terse report.

Shot-on-Both-Sides held up his hand, the column halted and dismounted while the Chief held a council of war with his son, the medicine man and, as a matter of courtesy, the visiting reserve officers of the army of France.

"The Great Lakes palefaces have their camp in Mondak, two days' journey away, and with their handcars will reach it in less than four hours. They are intrenched and armed and number only nine," the Chief said.

"Excuse me, *mon general*, I think there are only six effectives," said Dr. Toudoux. "Your son informs me that three were wounded by my countrymen, Schlumberger and Bonnet."

"The difference between six and nine, having in mind the un-sportsmanlike weapons now employed, is negligible," said Shot-on-Both-Sides. "I have never seen a machine gun in action, but from what my son tells me, it is among the more dastardly inventions of the whites, its only virtue being that it aids them in self-destruction. We must rely on cunning, and conserve the lives of our men, who, since they would throw themselves from the highest cliff if I asked them to, are worthy of intelligent direction. My opinion is that we should detail six braves to search for the black squaw and the *sok ko ma pe a ke kooin* (man-woman) who was sent away with her. The rest of us should ride until midnight, camp in the brush by the river, and plan to reach enemy territory at dusk tomorrow. The Great Lakes warriors, having stolen a load of fire-water, are likely to be drunk and possibly may prove to be easy prey. Their Chief, I have been told, does not drink, and to him shall be sent by messenger a snakeskin stuffed with arrows and a note informing him that we have his son."

Rain-No-More rose respectfully and asked permission to speak. "*E poo yeat*," said the Chief.

"*Eeeeee*" (thank you), Rain-No-More began. "I wished to remind the commander of the paleface taboo on blackmail," he said.

"As I understand it," replied the Chief, "the Great Lakes palefaces are in no position to apply for help to officers of the Great White Father, since the latter would promptly throw them into jail and apply the ordeal of the prickly heated throne."

Rain-No-More bowed. "You have spoken wisely, my father," he said. "Am I to instruct the men to refrain from scalping?"

"I beg of you, no," cried Frémont, jigging frantically and tearing his hair.

FAR TO THE SOUTH, well hidden in a crevice between ledges of lava were Tony Santo and his pal, Terry Gilligan, munching sulkily on a piece of raw gopher meat from which the fur had been partly removed. Near them squatted the Blackfeet braves who, as soon as night fell, would force them to continue their long trek into the badlands. The city shoes, of the famous brand of Oxfords that was to figure so prominently in the Cottoncreek murder trial, had been torn to shreds by sharp stones and spiny cactus and had been replaced by moccasins dyed black with the juice of meadowsweet. The resourceful Indians had found a way to induce their captives to march without resistance. They had simply slipped the noose of a lariat over the neck of each youth and attached the free end to the tail of the pintos on which the Indians were mounted. If the captives lagged or pulled back, the noose tightened and choked them into docility.

In the beginning, the two young men had tried to bluster and threaten, until their softer areas were dotted with scars from the medicine sticks equipped with rat-tail files. Just recently it had dawned on them that they were really up against a proposition that a mere telegram or cable to their doting fathers would not resolve. The fact that they had tried to bribe their escorts had resulted in their having been put on a diet of gopher, instead of toasted grouse and pemmican which was the Indian's fare.

"Zipper your trap," young Santo had cautioned Terry Gilligan, when he saw the stern expression pass over the faces of the braves at the suggestion that they should betray their Chief's confidence. "These mugs are untouchables."

"Come off it," said Terry. "The bozo doesn't walk who hasn't got his price."

"You don't get the drift," young Santo said. "These dopes don't go for the spondoolix. They don't even savvy what money is."

"Then we'll have to teach the dumb clucks," said young Gilligan.

21

Of Love and War, with Time Out for Victuals, Such as Could Be Had

IT MUST NOT BE THOUGHT that the financial transactions which took place at Opera Lodge interfered with preparations for the round-up. That the steers, dogies and calves now belonged to Weiss and not to Jim Leonard made little or no difference to the buckaroos. And the fact that the cowpunchers had been relieved of their money, and that they did not expect to see the color of it again in their lifetime, cleared their minds for action and spurred them on to make a good fresh start. Chuck wagons were loaded and departed, and Hjalmar's herd of two thousand head were feeding near a branding corral just east of Three Buttes. There the irons were heating in the fire, while the Professor and Slipnoose Pete were cutting out from the main bunch the cows with unbranded calves, who were mooing angrily and hooking this way and that as they milled around the corral.

Stenka, flushed and happy, caught a spry brindle calf and held him up, kicking, for Hjalmar to see. She had never read D. H. Lawrence, and neither had Hjalmar, but something struck a spark in their minds and eagerly they stole away.

Miriam, who was roping and cutting out the most obstreperous of the steers with a skill that challenged comparison with the best of the cowboys, had led Evans to the corral to watch the branding and was instructing him in the use of the rope when over the hill dashed a Blackfeet brave, his pony's belly not two feet from the ground, so furious was the pace at which he rode. Some of the wild cattle started running and for a moment all hands were busy preventing a stampede.

The Indian tried to give his urgent message in broken English until informed by Evans that he might use his native tongue.

"I am pleased," the brave said, which was a gem of understatement. "The Chief, Shot-on-Both-Sides wishes me to inform the paleface medicine man, one Evans . . ."

"I am Evans," Homer said.

"Good. The Great Lakes palefaces have attacked the train at Muddy Creek, chased certain of the occupants into the hills, taken others as hostages and prisoners, attempted to destroy the coaches, stolen a load of firewater, and generally comported themselves in a hostile manner. The Blackfeet, with the Chief and his son Rain-No-More in command, are on the march and will camp tonight along the Missouri, fifty paleface miles from Mondak. It would please the Chief if the paleface medicine man, a white squaw known to his people as Bird Cherry, and any braves who may be spared from the round-up, would join the party on the warpath, as it is expedient, in view of possible legal difficulties afterward, to have as many white men as possible involved. Otherwise the agents of the Great White Father will pin everything on the Blackfeet and do us further injustices."

"You have spoken well," said Evans. "Do us the honor to rest here, and eat before returning."

"I will accept a fresh horse, but cannot linger," said the brave, and in a moment was astride an unbroken broncho who was trying to rub him off against the fence of the corral. Within ten minutes, however, the Indian had subdued the animal and soon both were lost to sight.

Hjalmar, returning somewhat self-consciously with Stenka, whose laughter rippled like a pennant on the afternoon breeze, came up to Homer, grinning broadly.

"There's going to be rough stuff. I can feel it in my bones," he said.

"Let me in on it," begged Diluvio, who had succeeded in roping his first steer by the left hind foot and was winding his lariat around the saddle horn enough times to have held the *Ile-de-France* at its

moorings in a stiff offshore gale. Miriam was already off in search
of Jesse, Homer's outlaw roan, and the indefatigable Star.

The afternoon had been a trying one for Beatrice Diluvio, who
was a Baxter of Boston. First of all, Montgomery Ward had neglected to include a certain kind of darning cotton in a shipment
of goods from Chicago. Secondly, she had been depressed by the
spectacle of so many strong silent men being drawn into the stock
market. The Baxters had always stuck to conservative investments
which paid steadily and not too well, and it was only by accident
that the popularity of Moody and Sankey hymn books had put her
grandfather in the class of the vulgarly rich. To top it off, Anton,
her adored young husband, came bursting into the lodge to bid
her good-bye on the ground that it was necessary to give some
warring Indians a hand against a mob of gangsters. But, of course,
blood will tell. Holding back her tears, Beatrice smiled bravely,
soft-pedaled her sex appeal, and waved her handkerchief from the
kitchen porch as the combatants rode away. Afterward, to regain
the traditional Baxter composure, that in its best days had frosted
many a violet window pane on a bright sunny day of spring or summer, Beatrice put on high hob-nailed boots, as a precaution against
the rattlers, and took a walk alone.

"I should rejoice in my heart," she said to herself, "that I married a man, as well as the best interpreter of Vivaldi and Vieux-
temps who ever chinned a Guarnerius. Nevertheless, time is fleeting and I lost so much of it before I got properly started that each
moment is precious to me now."

Her steps, *marcato ma non troppo*, had brought her to the point
on the flower-dotted slope at which the last severe gale had left
the ruins of the former privy, in the lee of which lurked several
tumbleweeds. Inside the battered structure, Beatrice caught a flash
of red, white and blue, and peering through a knothole she saw
that the stock certificates of Old Glory Mining Company, of Red
Dog, Montana, were still intact, although faded. At once her mind
formed a plan. She was afraid, not understanding business, that
Weiss's scheme for the enrichment of Jim Leonard might flop, so
she worked out a conservative campaign of her own. The living

room was deserted when she returned to the house, her cheeks glowing from the exertion. Quickly she snatched the telephone and within ten minutes was talking with her old family lawyer, Fitz-Henry Fish, of Fish, Fish, Cabot and Saltonstall. It is to the credit of that smooth and experienced barrister that, while listening to Beatrice's instructions, he did not even blink.

"No trouble at all, my dear Beatrice," he said, for the Fishes and Baxters had been intimate before the Revolution.* "You wish, as I understand it, to have one of our young men inspect the premises of the Old Glory Mining Company, if any, at Red Dog, Montana."

"I want to find out if there is gold there, and, if so, in what quantities. In case there is little or none, I wish to have shipped, immediately, by truck, enough pay dirt to send Old Glory stock well up above par. This must be done discreetly, needless to say. Meanwhile, I want your office to buy up and send me by mail every bit of Old Glory stock that can be found. Never mind the expense, and don't trouble me with details."

"You wouldn't care to have me consult my partners as to the— er—advisability of this project?" suggested the cautious Fish.

"— your partners," exclaimed the precise Beatrice.

This alternative for the partners, amazed the former Miss Baxter as much or more than it did Attorney Fish, and also the partners when they were told, over a bottle of very decent port, at the Union Club that evening. In fact, the partners' guffaws brought about the resignation of six of the older members, one of whom was startled so severely by the sound of laughter that he had his second stroke right then and there. That the reader may not be left entirely in the dark, it may be said that the verb, used in the imperative form, contains six letters and was applied by Panurge to Herr Trippa, the astrologer, when the latter swore by all the stars that Panurge would be cuckolded in every style.

AT DUSK, A FLEET OF HANDCARS rolled into the railroad yards at Mondak, with Baldy Santo and what remained of his gang aboard.

---

* American, 1776-1781.

They had waited as long as possible for the return of Bird's-eye and the Paperhanger, but the condition of their three wounded men made it necessary to go on without the missing pair. Of the nine who had started out that day, only four were in commission, and the agitation of Baldy, the big shot, was more acute than ever, since no trace had been found of his son. Baldy knew that, however poignant his grief, the gang would have to make a night of it, so he instructed his men to take the liquor over to the local hookshop by the tracks, an establishment run by a huge fat blonde named Mona Mason and known from Frisco to Minneapolis as a none-too-strict disciplinarian. Mona's motto, in fact, was "Let's go."

"Tell Mona to lock up the joint," Baldy said, then hurried to the depot and ducked into a telephone booth. The connection with Cicero, Illinois, was established after a fusillade of assorted gong noises as coins dropped in all three slots. The gang leader got in touch with his lieutenant and ordered him to send out to Mondak every gangster he could find.

"I can use dozens, hundreds," Baldy said. "And tell 'em for cripes' sake to bring good strong boots, the kind with nails in the soles."

"I know. You want to massage a lot of wrongos' pusses," the lieutenant said.

"They'll need 'em for walking, but don't tell 'em that or they won't come," said Baldy. "They don't have taxis out here."

"I know. Covered wagons," said the lieutenant, and Baldy, disgusted, hung up the receiver.

HOMER EVANS, ON THE SPIRITED JESSE, glanced behind him as the ranch house was lost to sight and saw Moritz the dog, game but desperate, trotting patiently in the wake of the party. Reining up his roan, he stroked the horse's muzzle and spoke a few reassuring words. Then, to Miriam's astonishment, he lifted the panting Boxer to the saddle and mounted, with Moritz slung like a meal sack in front of him. The roan, a few short weeks ago an outlaw, stood up on his hind legs and Moritz, his frown deepening, glanced at Evans to see if he should jump down.

"Steady, Jesse. We've got work to do," said Homer, and the rangy roan stopped dancing on his hind legs and trotted complaisantly on.

Hjalmar was astride a huge gray named Legs, a wise old cow horse that did much to overcome his rider's reluctance to head right into the wind and make sweeping turns to avoid snapping off a rudder. Diluvio had a bald-faced bay and passed the time along the way trying to figure out how multiple hoof-beats should properly be orchestrated, if ever they should be orchestrated at all. He decided that he preferred the subtler treatment of Chopin, in the E-minor Concerto, final movement, which evokes the charging of cavalry, in defense of whatever cavalrymen hold most dear. Lvov Kvek and Grigori Lidin, their handsome Slavic faces alight with joy, rode their bronchos like clean-shaven centaurs and rejoiced at having been born. For the sabers they had ordered had arrived at the ranch that very day, in the shipment of goods that had proved disappointing to Beatrice Baxter, and many a new-blown lupine or gay tiger lily lost its head as the Russians swept along.

At Muddy Creek, which they reached in record time, Evans asked the others to ride on down the Missouri to the Indian camp, which they should not try to find until some brave appeared to escort them. Giving Jesse and Star to the Russians to lead, Homer entered the deserted special coaches, with Miriam and Moritz.

"We'll work on foot," said Homer, "and join you later at the camp."

In the Melisande, Evans found Hydrangea's colorful wardrobe and Zach's daintily perfumed clothes and gave Moritz a noseful of each. The Boxer, understanding he had a real job to perform, let out one short bark of glee and then got down to business in no uncertain way. But try as he could, the dog could find no scent to follow. He circled the coaches and nearly tore up the surface of the entire vicinity, sniffing here and there.

"No dice," said Evans. "Quite naturally, since they were on horseback."

In the shed, where the horses had been kept, there were many hoofprints and each of them was indicated to Moritz by Evans. The

Boxer caught on. He was to follow a horse, but which one? Evans, meanwhile, had entered one of his frightening phases of concentration so intensely that Miriam felt a chill in the air. If the Indian girls departed first, Homer reasoned, they would have chosen the fleetest mounts. The least promising would have been left for Hydrangea and Zach. Prone on the damp ground, Homer studied the hoofprints until he found one less steady and firm than the rest.

"Moritz, old boy. That's our horse," he said. And the Boxer sniffed and nodded. From that moment on, the progress was swift and sure. In the darkness they stumbled across the flats, keeping Moritz within hailing distance. Head low, nostrils spread, the dog trotted on and on, his large front paws placed carefully, his body swaying like that of a sailor on a rolling deck. But when he reached the point where Zach had freed himself, and smelled the, for him, somewhat over-laden fragrance of Molyneux No. 5, the dog pranced and cavorted with joy. Running back to join Evans and Miriam, the Boxer barked and wagged his stump of a tail, not twice, as was his custom, but time and time again.

Evans, following Moritz to the spot, found an uprooted sagebrush and a severed buckskin thong, then others that had been untied.

"Thank God they're safe," said Homer. "It's a miracle they didn't slip under the horses' bellies, to be kicked and dragged to death."

Suddenly Moritz bristled and growled. When Homer started onward, the Boxer took hold gently of his left trousers leg to detain him.

"What the devil?" muttered Homer, but he took heed of the warning. A second later, Moritz stiffened and hurled himself at a clump of sagebrush from which began to issue amazing grunts and yells. "Good God. An Indian," said Evans, and spoke firmly to Moritz to call him off his victim. The six Blackfeet braves, in full warpaint, who had been detailed to search for Hydrangea and the *sok ko ma pe a ke kooin* (concerning whom the Indians had a strong curiosity, never having seen a white one) had tracked the bronchos in a more laborious fashion and, upon hearing the approach of Evans and Miriam, had hidden to find out what was afoot.

The brave who had been bitten by Moritz was lost in admiration of the dog's tracking achievement and was most magnanimous. "The thinking dog, I am afraid," the brave said to Homer, "has smeared himself in line of duty with some of my paint. The red and black are both known to be harmless to animals, but the white is bad for them."

"Ah, yes. Zinc oxide, no doubt," Evans said, and carefully he scrubbed the white from Moritz's shoulder.

With Moritz in the lead, followed closely by the admiring Indians, the joint expedition was able to find without delay an old buffalo wallow. In the center of the slight depression Zach was sitting, shivering, while Hydrangea, too tired to care what happened, was sleeping near by. The Indians got out of sight, a maneuver they could accomplish as swiftly as Houdini, feeling instinctively that the sight of them, all red, black and white, bedecked with feathers and carrying weapons in both hands, might disconcert a colored girl awakening on the lone prairie.

Miriam spoke softly and Hydrangea opened her eyes.

"Oh, my God, another woman," sighed Zach, with resignation, but soon he discerned the figure of Homer Evans and was wild with relief and delight. "I knew you wouldn't leave us to perish in this awful place. I just knew it," the pickpocket said. "And I'm seldom wrong in sizing up men."

"We have six Indians with us," said Homer.

"The darlings," said Zach.

The Indians, who although invisible were watching Zach slyly, came out of their hiding places.

"Ugh," they said, in unison.

"I learned to 'Ugh' myself, when I was in the chorus and we did an Indian number. But we were taught to do it twice," Zach said. "No doubt we were wrong." It was his nature to be carefree. So the moment the others had arrived to take the responsibility from his shoulders he forgot his ordeal just past and all fears of the future.

THE READER NOW WILL BE WHISKED across the fiats and the raging Missouri to the foothills in which were wandering Sergeants Bonnet

and Schlumberger, the chef Corrigan, Waiters Cromwell and Washington, and their prisoners, Bird's-eye Cohen and Paperhanger
Stuntz. Were the reader more familiar with the country in question, he would be grateful to the author for affording him that literary method of transportation, for to cross that stretch of scenery by any other means than being whisked is not an act one would
care to contemplate.

The neighborhood coyotes were vociferous that night, having
filled the wrinkles in their bellies since the thaw, and it is a toss-
up among naturalists to decide whether the coyote sings more lustily from hunger or satisfaction, when the moon is bright or when
there is no moon at all. The waiters, Cromwell and Washington,
were by far the most sensitive to sound of any members of the party
and were just getting used to the wailing when they caught sight of
several pairs of gleaming eyes, green or amber in color, which
flashed on and off in a circle around the dying campfire. At last
Cromwell could stand the sight no longer and cut loose for the second time that day with the Thompson sub-machine gun. That time
he had better luck, for he bagged seven of the astonished coyotes
before the other twenty-five could lope away.

"At least, we shall have meat in plenty," said the mercurial
Bonnet, who had earned the name "White Lightning" from the Indian squaws. "How unlucky that we did not bring along at least
one bottle of Pinard," said Schlumberger, who was inclined to take
the darker view of things.

The coyotes were plump and meaty, although when stripped of
their fur did not look much larger than Belgian hares. The meat
was much stronger, however, and would have been improved by a
dash of salt and pepper, or practically anything known to man. The
French sergeants, by using buffalo bones tipped with bits of flint
had improvised fairly creditable medicine sticks, and when their
own hunger had been outraged if not sated by a mouthful or two of
roast coyote, they took partial revenge on the protesting gangsters
by making them swallow half a coyote apiece. Just before he was
about to collapse from thirst, Schlumberger remembered that in
certain sheltered spots a little snow remained and proceeded to

melt some in his mouth and swallow it, while Bonnet protested that the icy liquid would chill his stomach and cause fatal cramps. Schlumberger contended that the cramps were caused by the meat, not the water. The argument became general, but no one could be sure.

Washington, who wore glasses and was the intellectual among the attendants of the special train, had read a few Westerns in his day, before he took up philosophy, and seemed to remember that beds were made up, always with the loftiest of purposes, of evergreen boughs, interlaced in a manner he could not recall to mind. The nearest evergreen was about as far away from the foothills of the Rockies as Buffalo is from Times Square, excepting only a few balsams imported by Myra Patterson of Glendive in an effort to beautify her expensive new yard. Washington, not to be daunted, tried interlacing sagebrush and found the result distinctly disappointing. Finally he fell back on the bare damp ground.

A smooth chunk of lava rock was his pillow. The Frenchmen elected to sleep sitting up, back to back, as they had in the Battle of the Marne, only on the Marne they had slept much more soundly, because in the army they had had horizon blue pants while at the moment they had no breeches whatsoever. Corrigan stayed awake to prevent the gangsters from doing anything except cursing, which they did without cease until dawn, expressing the Irish chef's sentiments so eloquently that for once he was silent with admiration.

THE OUT-OF-DOORS SCENE just described contrasted vividly with what was taking place in Mona Mason's joint on the outskirts of Mondak. There the Santo gang were getting a start on what promised to be a red-letter evening. The doors of the hookshop had been barred, to discourage wayfarers from horning in on the party. Beer, whiskey and champagne were cooling on huge chunks of ice commandeered from the local ice-plant. Into the dance hall and reception room on the ground floor had been wheeled a huge four-poster bed from the alcove in which the madam usually slept, and in it had been installed the three wounded gangsters whose groans had diminished, then ceased, as the stolen liquor got in its merciful work. The capacious umbrella stand had been pressed into service as a gaboon and stood near by.

All three of the hookers were showing their stamina, dancing without respite with all comers, and rushing up and down stairs, as the exigencies of the occasion seemed to demand, their weariness, if any, concealed by vivid make-up, and their costumes, involving short skirts, corsets and old-fashioned long black stockings adding color to the scene. Their working names were, respectively, Rose, Violet and Lil. The madam was pouring and serving what were known as snake's drinks, so named because of their popularity with railroad switchmen. They consisted of a hefty slug of whiskey with a chaser of bottled beer. The "grape," as the champagne was called, was to be opened later, after all hands had laid a good foundation.

At the piano the professor, a battered but unbowed old rake with gray hair cut long behind, had in his day been capable of an Invitation to the Waltz that could not be beat in Omaha or Pocatello. But just then he was playing and singing, in a voice that gave testimony of a dissolute life, the following song, the first stanza of which takes the interrogatory form, with a Shakespearean connotation:

> "What did Rome-ee-oh-oh do to Jew-lee-ett
> When he climbed her balconee?"

Tastes differ tremendously, as the reader well knows. Some men collect orange wrappers or postage stamps, others twitter with glee at the sight of their first sweet pea breaking through the loam; golf, tennis and even Parchesi have their amateurs; there are wags who pinch plump neighbors in crowded subways. Proust has his readers, but then, so has Gertrude Atherton. Their name is legion who dote on comic strips, strip teases or teas for two with clothes and cocktails. Therefore, since Baldy's gangsters are snug and comfortable, not to say relaxed and content, let us leave them where they are for the present and peep through the brush fifty miles north, on the banks of the Missouri, where Chief Shot-on-Both-Sides and

his Blackfeet braves, reinforced by Frémont, Dr. Hyacinthe Toudoux, Kvek and Lidin, Hjalmar and Diluvio, are encamped for the
night.

Since the Indians were not being followed, they were able to
do themselves rather well. While the braves were polishing up their
equipment and getting their paint and feathers in shape for inspection, some squaws who had followed the main body of troops
found a clearing among the cottonwood trees, well screened from
above by wild grapevines, and difficult of approach by skulking
enemies. There a fire had been built and reduced to glowing embers and a meal was being prepared. There was venison, both fresh
roasted and smoked; grouse with checkerberries; store ham from
the Great Lakes region; and the *pièce de resistance*, the tribal sausage made by stuffing bear entrails, ritually cleaned and purified,
with chopped loin meat of the elk and white-tail deer. The braves
not on sentry duty ate their portions in silence, and as the night
sky deepened and the stars took their places one by one until the
constellations were at full war strength, the squaws ate what was
left, or as much as they could of it, and cleared the circle for the
evening of music and tale-telling that was to follow. Modestly the
princesses Tinted Cloud and Unreal Bear, concealing stoically their
anxiety about the French sergeants who had fallen into enemy
hands, directed the women's labors and accomplished their full
share.

"Since intrepid Frenchmen, whose names, dash it all, I must
remember to jot down, were the first Christians to explore this
noble country, I shall use all my influence to have these *Pieds Noirs*,
or Blackfeet, represented in our next Colonial Exposition in Paris,"
said Dr. Hyacinthe Toudoux.

Frémont could only keep from yammering by chewing hard on
a tree. "Merciful darkness and darker fate that cloak what is happening to my still darker Hydrangea," implored the stricken officer. "Descend also on my fevered brain. The immortal Hamlet was
not clear as to 'whether 'tis nobler in the mind to suffer the slings
and arrows of outrageous fortune' or to seek the final oblivion. He
had to deal with Danes, not Italians, and had lost, not my ebony

jewel of Harlem, but a pale neurotic aristocrat who could easily be replaced in any Department of France."

"Take heart," said Dr. Toudoux. "Remember that Monsieur Evans is looking after our interests."

At that Frémont began rocking from side to side and grinding his teeth together, having swallowed a mouthful of bark.

"Spare me, countryman," he begged. "A private detective, admittedly the best, nine times out of ten can only uncover the revolting details after disaster has happened. Better to be torn by uncertainty . . ."

"Peace, *neats ap pe kooin an ye sit*" (sorrowing Frenchman), said Chief-Shot-on-Both-Sides. "If this squaw of squaws should by chance return, and find out what she means to you, she might lead you such a life that the present moment will seem ecstatic in retrospect. Alas, I am old, I have lived and I know."

The old Chief rose and made a sign with his medicine stick and from their stations behind trees, the drummers and musicians stepped out, squatted in a circle and the soft insistent beat began rolling around from one to the other, in a clockwise direction, while brave after brave, in turn, performed a dance descriptive of what he intended to do when he caught up with the Great Lakes palefaces whose record had been such that they could not lean on the Great White Father for protection. It was an opportunity every young Blackfeet had longed for since childhood and that his parents had desired before him. Toudoux was fascinated and spellbound, and even Frémont was moved to the point where he sprang into the circle himself and cut a rigadoon until exhaustion overcame him. At last, the Chief held up his hand, the drummers toned down to a whispering pianissimo, and Shot-on-Both-Sides addressed first his visitors and then his tribesmen who hung on his words.

"Reserve officers of the *ni oks kum neats ap pe* (Third Republic) and gentlemen," he said. "I know you are loyal. I know you are courageous. Your dancing has testified to your enthusiasm for our cause, which is just and humane. What I wish to say to you is no reflection on your strength of heart and sinew. Hear me well.

"It is true that our enemy numbers less than a dozen, with possibly only four effectives. But warfare changes like the plains our tribal legends tell us were once the bottom of the great blue water, again were covered with forests two hundred feet high, were deep in muck, with monsters whose bones, indeed, may be viewed in our tribal museum. The palefaces, with apologies to the fortunate exceptions who are our guests and who must not take offense, were once a mighty race, but their power has dwindled, so that the general run of them are puny and have little resistance. The majority of them cannot find their own food or build their own fires. Their blankets are woven by strangers, their medium of exchange controlled by sorcerers beyond the reach of tribal law. As their muscles have shrunk their brains have distended like the livers of over-fed geese, and the intelligence that once brought them light and happiness has been perverted to the uses of destruction and greed. Enough of generalities. Let us consider our immediate and specific problem.

"The Great Lakes palefaces, our enemies, do not go abroad without new and cowardly weapons known variously as typewriters, machine guns or Tommy guns; also exploding missiles called pineapples, and stink bombs so potent that one whiff brings tears to the eyes of the strongest brave. We are to face, tomorrow, not a few evil-faced runts who, quite properly, value their lives at nothing, but an unknown number of the paleface typewriters, each one of which could kill a thousand men or mountain lions in less time than it takes a squaw to shake a blanket. Opposed to those engines of death, we have Springfields we were obliged to steal from a cinema company on location, while a film was being made of those happy days when Northern and Southern palefaces were potting one another in droves, because of a dispute concerning rights of tribes, in the form of federated government originated by the Massachusetts Indians.

"I ask you, every one, to be cautious and not to be led to folly by tribal stories of other conflicts in which your ancestors covered themselves with glory in hand-to-hand combat. First we must find out where the typewriters, or machine guns, are, and must capture and destroy them. I would go in sorrow to my grave were I to see a Blackfeet resort to such a weapon. Then let us settle the issue, man to man. My son, Rain-No-More, has seen machine guns in action, along with fourteen other braves who joined the paleface A.E.F. against my strict orders. Those men will hold a private council and later will instruct each brave what to do.

"*Kyi*."

22

A Clean Sweep of a Semi-Public Establishment

IN THE DESOLATE CORNER of Northwest North Dakota where Hydrangea and Galilee Zach had been found, the Blackfeet braves made swift preparations for the journey to the expeditionary camp. The superficial wounds of the brave who had been attacked by Moritz were rubbed with the juice of false dandelion, while the Boxer, aware that he had pulled a boner, watched penitently.

"Smile, beast with brains," the brave said cheerfully. "It is not against those with whom we have fought that the Blackfeet hold grudges."

Poles were cut from a scrub cottonwood by the wayside, and Hydrangea, protesting coyly, was slung beneath one by means of buckskin bands and was carried by two braves in single file. Zach, nothing loath, was transported in a similar way. The braves knew a trail across country that would save them many miles, and just before midnight the party, led by Homer and Miriam, approached the campfire by the Missouri.

"Who goes there?" asked a Blackfeet sentry, who had served with the 116th Engineers in the Argonne.

"A party of friends," replied Evans.

"Advance, friends, and give the countersign," the sentry said.

"*Sam it okh si u*" (Good hunting), said Homer.

"Pass and hunt," the brave said, giving the eye to Zach and Hydrangea who were being unslung at the time.

The reunion between Frémont and his sweetheart was so touching that the officer of the day caused the couple to be screened off with boughs in order that the braves might not be diverted from the business in hand. Miriam, at Homer's suggestion, rolled in with Tinted Cloud and Unreal Bear for a much-needed nap. Moritz busied himself with an elk bone and lapped some melted snow. He had made no complaint, but the pads of his feet were so sore that he had hard work keeping from wincing when he walked. Knowing that the adventure was not ended, the Boxer, after a bout of painful thinking, made his way to the lodge of Trout-tail III, approached the medicine man and held out a tender front paw, pads upward.

"Brother without words, I've just the thing for you," the medicine man said, highly pleased and flattered. And in a trice he made a salve of powdered ragwort, a little blue clay and a few drops from the white squaw Lydia's indispensable bottle and bandaged each of the dog's feet with cool grape leaves fresh from the overhanging vines. In a moment, the Boxer was stretched on his side, legs extended, snoring happily.

Homer Evans, however, had gone straight to the tepee of Shot-on-Both-Sides. The sentry announced him, then asked him please to enter. Evans stepped inside, saluted and sat in silence a full twelve minutes to collect his thoughts.

"Commander," Homer said, "I am happy to report that we have recovered the colored squaw and the *sok ko ma pe a ke kooin*, who, I may say, has behaved extremely well. The six braves you detailed were on the ground before me and should be given full credit for the rescue."

"I shall notch their coup sticks twice apiece," the Chief said.

"Concerning the attack on the Great Lakes palefaces," Evans continued, "with the Chief's permission, I have a suggestion to make."

"Speak freely," said Shot-on-Both-Sides.

"The men of the tribe of Santo, having stolen much firewater, will gorge and swill this night," said Homer. "The Chief intends to fall upon them this evening, and the way is long. Would it not be better to make a forced march before sunup and surprise them in the early morning, when they will be too drunk for organized resistance?"

"The leader, I understand, does not drink," said Shot-on-Both-Sides.

"For that reason he will be apart from the roisterers, in order to sleep peacefully," Evans said.

"You have spoken well," said the Chief, and arose.

Frémont, now the gayest man in North Dakota, was lost in admiration at the way in which the Blackfeet broke camp and got started on the warpath again. While squaws dismantled tents and folded blankets, braves found their ponies on the picket line. Braves in charge of quarters policed up the ground until no trace was left of the feasting and the council. Rain-No-More, with his A.E.F. veterans close behind him, set the pace, and single file the Indians and their allies stole through the brush and across the open prairie toward Mondak.

"If I could get the dragnet spread in Paris in twice the time it takes these savages to get going, I would merit a page in *Larousse* and the glorious history of France," Frémont said, to Dr. Hyacinthe Toudoux.

"I have planned at least six volumes in praise of their medical service and scientific acumen," said the doctor, taking a firmer grip on his pinto's mane. "We French are too provincial, too self-sufficient."

Kvek and Grigori Lidin, with Hjalmar and Diluvio, were roaring "Night and Day," which so resembled one of the old Algonquian melodies that the braves all along the line were able to join in. Rain-No-More glanced at his father and smiled.

"I shall make them all members of our tribe," the old Chief said.

Aurora, pink-fingered Goddess of the Morning, got an eyeful that April day as she touched the peaks of the badlands and the highest of the buttes. Across the cattle range, converging toward Leonard's ranch house and branding corrals, parti-colored herds were moving slowly, while the cowpunchers on the killpecker shift were nearing the end of their vigil and thinking mostly about chow. From the northwest corner near the reservation, three thousand head were creeping along Cottonwood Creek; the Professor's bunch of three thousand were nearing Three Buttes; two thousand had been collected near Mountain Sheep Bluffs; another two thousand from the Yellowstone side were being sorted and branded with the Lazy J, Leonard's brand.

At Opera Lodge the Chinese cooks were frying bacon and eggs and turning pancakes, which were served by Eugénie Toudoux and Beatrice Baxter, who had insisted on doing what they could in the emergency.

The pitiful sight in the foothills northeast of Bison Creek, when the first rays of the sun awakened the unskillful campers there, caused Aurora to itch beneath her dew-belaundered robes. The forlorn men began to clutch their cramped stomachs and gag at the thought of coyote meat, brush the dirt from their hands to their faces as they rubbed their eyes, and hustle in all directions toward clumps of sagebrush at the command of Nature.

"Perhaps it is fortunate that we have no pants," said Bonnet, one of the keenest sufferers.

"The ways of Providence are inscrutable," grunted Schlumberger from a near-by bush.

"Don't be blasphemous," said Corrigan. "You might bring worse luck to us."

"I doubt if that is possible," the Alsatian said.

Had he seen as much as Aurora was able to observe from her couch of fleecy clouds, the sergeant would not have been so hopeful. For over toward the N.P. tracks and headed toward Glendive a large two-passenger Curtiss biplane of an old but durable model was winging its way at a speed of more than one hundred miles an hour. The plane lost altitude as it approached the town just mentioned, and Cash-and-Carry Corkery, a mercenary flier who had been ruled out of the South American league of warring nations because of unethical conduct toward friend, foe and non-combatants in a dozen different putsches, glanced earthward.

"Well, the country is flat in spots. That's about all you can say for it," he remarked to Bat-ear McCluskey, his mechanic.

"Who'd you say this hick was who's hired us?"

"Gilligan's his monniker," Cash-and-Carry said. "And hereabouts is where he lives."

"He ain't bright, or he'd have picked some other burg, and he never would've hired you," was Bat-ear's contribution.

"He don't live in the burg itself, but out on Big Dry Creek, one hundred and fifty miles northwest by west. His house is the only one in that part of the country, so he said."

"Are we still in the States?" asked Bat-ear.

"That's the kind of money Gilligan hands out," said the pilot.

"I don't see how we can spend it here," the mechanician said.

THE ROSY-FINGERED GODDESS was just about to check out into the Pacific Time zone when Rain-No-More, at the head of the punitive expedition, sighted the rooftops of Mondak and cautioned the braves to pipe down. Chief Shot-on-Both-Sides and Evans held another council of war.

"Do my eyes fail me, or do I see, outside that small building on the edge of the railroad yards, some wooden boxes such as the pale-faces use for ammunition?" asked the Chief. Rain-No-More, whose eyesight was the sharpest, was summoned.

"There are several cases of empty bottles, which have contained several kinds of firewater and the malt fermentation used for chasers," Rain-No-More reported.

"Capital," said Evans. "That building, as you know, is the emergency squaw house, and it is natural that our enemies should choose it for their celebration. With the Chief's permission I will go ahead and reconnoiter."

"Agreed," said the Chief. "The railroad detectives might shoot an Indian, if they saw one, in the hope of getting a raise for vigilance. You are smartly dressed, therefore immune."

"Don't start any rough stuff until we all get there," said Hjalmar.

"Come along," Evans said. "But don't make too much noise."

There were no railroad dicks in the yards that morning, in fact, no one at all, but since the hookshop run by Mona Mason was on a broad flat, with no cover around it except dwarf sagebrush, it was not easy to get near enough to look in through the windows. Hjalmar was stationed behind a box car on a siding, while Evans got down flat on his belly and wormed his way toward the lupanar. The shutters were tightly closed, both doors were locked. But by means of a trellis over the back porch, Homer was able to climb to the second story and pry open a small window which proved to be on the stairway. Warily he listened, but heard no sounds except snoring. Tiptoeing down the stairs he peered into the dimness of the dance hall and saw, amid a litter of bottles and broken glasses, a pair of huge hefty legs in black silk stockings, spread wide in a posture of abandon. Above them he made out an expanse of white skin that would, if converted into leather, have made a binding large enough for the *Revised Laws of Montana*. The top half of the recumbent figure was clad in a Mother Hubbard of flesh-colored cotton on which four-leaf clovers had been printed indiscriminately. Approaching nearer Homer saw that Mona, for it was she, had tipped over backward into the nearly empty woodbox and, because of her ample figure, had got wedged in tightly and thus had fallen fast asleep. In the alcove near by was the professor, on the floor, with his old-fashioned night shirt pulled over his beer-stained working clothes of conventional black. The three wounded gangsters were still in the four-poster bed, also dead to the world.

Upstairs, in the various bedrooms, were the rest of the party, in no better shape than their hostess or their pals. Evans, with a smile of satisfaction, was planning to unlock the front door and rejoin Hjalmar, when a noise behind him caused him to leap aside and place his back to the wall.

"What day is it?" asked a husky Irish voice. It was the cook, Mrs. Keogh, who, from force of long habit, had awakened and was trying to pull herself together as she descended to the kitchen for an eye-opener. She had seen so many faces in Mona's joint, however, that the good woman did not tumble to the fact that Homer was an outsider, and he quickly caught on. Following her downstairs, he closed the kitchen door behind them, and when she turned her back to reach for the bottle he detached a clothesline on which were hanging several damp chemises, and bound and gagged her with all the gentleness the situation would permit.

In a few seconds he was across the flat at Hjalmar's side.

"They've all passed out except the cook, and I tied her up," Homer said to the big Norwegian. "Go back over the hill and bring a dozen braves. If you work quickly you can capture the entire gang and take them to the reservation. Baldy, the leader, as I expected, is not with them. I'll go through the town and try to locate him."

Hjalmar lit out in one direction. Homer started briskly in the other. The latter had not got farther than the depot when he saw the gang leader in the doorway of the former lunch cart not a block away. Baldy, after glancing at the cloudless sky and stretching his arms, slipped on his coat and started walking toward the station.

"The devil," Homer said. He assumed that the gang leader was headed for Mona's, which would interfere with the plans. In order to get out of sight, Evans ducked into the depot. The station agent was fast asleep at the telegraph desk. Cautiously Homer slipped off the man's spectacles and eyeshade, at the same time snatching a small phial of ether from his first-aid kit. He dashed a few drops of the anesthetic on a handkerchief and held it near the operator's nose, then, just as Baldy Santo's steps resounded on the board-walk outside, Homer rolled the agent underneath the desk and sat in his place, clicking dots and dashes with the key.

Instead of passing the window, as Evans had expected he would, Baldy entered the waiting room and went straight for the telephone booth. Evans' mind was working rapidly and he had just about decided to take the hammer and some nails he saw handy and nail the mob chief into the booth when Baldy backed out and approached the office.

"Got any chicken feed?" asked Santo, tossing out a hundred dollar bill.

Evans, an excellent mimic, assumed the voice of a railroad employee. "I can't change the bill," he said. "Why don't you use the comp'ny phone, then pay me some other time?"

When he saw Santo hesitate, he added: "I'm going to the baggage room for a minute, anyway, if you've got something private to say."

"Keep the change," said Santo, tossing over the bill.

"Thanks, brother," Evans said, and left the office.

The phone was on the wall, so that in order to use it Santo had to stand with his back to the desk and did not notice the pair of shod feet sticking out from under. Also, having been in the beer racket so long, he did not smell the ether. He got the operator and asked for Chicago, but once the connection was completed he lowered his voice so that Evans, in the baggage room adjacent, could not hear what he said. The conversation lasted long enough, however, to give Evans time to think of an expedient. As soon as Baldy hung up the receiver, Homer sauntered in, the eyeshade well down on his brow.

"You from back East, brother?" Evans asked.

"What's that to you?" asked Santo suspiciously.

"Oh, nothing, brother. No offense. I was just a little bothered, that's all."

"What's eatin' you?" Baldy asked.

"Well, it's thisaway," drawled Evans. "Some fellas from somewhere back East, Minneapolis maybe, they borrowed the big handcar from the shed. Had been hittin' up the booze, I guess, because three of 'em couldn't stand. They had some hookers with 'em, too."

"Yeh?" said Baldy, now showing keen interest. "What about 'em?"

"Oh, nothing," said Homer. "Only that handcar is charged up to me. I'm responsible, see? I wouldn't a let 'em take it, only they said they just wanted to take a little ride and would bring it right back."

"Which way did they go?" Baldy asked.

"They went east, and on the wrong track, too. And that ain't the worst of it. Just before they got started, mister, one of 'em waved to me and said: 'So long, appleknocker. We're fed up with this God-forsaken country and are heading for home.'"

"The hell you say. How many were there?"

"There were four who could navigate, three others lying down, and three of the girls from Mona's. And they had a case of something they called grape."

"When did they leave?" asked Baldy, whose dark eyes were burning with indignation. "Believe me, friend, I'll fan 'em good when I catch 'em."

"But how can you catch 'em? Of course, there's the motor handcar, but I wouldn't want to let that go. I'm charged up with it. Understand? The comp'ny holds me responsible. See? I'd have to pay if you didn't bring it back. Do you get me? They'd take it right out of my wages. That's the way the comp'ny is, and after all, you can't blame 'em."

Baldy had stopped listening. He was reaching into his pockets and pulling out hundred-dollar bills, a sheaf of which he shoved into Evans' hand.

"Pay 'em out of that, if I don't show up," he said. "Keep the change. Buy some stock in the God-damned company, if you like, then you'll be making some profit on your own labor an' drawin' pay from yourself besides."

"Gee, thanks, brother," Homer said, pocketing the greenbacks without counting them. "Shall I help you get the thing going? You can catch 'em all right, but you'd better go on the eastbound track. If they meet a freight it's all up with 'em."

"I hope they do," said Baldy, "and when I catch up they'll wish they'd been run over by the Limited, instead."

The motor handcar was on the track in a jiffy and the dapper Sicilian rode away, while the barks of the engine rent the morning air.

"Now for a look at the hideout," Homer said to himself. There remained the problem of the unconscious telegraph operator, but that was quickly solved. Evans propped him back in his seat, took his pulse and smiled. "He'll never know, when he wakes up, what gave him a headache," he said, and started down the street to the weed-covered lot on which the old converted passenger coach occupied by Baldy was standing.

Meanwhile Hjalmar had streaked it back to the coulee in which the Indians were waiting. He gave the Chief Homer's message and the braves showed disappointment. So did Diluvio and the Russian contingent, not to mention the French.

"I shall run them through the moment they wake up," said Frémont.

"Do it neatly," said Toudoux. "If you twist the blade, or stick it in obliquely, it will take me longer to patch them up."

Chief-Shot-on-Both Sides told off twelve men to steal up to the hookshop and bring back its sodden occupants. Hjalmar, Diluvio, Kvek, Lidin, Toudoux and Frémont were given places in the detachment, with six of the most deserving braves, headed by Rain-No-More and Trout-tail III. Miriam, who was curious to see what a hookshop was like, inside, asked permission to accompany the expedition as sharpshooter.

"Go, if you must, but don't tell your father. I'm responsible, in a way," said Shot-on-Both-Sides.

Being thorough men, the members of the detachment, in the absence of exact instructions, lugged across the flat not only the seven gangsters, three wounded and four as effective as men could be after what they had drunk, but the madam, the professor, all three hookers and Mrs. Keogh, the cook, whose words, if the gag had permitted her to utter them, would have wilted the buds of the fragrant sage. In the case of Mona, it was agreed that it was easier to carry her wedged into the woodbox as she was. So two braves caught up two corners apiece and thus she was transported across the flat, while flies buzzed merrily around her exposed areas. It was an even bet as to who was painted the more gaudily, Mona or the braves who acted as her porters.

The other captives, male and female, were slung like sacks over the men's sturdy shoulders.

"How tired the women look," said Miriam. "Still, I suppose it's better than standing on their feet all day in some factory, or being cooped up in a bank."

"At least, they meet more interesting people," said Diluvio.

"You said it," roared Hjalmar, appreciatively. He was lugging the professor and planning to go back for the bullet-pocked piano, since one would be handicapped without the other.

23
At Death's Door

IN THE DESERTED LUNCH CAR which had been used by the gangsters as
a hideout in Mondak, Homer Evans found nothing at first glance
that seemed of value to him. Like so many executives of the old
school, Baldy Santo kept few written records, preferring to have
dangerous information contained safely in his own brain rather
than committed to paper. There were innumerable suits of clothes,
all expensive and in execrable taste; pairs of shoes, all of the Oxford pattern that already had attracted Homer's attention; shaving and toilet articles in profusion; a hydrometer for diluting liquor, a process known as "baptism" in the profession; bolts and
nuts for massaging victim's faces; small bills and change that had
been cast aside; *marijuana*, cocaine and heroin in moderate
amounts; copies of *Detective Magazine*; canshooters and a stethoscope for listening to tumblers in locks; assorted inks and forging
pens for the absent Paperhanger; weapons, including sharp and
blunt instruments, in various stages of disrepair; cards, dice and a
roulette wheel; in short, articles for use in the gangsters' trade and
for their personal amusement, but nothing that afforded Homer a
clue to Gilligan's intentions.

At last, however, tucked into a package of safety-razor blades
near the tidiest bunk, which Evans assumed must be that of Baldy
Santo, he found a list of Chicago telephone numbers, six of them,
written neatly but with no accompanying names.

"Either women, doctors or lawyers, perhaps all three," Evans
said as he copied the numerals and letters and checked them with
the original. "Who knows? They may prove to be enlightening."

Not wishing to be seen around town, Homer sat in a swivel chair behind the battered cash register and indulged in a bout of random thoughts, and his eye, wandering idly around, caught sight of a bundle of Chicago *Tribunes* of recent date. He picked up the latest one and chuckled, for on the front page was an indignant statement by the British consul concerning the demise of Montmorency Lewson-Phipps, the British subject who had met his death on the day Evans and his party had left Chicago.

"Persistent chaps, the British," said Homer. "Now if an American in London . . . Ah, well. Advantages either way. Official scrutiny often proves embarrassing, one must admit." In his formative years, Homer had developed the ability to read, not a word at a time, but an entire line. Thus it was the work of a moment to assimilate the contents of the article. The British Consul had called upon his Ambassador in Washington, who, in faultless morning clothes and with silk hat in hand, had flown to Chicago and given the Mayor, the Chief of Police, the District Attorney and all the newspaper owners extremely bad half hours.

ENVOY DECLARES PHIPPS
MURDER PROBE HAS
BEEN NEGLECTED

Phones in Doubletalk to
10 Downing Street;
"Thick," Says King

Suddenly Evans stood erect and slapped his knee. "At last an inspiration," he said. "In this case I have indulged too freely my passion for violent action, at the expense of ratiocination. Still, my luck does not desert me. Fancy any good coming from British officials, but here it is."

The well-worn lunchroom pay station stood in a corner, and within five minutes Evans was in communication with the branch office of Fish, Fish, Cabot and Saltonstall, all of whom had been friends of Homer's late father. Fitz-Henry Fish, Jr., the son of Fitz-Henry, who was Beatrice Baxter's attorney, had just graduated from

Harvard Law School and, having got himself involved with a waitress in the Congregationalist Cafeteria, had been exiled to Chicago.
The young man, however, was as bright as he was wild and had
done odd jobs for Evans before.

"Fitz," Evans said, "I want you to sound out the Mayor and the
Chief of Police about this Lewson-Phipps affair, also talk with the
British Consul, who is at a loss just what to do. You may tell them
that if they will make me a deputy sheriff—that can be arranged—
and send me by air mail extradition papers to be served on Baldy
Santo and all his gangsters—you can get the list from the *Tribune*—
I will solve the murder of the Englishman beyond a doubt."

"They'd give you the keys to both London and Chicago, old
man," young Fitz-Henry said.

"You'll attend to the matter this morning? And not a word in
the press?" said Evans.

"Right-*O*," Fitz-Henry, Jr., said. "Will nickel do for your badge,
or must it be sterling?"

"Nothing ostentatious," Homer said.

The bark of a one-lunged engine came to his ears, pianissimo,
then mounted a crescendo. "The devil," said Evans. "Our friend
Baldy's back."

There was no time to cross the lot without being observed. So
Homer was forced to get into the telephone booth and crouch beneath the level of the glass in the door. He had barely got himself
out of sight when Baldy came stamping in, his eyes glowing angrily, his face cherry red. Outside, on the tracks, the motor of the
handcar was still running. The gang chief made a dive for a pile of
weapons in the corner, picked up a sub-machine gun and a belt of
ammunition and dashed out to the handcar again. It dawned on
Evans instantly what Baldy was about to do. The innocent station
agent, already afflicted with an unearned headache, was about to
breathe his last.

"Dash it all. I should have thought of that before," Evans said,
and at once got into action. Baldy, showing an agility most amazing in a man of his habits, had vaulted on to the handcar and already the vehicle was in motion. Evans, while at the university,

had established a record for the hundred-yard dash. He lit out in pursuit, handicapped by the spacing of the railroad ties and proceeded to set a new mark which, unfortunately, was not recorded. Slowly he gained on the unsuspecting Santo, but Baldy never let too much time elapse without looking behind him so he soon caught sight of his pursuer and let out an oath as he recognized him. The gang leader pivoted the machine gun and was about to let fly when Evans tripped on a misplaced tie, described an arc through the air and crashed head-first against a rail.

"What a break," said Santo, as he slowed down the engine, dismounted and, with an effort, lifted the unconscious Evans to the platform of the handcar. The gang chief, however, had not connected Homer's appearance with the incident in the depot that morning. He felt of Evans' skull, took his pulse, and decided that he would live, but would be unconscious for several hours. There was no reason, therefore, why Baldy should not continue with the business in hand. He started up the handcar, got the machine gun into position, and chugged slowly past the depot, riddling the structure with bullets. The bewildered agent, too startled to duck, received a row of wounds across his narrow chest and died instantly. But Baldy's blood lust was aroused. So he reversed the handcar and rode back and forth three times, firing until the first belt of cartridges had been used up. Then he took the Tommy gun under his arm and started on foot for the hookshop, but the townspeople, startled by the sound of gunfire, had started running, some toward and others away from the depot, according to their temperaments. Baldy, not wishing to be mobbed, gave up his disciplinary project and hopped on the handcar again. It was headed east and picked up speed before the local constable and some other men could block the way.

"Ta ta, shorties," yelled Santo. "If you need someone to be the goat, pin it on those mugs in the cathouse. They've got it coming, anyhow."

THAT EVENING AFTER SUPPER, which was relished by no one, a solemn group sat in the huge living room of Opera Lodge. Gone was the zest that had attended the fight against larkspur, the preparations for the round-up, the ride to join the Blackfeet on the warpath. Miriam, dry-eyed and pale, sat beside her father, looking straight ahead and seeing nothing. Jim Leonard, torn by his only daughter's grief and desolate on his own account, for he had grown to love Homer Evans and to understand that some day . . . Well.

"We've got to stick it out, my girl," he said, but it came over him that he was old, a thought that seldom entered his mind. The piano stood silent in the corner, lid down. From the kitchen the Chinese glanced furtively in and spoke to each other in whispers. Out by the stable, the wailing and sobbing of the Russians, with Stenka's shrill treble, could be heard. Hjalmar, without realizing it, was tearing a Sears Roebuck catalogue into shreds. They had been informed of what had happened in Mondak, or as much of it as the bewildered population had understood. Every town on or off both railroads had been notified to be on the lookout for the fugitive gangster and his injured victim, but no news, not a word, had come to them.

Santo had vanished, and every hour that passed gave him more of a start.

As sometimes happens in such emergencies, the man who often was hysterical over trifles was the only one who could view the situation with equanimity.

"Me, I might worry about this *voyou* Santo if I loved him, but not about Monsieur Evans," Frémont said.

Miriam, at the sound of his words, threw her arms around his neck and was relieved by the tears that flowed freely, for the first time since it had become evident that Evans was in enemy hands.

"There, Mademoiselle Montana," the Frenchman continued soothingly. "You and I should know, having seen our friend in action, that even unconscious he could take care of himself somehow. Did he not go straight to my Hydrangea, who was lost on the prairie? Would Monsieur Weiss be with us here tonight? In fact, how many of us owe our lives to Evans, on how many occasions?"

Hjalmar reached for his hat. "I'm going to the hideout in the badlands and work on those gangsters," he said simply, and Diluvio, Kvek and Lidin nodded and started after him. Before they got across the porch, however, they were halted by a sharp tearing sound high in the air, a drone that gained in volume, then diminished.

"Sounds like a plane," Hjalmar said. The others, inside, came running out.

"It is a plane," said Miriam. "And close. Oh, Dad, I hope . . ."

But already it was clear that the hope was futile. A low rumbling from the darkness on the ground increased little by little, as the aviators continued their noisy power dives, until the concerted thud of hoofbeats and bellowing of terrified cattle increased to a frightening roar.

"Good God, the whole herd's stampeded. And they're coming this way," Jim Leonard said. From the stable and the corrals came the frantic whimpering of panic-stricken horses. Dust rose in a cloud from the side of the western butte and dimmed the stars. How long it lasted, no one present could have said. The rumble and the dust cloud moved relentlessly toward them. The men and women rushed indoors and cowered there, waiting. On swept the herd, thousand upon thousand, packed tightly shoulder to shoulder, blind, deaf and crazy with fear. Overhead the plane dived, roared, stuttered and climbed again to repeat the process. Miriam, rifle in hand, fired constantly at the tail light, but, of course, in vain.

"No use, girl," her father said sadly. "This is Gilligan's work."

Crash! An outbuilding, in the path of the maddened steers, was demolished and trampled. The corral fence was down. All around the lodge the great herd swept forward, destroying everything that could be knocked over and breaking their stout necks against objects immovable. The dust and clatter, the beat of hooves, tang of animal sweat and lather was overpowering. Then the sounds diminished and grew faint toward the north on Bison Creek.

Before anyone regained his presence of mind, Wing Lee, the cook, ran into the living room and threw himself flat on his face on the floor, convulsed with grief.

"Wing Sam 'e one-piece dead fella," he shrieked, making motions with his hands to indicate his cousin was flat, like a pancake. For Wing Sam had been crossing the yard when the stampede hit the ranch and, not knowing what to do or where to turn, had been trampled. On top of that, the Professor came riding right up on the porch, eyes bloodshot, face streaked with dust, voice trembling.

"Pete got it," he said, and the men took off their hats while the women turned away.

It was then that calm was restored by Dr. Hyacinthe Toudoux.

"Ladies and gentlemen," the doctor said, in his best professional manner, "for the present I shall expect you all to act on my orders. Wing Lee, makee plenty hot watta, catchum plenty towels now you boil 'em. Miriam, Eugenie, Madame Diluvio, get on suitable white clothes and sterilize your hands. Hjalmar and Kvek, Diluvio and Lidin, improvise stretchers from the spare cots in the bunkhouse and, under the direction of Frémont, who knows how injured men should be handled, bring the victims to me. I shall prepare the table. That's all just now."

Everyone sprang into action, imbued with a sense of discipline and responsibility. The first trampled body to arrive was that of Wing Sam. Gravely Toudoux took out his stethoscope and listened for the beating of the Chinaman's heart. Around him, the women waited, faces pale and strained. Wing Lee was praying in Chinese, and, also according to the instructions of the missionaries, with no noticeable partiality.

"Topside joss, now Wing Sam get well, I chuck plenty wages in mission bokis. Ancestors! Can do or no can do?" wailed Wing Lee.

"He is alive. I'll do the best I can," said Toudoux. "Miriam, do what you can to clean the patient and stanch the flow of blood. I hear the others coming with another case."

The other case was what remained of Slipnoose Pete, and part of his horse with which the cowpuncher had been scrambled.

"Well, Doc?" asked Jim Leonard, tears streaming down his weatherbeaten face.

Toudoux sighed and felt Pete all over. He tried the pulse and shook his head, fished for his stethoscope and listened, once, twice, three times.

"Pulse weak, heartbeats barely audible. Mr. Jansen, prepare yourself for a blood transfusion. Professor, light a signal fire and start someone from Muddy Creek for Trout-tail III. I shall have need of a consultation," the doctor said.

No one present ever could forget the nightmare that ensued, the gauze-covered faces, gleam and odor of blood, sight of mangled bodies and limbs, the frail China boy looking like a doll on the huge table, end to end with Slipnoose Pete. From one to the other stepped Toudoux, enwrapped in a frightening calm. The sharp smell of antiseptics filled the lodge, but there were no groans or cries, no need for anesthetics. At some late hour in walked Trout-tail III and wordlessly nodded and got into action, supplementing the movements of his white colleague, once or twice making a respectful suggestion which was heeded and acted upon.

Hjalmar, who had given a full two quarts of blood to take the place of what Slipnoose Pete had lost, when informed that Wing Sam also needed a transfusion, stuck out his other arm. Everyone, man and woman, at the lodge volunteered, but Jansen waved them away.

"Shucks," he said. "It won't take much to fill up one Chinese, and if I stick it out, Doc can save some time."

At dawn, it was reported that the herd had quieted down and scattered again in the vicinity of the Missouri basin.

"How lucky I took the precaution of insuring the stock at a top-notch figure," Weiss said. He scribbled a few numbers and looked up, crestfallen. "Damnation," he added. "I shall come out ahead on the deal, allowing plenty for damages to Leonard's property, for which I'm legally responsible."

Jansen, sitting patiently while his stout heart was pumping its vigorous stream into the pitiful Chinaman, let out a happy yell. "I saw his eyelids move," he said. The doctor nodded and Wing Lee again crashed to the floor, overcome with relief and joy. Half an hour later, Pete showed faint signs of returning consciousness.

"I am pleased to announce," said Dr. Hyacinthe Toudoux, "that both patients have a fair chance of recovery. Convalescence will be long and tiresome, but . . ."

His words were drowned by the noise from the piano, where Lvov Kvek, unable to express his ecstasy in any other way, was banging with both fists on the keys.

Trout-tail III, who, having set several important bones, was starting in on the minor fractures, called to Dr. Toudoux.

"There," he said, pointing to a place where a rib had pierced Wing Sam's left lung, "is the danger point. We must avoid, if possible, pneumonia. For that reason, a general anesthetic is not advisable, although the patient will suffer much pain for a while. In such cases, we Blackfeet have found that tribal drumming is helpful, as a counter-irritant for the nerves."

"*Chèr colleague*, an excellent expedient. I shall take copious notes, and report results to the Sorbonne. By all means, drumming. *Vive le son, mon frère. Le son . . .*" And Toudoux, from sheer fatigue, collapsed comically into a chair, to be fairly smothered with wifely attentions from Eugénie.

In the kitchen, Wing Lee had cleared the pastry board, set up on it a Gideon Bible, before which joss sticks were burning amid Chinese charms and prayers on fragments of colored paper. From his bunk in the alcove, the cook brought out his wad of savings and chucked them on the pile.

"I'm God blasted if I wouldn't do the same, if I wasn't stone broke," said Hank.

"Pass the whiskey," roared Hjalmar. "I got to get my strength back, *pronto*."

24
Of Social Life and Justice on the Last Frontier

ON THE EVENING DESCRIBED in the previous chapter, while violence and tragedy pervaded Three Buttes, a hilarious meeting was in progress at Glendive, in the spacious new home of Judge Patterson. At the head of the polished mahogany table, facing an eight-foot Maxfield Parrish "The Garden of Allah," sat Larkspur Gilligan, coat discarded, vest unbuttoned, store fore-in-hand awry. A long cigar, of expensive aroma, jutted from a corner of his mouth at a triumphant angle. The Baluchistan rug* on the hardwood floor near by was getting a memorable going-over as the judge, frock-coated and horn-rim bespectacled, paced to and fro. In the white-enameled kitchen, Sheriff Hockaday was opening a can of beans with his hunting knife, not having been able to relish the caviar and rare duck smothered in oranges that had been served at dinner.

The hostess, Myra, whose temperament kept her continually on the *qui vive*, was not at home. In fact, she was with Tom Jackson in his den at the Hotel Jordan, to which they had repaired at the children's hour in order to discuss the women's page. The telephone rang and at first neither Tom nor Myra heard it, but eventually it had to be answered.

"Jackson," said Jackson peevishly.

"You know who this is," said Gilligan. "Come over to the judge's. We've got to get out another extra."

* Montgomery Ward, Catalogue No. 72C589.

"He's got a nerve," said Tom to Myra, after the sheepman had hung up. "'We've got to get out an extra,' he said. Well, if a guy buys a cake, he's got to eat it, I suppose. So long, sugar."

"I think he's mean," said Myra. She was not thinking at the moment of Gilligan's role as debaucher of state and county governments. The larger aspects of the activities of her male acquaintances seemed to interest Myra less and less, as her acquaintance with Tom ripened. Being the First Lady of Montana or even of the United States no longer tempted her. Indeed, the wholehearted way in which she had entered into her new work had given Tom a few anxious moments, what with one thing and another.

To grasp the full significance of the meeting Tom Jackson was about to attend, the reader should know that Larkspur Gilligan had received a call from Baldy Santo late that morning and since that moment had been in excellent spirits. For, as has been made clear already, Gilligan was a father first and a conspirator afterward. The fact that Santo had Homer Evans in his power meant to Larkspur that whoever had Terence, his son, would refrain from knocking him off because of possible reprisals. The elder Gilligan did not mind so much having Terry away for a while. He found it easier to build up castles in the air for the boy in his absence than in his company. But a weight of woe and worry had been lifted from Larkspur's inventive mind. Now nothing should hold him back, he resolved.

First of all, he was determined that Jim Leonard should be tried and convicted without delay, while Evans, the only man who could engineer a defense, was safe in Baldy's hands. That the aviators, Cash-and-Carry Corkery and Bat-ear McCluskey had been instructed to stampede Leonard's herd, in order further to demoralize the Three Buttes outfit, the reader already knows, and also the deadly effect of the maneuver.

"Judge," said Gilligan to Patterson, "rest your legs a minute and sit still. I want to talk to you. We've got to put this here trial on some high-sounding basis, something that'll look well in the paper, if you get what I mean. You're good at that kind of thing. That's why you're in on this. Can you think up something before Jackson gets here?"

Patterson stood still on the rug, wove the fingers of one hand between his vest buttons, and began speaking so sonorously that Hockaday, in the kitchen, tossed a forkful of beans into a cage of lovebirds on a windowsill near by.

"Fellow citizens," the Judge said, "why should Arizona and New Mexico enjoy a monopoly of the tourist trade, when Eastern Montana possesses the natural advantages? I do not refer to the national parks, which any American worthy the name would visit anyway. I am speaking of the Lower Yellowstone, that miracle wrought and rewrought by prehistoric ages and whose civilized history has so auspiciously begun.

"Why? I repeat. And echo answers 'Lawlessness.' The tourist in the East, with purse strings open, eschews the wonders of the badlands and the prairies, and supinely contents himself or herself with the inferior Indians of the Southern States while the manly Blackfeet, the Crows, the Sioux and the Cheyennes doze and degenerate where once the bison and their fathers trod. Alas, fellow citizens, we must face the facts. As long as visitors have reason to believe that our justice walks on leaden feet and smacks of the frontier, just so long shall the charms of Eastern Montana, like 'many a gem of purest ray serene,' be born to blush unsung. And the coffers of New Mexico and Arizona shall ring with the tintinnabulation of gold on counters while through trains bear vapid faces at their window panes across our glorious county and peerless State. . . . Will that do, Gilligan?"

"It beats hell what they swallow," said Gilligan, and slapped his knee. "You'll have to run through it again when Tom shows up. I don't see what's taking him so long."

"Tom's wonderful company for Myra," Judge Patterson said. "Too bad she isn't here."

As soon as Jackson put in an appearance, the judge explained in fewer words what he had just let fly about the tourist trade and law and order. Then he went to the wall telephone and asked Tom to listen.

"Let me see. It's Tuesday. Set Jim's trial for Thursday, to give him time to get in. If you put it to him right, he'll come of his own accord. Likes to stick to Hoyle, Jim does. Still thinks it pays," said Gilligan with a tolerant sigh.

Patterson asked for the Leonard Ranch and soon had Jim on the line. The rancher took the call in his bedroom, because the living room had been converted into a surgery.

"That you, Jim?" Judge Patterson began.

"What's your business?" asked Leonard. He was determined to say nothing about the stampede until after an investigation.

"It's this matter of your trial. Mere formality, you know, but we ought to get it over with. We're keeping witnesses here at the public expense, and you don't want to be under a cloud."

"Never mind about that," said Leonard. "What day shall I come in?"

"I'm right glad you're reasonable, Jim," the judge went on. "Now how would Thursday do? Would that give you time? I suppose you'll want a lawyer."

"I'll attend to that," the rancher said. "Anything else on your mind?"

"Thursday, then, at ten o'clock. The moment you show up, we'll release the fifty thousand," said Patterson.

"Who's we? You and Gilligan?"

"Now, Jim."

There was a click as the rancher hung up the receiver and, after sitting wearily on the edge of his cot to master his emotions, he returned to the operating room, saying nothing to anyone about the summons he had received.

The preparation of an extra, with the announcement of the trial and the editorial in praise of tourists and prompt justice, meant that Jackson would have to work all night. He excused himself and hurried to his office. The tone of the story was not to be inflammatory, Gilligan had explained: a summing up of the history of the case to date, with pictures of Donniker Louey, touched up in a way to win public sympathy; the announcement that the stricken father would be the State's principal identification witness; and that the sheepherders, Stumpbroke and Jill, would be unable to appear, since both of them were in the Glendive hospital with severe cases of tick fever. That the ticks, after expert microscopic examination, had been planted on the two men by Gilligan himself was not disclosed.

"Well, the set-up seems perfect," said Gilligan, content to know that the presses soon would be rolling. "Jim'll bring in his daughter. That's certain. Then I can talk turkey to her, with the cards all in my hands. . . . You know, Judge, I feel sorry for Jim, so help me Moses. If he'd only have sense enough to quit, and go to Californy, things could all be nice and peaceful here."

"Be careful about boosting California," the judge said, uneasily. "That would sound bad, if it got to the voters."

What Gilligan suggested regarding the voters was so impractical, considering the number of them and the diversity of their sexes, ages and temperaments, that it is not worth recording here. Suffice to say that it caused Judge Patterson to repress a smile, he having been acting along those lines for quite some time.

THE SCENE CHANGES to a dim caboose in Wibaux, Montana, a small town eleven miles from the Dakota border, with an altitude about four and one-tenth times higher than the number of inhabitants. The caboose was backed up against a bumper on a side track little frequented and its windows were screened heavily. It was there that Baldy Santo had taken refuge with the unconscious Evans. The latter, when he opened his eyes after twilight, saw nothing but a kerosene lantern around which a few moths were fluttering, a few old clothes and track tools on the wall, and the smug face of Santo, who sat watching him from a keg in the corner. The smell of cinders and garlic was modified if not improved by Baldy's bay rum and Fatimas, and proved to be distressing to a man who had sustained concussion of an extraordinary brain. Homer tried to move and became aware that he was in a strait-jacket that had been expertly adjusted.

"You're taking no chances, Mr. Santosuosso," Homer began.

"Not likely," the gang leader said. He had not been addressed as mister for so long that it threw him off his guard.

"How is Wibaux in the spring? Diverting?" Evans asked. He had assumed that Baldy would have taken him somewhere across

the North Dakota line into Montana, because of the magic influence enjoyed by Gilligan there. Wibaux was the first town, also
Santo had been there in hiding before.

"Wise guy, eh? Well, I'm going to kill you, as soon as I get some
information," said Baldy, picking up a wrought-iron jimmy and
standing over Evans menacingly.

"How absurd, Mr. Santosuosso. You must pull yourself together. You are accustomed to dealing with the lower orders of
mentalities, and I suppose you form careless habits that way. But
in my case, although I am by no means puffed out with false pride,
I can put two and two together. And I rate you higher, apparently,
than you do me. In case you wish to know why you will not kill me,
let me remind you that your son and heir, a youth who has plenty
of guts, as you call them, is somewhere beyond your reach or protection, and if anything grave should happen to me at your hands
or in any way at all, your offspring would be cut off long before his
time. You would never see him again. Furthermore, your friend,
Mr. Gilligan, is in a similar situation. Think it over. . . . But of course
you have. Only let's have no more nonsense about my span of life,
or information I possess and you desire."

"Wise guy, eh?" said Santo, and bit his lips when reminded that
he had said the same thing before.

"A little variety would help in our conversations, since we are
to spend some time in each other's company. But let me warn you that
the longer that period is protracted, the worse for you in the end."

"Say, who in hell is prisoner here, anyway?" demanded Santo.

"'Each his own prison,'" quoted Homer, and asked for a glass
of water, and a bandage for his aching eyes. Santo debated with
himself, found to his annoyance that he was not enjoying his usual
self-confidence, and decided to observe the amenities for the time.
He poured the water from a jug into a tin cup, wet a brand-new
shirt that had set him back eighteen dollars, and tied it around
Evans' forehead. Homer relaxed and Baldy, whose dislike of being
alone amounted to a mania, did what he could to keep him awake.
Hurriedly he unlaced the straitjacket and lighted the oil stove, on
which he heated a can of soup.

"Sit up and eat a bite, if you can," Santo said. "And bear it in mind that I didn't gonk you. You fell of your own accord."

"It was fate," Evans said, sitting up with difficulty and removing the shirt, which already was steaming on his heated brow. "And fate, my dear companion, has frequently been kind to me. Who knows? Perhaps this new contact will be valuable, if not to you, to me. There are many things I'd like to know that you could tell me. Suppose I outline them tentatively."

"Save your breath," Santo said. "I'll stand on my constitutional rights, like my legaler taught me. That's the nuts of a formula to keep from being pumped."

"This time you're going to burn," said Homer sternly.

Santo spilled hot soup all over his well-pressed pants

"Cripes, don't say that. Knock on wood," he said, on the verge of panic.

"There's only one concession I would make to you," continued Evans. "That is, if you are reasonable. I'm not keen on capital punishment. I'll see that you get off with life, what you call a 'hearse rap' I believe. But only if you're reasonable."

"I'm sorry I didn't chuck you into a coulee when we crossed that trestle. You make me nervous," Baldy said. "On the level, you ought to take it easy, after the crack on the conk you got today."

"The routine of prison will tend to calm you, as talking soothes me," was Evans' rejoinder.

IT HAS BEEN SOME TIME since the reader has had news of Bonnet and Schlumberger, who with their prisoners and companions, were eking out a miserable existence just south of the Missouri, on roast coyote and snow, with rocks for pillows and only the stars overhead. They were camped, if that is not to cozy a verb, so far from Three Buttes that they knew nothing of the stampede. But imagine their delight when they saw, soaring over their desolate stretch of country an airplane, with front and back lights twinkling and a motor running smoothly.

"We are saved," yelled Bonnet, waving a firebrand until sparks threatened to make the conflagration general.

"The fliers know nothing of our predicament," Schlumberger said. "They will think we are a prairie fire and for that reason will shun this area, because of the inflammability of petrol."

"For God's sake, let's do something," yelled Corrigan.

"I have a plan," the waiter, Cromwell, said. "In the War I was in the signal corps. Ten to one the aviators can read semaphore."

Grabbing up two impromptu torches from the blaze, the waiter lay flat on his back and waved H-E-L-P so assiduously he succeeded in attracting the attention of Cash-and-Carry Corkery, who was congratulating himself on the success of his first stampede.

"What's loose down below?" he asked of Bat-ear.

"Looks like someone in a jackpot," Bat-ear said.

Cash-and-Carry was struck with an idea. "We could soak 'em plenty for a rescue, in such a God-forsaken country. They must have money, or they couldn't get so far from home."

"It won't cost us much to land," said Bat-ear. "You could make an airfield anywhere around here, with a brush-hook, in half an hour."

"Hold on tight," said Cash-and-Carry. "I don't know how sagebrush and wheels act together."

"We'll soon find out," the mechanician said.

Imagine the joy in the camp below when the plane circled in a speculative manner, veered neatly to starboard and began to descend. The sagebrush was scrubby and weak and the terrain as flat as a table, so Corkery had no difficulty in landing.

"Did you mugs want something?" he asked, then burst into raucous laughter as he neared the campfire. The two French sergeants, their voluminous shirt-tails waving in the breeze, were covered with soot and dirt and too excited to attempt to speak English. The gangsters were silent, because of the proximity of Corrigan with a medicine stick, but also were smeared with black. The Negroes, on the other hand, were patched with powdered sandstone and white alkali.

"Let's go back up," said Bat-ear disgustedly. "They haven't got pants, let alone heavy dough."

It did not take the French officers long to pull themselves together and at once they decided that the airmen were not in the service of any constituted government, but rather were in the class with the Great Lakes palefaces they had met. The prompt decision they arrived at independently is to their credit.

Bonnet grabbed the Tommy gun, while Schlumberger picked up a pineapple bomb in each capable hand.

"Stick 'em up," the sergeants said in unison.

The outraged expression on the faces of the aviators as they reached for the stars was comical to behold.

"Tie up the smaller one," ordered Bonnet, and the waiters trussed up Bat-ear, in a manner that would have stopped Houdini, and tossed him over with his social equals, Bird's-eye and the Paperhanger.

"Disarm the big one," said Schlumberger gruffly, toying with the pin of his hand grenade.

The sergeants held a whispered consultation, then Bonnet addressed their comrades as follows:

"One of us will replace the mechanician, while this man" (indicating Corkery) "flies us to Three Buttes, if he cares for his life. He will be covered at all times and will be shot in several vital spots at the least false move," the sergeant said.

"Have a heart. Not Three Buttes. Let's go to Glendive," Corkery said.

"Three Buttes is an excellent place. You will be hospitably received," Bonnet continued, and was interrupted by a roar of laughter from Bat-ear.

"That's right, Frog. He'll get a hot reception, all right. Well, this was all your idea, you big palooka," he added to the pilot. "You tried to chisel me more than once. I wouldn't weep if you got yours."

"You will take me to Three Buttes, and promptly," said Bonnet.

"Let me go," urged Schlumberger. "I don't enjoy life as much as you do anyway."

They compromised on tossing a coin and the Alsatian won. Pineapples in hand, he prodded the reluctant flier into his seat and got in beside him.

"Courage, men," he said, as they were about to take off. "A few short hours will bring you relief, and proper trousers. As for me, do not be inquiet. My father warned me, when first I joined the force, that there were many hazards, and although he did not mention this one specifically, no doubt he would have done so, if he had possessed a more imaginative mind. *Au revoir*, or *adieu*, as the case may be."

The propellers whirled, the plane throbbed and trembled and taxied briskly across the flat.

25
Of the Quality of Mercy

TOM JACKSON, STILL VAGUELY DISGRUNTLED because his conference with Myra Patterson had been interrupted, and troubled by Gilligan's air of confidence, had barely got his eyeshade on and his shirt-sleeves rolled up before he saw a whiskered face peering through the window pane.

"Come in, you old desert rat," he shouted, and in came Tumbleweed O'Flaherty, the former sheriff who had been defeated after years of service by Hockaday, in a manner best known to Larkspur himself.

"Did you know that an airplane stampeded Leonard's herd last night, on purpose?" the old prospector asked, aiming at an office cockroach with a jet of tobacco juice.

"The hell you say?" asked Jackson.

"That ain't all. That gang boss from Chicago shot up the station agent in Mondak and kidnapped Homer Evans. I got it straight from them as knows," continued Tumbleweed.

Jackson, regardless of curious ears in the telephone exchange, grabbed the instrument and asked for Three Buttes. In a moment he had Miriam on the line. The tone of her voice confirmed Evans' misfortune before she could pronounce the words. And she made it clear that the stampede was no accident. The fliers had poised the plane high over the main herd, at the crucial stage of the round-up, and executed power dives again and again, she told Jackson. Everything around the lodge had been demolished except the strongest buildings; hundreds of shorthorns had lost their lives; one cowpuncher, Slipnoose Pete, and the China boy, Wing Sam, had been trampled and were by no means out of danger.

"And what about your father's trial? It's set for day after to-morrow," Tom said.

Miriam screamed and dropped the receiver, then recovered it quickly. "Hold the line, I'll ask Dad," she said. After a short delay she was back. "Dad promised to show up at Glendive. He didn't say a word to us about it," she said. "What shall we do?"

"Let me talk with Weiss," Tom said. When the multi-million-aire got on the line, Tom suggested that they print the extra, making everything public that they knew or suspected about Gilligan, distribute the papers all over the country, then shut up shop.

"Better wait until we hear from Evans, or know for certain that he won't come back," said Weiss. "I heard him say, once, that he was giving Gilligan rope enough to hang himself. We'd better stick to those general lines."

"Leonard'll be convicted. The whole thing's framed," said Jackson. "I wish you could have seen Gilligan. He looks like a June bridegroom."

"Frequently the tables are turned on June bridegrooms, in a manner of speaking," said Hugo Weiss.

So the extra, extolling the virtues of law and order and prompt trials promptly arrived at, was rushed through the presses. Half the front page of the *X-Ray* was devoted to the life and death of Donniker Louey, the defendant, the witnesses, and the spot marked "X." The other half, with illustrations improvised from stills of forgotten horse operas shot in Hollywood, told of the stampede: how a stray airplane now being traced by government officials had frightened the herd, causing damage to persons and property. An old boilerplate of the wife of Dr. Wellington Koo was doctored up to look like Wing Sam, and an extra cowboy in the Covered Wagon served as Slipnoose Pete, who had sustained a total of forty-seven fractures and so many contusions that the final figures were not available at press time. The editorial about the tourist trade for Eastern Montana was set off with an evergreen border filched from an old Christmas ad of the Bon Ton Dry Goods Store.

Old Tumbleweed O'Flaherty read proof with grunts and oaths of mingled rage and admiration. Then he hitched up his belt and started for the door.

"I'm going to outfit myself with grub and find Evans," he said. "And I won't come back until I do."

"Any idea of where he might be?" Tom asked.

"Well, he won't be in North Dakota, and he won't be anywhere along the Great Northern, on account of the insurance company dicks. That Wop couldn't go back to Chicago, the way things are just now. He must be in Montana. That's what I calculate," the old man said.

"Montana's almost as big as France and a damn sight harder to get around in," Tom said.

"There ain't many ways to get into the State from Mondak, and Gilligan has the N.P. eatin' right out of his hand. I'm going to head for Wibaux and start prospectin' from there."

"I'm worried about Homer," Jackson said.

"Who ain't?" said Tumbleweed, and slammed the door.

As the old sheriff and prospector hoofed it across the sagebrush flat he had the advantage of Sergeant Schlumberger, of the Paris police, who was fifteen hundred feet above the surface of the ground, slightly north of Opera Lodge. Peering down with one eye, while he kept the other on Cash-and-Carry Corkery, the Alsatian saw lights blazing, not knowing what dramatic scenes were unrolling in the living room.

"Land right down there. There's a plowed fire strip plenty wide enough," Schlumberger said.

"On the level? Why stop at this farm house? You ain't a traveling man, and ten to one the old man hasn't got no daughter. Why not go on to Glendive? It only takes twenty minutes. You can rustle up a rescue party there in town," the pilot said.

For answer the sergeant jabbed his medicine stick so smartly in the aviator's giblets that the plane went into a tail-spin from which Corkery barely jerked it out in time to hit the dirt right side up. But the mercenary flier was as skillful as he was unscrupulous, and more by instinct than in the hope that it would improve his situation, he avoided a smashup and brought the plane to a halt after taxi-ing almost to the barn.

"Stick up your hands and get out," Schlumberger ordered.

Corkery got out and tried to bolt into the darkness, only to be brought down heavily with a slug in the calf of one leg.

"I can't walk," he pleaded, when prodded again with the medicine stick.

"Do not talk rot," Schlumberger said, with another jab of the stick. "I have seen men twice as badly wounded march day and night on the Marne."

Protesting, the aviator struggled to his feet and limped along, with Schlumberger close behind him. They were halted sharply by Laramee Bob and the Professor, who had been detailed to stand guard outside the lodge while the surgical work was proceeding inside.

It should not be overlooked by the reader that out behind the stable, before the stampede, had stood an impromptu snake corral which had been trampled flat by the crazed and fleeing shorthorns along with most of the surplus rattlers the doctor had collected. The remaining serpents were roaming at large, and in a peevish mood, to put it mildly.

A piercing yell was heard from Cash-and-Carry Corkery.

"There's something moving there. I can see it, on the ground," he shrieked.

"Be quiet, can't you?" the Professor said. "There's men at death's portals right inside."

But the flier could not control himself. "I see another. It's crawling. Don't let 'em get me," he begged.

The cowpunchers, who had on high boots, laughed aloud. "Don't take on so. We're going to hang you, anyway, before you suffer much," Bob said.

"That's fine," said the Alsatian, "but it doesn't solve my immediate problem. I not only find myself without proper footgear, but lack trousers also, gentlemen."

"Get back into the plane, till we can bring you some," said Bob, getting out his rope. Casually he slung the noose around Corkery's shoulders and tied him in the Laramee style to the propeller. The

Professor stood guard, while Bob hustled over to the bunkhouse for an outfit to give Schlumberger.

"What'll we do? We can't go busting in while Doc's operating," the Professor said.

"We'll wait right here, till we know if Pete's goin' to pull through," suggested Bob, and Schlumberger agreed.

After dawn, which took the sharp edge from the pilot's fear of meandering rattlers, the door of the ranch house opened and Miriam stepped out on the porch for a breath of air, followed by her father, Hugo Weiss, Hjalmar and the other men. The sight of the plane on the ground brought them all to the spot, guns and clubs in hand.

"The Frenchman brought him in, God knows how," explained the Professor admiringly. Schlumberger, in a burst of eloquent French, gave Miriam the details, which she translated breathlessly. Star, her favorite mount, having saved herself from the onrushing herd, had come back to the stable of her own accord, followed by the former outlaw, Jesse. Miriam was on the mare in a moment and started rounding up what other horses she could find. Laramee Bob, a rider whose reputation as a broncho buster extended over four or five States, tried to throw a saddle on Jesse. The rangy chestnut sidestepped, reared and made a pass at Bob with both front feet. The Professor, no mean horseman himself, vaulted on his bare back from the wrong side and was tossed six feet into the air and landed sitting down.

"It's no use," said Jim Leonard sadly. "He won't let no one but Evans ride him."

However, Miriam succeeded in collecting a half dozen saddle horses and quick preparations were made for the rescue of Bonnet and the other members of the distressed contingent in the northern foothills. Before the cowpunchers set out, a council was held and it had just about been decided to hang Corkery from the hay derrick on the barn when Hugo Weiss, always slow to act on impulse, asked permission to say a word before the vote was taken.

"Men," he said, "I should enjoy seeing this man swing as keenly as any of the rest of you. The question is: can he be of further use

to us, alive? Now we may have need of an airplane, for transportation
to distant points and patrolling the range, in view of what has occurred.
May I ask if any among you know how to fly this machine?"

The buckaroos and all the others shook their heads with chagrin.

"Why not hold this scoundrel and his plane and press him and
it into service? Then later, after Evans has returned and our difficulties have been resolved, we can hang him at our leisure, although
I should remind you that, technically, he is not guilty of murder,
only attempted murder, the maximum penalty for which in Montana is . . . let me see . . ."

"Twenty to thirty years at hard labor," said the Professor
promptly.

"Twenty would be enough," said Weiss thoughtfully. "Is it not
ironic, gentlemen, that this man, who perverts a noble new profession to unworthy uses in order to avoid heavy work, should be
destined to crack rocks, twist hemp or perform similar monoto-
nous tasks throughout 7,300 consecutive days, except Sundays, on
which church attendance is obligatory?"

"Damn my soul," said the Professor, "we'd be doin' him a favor
to string him up. By all means, the rock pile and the meeting house."

"Is that the consensus, boys?" asked Jim Leonard, who was
presiding.

Every hand went up, including that of Corkery, who had to
strain at the ropes in order to record his vote.

The ensuing day was a sad and busy one. The rancher got out
his old black suit, white shirt, stiff collar and detachable cuffs, black
necktie, collar buttons and studs, the sight of which always filled
him with deep melancholy.

For the ride to Glendive, Miriam chose a flannel shirt that but-
toned down the front, an embossed leather belt equipped with holster, a short corduroy skirt, split conveniently, lisle stockings and
tan riding boots. For use in the court room she carried behind her
saddle a simple frock of non-crushable midnight blue, relieved only
by a plain gold clasp at the front.

It had been agreed that only Miriam, Frémont and Dr. Hyacinthe Toudoux were to accompany her father at the trial, since

every man was needed on the ranch to round up the stray cattle again, to organize a search for Evans, take care of the injured men and guard the prisoners. Bird's-eye, the Paperhanger and Bat-ear McCluskey were confined with Corkery in the ruins of the snake corral, and the rest of the Muddy Creek contingent returned to the special train, which had been shunted back on its sidetrack.

IN THE LODGE OF SHOT-ON-BOTH-SIDES across the angry Missouri a discussion was taking place between father and son. In his hand, the young Blackfeet leader had a copy of the Glendive *X-Ray*, still wet from the press, as it had been rushed across country by a relay of the fleetest Indian couriers.

"In the absence of Homer Evans, surrounded by false witnesses, before a packed jury and a corrupt judge, the friend of our tribe is to be tried. Unless I do my duty, he will be convicted. I have one request of my father—the scalp," said Rain-No-More.

"If you wish to serve Jim Leonard, you will do better to take up Evans' trail from Mondak and follow where it leads. Have I trained you so badly that a Great Lakes paleface can show you his heels? Do you think Evans, the moment he regains consciousness, will fail to leave messages all along the line, signs which only the Blackfeet would observe? Who will be the first man our friend will expect to follow him? Not I. I am too old. No paleface. For their talents lie in other directions."

"True," agreed Rain-No-More.

"Furthermore," continued the old Chief, "the customs of the palefaces are not like ours. Once they have convicted a man and decided to kill him, they do not proceed to do so, but torture him with false hopes and the sounds of the lamentations or execrations of other condemned men for a certain period before ending his life. Such cruelty would be unthinkable with us, but in this case it gives us more time."

"I shall pick up Evans' trail this very night and will not rest until I overtake his captor," said Rain-No-More.

The distance from the Indian lodge to Mondak, along the river trail, was one hundred and fifty miles. By way of Three Buttes, through the foothills and across tablelands, the mileage was higher but the going easier, to one who had Rain-No-More's sense of direction. Also, the young Blackfeet had need of the thinking dog. After swimming his tough pinto across the Redwater ford, a chance few men would take at that season of the year, Rain-No-More made a bee-line for Opera Lodge and got there just as Miriam was about to depart. To her he recounted the talk he had had with Shot-on-Both-Sides and his decision to camp on Santo's trail.

"My eyes and ears are sharp. They will miss nothing," said Rain-No-More. "If likewise I may take advantage of the nose of Moritz, we could follow an eel through the great blue water, and give him two days' start."

Moritz had eaten nothing since sadness had enveloped the ranch and its occupants. He would watch Miriam with compassionate eyes for a while, then roam the yard and sniff around the ruined outbuildings, avoiding warily the roaming rattlers and lurking for hours near the prisoners' corral, in the hope that one of them would merit a going-over. When Miriam explained what was wanted, placing her hand on Rain-No-More's bare shoulder, then pointing far away toward the badlands, the Boxer's gratitude was touching to behold. He walked straight over and sat beside Rain-No-More, where the Indian was standing, and when the Blackfeet moved, so did Moritz. When Jim Leonard, Frémont, Dr. Hyacinthe Toudoux and Miriam mounted their horses and rode away, watched furtively by the cowpunchers and the others, who knew the boss dreaded any kind of scene, the frown deepened on the Boxer's forehead, but he stuck with his assignment just the same. Once the party was out of sight, he hopped up on the pinto in front of Rain-No-More and they also were away.

ON THE EDGE OF THE PETRIFIED FOREST across the Yellowstone from the mouth of Beef Slough, Terence Gilligan and the younger Santo were experiencing a boredom the like of which they never had suffered before. It is true that the grotesque shapes around them, huge pre-historic trees heaped like jackstraws and turned to stone, would have been of interest to savants who cared for that sort of thing. The spectacle, however, left the two young desperadoes cold, as did their flimsy city clothing on the sharp spring nights. The water was faintly alkaline, and scant. The grub was easier to prepare than describe, and far easier to describe than to swallow. Aurora and Luna, with their best efforts at heightening the colors, got no response from the blasé young men except to be wished in hell. One Blackfeet sat silently on guard while the other hunted or slept, according to his taste or need. Conversation ran low, and lower ran the prospect of relief.

Imagine the joy the two sons of conspirators felt when a sizeable party, traveling with the utmost difficulty at barely discernible speed, was sighted at a distance, where the faint trail brought them into view for a brief half hour.

"The old man's found us," said Gilligan. "I knew he'd come through."

"Then why isn't this bloody Indian on the lam?" asked young Santo.

"Cripes. Maybe they're friends of his," Gilligan said.

"At least, they'll be company," was Tony's comment.

The young men's amazement when the party got nearer was unusual, for them. For tied hand and foot in a string, in such a way that they could walk but not make a break of any kind, were four gangsters of the Santo mob, in a state of demoralization that would have touched the hearts of more tender observers. These were followed, all escorted by Blackfeet braves in full regalia, by litters on which were borne by sturdy Indians the three wounded gangsters, Mona Mason, who was puffing and fanning herself with a fan made of buzzard feathers; the three hookers, Violet, Rose and Lil; the white-haired professor in a greenish-black jib-swinger; and a battered and dismantled piano.

The two Blackfeet entrusted with the custody of Terence and Tony held a powwow. Their Chief had told them to keep the prisoners out of sight. So the protesting young pair were hustled into a dim natural cave, where stalactites and stalagmites vied with one another in making the place uncomfortable, while the newcomers camped on the edge of a patch of squirrel grass out of sight and some yards distant.

"They say men go nuts in the desert," said Tony. "It ought to be twice as easy in a place like this."

Terry Gilligan, accustomed from birth to having his way, could not repress his irritation any longer. "Aw, button up your kisser," he said. "*Your* old man'd do something to get us out of soak if he was half as bright as you say he is."

"We ain't in Chicago. We're in *your* fam'ly's territory, and, by Jeez, it looks it, too," was Tony's spirited rejoinder.

The Blackfeet, listening outside, turned to one another and nodded.

"*Ai peix ksis kat*," said Blackfeet A, meaning that the boys were cracking.

"I am pleased" (*Nit okh si tuk ki*), said Blackfeet B.

26

In Which the Voice Proves Mightier Than the Gavel

LONG BEFORE THE HOUR SET for the opening of Jim Leonard's trial the court room in Glendive was crowded to capacity with residents, storekeepers, clerks and employees of the town and the railroad men with their daughters and wives. Every hitching post in the main square and behind the depot was lined with bronchos and cayuses, while rigs with driving horses tied to the hind wheels dotted the vacant lots and monopolized the few shade trees which had been planted by the association started by Judge Patterson's wife. Sheriff Hockaday, in a brand-new cowboy's outfit with ornamental leather belt, embossed gauntlets, shiny boots and silver spurs, all topped off with a shirt striped blue and yellow and a Stetson with stiff brim and beaded band, was much in evidence. Myra Patterson, by using all her wiles, had reserved the front seat for herself and intimate women friends, who made up the livelier set. The church people were gathered in drab little groups in the balcony.

The spring sun shone brightly and not a cloud marred the sky, which was taking on that pale shade of blue that matched the faded colors of the prairies and the badlands. Also the air was mild with the fragrance of cottonwood buds. Meadowlarks, having learned that rustling was easier in town than on the plains, hopped boldly along the sidewalks and in yards.

In order that more citizens might see or hear the proceedings, Judge Patterson, always responsive to the voters' interests, had directed that the windows be opened.

The general feeling among the inhabitants of the valley, some of whom had traveled two hundred miles or more to be present when the rancher was tried, was one of bewilderment. There were many whose old loyalties to the cattle trade and whose abhorrence of sheep gave them a violent prejudice in Jim Leonard's favor, particularly those who had known him as a square-shooter who had lived in the valley a full half century. Others, and especially some of the younger business men, made a living from the sheepmen and dry farmers, and supported the ministers' drive to curb the wild buckaroos and limit their traditional forms of amusement on holidays. To each and every man, however, there was something off-color surrounding the entire affair. The victim, Donniker Louey, to those who had seen him, had never seemed prepossessing. Until the aged stricken father had appeared on the scene, and been thoroughly advertised, public sentiment had not been aroused. After that, many settlers, although sorry for Leonard, believed that the law should take its course.

Jim Leonard and his party had put up, as usual, at the Hotel Jordan, where the pro-cattle sentiment amounted almost to an avocation. He had dressed in his old black suit and was champing at his stand-up collar, while Miriam, in the next room, slipped off her riding togs and into the midnight blue that had lived up to the Paris couturiere's promise as to uncrushability, and did much to counteract Miriam's outdoor complexion with an effect of pallor. On the bed lay Miriam's automatics, but she decided against them, at least for the opening session, until she got the lay of the land. That no one should lead her father to the gallows while she had fingers and there still were triggers, she was determined, but she was making a heroic effort to control her impulses and, as Evans would have counseled, to bide her time. Being unaccustomed to legal processes, she could not believe that right and justice would not prevail. She had learned it in school, and done much on her own account to uphold those abstract ideals in an amateur way. But as she glanced at herself in the mirror, she knew that where her heart should be was an aching emptiness and that her courage was diluting itself to take up the extra space.

Frémont and Dr. Toudoux were getting out note paper and sharpening pencils, intent on gleaning some first-hand data on American procedure. And, like Miriam, they were vaguely troubled by Jim's insistence that he needed no lawyer.

"I didn't do it. Nobody says he saw me do it. So what can a lawyer do or say?" the rancher had repeated again and again. He did not know that while he was waiting for the clock to reach the hour, Larkspur Gilligan was in the Glendive Hospital, with typed depositions in his hand which were being marked with crosses above the dotted lines by the feeble sheepherders, Stumpbroke and Jill, neither of whom could read or write their names.

The morning train came steaming in from the East, and played to an unusually crowded platform that day. No one in the throng, however, could identify the tall distinguished-looking tenderfoot, dressed in faultless morning clothes and carrying his black leather brief case with an air of authority.

"Looks like some big lawyer," was the general comment, and it proved the perspicacity of the free and common man, for the newcomer was none other than Fitz-Henry Fish, Sr., of Fish, Fish, Cabot and Saltonstall. The clerk of the Jordan, liking the look of the stranger, helped Fish with his baggage and escorted him in person to the hotel. The moment the register was signed, the clerk mounted the stairs two at a time and knocked on Miriam's door.

"There's an Eastern lawyer downstairs who just asked for some friends of yours," the clerk said, knowing Miriam had been worried about legal representation.

"What friends?" asked Miriam, as her heart leaped in anticipation.

"Well, that good-looking chap named Evans, for one. Says he knew Evans' father. Then he asked for a Beatrice Baxter, who's married to a 'violin Johnny,' I think he said. I've heard the boys say you got a pippin of a fiddler at Three Buttes. Maybe he's the one, if he's married."

A sudden resolve shook Miriam. Just the mention of Homer's name had given her hope and assurance. "Will you ask Mr. Fish if I may talk with him, in the upstairs reception room?" she said.

"You bet," said the clerk, and hustled down the stairs.

The lawyer, relieved at making an immediate contact, walked suavely up the stairs.

"I'm Miriam Leonard, friend of Homer Evans," the girl said diffidently.

"How fortunate," said Fitz-Henry, Sr., extending a steady hand that made her own look definitely brown. "I learned from my son in Chicago that Homer was in these parts and I couldn't go back without seeing him."

"He's been kidnapped, perhaps murdered in cold blood," gasped Miriam.

"Oh, I say. Now I can't believe Homer's been murdered. In the first place, no one would want to kill him. He's simply topping, as I daresay you're aware. Besides, should anyone want to murder him, he wouldn't let him, you know. He's deucedly clever, quite abnormal, one is tempted to say. I doubt if any criminal could get the best of him."

"You must help me," Miriam said. "My father's being tried for murder, this very morning . . ."

"You don't mean . . . Oh, really . . . It couldn't be that your father . . . Dear, dear, now. Of course, I've read how it is about fathers in this country . . ."

"My father didn't kill Homer, if that's what you're getting at. They're the best of friends, *Dieu merci*," interrupted Miriam.

"Then your father killed another duffer?"

"Wait. Listen," said Miriam, tapping with her foot in despair. "Dad wouldn't kill anybody. But they're trying him just the same."

"A violent community, and no mistake," said Fitz-Henry. "I'm Fish, of Fish, Fish, Cabot and Saltonstall. We handle civil cases, questions of investments, wills, relatives who go dotty—that sort of thing."

"You must act for my father. He's innocent, and they're trying to get rid of him," Miriam continued. "If Homer were here . . ."

"Of course, Miss Leonard. I'd do anything for Homer, but as likely as not I'd make a frightful hash of it. This is not in my line."

Nevertheless, within ten minutes Jim Leonard had been persuaded to change his mind and accept the services of counsel,
by the combined entreaties of his daughter, Frémont and Dr.
Hyacinthe Toudoux, who had been subpoenaed as witnesses for
the State. The story of the disappearance of Dunniker Louey, the
indictment, the enormous bail, the finding of a body on Cottonwood Creek, the bereaved father, and what could be conveyed in
the brief space of time available about the sheep and cattle war
impending, was told Fitz-Henry, Sr., whose brow for the first time
in years grew damp with perspiration, so hard did he try to receive
and assimilate facts and conjectures off the bat, without the deliberate consideration he was accustomed to bestow on the minutest
details. When told about the stampede of ten thousand shorthorns,
the attempted wrecking of a train, the Indians on the warpath, and
the gangsters in the dells, he fairly gasped for air. His clients among
the Boston aristocracy were outstandingly eccentric, and had told
him some harrowing tales, some of which had and others had not
proved to be substantial. The great West, he concluded, had also
its whacky aspects.

Obviously it was impossible for any attorney, and especially
one with a strictly civil practice, to get into the swing of a murder
case as complicated as Jim Leonard's was turning out to be, between train time, 9:14, and 10 o'clock. But for generations it had
been the custom of Fish, Fish, Cabot and Saltonstall to open any
trial with a request for a postponement, in order that the defense,
or the counsel for the plaintiff, might have time to pull themselves
together. Being an old conservative firm, time always seemed to
operate in its favor.

"I shall ask for a postponement," he said.

"I'm ready, right here and now. I've nothing to be ashamed of . . ."
Jim Leonard began.

"Be still, Father," said Miriam. "We need a postponement in
order to find Homer."

"Quite," said Fish, and tried to figure out off-hand how that
could be worked into the argument.

"He's a small arms expert, qualified in Massachusetts," went on Miriam. "Will that help?"

"No judge would refuse us time, in that case," Fish said, and dabbed at his forehead with his handkerchief. "By the way, is there any feeling, any sectional feeling, I mean, against Easterners? I could put on camping or shooting togs, if I could find any here, but do you think the jury'd resent my inflection? It's Harvard, no use denying it. When our firm has to face a jury composed of Jewish and Irish citizens, for instance, in Boston, we send associates of appropriate races into court to make the actual plea. Could I, perhaps, find a young local chap who can be trusted . . ."

"No one can be trusted in Gilligan's town," Jim Leonard said. "At least, no lawyers."

"Excellent," said Fish. "On those grounds I'll ask also for a change of venue. We can argue for days about that."

"I want to get back to the ranch," Jim Leonard said anxiously, but Miriam soothed him by stroking his hand.

"I have detected no departure from French procedure as yet. Have you?" asked Frémont of Dr. Hyacinthe Toudoux.

At ten minutes of ten, the bellboy of the Hotel Jordan brought the horses around from the livery stable, with an extra one on the saddle of which the stirrups had been shortened for Fitz-Henry Fish, Sr., who perched up with his knees under his chin, English style. Jim Leonard mounted Legs, the gray, in spite of the danger of getting white horsehairs on the black store suit; Miriam was on Star, while Frémont and Dr. Toudoux rode a pair of gentle geldings. The distance from the hotel to the court house was not much over two hundred yards, but no one even remotely connected with the cattle business will walk that far in town if he can help it.

As the defendant's party approached the court house, the assembled spectators began to murmur and stir, and the excitement was communicated to the bronchos at the hitching post, who began to kick, snort, pull back, throw themselves and squeal.

"Here he comes," said Gilligan, *sotto voce* to Judge Patterson. Jim Leonard, looking grim, indeed, was seated on the prisoner's bench, and Myra Patterson, after an admiring glance at Tom Jackson at the press table, displaced three of the townswomen who had sniffed at alligator pears in the course of her last club luncheon, to make room for Miriam, Frémont and Dr. Hyacinthe Toudoux. Fitz-Henry Fish, Sr., proceeded to the bench, and after a whispered consultation with the judge, who seemed ill at ease, was registered as counsel for the defense. Then Judge Patterson left the court room to make his official entrance, after the jury had filed in.

The foreman of the jury was August Tisdale, of Tisdale and Andrews, who ran the dry-goods store. Next to him sat his partner, Andrews; a trouble shooter for the telephone company; the proprietor of the Criterion bar; the cobbler and saddle-maker; Doc Shields, the prescription clerk at the drug store; a hardware dealer; one old prospector who had need of a grubstake for the summer; an insurance agent who doubled in lightning rods; a contractor and builder and one of his rough carpenters who was unable to work just then because of a broken arm; and the principal of the Glendive High School. At the sight of them, Miriam flushed with indignation and whispered to Fitz-Henry Fish. For, although none of them dealt in sheep directly, not one did not benefit from Gilligan's trade or his largesse.

"Old Larkspur's takin' no chances," said a grizzled pioneer three rows back, and Judge Patterson rapped smartly for order, and warned the spectators that if any demonstrations occurred, the court room and adjoining lots would be cleared. As if to back the judge's threat, Young Hockaday, the sheriff, stood up and let himself be seen.

Fitz-Henry Fish, Sr., rose in his place at the counsel's table as soon as the opening formalities were over and the witnesses sworn in.

"Your honor," he said, "in view of the fact that I arrived in town this morning, I ask that consideration of this case be postponed until one month from today. As your honor is aware, however flimsy the evidence on which this indictment was made, the life of a citizen is at stake and under our Bill of Rights and Federal Constitution, as well as the Constitution of this Sovereign State, and the customs of civilized communities dating back to the Magna Charta . . ."

"I object," the prosecuting attorney, known as "Highpockets," said, but the judge waved him aside. The judge had not had time to pull himself together in order to deal with the unexpected development. Fitz-Henry Fish simply radiated assurance and distinction. Tom Jackson had been asked by the A.P. to send out the story in full, for the Eastern dailies. A slip might jeopardize the judge's political career.

The upshot of it was that at one o'clock Fitz-Henry Fish was still on his feet, not even groggy, and half the audience, a large number of the jurymen, witnesses including the father of the deceased, and even the bronchos at the hitching posts, were dozing in their seats, if they had them, and if not, on their feet.

Jim Leonard's face was a picture of woe. He had hoped that in fifteen or twenty minutes the case against him would have been dismissed, for lack of direct evidence. And his spirits were not lightened when, parenthetically, just before the noon recess, the attorney for the defense gave notice that when he had finished his argument for a postponement, he would ask for a change of venue. The Boston barrister, who relished a chance to let himself go, had done a scholarly job on the Magna Charta, the conquest of the plains (in which he had used quite a bit of historical data on the Pilgrim fathers, adapted for Western consumption), the growth of the custom of trial by a jury of one's peers, the gradual restrictions self-imposed by States on capital punishment, and was starting in on precedents regarding circumstantial evidence when a halt for lunch was called.

"This here case is more serious than I'd calculated," said a plainsman, as his wife handed him a chipped-beef sandwich and a bottle of St. Louis beer. "I didn't know they had so much on poor old Jim."

"The professor's *for* Jim, not aginst him," said the wife, who had taught school in Virginia before coming west, through the agency of the Montgomery Ward marriage bureau.

"He sure can shoot off his face," was the husband's reply. "He had them all pullin' leather, no matter which side they were on."

In the back room of the Criterion bar, a heated conference was taking place between Judge Patterson and Larkspur Gilligan, with

Sheriff Hockaday and the prosecutor, Highpockets, sitting in. The judge would have preferred a safer place, but Myra was entertaining in the palatial dining room of the judicial residence and had offered Miriam the seat of honor, which she had declined in order to be with her father.

"Judge," said Larkspur, his weather-beaten face flushed turkey red and his handle-bar mustaches twitching, "you got to hogtie that tenderfoot lawyer. I don't care how you do it. But it's got to be done."

"But, Mr. Gilligan," objected Patterson, "he's well within his rights, I think. And the attention of America is focused on our humble little court room. Mr. Fish, according to Myra, is from one of the most prominent Boston families."

"Maybe you'd like to move to Boston, and run for Senator back there," said Gilligan, whose patience was worn ragged.

At the Hotel Jordan, Fitz-Henry Fish, Sr., was soothing his vocal cords with some No. 1 Bass ale and giving them some variety by conversing in clipped French with Miriam, Frémont and Dr. Hyacinthe Toudoux.

"Don't mind me," Jim Leonard had said. "I don't get what you're driving at, no matter what language you speak. Me, I didn't kill a man, and that's all there is to it. I want to hear what Gilligan and his gang of fourflushers have got to say for themselves."

"But, Father," said Miriam, "every moment we can save will give Rain-No-More that much time in which to catch up with Homer."

"I must get a copy of that Magna Charta," said Frémont, anxiously. "Is it, perchance, like the reforms of Julius Caesar or Code Napoleon?"

"Ah, capital. Thank you, sir," said Fitz-Henry Fish. "I shall touch on those epoch-making codifications this afternoon and part of tomorrow."

The defendant groaned and gave up trying to swallow the business men's lunch at the Jordan, which, under ordinary circumstances, he could have disposed of in double portions, with a steak on the side.

Back in the Criterion, Larkspur Gilligan had not ceased to apply the heat to the shuddering presiding justice. "Call up Lawyer

Anderson in Minneapolis. He'll tell you how to muzzle this dude, and give you chapter and verse," said Larkspur. The judge passed up his dessert and hung for twenty minutes on the wall telephone, while sheepmen in the bar kept up such a commotion that the judge could not be overheard. In fact, he could barely hear himself and the voice of Lawyer Anderson.

When the audience was settled for the afternoon session and the jury filed in, however, Judge Patterson rapped sharply with his gavel and got the jump on Fish, who was fumbling with his notes on the Code Napoleon.

"The court wishes to state," he said, "that no postponement of this trial will be granted, on the grounds put forward by my distinguished colleague . . ."

"They're all in cahoots, as I always said," muttered one of the old timers, who had lost a homestead suit in the same room eighteen years before.

"Order," the judge shouted, and this time broke the handle of the gavel, the head of which hit the court stenographer's fountain pen and ruined six pages of the record. "I repeat, the request for postponement is denied. The defendant has had ample time to secure counsel, and until today has refused to avail himself of that privilege."

"That's right, judge," said Leonard, who, above all, stood for absolute fair play.

"We are asked by my distinguished colleague" (indicating Fish) "to obstruct the wheels of justice, on the ground that he has had no time to prepare his case . . ."

Fish, who was quick on the trigger, rose in his suavest manner, took off his spectacles, and smiled benignly.

"Your honor," he said, knowing he would have to change his tack, "in the course of the noon recess I have had the opportunity to examine the records of this case to date, and had I realized how transparent were the pretexts on which my client is being tried, I should not have asked for a simple postponement but an out-and-out dismissal of the case."

The judge made a grab for the gavel and remembered too late that it had been demolished, and his hesitancy gave Fitz-Henry time to get into action in a way that better courts than that of Dawson County had found difficulty in blocking.

"The question is, therefore: shall Jim Leonard, your law-abiding and respected fellow citizen, my client, and the defendant in this trial, be brought before the bar of justice at all," the attorney began. "On that point, I should like to quote Montana vs. McGregor, 1910; Commonwealth of Massachusetts vs. Standish, 1810. In fact, I could give you a list of precedents as long as the court calendar for the entire session to support my contention, which is, in a nutshell . . ."

And he went on to argue that the indictment had been made before a corpse was found, when Donniker Louey, in fact, had merely disappeared. That disappearance was not proper grounds for legal action, and that the indictment so drawn was irregular and had not been superseded or corrected at the time the body was found on Cottonwood Creek, or at any subsequent time, was stressed by Attorney Fish, with variations. Judge Patterson, meanwhile, glanced furtively and helplessly at Gilligan, who merely glowered. The lawyer for the defense was still going strong when the hour for adjournment struck, but long before that the jurymen, who had counted on an easy three dollars for a morning's work and had business to look after, began to hem, haw and wriggle like pigeons in a crate.

"Does it not seem," asked Dr. Hyacinthe Toudoux of Frémont, "that our friend from Boston is running the chance of antagonizing the jurymen? Evidently they are not accustomed to oratory, in large doses and in abstract terms."

"The American juryman," wrote Frémont on his empty pad, "is more restive under stress of long technical arguments than his counterpart in France, but once wearied, gives vent to his boredom in similar ways. It is gratifying to a French observer to note, however, that frequent references are made to the Code Napoleon, which in the first day of the process known as Dawson County vs.

Leonard has overshadowed the British Magna Charta by at least twenty references, although our entry got a very bad start."

The crowd dispersed, some spectators returning to their homes, others repairing to bars and saloons, which did a land-office business that evening, still others seeking shelter in the crowded hotels, and the remainder making preparations to camp on the flats, the weather being mild.

Tom Jackson, editor of the thriving *X-Ray*, had not put pencil to paper that day, and, suspecting that Gilligan would call him into consultation, he made himself scarce to gain time to think over the situation.

The Patterson dining room was available to the judge that evening, since Myra had to call on several of her friends to pick off items for the social column. The Baluchistan rug not only got a workout by the harassed judge who had paid for it, but from the hobnails of Larkspur Gilligan who was laying down the law, not that of the statute books, which after Fitz-Henry's efforts of the day was hanging on the ropes, but the law of the sheepmen's jungle, over which Larkspur reigned unchallenged.

"I'm here to tell you that you've got to throttle this wise guy from Boston," Gilligan began.

"If you don't, we won't get nowhere," the sheriff said.

"Can't we get together a few of the boys and ride him out of town on a rail?" the station agent suggested.

"But, gentlemen," protested the judge, "the A.P.'s asking for the story. 'Let it run. Send pictures.' I saw the telegram myself. What position would I be in, if there should be an abduction? Remember, when he gets through his dismissal plea, if any of us are still alive, he then will have the right to argue a change of venue. Should he be ridden out on a rail, his successor would have the best possible argument for a change of venue."

"Talk plain American," growled Gilligan.

"I mean to say, a transfer of this trial to another locality where feeling is not so high," the judge said.

"I'm going home," said Gilligan. "And tonight I'm going to decide who'll be candidate for State Senator from this here district, in case we don't get down to brass tacks in the court room tomorrow morning. And that's flat."

And in spite of Judge Patterson's frantic yammering and clutching at Larkspur's coat-tails, the latter strode from the judicial mansion and out into the night.

27
In Which Lawyers Come and Go

WHEN RAIN-NO-MORE, with Moritz at his heels, dismounted from his pinto in front of the Fur Traders' Rest in Mondak, he found that small community in an uproar. The murder of the station agent in cold blood, entailing also the riddling of the entire depot with machine-gun bullets, had stirred that frontier town to its fundamentals. Grim citizens, to the number of sixty, were patrolling the streets, fully armed and disposed to shoot first and ask questions afterward. Posses were scouring the surrounding flats and foothills. Furthermore, feeling was running high because of the abduction of Madam Mason and her hookers by Indians. Consequently, Rain-No-More was immediately surrounded by an angry mob and showered with threats. Had not Moritz taken a definite stand, and refused to let anyone approach his partner, the result might well have been tragic.

However, Rain-No-More was known to many Mondak business men who had traded with the Blackfeet, and his acquaintances held back the more impetuous members of the mob until the son of the Chief could make himself understood.

"The outrage which has left your town in an unenviable situation was perpetrated by outlaw Shoshones, not by the Blackfeet, your friends and neighbors," Rain-No-More said. "Their leader, one Tall-Horse-in-Flytime, has taken your emergency squaws across the line into Wyoming, according to information I have received. In the name of my tribe, I promise that the squaws shall be recovered and returned in the best condition possible under the circumstances."

A cheer went up from the crowd. "We'll get up a good purse for whoever brings 'em back," a man shouted, and was generally acclaimed.

Rain-No-More, after promising again to look out for Mondak's interests, turned his pinto loose to graze his way home and hastened to the livery stable to buy another. From his belt he took a sack of gold dust and, after bargaining, weighed out the price on the drug-store scales near by. Then he hurried to the railroad station to pick up what information he could.

The evening train was just steaming in from the east and Rain-No-More's attention was attracted by a personable young man in college clothes who got off and peered up and down the platform.

"Can I help you?" Rain-No-More asked.

"Well, rather," said Fitz-Henry Fish, jr., for it was he. "I'm looking for my friend Homer Evans. A large order, what, considering the vastness of this country. Ripping sort, old Evans, but likely to be anywhere."

"Come with me," said Rain-No-More simply, and, followed closely by Moritz, the pair made their way down the street. "I, also, am a friend of Homer Evans and his situation makes it necessary for me to ask you some questions," the Indian continued.

"Right-_O_," said young Fitz-Henry. "Pop away."

"Will you tell me why you thought you might find Evans here in Mondak?" asked Rain-No-More.

"Why, certainly, old chap. I talked with him day before yesterday, and he wanted me to bring him certain thingumabobs and documents from Chicago. Confidential stuff, of course. I'm his lawyer, in a way of speaking, unthinkable as that may seem. Copped the old degree, after a struggle, and the governor shipped me west. Got in a bit deep with a waitress, if you know what I mean."

"Of course," said Rain-No-More urbanely. "I'm California, '29."

"No doubt you made your letter," young Fitz-Henry said. "You outdoor chaps are demons on the field. The best I could do was to captain the chess team. Silly game, but I had to do something for old Harvard, you know. The Fish always have."

"We have a similar custom among our young men," said Rain-No-More. "What you indicate with letters worn on sweaters, we record with coup sticks. Notch 'em, you know."

"Dashed ingenious, that. Concise and to the point," said Fish, Jr., heading straight for the Fur Traders' Last Hope, which was the nearest saloon. In the back room, after Rain-No-More had slipped on an extra slicker that was hanging on the wall, as a gesture toward the law which forbade the bartender to serve Indians, the Blackfeet told young Fish about the murder of the station agent two days before and Evans' disappearance on a handcar run by Baldy Santo. Fish, in turn, confided in Rain-No-More the nature of his errand, how he had received the call from Homer and had secured a badge giving the latter authority as an assistant district attorney of Chicago. The extradition papers for individual members of the Santo gang were contained in two large brief cases, one hundred and fifteen in number, each covering several aliases.

To make sure no news about Evans had been received at Three Buttes, Rain-No-More telephoned the ranch, and while he learned nothing about Homer's whereabouts, he was encouraged because the trial had barely got started in the course of Leonard's first day in court. Hank, incidental to the main conversation, let it slip that an attorney named Fish had been retained by Jim.

"Fish, did you say?" repeated Rain-No-More.

"Fitz-Henry Fish. That's the bird," said Hank.

"But, dash it all, that's the *pater*," said young Fish, when the information was relayed to him. "I knew he was planning a trip west, about some ripping old mine a client got nicked with. I'll toddle up to Glendive and pay the filial respects, since you've got a hard bit of cross country stuff ahead of you."

So it was agreed that Fish, Jr., should take the morning stage to Glendive next day and tell Miriam and Fish, Sr., about the extradition papers and Evans' mysterious promise to the British Consul in Chicago to run to earth the slayer of Montmorency Lewson-Phipps. Just after sunset, Rain-No-More put Moritz on his new pinto, a process which required ten minutes of strenuous effort and won the plaudits of the crowd in the square. Then he started grimly eastward along the Great Northern right of way.

According to all reports, Baldy Santo had not passed through Williston with his handcar on his trip with Evans aboard. All the railroad men were positive of that. Williston was the next town east, situated twenty-six miles from Mondak. There was nowhere to hide in the flat stretch of country between the two towns except in the brush near the junction of the Missouri and the Yellowstone. What could a Chicago tenderfoot do with an injured man in the brush? the Blackfeet asked himself. The answer was: Nothing at all, unless the helpless prisoner was abandoned. That was unlikely, since Santo's son was being held as hostage.

A few miles along, there stood a grain elevator and a sidetrack had been recently built to serve it. There Rain-No-More learned that a string of empties had been picked up by the east-bound freight the same morning Santo had fled. All were slat cars, and sealed, except for one gondola.

"Beast with intelligence! Our men went east in that gondola," Rain-No-More said to Moritz, who wagged his tail, left-right. "Consequently," the Indian continued, "the handcar must be hidden hereabouts."

The country around the grain elevator was flat, and large areas of it had been plowed. No one had been near by when Santo had passed that way.

"How long since that derrick has been used?" the Indian asked.

"It hasn't been touched this season," the switchman said.

Rain-No-More examined the hand derrick more closely and gave a grunt of satisfaction. At his request, the switchman pulled back a lever that released the drum and Rain-No-More unwound a yard or two of cable.

"Strange that a foot of cable, rusty on the underside, should have been wound on the drum, while the rest of the unexposed wire is well greased and free from rust," the Indian said. "Let's have a look in the grain bin."

There, covered with wheat, was the handcar. The Indian, after lowering the vehicle by means of the derrick, put it back on the tracks, with a silent tribute to the strength of the diminutive Santo who must also have lifted it. Rain-No-More filled up the can with gasoline, then roped his pinto and loaded the frantic beast, who nevertheless could not move his legs, onto the vehicle. Moritz, catching on, found himself a place. In a jiffy they were chugging into Williston, where Rain-No-More explained his errand to the railroad men and found out that the gondola in question had been bound for Oakland, California, via Bismarck. That was enough for Rain-No-More. To go back east to Jamestown Junction and then head west on the N.P. on the handcar would take longer than the journey overland, along the Yellowstone and through the badlands. So it was the latter course on which Rain-No-More decided. He released the outraged pinto, who immediately attacked him with all fours and his teeth, and only subsided when Moritz took a firm hold on him above the shoulder and clamped down hard. Then the Indian mounted, the dog hopped up in front and they were off again. Aurora, whose interest in the valley had been heightened by what she had seen there lately, touched with her rosy fingers the spotted rear of the resentful pinto and the noble head and shoulders of Rain-No-More on the east bank of the raging Yellowstone, just across from Leonard Creek.

A FEW SECONDS LATER, when the goddess got around to the Hotel Jordan, she saw at an upstairs window the wan face of Jim Leonard, who, as usual, had awakened before dawn and was looking forward to several lonely hours before his daughter, his guests and his new attorney would get up. If any of them failed to do so, Jim was thinking, it had better be the attorney, for Fitz-Henry, Sr., had explained to him the evening before that the preliminary arguments on the question of dismissal of the case because of an illegal indictment would occupy several days. To kill time, the rancher called Three Buttes and got Hank on the line. The news he heard was far from reassuring. He was pleased, of course, to know that the roundup was progressing in a satisfactory way, that most of the stray rattlers had been rounded up by Wing Lee, that both patients were as well as could be expected and that Rain-No-More, with Moritz, was hot on Evans' trail. What caused an extra wrinkle to furrow his brow was the information that another member of the firm of Fish, Fish, Cabot and Saltonstall had been sighted in the lower end of the valley and was bound for Glendive with two or three well-laden brief cases.

"This lawyer of mine don't give the rest of 'em a show," said Leonard. "I don't even know yet what I'm up against, and the jury's gettin' hot under the collar."

"You just keep your shirt on, Jim," said the foreman. "That Boston man's sure to get tuckered out pretty soon. A fella can't talk for days on end."

"You don't know Fish," said Jim. "And if what you say is true, he'll soon have another fella to spell him. I'm going to ask the judge if I can't go back to the ranch until my lawyer gets through. They've still got the fifty thousand bail."

The second morning of the trial was much like the first, except that Gilligan was madder, Judge Patterson was on the verge of hysteria and the jurymen were more obviously bored. The court room was well filled inside, but most of the men in the vacant lots preferred to stay in the saloons, leaving a few young boys on guard to let them know if anything broke loose in the trial.

"That *hombre* with the sideburns from back East just rung in a new wrinkle he calls *habeas corpus*," one of the messengers reported about ten minutes before the noon recess.

Judge Patterson ate no lunch that day, and neither did Larkspur Gilligan. The latter was just about to reconsider the station agent's offer to ride Fitz-Henry, Sr., out of town on a rail, well-tarred and feathered, when Patterson, who saw his dreams of political advancement melting like mirages, had an inspiration.

"Why can't I set a limit on the time for argument on the question of dismissal? I'm not going to grant the request, anyway," the judge said.

"You better do something," said Gilligan.

Thus it was that the judge, beating the rap of the gavel by a split second, got away ahead of the counsel for the defense and said:

"The court has been patient in listening to argument, but it must be remembered that these Jurymen" (he indicated the jury with a sweep of his hand) "have laid aside important private affairs in order to serve the county in this capacity. The court has decided, therefore, to limit the time in which the learned counsel may present his reasons for a dismissal. At three o'clock, the ruling will be made, willy-nilly."

Fitz-Henry Fish, Sr., did not bat an eyelash. "It is within the power of this honorable court to impose certain limitations on the time consumed by counsel, but your honor will not mind if I call it to his attention that the power of limitation he is about to exercise is defined rather broadly by the statutes. In the cases of Pennypacker vs. Brigham Young, et al.; Chute and Leavitt vs. Simard; Pedro Montana vs. Armstrong; in fact, I could cite at least a hundred cases; the higher court has ruled that county courts may pass on the questions of the legality of subpoenas, summons, writs of replevin, indictments and/or depositions, sworn statements, written testimony, and related matters, only after the defense has had ample time to present its contentions, allegations and remonstrances, either orally or in writing.

"I am willing to argue the restrictionary powers of the court in the present instance, with the understanding, of course, that the time thus employed will not be deducted from the two additional hours the court has already granted, or is considering granting, for me to conclude my arguments on the question of dismissal. Is that understood?"

"Glub," said Judge Patterson, who was trailing by several paragraphs and thus was caught napping again.

"Thank you, Your Honor. I was sure you would be eminently reasonable," said Fish, Sr. "Now on the question of the court's right to limit arguments concerning the legality of the indictment, I should like to tell an anecdote, if I may, that involves the late Chief Justice Marshall of the United States Supreme Court. It seems that the justices of that august tribunal, just after the War of 1812 . . ."

"Holy cracky, he ain't got as far as the forty-niners yet," said one of the dry farmers in the audience. "I'm goin' back to the homestead and get in my oats before the witnesses are called."

"Can't you submit a brief?" asked the judge, of Fish.

"Of course I shall do that later, and in it I will amplify my argu-ments. Now, the Justices of the Supreme Court, just after the War of 1812, formed the habit of having a pitcher of grog on the table while court was in session . . ."

Bang! resounded the gavel. "I fail to see what grog in 1812 has to do with the death of Louis or Luigi Flato, alias Donniker Louey," roared the judge.

"I was coming to that," said Fitz-Henry, Sr., and smiled.

At three o'clock the versatile attorney was still coming to it and Larkspur Gilligan, unable to accept a passive role any longer, sprang to his feet.

"Your Honor," Larkspur began.

"I trust the court will preserve order," said Fish, Sr. "In the case of Pratt vs. Pratt, et al., Nevada, 1902, a mistrial was granted because of disorder in the court room."

The sheriff got into action. "He insulted the court, Judge. He said you couldn't keep order. Shall I run him in?"

Gilligan began to swear, the sheriff got out his six-shooters, Judge Patterson rapped with his second-string gavel until it also was shattered, but Fitz-Henry Fish, Sr., kept right on talking, ex-cept that he had switched from the story about the grog in 1812 to the question of mistrials because of public or private demonstra-tions in court rooms. Outside, the young boys who were watching through the open windows started running full speed for the sa-loons to fetch their elders.

"There's something goin' to bust. Four of 'em are talking at once now, and the sheriff's pulled his gun," one kid said, and streaked back to the scene of action.

"May I make a statement?" the foreman of the jury asked, but failed to make himself heard. The uproar had spread to the bal-cony and the vacant lots outside.

The court stenographer, who had been put through such a test of endurance by Fish, Sr., that she was on the verge of a break-down, began twitching and screaming. Two women fainted and were lugged out feet first. It took the combined efforts of the court officers, extra police, county employees and several volunteer first-aid workers to restore a semblance of quiet, and the moment the room was still, Attorney Fish resumed as if nothing had happened.

"The grog, which now was served only on rainy days . . ." he began.

The sheriff made a dive at his legs from behind while several deputies tackled Fitz-Henry from the front. Now the Boston attorney, while at Harvard, had pulled a mean oar in the 'varsity scull and the strength he still had in his elbows and shoulders was attested by the fact that he sideswiped Hockaday in the schnozzle, flooring that young official and putting him out of the free-for-all, while with his right toe, which had been instrumental in beating Yale 4–0 in 1908, Fitz-Henry booted the station agent all the way over the press table to the bench. Had not the foreman of the jury reached over, grabbed the judge's gavel and dealt the fighting Fish a wallop on the top of his head, there is no telling how the melee would have resulted. As it was, Fitz-Henry, Sr., decidedly *hors de combat*, was lugged off to the hoosegow, having been charged with contempt of court.

"Now we can get down to business," Jim Leonard said, and sighed.

"First witness for the state," roared Judge Patterson, visibly cheered. The senatorship had drifted back over the horizon—not far back, but still it could be seen.

The first witness was Larkspur Gilligan, and Highpockets, the prosecuting attorney, rose in his place to conduct the direct examination.

Q. "Your name?"

A. "Patrick Gilligan."

Q. "Profession?"

A. "Oh, what the hell's the use of all that stuff? You know who I am, where I live, and as much as is good for you of what I do . . ."

"The counsel for the State will be as brief as possible," Judge Patterson said severely.

Q. "Where were you, Mr. Gilligan, on the 28th of November last?"

A. "On my sheep ranch."

Q. "Did you hold any conversation there with the deceased, Donniker Louey?"

A. "I did."

Q. "What did he say?"

A. "He said he was going to Three Buttes to talk with Jim Leonard."

Q. "Did he tell you what he was going to talk about?"

A. "He was going to ask him, for me, if Jim would sell his water rights."

Q. "Did you ever see the deceased again?"

A. "Yes and no. I saw him in a grave on Cottonwood Creek, a couple of weeks ago."

"That's all for the present, Mr. Gilligan," Highpockets said.

"In the absence of counsel for the defense, will the defendant waive cross-examination of the witness?" Judge Patterson asked benignly of Jim Leonard.

The rancher was bewildered. "I didn't kill the deceased, or anyone else, since 1910," he said.

"All in good time, you will be permitted to testify," the judge said. "Just now I am asking if you will waive cross-examination."

"Not on your tintype," said a cheery voice in the rear, and young Fitz-Henry Fish came down the center aisle, waving some documents in his hand. He had got in on the afternoon stage from Mondak not five minutes before and had been informed, briefly, at the Hotel Jordan, what had happened to his father.

"Order," yelled the judge.

"I'm Fitz-Henry Fish, Jr., of Fish, Fish, Cabot and Saltonstall, counsel for the defense," the young man said, and a murmur arose in the court room while faint cheers sounded in the vacant lots.

"Your credentials," snapped the judge, at loss as to what to do.

"Oh, I brought along the old sheepskin, all right. Had a close call getting it, but here it is," said Fish, Jr., and spread his diploma

from Harvard Law School and his Massachusetts certificate of ad-
mission to the bar on the counsel table.

"You wish to cross-examine the witness?" the judge asked.

"First, with Your Honor's permission, I should like to ask for a
postponement. I just got in, on the stage, and therefore am unprepared."

"Be Jesus, it's startin' all over again," said a fur trader in the
balcony, and got up to leave the hall.

The judge rapped, the foreman of the jury and the sheriff pulled
their guns and the court stenographer began to twitch and shudder again.

"The court has ruled," Judge Patterson said, "that no postponement will be granted on the grounds that the counsel for the defense is unprepared."

"Sorry, Your Honor," said young Fish. "And don't think I hold
it against you because the *pater* got the bum's rush. If anyone can
get the best of the *pater*, Fitz-Henry, Jr., knowing the difficulties,
steps right up and says, 'More power to him.'"

"The defendant," Judge Patterson said, "refused stubbornly to
employ counsel until the eleventh hour. Now we are showered with
attorneys."

"It isn't my fault, Judge," Jim Leonard said.

"I hereby give notice," said young Fish, "that when I have finished with the witness who has just been examined by the prosecuting attorney, I shall argue the question of dismissal of the case,
and after that the change of venue. This afternoon, however, while
the direct testimony, if that is not too dignified a word for what
was offered by Patrick Gilligan, is still fresh in the minds of the
jury, I shall cross-examine him."

"Mr. Gilligan, would you mind taking the stand again?" asked
Judge Patterson.

"Am I to understand that it is optional with Mr. Gilligan?" asked
Fish, Jr. "Is he, perhaps, entitled to some special privileges or im-
munities not usual in a court of law?"

"You're a fresh young punk," said Larkspur, draping his lanky
form over the witness stand once more.

"I shall argue that question after the change of venue has been discussed," said Fitz-Henry, Jr., good-humoredly, and in spite of himself, the old prospector on the jury chuckled. Miriam, sitting tensely in her place, began to feel a certain confidence in the irrepressible college lad who had come upon the scene so unexpectedly.

"Begin the cross-examination, if you please," said Judge Patterson.

"Right-O. We're off," young Fish said. "First of all, Mr. Gilligan, I wish to ask you if you are sure that you talked with the deceased on November 28?"

"I've already said so," replied Gilligan.

Q. "Was that the first time you ever saw him?"

A. "No. He'd been around the ranch quite a while."

Q. "Purely by chance, or did you send for him?"

A. "A friend of mine in Chicago sent him out. Said Louey needed a job."

Q. "Did he bring references from any persons or concerns for whom he had worked?"

A. "No."

Q. "Who was the friend who recommended him?"

A. "Baldy Santo."

Q. "What is Mr. Santo's profession?"

Gilligan, annoyed, turned to the judge. "Is this stuff pertinent?" he asked.

"I must ask the counsel for the defense to state where this questioning is leading?" the judge said.

"Well, of course, I've only been on this case five minutes or so, but it struck me as being strange that a man of affairs like Mr. Gilligan would employ a gangster under indictment for several murders in Illinois, on recommendation of one of the most notorious gang leaders in America, to ask a simple question of a neighbor Mr. Gilligan had known fifty years," young Fitz-Henry said.

"That's my business," said Gilligan.

"Quite," said Fish, Jr. "Now perhaps you will tell us how it happened that the chief identification witness for the State, the father, self-styled, of the deceased . . ."

"What do you mean, self-styled? A man knows his own son, doesn't he?" demanded Larkspur, aroused.

"We will come to that later. First I want to know if witness Flato, we will call him (all these Chicago chaps seem to have a variety of names), was your guest for several days before he was asked to identify the body?"

"He was," Gilligan said. "I felt sorry for the old man and asked him to stay at my place, that's all."

"You didn't prime him a bit, by any chance?"

Bang! The gavel hit the table, and the stenographer ducked. "That question will be stricken from the record, as impertinent and insinuatory," said the judge.

Young Fish turned to the jury. "Do your duty, men, and try to forget it," he said, and smiled.

Larkspur Gilligan turned a shade of purple something like a hail cloud.

"If I have to caution the counsel for the defense again, he will be barred from the court room," the judge said.

"By that time the *pater*'ll be out on bail. We Fish are known as stickers. Not brilliant, but persistent, if you get what I mean. Now, Mr. Gilligan. You have testified that you wanted the defendant's water rights. May I ask what for?"

"Look here, Judge. Can this young rah-rah boy ask me about my private business? All I got to say about this case is that Donniker Louey left my place November 28th, bound for Three Buttes, to ask Jim Leonard if he'd sell his water rights. Donniker Louey never came back, and just this spring we found he had been shot, with a gun like Jim Leonard's, and buried on Cottonwood Creek."

Judge Patterson cleared his throat. "The cross-questioning must be kept within proper bounds. The only matters before us have to do with the death of Louis Flato, or Donniker Louey."

"But, Your Honor," objected young Fish. "If I can show that Mr. Gilligan was anxious to get the defendant out of the way . . ."

Another gavel was shattered. "This is my last warning," said the judge.

"I trust that Your Honor does not intend to apply the doctrine of *omnia praesumuntur rite esse acta* to the witness now on the stand," Fitz-Henry, Jr., said.

"I beg your pardon?" the judge said, obviously rattled.

"I should like to ask the Court, for the purposes of the record, in view of the fact that this court room is the focus of all eyes throughout the breadth of our land, whether or not the doctrine of *omnia praesumuntur rite esse acta* is to be applied to Mr. Gilligan."

"Anybody who starts in applying any of this high-falutin foreign stuff to me will have to fight," Larkspur Gilligan said.

"No offense," continued Fish. "I did not go so far as to ask for *omnia praesumuntur contra spoliatorem*, but I should have to file an objection—it would be my plain duty to my client" (he glanced around at Jim Leonard, who winced) "to contest the theory of *omnia praesumuntur rite esse acta*. I should like also to ask my distinguished opponent, the prosecuting attorney, what his feelings are in the matter. Would he be willing, with the consent of the bench, to compromise on something about half way between those opposing doctrines?"

The prospector on the jury, seeing the woebegone expression on the face of Attorney Highpockets, burst out laughing, in which he was joined by the trouble shooter and the lightning-rod salesman.

"The kid's sure boiled over and wrinkled his spine. They'll have to rake and thumb him, sure 'nough, or he'll bust 'em in two," the old desert rat cackled.

"His old man rung in grog dated 1812, now the kid's got 'em dizzy with mumbo jumbo. Say, what is this here *omnia prae*-something or other? I think the jury ought to know," said the trouble shooter. Young Fish was in his element. "Perhaps I can make myself clearer," he said. "What I am getting at is that the weight of a witness' testimony depends on the character of the said witness. If I can establish, for instance, that none of Mr. Gilligan's intimates in Chicago, where he transacts the bulk of his business, are *absque fraudem* . . ."

"There he goes. He's a-buckin' and a-pitchin' again," chortled the old prospector. He was one of the few on the jury who wanted the job, at three bucks a day, to continue indefinitely.

Judge Patterson turned shell pink, which clashed with the Gilligan mauve. "If any demonstrations of approval or disapproval occur, the court room will be cleared," he shouted.

"Can't kick out the jury, or there won't be no trial," the desert rat said. In leaner years, he had been forced to set prairie fires and then get himself sworn in as deputy fire warden in order to make both ends meet.

Young Fish, meanwhile, was grinning at Tom Jackson, who had been aroused from his semi-stupor by the forcible ejection of Fitz-Henry, Sr., and was dashing off a colorful item for the A.P. BOSTON FISH NIXED BY HIX was the way he had started it off. To the newspaperman's delight, the young Harvard graduate assumed his blandest smile and walked over to the bench, beckoning the prosecuting attorney to follow him. Soon the judge, Larkspur Gilligan and the two lawyers were in a huddle.

"I tell you what I'll do," said young Fish, with disarming aplomb. "I'll soft pedal the Latin if you'll give me a bit of leeway. Otherwise, I'll have to insist on a ruling between the doctrines of *omnia* . . ."

"The court wishes to be fair," said Patterson, who did not relish an A.P. story to the effect that the future candidate for State Senator, Governor, United States Senator and even higher offices was stumped by schoolboy's Latin.

"I want to ask Gilligan about his friends in Chicago. Do I continue, in English, or shall we go into a brace or two of doctrines in Latin? Not only could I ring in the *omnias* already in the record, if the old gal with the Gibson *coiffure* really got what I said, but a few odd items like *billa non vera, coram non judice, lex loci delictus, de minimis non curat lex* . . ."

"Why not let him ask the questions, then rule 'em out afterward?" suggested Highpockets, who, while no Latin scholar, was a trader from birth.

"Topping, my cherished old opponent," said young Fitz-Henry, and the questioning was resumed. To the horror of the judge, the majority of the jury, the witnesses, the spectators and particularly the defendant, the young man pulled from his briefcase a telephone directory of Chicago, which he had brought along for his own convenience in keeping in touch with various loose young women.

"*Nom de dieu. Il commence avec les 'A',*" said Frémont to Dr. Toudoux.

"*Naturellement,*" the doctor replied. "*Ça c'est parfaitement togique, pas?*"

"Do you happen to know Miss Amelia C. M. Aaberg, of 1659 North Humbolt Street, Mr. Gilligan?" asked Fish, Jr.

"Never heard of her," said Gilligan.

The same question was asked regarding Carl Aabye, of 12234 S. Egelston Street; Othella Aadland, of 2701 West Lunt; Lars Aadnesen, 2529 North Kimball; and so on through the "A's." By quitting time, the audience had thinned out to a faithful few, Gilligan was on the verge of a fit, and the judge's prospects of political advancement had been reduced to nil, minus the heavy mortgage Gilligan held on the palatial judicial residence and the articles of furniture and personal property, both tangible and intangible, contained therein.

"I'll have to ask one of the boys to ride in from Three Buttes with a shirt and a change of underwear," said Jim Leonard dismally, when the session was adjourned.

That young Fish was highly elated was evidenced by the snorts of satisfaction that came through the thin walls of his room at the Hotel Jordan when, late that night, he was still poring over the records and mapping his campaign for the morrow. He had called to see his father through the bars and had slipped Fitz-Henry, Sr., a package of peanut brittle, of which the famous attorney was inordinately fond, then excused himself in order to continue his work on the case, leaving his father spluttering with indignation. The matter of wiring for his father's bail, he said, would be attended to as soon as certain promises regarding transfer to the Boston office of Fish, Fish, Cabot and Saltonstall had been committed to paper in proper form and signed.

The third morning of the trial was sparsely attended, and nothing was accomplished except to get as far as Dhargomozhyskov, Bill, of 1465 Canal Street, whom Gilligan did not know. At two-thirty in the afternoon, however, the messenger boys started running toward the saloons. A break had occurred.

Monotonously young Fish had plowed through the Dh's and the witnesses were, for the most part, fast asleep.

"Mr. Gilligan," the young lawyer asked, "do you know one Michelangelo Diocanne, of 6005 South Albany?"

"No," snapped Gilligan. He had just made up his mind to have both Fish tarred, feathered and bounced half way to Billings on rails from which the splinters had not been planed, and be damned to the A.P. and the eyes of the nation.

"Let me put the question in another form," persisted Fish, Jr. "Have you ever heard any of your friends mention the name of Michelangelo Diocanne?"

"Never," said Gilligan. "And I'm getting fed up with this horse-play. I'll answer your fool questions until quarter of three, and not one minute longer."

"Sufficient unto the moment . . ." paraphrased Fitz-Henry, Harvard '30. "I wish to call the attention of the Court and the patient members of the jury to a strange state of confusion in the witness' mind. He has repeated twice, fully *compos mentis* . . . I beg your pardon, Judge. Just a slip. Unintentional, I assure you. The witness has repeated that he does not know one Michelangelo Diocanne, although Mr. Diocanne has spent weeks at his home, and at the present time is peacefully snoring within six feet of Witness Gilligan."

"That's Mike Flato," Gilligan said.

"I am aware that the gentleman is on record here as Michel Flato, fruit dealer and bereaved father of Louis Flato, alias Donniker Louey. It happens also that he is Michelangelo Diocanne, shoemaker, of 6005 South Albany Street, and that the Chicago Grand Jury found sufficient cause to indict him, just previous to his visit to Mr. Gilligan, for having stabbed with intent to kill one Adolph Percolese, of the Capone faction, against whom our Baldy Santo had waged unremitting war."

The old man, Flato or Diocanne, began to groan and roll his eyes. "I gotta one by Jesus Christa bigga pain," he said, clutching his abdomen, and Judge Patterson, spurred by the emergency into some rapid thinking, adjourned court until the following day.

28

Of the Mental Attributes of Sheepherders

THE THIRTY-ONE TOUGH MILES from Glendive to Wibaux, across flats and badlands, were covered by Tumbleweed O'Flaherty in a single night, and morning found him camped on Beaver Creek, frying sow belly and making sourdough bread, his pan, prospector's hammer and spade beside him. He had not discovered that Homer Evans was held prisoner by Baldy Santo, or that Homer's nicely adjusted brain had suffered by collision with an iron rail. Santo kept under cover during daylight hours and the windows of the old caboose were skillfully shaded. The deposed sheriff, and seeker after the legendary fleece, however, took a turn through the town, on the pretext that he needed to buy salt before hitting for the high hills.

In the general store the conversation, while not confined to Yea-yea and Nay-nay, might as well have been, for all the information it contained. But while passing the depot, Tumbleweed heard the voice of the freight agent who shared the popular belief that by shouting into a cracked phone he could counteract the instrument's deficiencies.

"That's what I said, Tank water. Tank. T-a-n-c. There's a train load, mebbe two trainloads o' stinkers comin' through from Ideeho," was the text of the agent's communication.

"Yeah. They gotta drink. The grass ain't green enough yet so they can travel long stretches without water," the agent continued.

Tumbleweed O'Flaherty was all ears. The only big sheepman for hundreds of miles around who wintered his flock in Idaho was Larkspur Gilligan, and it was a full month before the season when

Gilligan usually moved his sheep to the summer range on the Yellowstone. A little later, he saw a string of slat cars, empty and sealed, marked for Oakland, California, and a railroad man was walking along and changing the destination of each with a piece of chalk. The one gondola was left as it was, with the Oakland label. As soon as he could, Tumbleweed ambled down the tracks and inspected the new marking. The slat cars had been re-routed to Ashton, Idaho, on the Oregon Short Line. That was Gilligan's winter range.

"Now, durn and blast it all. I've gone and hoofed it all the way from Glendive to here, and now I've got to hoof it back again," Tumbleweed said. He didn't dare trust the telephone and he had to get in touch with Jim Leonard without delay.

What did Gilligan have in mind? It was clear to the old prospector that the unseasonable return of the sheep from Idaho had been timed to coincide with Leonard's trial and the stampede brought on by the airmen. So Tumbleweed picked up his tools and, in the heat of the strong spring sun, started walking the track back where he came from.

OF THE PAIR WHO WERE CAMPING in the old caboose, Homer Evans was by far the more tranquil. The injury to his head, he had concluded, was not a permanent one but was severe enough to make it necessary for him to lie quietly and postpone arduous thinking until he was somewhat stronger. He knew nothing of the trial in progress in Glendive but was concerned about the badge of authority and the documents he had ordered from Chicago. If young Fitz-Henry sent the papers by air mail, addressed to Three Buttes, Homer assumed that Miriam, in his absence, would open the envelopes. Just what she would do after that, he did not try to guess, for a preliminary sally into that field of conjecture started his head throbbing in an admonitory way. So he devoted himself to the lighter task of badgering the restive Santo.

On the second day of the trial, however, just about the time Fitz-Henry, Sr., was hearing the clang of the cell door, Evans felt a change for the better. He wondered, in an experimental way, what steps, if any, were being taken for his rescue, and immediately, unaccompanied by migraine or other distressing symptoms, his convalescent brain rewarded him with the answer: Rain-No-More. Hitherto Homer had been unable to leave any signs along the route, but to that end he quickly applied his extraordinary powers. Day and night, except at meal times, he was trussed up in the duck straitjacket* and bound in such a way that he could not leave the bed. When it was necessary to visit the john, his bonds were loosened so that he could shuffle to the end of the caboose. But Santo, whose nerves were being rubbed raw by the period of enforced inaction, devoted all his ingenuity to keeping Homer helpless and to that end had removed the door of the W.C. and sat opposite with a machine gun trained on the humble throne whenever Evans was in occupancy. Nevertheless, Homer did not despair.

First he suggested, as a pastime, a simple gambling game originated in the Yale Theological School. Two cockroaches, one marked with a bit of colored string, the other with a plain white thread around its middle, were placed on the board that served as a tray. Baldy Santo, who loved games of chance, fell in with the idea at once and chalked three circles on the tray, one in the center, and one in each of diagonally opposite corners. In the central circle, covered with an inverted tin cup, the two labeled roaches were placed, one backed by Evans, the other by Santo. The roaches were kept in the dark enough to allow the pupils of their eyes to expand, so that when suddenly they found themselves in bright light they were bewildered and made a dash for safety. Several classes of bets could be made on the outcome. The first man whose corner circle was crossed by a fleeing cockroach won a small prize, which was doubled if the insect remained outside three-fifths of a second. If the roach which chose Baldy's circle was his own entry, for instance, the gang chief got a double premium. At once, the watchful Santo became fascinated, and was particularly enthusiastic because at first he won consistently, to the point that Homer was obliged to sign a stack of I.O.U.'s.

---

* Brooks Appliance Co., Inc.

Now and then, of course, a roach would escape and had to be replaced with another, which offered no difficulty, since the caboose was amply supplied. Gradually Homer, whose hand was quicker than Santo's eye, was able to catch, squeeze into insensibility and stow beneath his blanket a number of the insects and also several of the score sheets. At night, while he was feigning sleep, Evans scrawled on the fragments of paper thus acquired a number of Indian signs indicating where he was, who was with him and by what route they had come to Wibaux. The blood of the roaches served as ink.

Having a photographic memory, Evans was able to reconstruct the small town and its sidetracks, having passed through it on his way to Glendive some weeks before. The siding on which his caboose stood faced northeast. Across the tracks, at the junction with the main line, was a long snow fence blocked up with tumbleweeds. Homer waited until the wind was high, which never was much of a wait in Wibaux, and was able to detect the direction of the strong air currents by the rattling of the windows of the car. Thus, straitjacketed and covered with a Tommy gun, in full sight of his captor, he was able to drop his messages through the toilet tube at moments when the wind from the southwest was blowing steadily. Of course, the telltale pieces of paper, on which he had written with roaches' blood what he wished to convey, brought up against the drift barrier along the main line tracks and clung there. And once the countryside was well strewn, Evans concentrated on detecting Santo's method of nobbling his entries, double-crossing the gang leader with his own tricks, and won back his I.O.U.'s and a substantial sum besides. He might soon have need of ready cash, he believed.

IN THE MEANTIME, Tumbleweed O'Flaherty got back into Glendive under cover of night, and by rapping softly on Tom Jackson's door upstairs in the Hotel Jordan came very close to causing two fond hearts to cease beating as one, or at all, for that matter.

"It's me. Tumbleweed. Let me in," the former sheriff whispered.

Jackson's reply contained several elements, including profanity, relief, social falsehood and the request to wait a minute. However, the newspaperman and the old prospector were soon in conference with Miriam and Jim Leonard, who received the news that Gilligan's sheep, numbering thirty thousand, were on the move from Idaho a month ahead of time.

"He's going to pull a fast one," Jackson said, and Miriam, pale and determined, strapped on her automatics.

Since Jim Leonard could not leave Glendive while the trial was in progress, he telephoned Hank and asked him to ride into town the next day, with all the men available, for a council of war. Hank gave the word, the triangle clanged at Three Buttes, there was another quick phone call to Muddy Creek, a signal fire was lighted near the hot and cold springs to warn the Blackfeet and summon the Chief and the medicine man, and, by moonlight, down the Leonard Creek trail rode a grim and determined body of men and women of assorted races and backgrounds but with a firm single purpose, namely, to meet force with force and get the best of Gilligan. They rode in a column of twos, as, follows:

Hank, the foreman	The Professor
Colonel Lvov Ivanovich Kvek	Captain Grigori Hippolito-vich Lidin
Hjalmar Jansen	Anton Diluvio (*né* Andrew Flood)
Chief Shot-on-Both-Sides	Trout-tail III, I.M.D.
Sergeant Bonnet	Sergeant Schlumberger
Chef Corrigan	Galilee Zach
Sterling Cromwell	"Big George" Washington
Stenka Ivkich	Hugo Weiss (incognito) in Blackfeet costume
Princess Tinted Cloud	Princess Unreal Bear

Back at Opera Lodge was left on guard the unlucky Laramee Bob, who had lost the determining hand of poker, Eugénie

Toudoux, Beatrice Baxter Diluvio, and Wing Lee—all resolved to carry on with the utmost vigilance. Beatrice, a fair shot, sat in the plane with a sawed-off shotgun across her enticing silk-clad knees; Madame Toudoux, as calm and withal as wary as if she were in a salon in the Faubourg St. Germain, stood on guard on the western butte from which she could survey miles of the surrounding country; the buckaroo from Laramee kept watch over the prisoners, who had sensed trouble was in the wind; and Wing Lee took tender care of the invalids.

Through the watches of the same eventful night sat in grim conference Larkspur Gilligan, the wreck of the dapper Judge Patterson and Sheriff Warren Hockaday, with a shiner from Fitz-Henry, Senior's, elbow that would have won a prize among the watercolors in the Independent Show. The irate sheepman was laying down his final dictum, which he emphasized with bouts of table pounding that shook the judicial mansion to its foundations.

"Tomorrow the case goes to the jury, and no monkeyshines," said Gilligan, fixing the judge with a baleful eye. "And, furthermore, I'll give the jury just twenty minutes to bring in a verdict. If you can't hooley-ann that college kid, you won't represent this State in the Senate or anywhere else. You'll find yourself one of the People you talk so much about, and I'll foreclose the mortgage in the bargain."

"But, Gilligan. He'll ask for a ruling on that . . . er . . . *omnia praesumuntur* business that even Lawyer Anderson in Minneapolis never heard of," said the quivering judge.

"He won't do no such thing, because that *omnia* stuff, whatever in hell it is, he's trying to pin on me. I won't be there. I shall have been excused, on the ground of pressing affairs outside the State. And that Wop we got for a weeper will be in the hospital, indisposed, and you'll accept his deposition. That, with the sheepherders' story, ought to be enough for the A.P. and the eyes of the whole bloody nation, and if it isn't, let 'em all get glasses. I want action and I want it pronto," said Gilligan, in part.

Therefore, when the trial opened at ten next morning, Judge Patterson, wan from a sleepless night, called to the bench the defendant and the opposing counsel, one of whom was holding the telephone directory in a meaningful way and was muttering what he remembered of the first book of Julius Caesar, padded out with a few Kyries and a Sanctus or two.

"Now listen, folks," the judge whispered. "Jim here's anxious to get through with this trial. He's said so himself, haven't you, Jim?"

Regardless of the pressure on his right big toe from the shoe of his vigilant attorney, the rancher said: "You bet."

"Mr. Gilligan, who was on the stand, has been called away," the judge continued. "I want to open up this morning with a few depositions, just to get 'em out of the way . . ."

"I should like to examine them first," said young Fitz-Henry. "In the absence of the *pater*, I'm *curator ad hoc*, in a manner of speaking, of the defendant's interests. Should there be anything contained in these documents touching on or constituting *damnum absque injuria, dedimus potestatum* . . ."

"You're wanted on the telephone in the ante-room," said Sheriff Hockaday, pulling his gun.

The young lawyer did some rapid thinking. With one Fish in the jug and another drilled full of holes, and Cabot and Saltonstall two thousand miles away, the case would go to pot, he concluded, and reluctantly followed the direction indicated by Hockaday's Smith & Wesson. As he had suspected, the phone call was not for him, but when he got back the trial was in full sway. First, Mike Flato's affidavit that he had identified the body of the deceased as Donniker Louey, his son, was read and explained to the jury, who drank it in avidly as an indication that the end was near.

But the trump cards produced by the prosecutor, Highpockets, were the depositions of the sheepherders, Stumpbroke and Jill. They were identical, signed untidily with an "X," and set forth:

"That on the 28th day of November the undersigned was in possession of his faculties . . ."

"I object," said Fitz-Henry, Jr., waving a sheaf of papers under Highpocket's nose. "From information I have at hand, neither of these sheepherders has been in possession of his faculties since early childhood, if at all. On the question of *non compos mentis* . . ."

Six-shooters started waving in his direction like cornleaves in a breeze.

"Objection overruled," snapped the judge, who was more bold when cornered.

The reading of the depositions was continued. The sheepherders, according to their sworn statement, had been at the head of Cottonwood Creek on November 28th, late in the afternoon; had seen the deceased, then living, on an old white horse. The defendant, Jim Leonard, they stated, had ridden in from the direction of Three Buttes and after an altercation with the deceased had plugged him with a rifle, then buried him. The witnesses, afraid of the vengeance of the disorderly element among the cattlemen, had refrained from telling the authorities what they had witnessed until assured of full protection of the law.

An automatic barked and deposition No. 1, that of Stumpbroke, went flying into the air.

"It's a lie," said Miriam, the gun smoking in her hand.

Amid the tattoo of the gavel, shrieks of women and mingled shouts of men, her arms were pinned from behind by a squad of deputies, while two others slipped handcuffs over the wrists of the roaring and struggling Jim Leonard. After his first fit of rage had subsided, however, the rancher's law-abiding instincts regained the upper hand.

"Sit tight, my girl," he cautioned. "Let's hear it all before we make another move."

"I insist on being heard. I stand on my rights as a citizen and a member of the bar," said young Fitz-Henry, ignoring the muzzles of the Smith & Wessons. "Shoot if you must this jolly old onion, but as long as it sits on the shoulders of a Fish, he will assert and reiterate the doctrines on which American jurisprudence has leaned, to become the envy and admiration of the civilized world."

He was muzzled by what seemed to him a multitude of extraordinarily heavy hands.

Judge Patterson, trembling and sweating like a Trojan, got into action. "The counsel for the defense has been warned repeatedly by the Court for infringements of legal procedure. Already I have had sufficient grounds for excluding him from this court room and his conduct this morning has forced me reluctantly to come to a decision . . ."

The judge paused, turned a shade of cheese green, and his eyes protruded from their sockets. For unlike the others in the room, he was facing the rear and was seeing, entering grimly and lining up in formidable array, left to right:

Hank, the foreman; the Professor; Colonel Lvov Ivanovich Kvek; Captain Grigori Hippolitovich Lidin, Hjalmar Jansen, and Anton Diluvio.

That would have been plenty to give pause to more courageous judges than Patterson, but in the bargain were facing him:

Chief Shot-on-Both-Sides and Trout-tail III in full paint and feathers; Sergeants Bonnet and Schlumberger of the Paris police; Corrigan and Galilee Zach; the two colored waiters; Stenka Ivkich, Hugo Weiss, in Indian disguise; and the Princesses Tinted Cloud and Unreal Bear.

With frantic effort, the judge cleared his throat and faintly at last the words came:

"On the other hand," he resumed, "it is the wish of this Court to give fair play to every man, however impetuous, and for that reason the attorney for the defense may proceed."

"That's sporting of you, Judge," said young Fish, surprised but not bewildered, and within two-fifths of a second he was launching into one of his outstanding efforts which began:

"On the question of *non compos mentis* as applied to absent witnesses, known respectively as Stumpbroke and Jill, I should like to point out to the honorable court the decision of the higher court of the Hall-Mills case involving Simple Willie Stevens; and that gem of American jurisprudence, the opinion of a minority of the justices of the United States Supreme Court in their review of Peaches vs. Browning.

"The court will remember that Browning, defendant, was addicted to certain childish games in the course of which he romped on all fours and emitted creditable 'woofs' in imitation of a grizzly bear."

The stroke of noon, which marked the end of the morning session, interrupted, but only for an hour, young Fish's list of pertinent citations and precedents, which, he contended, clearly disqualified fever-stricken sheepherders until such time as the defense could produce capable alienists and psychiatrists to pass on their mental condition.

In the jury box, the old prospector, who had bribed one of the attendants to slip him a bottle of Jamaica ginger, which he preferred to the more effete bottled liquors, was standing and cheering the young Harvard man with undisguised admiration.

"Twist 'em! Kettle 'em to a fare-ye-well. Keep your lunch hooks clear of that horn," the old juryman yelled. "I got nine dollars comin' from the county that says you can ride 'em, kid, straight up and handsome. Whoopee!"

In which yell Hjalmar Jansen, the Russians and the Indians joined lustily.

29
In Which Furniture Is Moved out and in While Trench Warfare Looms, Not to Mention John Marshall and Sigmund Freud

IN HIS TREK THROUGH THE BADLANDS Rain-No-More, together with his pinto and Moritz the dog, were astonished to hear, borne faintly on the southwest wind, the strains of an out-of-tune piano on which was being played, with some authority, a ballad entitled: "A Whistlin' Train Came Down the Track, She Blew, She Blew!"

"*Nit se pop pow ka*," the young Indian exclaimed, which may be translated variously as: "Am I dreaming?", "Od's bodkins," or "Blast my timbers."

Moritz, although inarticulate, expressed the same idea with a lift of his eyebrows. What the pinto did has no real place in the story, but it seemed to please him just the same.

Although reluctant to leave the tracks for an instant, Rain-No-More let his curiosity persuade him to investigate and thus came upon the hideout where his tribesmen were concealing from the buzzards *et al* the son of Gilligan, ditto of Santo, the two young men being no longer on speaking terms; four able-bodied gangsters who begged intermittently to be allowed to go back East and face the electric chair, in a way of speaking; three wounded ones with similar inclinations; and last, but not least, Mona Mason, the hookers known as Violet, Rose and Lil, and the piano professor who was grinding out the aforementioned tune.

Madam Mason, whose high place in her profession was due to her ability to adapt herself to circumstances, had received permission to set up her establishment in a commodious cave from which stalactites and stalagmites had been cleared. The braves off duty, and such of the prisoners who earned the privilege by good behavior and were in funds, were allowed to patronize the place between the hours of four in the afternoon and dawn, it having been wisely decided that the girls were entitled to the remaining hours for purposes of rest.

Rain-No-More consulted with the Blackfeet in charge of the encampment but could get no information regarding the gondola No. 354768, bound for Oakland, California. So reluctantly he refreshed himself and hit the trail once more. On and on he pressed, at intervals mounting the pinto, at other times leading the weary animal at a faster pace than could be maintained with Rain-No-More on his back. No longer did the pinto rear and snort when approached by Moritz the dog. In fact, so thoroughly tuckered was the piebald little horse that a child could have slung a live crocodile across its back without eliciting a blink of protest.

When the Indian was nearing Wibaux, he sent Moritz ahead to reconnoiter and was pleased to see the Boxer running back to meet him, visibly elated. Following Moritz's eager gallop, Rain-No-More came upon the first bit of paper Homer Evans had let fly, carefully folded on the glider principle and marked with exactly what Rain-No-More wanted to know. But just as the Blackfeet was about to investigate the caboose cautiously, a shrill whistle warned him of the approach of a passenger train from the east and he was dismayed to see descending to the depot platform an assortment of Great Lakes palefaces in city attire, to the number of ninety-three.

The newcomers stood by the tracks, cursing and shouting ribald comment as the train steamed away toward Glendive and the west.

Rain-No-More knew that he must act quickly, but before he could formulate a plan, he saw Baldy Santo step down from the caboose, glance furtively around, and hit out for the mainline tracks. Baldy never knew exactly what struck him, but when he regained consciousness he was tied up and gagged, in the midst of a large clump of sagebrush with Moritz standing guard in his wistful yet determined way. Homer Evans, lying helpless in the caboose, heard a sound at the door and was overjoyed to see, not the famil-

iar face of Baldy Santo but the imperturbable countenance of Rain-
No-More. With a few slashes of his hunting knife, the Indian cut
Evans loose and explained in a whisper their situation. Two minutes later they were crawling through the brush toward Baldy
Santo, and while the assembled gangsters were still milling around
the center of Wibaux, their leader was being hustled back into the
badlands at double quick time. The abandoned pinto, left to his
own devices, limped disconsolately behind. Around them were
crumbling sandstone, mounds of rust-colored ashes, terraces of
lava rock, in ledges and chunks. A few lichens clung to the firmer
boulders and in mangy patches scrub sagebrush and false dande-
lions continued their losing struggle. The sun beat down, gusts of
wind stirred the alkali dust.

BUT IF THE READER thinks the foregoing panorama is desolate, what
would he have thought had he been at the same moment on Custer
Avenue, Glendive, in front of the residence of Judge and Myra
Patterson where Sheriff Hockaday, in a desperate effort to save
his own skin, was carrying out Larkspur Gilligan's instructions to
the last Chippendale? Two squads of deputies, in fact, had backed
up as many huge moving vans and were lugging through the open
doorway, from which the John Hancock grill work had been detached, carved bedsteads and billowy Ostermoors; framed chro-
mos and reproductions ranging from Botticelli and the Landscape
with Mill johnny to Maxfield Parrish and Rosa Bonheur; Morris
chairs, Grand Rapids sofas; china and crockery stamped Wedgwood
or Montgomery Ward; a grand piano in the bench of which popular songs of the epoch were flapping, *Hallelujah, Blue Heaven* and
the *St. Louis Blues*; highboys and lowboys; the kitchen range and
all sorts of enameled receptacles marked coffee, tea, etc.; pots,
pans, colanders, calendars, incinerators, Frigidaires, bridge tables
with attachments for holding drinks, ash trays, established brands
of playing cards, chafing dishes, night tables, back scratchers of
exotic models, signed photographs in fish nets, college pennants,
and articles of clothing and toilet necessities too intimate to be
catalogued here.

And in one corner of the nearly empty living room, from which had been snatched the Baluchistan rug, sat Judge Patterson, head in his hands, a crushed and sorrowing man. For at the hour the whistle had blown, young Fitz-Henry Fish had been reciting in court "Tom's a-cold" from *King Lear*, in an effort to draw a triple parallel between Sheepherder Stumpbroke, the Shakespearean fools and Simple Willie Stevens, of Hall-Mills fame, pausing only to serve notice that the next day he would ring in Freud, Jung and Adler in order to prove conclusively that the mother and grand-mothers of the fever-ridden sheepherders must have been as whacky as their sons. The case had not gone to the jury, as Gilligan had ordered, and few among the spectators or even the principals still clung to the belief that eventually it would. Therefore, true to his word, Larkspur had foreclosed the mortgage and seized Judge Patterson's movable goods, and had sent to Butte for a couple of accountants to find something wrong in all the corporations to which Judge Patterson had lent his name.

The judge was up against it, but he had only a shade on Tom Jackson who was comforting the impetuous Myra as best he could. The latter, once the pride of Northern Michigan, was taking the judge's reversal of fortune right on the chin without weakening.

"At least we have each other," she was saying to Tom Jackson, and the reporter could think of no rebuttal until too late. More-over, the evening train had already departed and he was under obligations to Hugo Weiss to stick with the *X-Ray* and see the matter through.

"You might go back to your folks for a visit," Tom murmured weakly.

"No. I shall have the courage to follow the dictates of my heart. How wonderful, Tom, no longer to be obliged to dissimulate—to be able to defy those narrow-minded women who sniffed at my alligator pears and who have never known the frank companion-ship of a man of letters like you," Myra said intensely, as, glancing through the curtains she saw the deputies loading an oil burner and a few spare kegs of nails on top of the Duncan Phyfe table from the library. The Three-Foot Shelf, with sets of O. Henry and Kipling and the Modern Library were being separated from their shelf companions in order to fill voids between the larger articles.

Jim Leonard and his buckaroos and friends were in session in the upstairs dining room of the Jordan when definite word came mysteriously from Wibaux that two trainloads of sheep were due there next morning, with more to follow at intervals of a few hours. Also that nearly one hundred suspicious-looking strangers, probably Chicago gangsters of the Santo mob, had got off the westbound train there and bade fair to terrorize the town, already known as an extremely tough one.

Miriam, when she was handed the telegram in code, sat down limply and began to cry, not from anguish but because her long suspense was over. None other than Homer Evans could have dispatched that message, and that meant he was alive and in charge of things again. Her father, always embarrassed by a show of strong feelings, sat uncomfortable and helpless beside her, patting her shoulder from time to time.

"Steady, my girl," he said, and brought the meeting to order in an informal way.

The first to speak was Hank, the range boss.

"Boys," he said. "When we come by the head of Indian Coulee this mornin', about dawn, I took a good look across the deadline and the bluffs are covered with larkspur, right in its worst season. Do you reckon Gilligan's crazy enough to put a bunch of hungry sheep there now?"

"I can't figure out his game," Jim Leonard said. "Unless he plans to run 'em across our cattle range and drive us out of the country. What else would he have those gangsters for?"

"You hit the nail right on the head," Hank said.

"There's going to be rough stuff," said Hjalmar gleefully. Kvek and Lidin drank and smashed their glasses, which was the signal to the waitress downstairs to bring more liquor.

In the midst of the excitement calmly rose Shot-on-Both-Sides, whose braves, in the absence of the Leonard outfit, had kept the

herd of shorthorns together and worked them gradually toward
Mondak, in the northeastern corner of the range, near the shipping corral.

"Gilligan, unlike most palefaces, is a one-man powwow. He
talks little, acts promptly, thinks all the time. He has divided our
forces, with the cattle and my braves toward the rising sun and the
northern railroad, while we are here entangled with the agents of
the Great White Father. I shall tell you what Gilligan hopes to do.
With the aid of the Great Lakes palefaces he will drive his sheep
on the cattle range, armed also with papers stamped with strong
white man's medicine and colored seals. The sheep will nibble the
grass and everything eatable, even to the roots in the ground and
for fifty or sixty moons not even the lizards will find nourishment
where now there is good grazing.

"Where will the sheepmen cross the deadline? Not on lower
Redwater Creek, which is raging. Not across Indian Coulee, or the
Yellowstone or the Missouri."

The old Chief paused and advanced toward a blackboard which
had been used in a university extension course that had died a
natural death, leaving relics behind. Swiftly he sketched the cattle
range and pointed to the vulnerable spot.

"There," he said, indicating the gap between the head of
Redwater Creek and the range of Mountain Sheep Bluffs, "is where
a sensible man would make the sally, and Gilligan is not a fool."

The Chief sat down, and the telephone rang.

"They're talking Indian," said Jim Leonard, after a bewildered
effort to understand.

"Permit me," said Shot-on-Both-Sides. Then after an exchange
of monosyllables he interpreted, phrase for phrase, what Rain-No-
More, who with Evans' aid had tapped the line along the N.P. right
of way, was saying:

"Greetings, my father."

"*Nit okh si tuk ki*" (I am pleased), replied the Chief.

"Evans is near by, and well."

"*Nit okh si tuk ki a kan o*" (I am *very* pleased).

"Sheepmen, with Great Lakes palefaces and medicine papers from Great White Father, will attack just northwest of Mountain Sheep Bluffs, with Circle as base."

"*Nit okh si tuk ki na pi a—na pi u uk*" (We all are pleased).

"Friend Evans says *neats ap pe kooin* (Frenchmen) know stump hole fighting."

"What's he say?" asked Jim Leonard.

"Stump hole fighting. He must mean trenches," said Miriam.

"*Ah, les trenchées*," said Frémont. "*Les trenchées! En avant!* Over ze top! *Vive les vâches! A bas les moutons.*" His enthusiasm was so spontaneous that it was communicated to Hjalmar, Diluvio, the Russians, colored waiters and especially the French police sergeants and the Princesses Unreal Bear and Tinted Cloud.

Shot-on-Both-Sides held up his hand for silence.

"We are pleased and some of us are drunk," the Chief explained into the transmitter.

"I am sober," said Rain-No-More.

Knowing that the Glendive exchange was in Gilligan's sphere of influence and that all important conversations were reported to him, Evans took the wire and gave instructions to Miriam in Blackfeet, through Shot-on-Both-Sides. He asked that a line of trenches and pill-box machine gun nests be dug and constructed immediately, covering the exposed gap between the bluffs and the Redwater. The work should be done at night, carefully camouflaged and, if possible, kept secret from Gilligan. Miriam noted down the orders patiently, but in the end could not refrain from asking: "But when shall I see him?"

Evans, of course, had learned about the stampede and the capture of the airplane from Rain-No-More. He asked that the plane be sent to the old gangsters' hideout in the badlands, where the train had been marooned and the squirrel meadows made landing feasible. The mercenary flier, he said, should be accompanied by a Blackfeet brave who could take care of himself alone in the badland country. Evans would then replace the brave in the mechanician's seat and carry on from there. He asked especially

that a copy of the *X-Ray* with full account of the trial to date be
dispatched with the plane.

It was a rollicking company, indeed, that set out from the Jordan bar a scant half hour later, hopped on their waiting bronchos,
and rode hard to the north to prepare for the battle. Jim Leonard
watched them wistfully as they drummed across the long bridge
over the roaring muddy Yellowstone. Only Hugo Weiss remained
behind, to get the news of the market on the morrow and to order
ammunition and supplies in code.

The rancher, always troubled by possible legal complications,
was ill at ease until Miriam found out what was on his mind.

"But if Gilligan's got government papers . . ." Jim objected.

"Oh, those," said Weiss. "No doubt Evans has already fixed us
up with some papers, too. If not, I'll have the boys in my office get
in touch with Washington. We'll both have plenty of documents;
then, if we want to, we can string the case along in court until hardly
a sheep now living is still fit for consumption. Don't worry about
that, Jim. That's a question for specialists. Let them fret. That's
what they get their money for."

In another room in the same hotel, a touching reunion was taking place between the Fish, Fitz-Henry, Sr., and Fitz-Henry, Jr.
The former had finally signed the necessary papers about the transfer of the latter from Chicago to Boston, with a generous settle-
ment for the waitress in the Congregationalist Cafeteria. The bail
had been forked over by Cabot and Saltonstall, not without some
broad "a" beefing, and both Fish were planning their orations for
the following day. The elder was going to continue his anecdote
concerning the grog in 1812, while the younger was going to inject
into the trial the virus of psychoanalysis, one complex at a time.

But none of them reckoned with Judge Patterson's consuming
ambition, which made boot-polish and tutti-frutti ice cream practically indistinguishable. The judge was on his way to Gilligan's
sheep ranch in the fastest hack of the Glendive Livery Stable and,
once admitted by the scornful sheepman, Judge Patterson poured
forth alternate pleas for mercy and promises that the jury should
get the case before closing time next day, if both of the Fish had to

be chucked into the Yellowstone with millstones around their necks. The judge had millstones handy, he assured Gilligan, since Myra had thought they would be decorative along the driveway.

"All right. I'll give you one more chance," said Larkspur, and barked into the phone an order to the sheriff to have the furniture put back into the judicial mansion. So until dawn the deputies lugged in antique and Grand Rapids numbers, including the Steinway and the Ostermoors, the *St. Louis Blues*, highboys, lowboys, hot water bottles, douche bags, chafing dishes, photos in fish nets, and the judge's and Myra's extra clothes. Myra, advised of the change, was weeping on Tom's shoulder and swearing she would rather die than go back, while Jackson was arguing that going back, for appearances' sake, would be a noble gesture and that they still could be friends, if they were very careful.

At dawn, viewed only by Hydrangea, Wing Lee, Bat-ear McCluskey, Bird's-eye Cohen, Paperhanger Stuntz, Eugénie Toudoux, Beatrice Diluvio, the curlews below and the turkey buzzards overhead, the plane known as the *Honi Soit*, pronounced by the pilot "So what?", was filled with gasoline, the propeller spun, then whirled; the wheels began to roll, and gradually the plane lifted itself and its bi-racial contents from the sagebrush flat, all but brushed the rim of the western butte and in an hour was over the squirrel meadows in the badlands and descending to earth again.

"Good morning," said Homer Evans pleasantly. "You will keep the motors running, if you please."

"Don't be so damn polite," said Cash-and-Carry Corkery, but he obeyed. And without delay, the *Honi Soit* taxied across the meadows, gained momentum, left the ground and was in the air again, with Evans aboard, a copy of the *X-Ray* in his hand. As they sped toward Glendive, over Wibaux, Homer read hastily the last developments and grinned with satisfaction. If Fitz-Henry, Jr., was on hand, he must have the Chicago credentials and the extradition papers to be served on the gangsters. That would give Evans the right to deputize his whole gang and take the fugitives by force, if they wanted it that way. Gilligan, left without cohorts, would have to fall back on the outlaw Shoshones, led by Tall-Horse-in-Flytime and his lieutenant Noisy Snake.

"Ah, spring!" murmured Homer aloud, to the utter disgust of Cash-and-Carry Corkery.

"Aw, nuts," the mercenary flier said.

30

A Case in Which an Asbestos Roof Proves Ineffective

HOMER EVANS' FIRST ACT, after greeting Miriam with a warmth that sent the blood tingling to the tips of her fingers and toes, on which the faintly tinted nails curled gently in response, was to shake Jim Leonard's hand.

"Now that you're here, maybe you can harness-break this team of ornery lawyers and get me out of this," the rancher said hopefully.

"You are as good as free," said Homer cheerily, "but first I must speak with Gilligan." He reached for the phone.

"Gilligan?" he asked, when the connection was established. "Evans."

"What the hell do you want?" asked the sheepman peevishly.

"I thought you'd like to know I was around," Evans said. "I even hoped it might influence you in your plans for the near future. Your son, whom I saw just recently, is anxious, I am sure, for you to behave circumspectly."

"You wouldn't hurt the boy?" slipped out from Gilligan, with touching solicitude.

"We don't want to hurt anybody," said Evans, "but there's a limit to what we will stand. I wanted to advise you, free of charge, not to try to cross the deadline with any of your sheep or sub-human companions."

"And what if I do?" demanded Larkspur, infuriated by Homer's bantering tone.

"We won't use you easy," said Homer. "And furthermore, put out of your fertile mind any notions you might have about convicting Mr. Leonard. It's not in the cards. Not by any stretch of the imagination."

"Look," said Gilligan. "I wasn't born yesterday. You're one of them humanitarians, a kind of blue-ribbon scout master, if you get what I mean. You wouldn't kill my kid, in cold blood, and you don't know what hot blood means. So don't try to get around me that-a-way."

"I offer no apologies for the control I have gained over my temper," said Homer, "or for any of the softer instincts you disdain. I'm merely giving you a chance, before it's too late."

"You're giving me a chance. Say, young fella. You ain't been out in this country long, and you're not going to stay here much longer. Now get down to business, if you've got something to say."

"Nothing more," said Homer, and hung up the receiver.

Gilligan, on the other end, restrained himself just in time from place-kicking his pet cat into a patch of wild sunflowers just outside the open window. "Dang me if I don't wish I had a bright young man like that. He almost got my goat, and no mistake. I wonder if he'd run for Senator," Larkspur Gilligan said.

What Evans did next was to send a bellboy down to the county surveyor's office to borrow a slide rule and some paper divided in millimeter squares. While Jim Leonard watched with some misgivings, Homer took out his reading glass and measured carefully the lens, consulted an almanac in the chapter where data concerning the sun was contained, experimented with some cigarette papers and then began to jot down equations and computations that made Indian signs look like foursquare Gospel.

"Capital," said Evans, and excused himself for a conference with the attorneys, man and boy, retained by the defense. What he asked of the Fish did not concern either the Supreme Court's drinking habits in 1812, nor yet the Freudian complexes, inhibitions, libidos and dream interpretations with which Fitz-Henry, Jr., was primed. Hastily he checked his mysterious computations and said:

"Let the case go to the jury at two thirty-six, or as near that hour as you can," said Evans.

"But the questions of postponement, change of venue, dismissal of the case, *billa falsa* . . ."

"We shall have to pass them up this time," said Homer. "There's weightier business afoot."

At ten o'clock, in the court room, Judge Patterson, more dead than alive, made a feeble pass at the stack of depositions, expecting any moment to be assailed by both the Fish, and in the bargain the chap named Evans who, it seemed, was also a member of the bar in good standing, although he usually kept the matter dark. Instead, the defense, which had kept all heads reeling during four harrowing days, was ominously calm.

"Come on, kid! Ride 'em bareback, and pour in the leather! Bulldog 'em! Scratch and squeeze 'em! Let 'em hop for papa! Swing your partners! First couple to the wall and balance off!" yelled the prospector juryman, who had got a fair start with the Jamaica ginger before court was opened and wanted action before the edge wore off.

Even that encouragement did not get a rise out of the Fish.

The prosecutor, Highpockets, read the depositions in a sing-song manner, while both Miriam and her father, the defendant, writhed and ground their teeth in rage and alarm.

"Oh, Homer, are you sure?" asked Miriam, breathlessly.

"Unless I've forgotten my higher algebra," he replied, and smiled reassuringly.

"But the jurymen. Every one is fixed by Gilligan. The judge has a mortgage hanging over his head," Miriam gasped.

The judge did not even rap for order. He was living in a dream. Back over the horizon was drifting the stern of the judicial mansion and the bow of the senatorship, propelled by a following breeze. Tom Jackson, at the press table, was tearing off copy for the A.P., and was as nervous as Miriam about the way things were going. Before noon, the statements had gone unchallenged to the jury, to the effect that the old Italian was Louis Flato, fruit dealer, and father of the deceased, who was identified as Donniker Louey. Two sheepherders were eyewitnesses to the slaying. There was no more talk of improper indictments, not a word about *omnia praesumuntur*, *lex loci* or *lex talionis*. The Supreme Court in 1812 could have guzzled ice-cream sodas for all the senior Fish seemed to care, and Daddy Browning might "woof" to his heart's content, as far as Fitz-Henry, Jr., seemed to care.

Early in the afternoon, Highpockets summed up for the prosecution and was at the end of his rope by 1:45.

"That leaves us fifty-one minutes. Shall you coddle the jolly old jury, or dare you leave it to your willing offspring?" asked Fitz-Henry, Jr.

"You take it, if you wish," Fitz-Henry, Sr., said.

At two thirty-six, at a sign from Evans, the young lawyer smiled upon the jury and said: "You've been my first jury and I like you. Go on in, and may God have mercy on your souls."

The judge waved feebly toward the jury room and the foreman rose to lead the way.

Fitz-Henry Fish, Sr., excused himself and sauntered over to the Jordan, from which point he held a telephone conversation with Beatrice Baxter Diluvio at Three Buttes and for the first time that beautiful and gracious heiress got the complete attention of Wing Lee. For after asking the China boy for a kettle of hot water she carried it across the slope to the ruins of the ancient privy and began steaming colored stock certificates from the inside of the weather-beaten walls.

"One-piece Mary 'e unstick 'em Clistian plaires flom topside john," he confided in Wing Sam, who had improved to the point where he could hold conversation.

"Maybe one-piece Mary 'e need 'em," was Wing Sam's tolerant comment.

Now the Dawson County court house on the flat in Glendive was a rambling structure built of wood, two stories high. During the Leonard trial, however, all county offices had been closed in order that the employees might attend. So at 2:36 the building was unoccupied, except for the court room, which was served with huge double doors; the balcony, which was equipped with direct exits by means of outside stairways; and the ground floor room at the northwestern corner in which the jury sat down to deliberate, if that is not too elaborate a word for what Gilligan had instructed the talesmen to do.

To keep up appearances, the foreman, Dry-Goods Merchant Tisdale, and his partner, Andrews, had decided to use the entire twenty minutes allotted them to bring in a conviction. Consequently, after plying the old prospector with a large swig of Jamaica, the foreman began reading the various depositions, which constituted the case for the State. He had got as far as Sheepherder Jill's story of having seen the defendant burying the party of the second part, secretly and with felonious intent, when the nose of the trouble shooter began to twitch in an admonitory way.

"Mr. Chairman," he interrupted.

Foreman Tisdale, who had borrowed the judge's fourth string gavel, began to bang in brisk two-four time.

"But, Mr. Chairman," the trouble shooter persisted.

The banging went into six-eight and *presto*. Tisdale was taking no chances. He had remarked that the electrician had taken a shine to young Fish.

"All right then. Roast alive, you fathead. As for me, I'm leaving," the trouble shooter said.

A burly court officer with his back to the door drew his gun. "Everybody stays," he growled.

Just then Andrews, the more conservative of the dry-goods partners, nudged Tisdale and whispered something in his ear.

"I smell smoke, Ezra," was the text of his communication.

The foreman sniffed and started chewing the gavel. Not only did he smell smoke, but saw tender young flames shooting up like crocuses through the cracks of the board floor.

Panic ensued in the jury room, all members being affected except the prospector, who was waving the Jamaica bottle and singing: "We drug him round the room."

The court officers at the two exits, both having families to support, were at a loss as to what to do, but at last decided that even

Gilligan, exigent as he was, would understand that a grilled jury would be of no use to anyone. So the jurymen, two with coat-tails afire, dashed out in all directions, some through the audience in the court room, others through the windows into the crowd outside.

Homer Evans rose, and said calmly: "File out quietly, please. There is ample time for each and every one to escape." And, seeing a cowpuncher with a mouth organ, he asked the buckaroo to step up to the bench and play "Turkey in the Straw" while the spectators, four abreast, poured out through the double doorways in fair order.

Judge Patterson, his visions of promotion dissolving in the angry flames, ran here and there trying to catch jurymen, as if they were hens who had broken out of their coop. Meanwhile, young Fish, who was by no means slow to catch on, was gathering all the records of the case and slyly chucking them into the fire.

It was a matter of moments for the building to be cleared, and before the firemen could get back to the station, all of them having been in the balcony of the court room, the conflagration had spread to the upper story, where the boards, thoroughly dry from days of strong sun, blazed like tinder. Laterally the fire ate its way to the bench. The heat drove the crowd back on all sides and to and fro ran the frantic Judge Patterson, wailing and clutching at his hair. He knew that, with the eyes of America on the ruins of his court room, the records consumed by the flames, and the jurymen dispersed from hell to breakfast, conversing with all and sundry, a mistrial was a *fait accompli*. Without even glancing at the judicial mansion, or waiting to face Gilligan, the judge, with what money remained in his pockets, chartered the fastest hack in town and lit out for the State border, a man without present or future, and with a past he hoped in vain to leave behind.

Tom Jackson was in the *X-Ray* city room, pouring vivid word pictures into the long-distance phone, while Myra stood by with a palm-leaf fan and a highball, to cool his brow and his throat, respectively. Jim Leonard, the ex-defendant, was being carried on the shoulders of his friends to the Jordan bar. And in an upper hallway Miriam was sobbing happily on Evans' shoulder.

"How could I have doubted you for a moment?" she said.

"The problem was a simple one," Evans said. "The jury was fixed. No matter what was said in court, they would have brought in a conviction. Hence it became imperative to get rid of the jury as mercifully as possible. Fortunately no one was injured."

"But, Homer. How did you know that exactly at two thirty-six . . ."

Evans smiled and held her close once more. "That, darling, was a matter of my reading glass, placed at just the right angle to catch the rays of the sun and focus them on some cigarette papers, which in turn ignited oil-soaked waste, the floor boards, and ended in destroying the building, the court records, all the evidence, and forcing the jury to put itself out of action by mingling with the public before a decision had been reached and signed. As for me, I shall have to buy another reading glass, but not just now. It might put a bee in Gilligan's bonnet."

"And to think you have remembered your algebra all these years," gasped Miriam, admiringly.

"Of course, there were physical factors as well. The ignition time of rice paper under a slowly increasing degree of calorification, the prevailing wind direction, the safety of the crowd. You will notice that while the blaze went upward, it did not threaten any of the exits."

The telephone rang, and through the transmitter came the voice of Larkspur Gilligan.

"You win this time," said the sheepman to Evans. "Now why can't you and me get together? I can promise you that you'll be State Senator in the fall. . . ."

"I'm magnanimous," Evans said. "Your one remaining chance is still open to you. Just stay west of the deadline, and refrain from further gardening activities, meaning planting of *delphinium*. Also call off all future stampedes, caused by airplanes or other devices. That's all I ask, and everything else will be forgiven."

That time it was not the sheepman's cat but a potted rubber plant that went sailing through an unopened window. "I'll get you, if it's the last thing I do," shouted Gilligan and, perceiving that he was talking into an empty phone, he pulled the instrument out by the roots and started whirling it like a Balearic sling above his head, while his feet beat out a rigadoon. From clumps of sagebrush in which they had taken refuge, the employees of the sheep rancher looked on in awe and trembling.

"I've never seen the boss so het up," one of them said hoarsely.

Part Three

The Sheep and Cattle War

31

The War Clouds Gather

THAT NIGHT IN GLENDIVE will be remembered by everyone concerned except Judge Patterson, who was not there. With the deepening of twilight, hacks began rushing back and forth between the main square and the red-light district, which was fenced off and lighted with colored lanterns, according to Western custom. Bars were filled to overflowing, as were a majority of the customers. Cowpunchers, elated by their victory, rode up and down the streets and the stairs, and in and out of public and private buildings, yelling like Indians and firing wildly into the air. The church element, never very dangerous in Glendive, kept to their homes, with doors bolted and shutters lowered.

At first Sheriff Hockaday tried to throw his weight around, but after Hjalmar Jansen, who had ridden in from Mountain Sheep Bluffs for a consultation with Homer, had taken the sheriff's badge away, along with his striped blue and orange shirt, his embossed leather belt, his firearms, bandana handkerchief and other small articles, Hockaday subsided. Of course, the fact that Hjalmar knocked out three of his front teeth and jammed him into an ashcan was also a factor in the officer's decision.

But all was not merriment in Dawson and the surrounding counties. Grim work was afoot, and Larkspur Gilligan, although he seemed to have surrendered the county seat to the cattlemen that evening, was busier than the proverbial bee, the one-armed paperhanger, and Gunga Din combined. He was, in fact, in Wibaux, near the North Dakota line, where a search was being made for the

missing Baldy Santo, on whom the sheepman had relied to keep
the ninety-odd gangsters in order. Santo, of course, was nowhere
to be found, but Gilligan, who could read Indian signs, came upon
one of Homer's wind-tossed messages and deduced from that how
the rescue was effected.

"Ah, God blast it, what a Senator that fella would make, if only
he'd listen to reason," muttered Gilligan, but also he felt his blood
begin to boil. He had never been in contact with a man before who
aroused simultaneously his hatred and his admiration, who made
him blow hot and cold, place-kick well-meaning cats, demolish
rubber plants and otherwise behave like a two-year-old.

Between the gangsters and the sheep who were overrunning
Wibaux and the Beaver Creek canyon, an unfortunate relationship
seemed to have sprung up. No, reader, I do not mean the one that
first comes to mind, but merely that the gangsters seemed to take
a delight in bullying and scattering the woollies, while on their part
the woollies had developed a pardonable fear of the Great Lakes
palefaces and lost what sense they had when one of the same
lurched into view. Several sheep had been shot and a few had had
their backs broken over boastful gangsters' knees. All decent
women in Wibaux had fled in one of the town hose wagons, and
the others were wantonly carousing in a manner that scared the
coyotes farther into the crumbling volcanic hills. Into this confused
situation, Larkspur Gilligan was trying to bring a semblance of
order. The fact that he succeeded, without killing more than a scant
half dozen of his Chicago adherents, is a tribute to Larkspur's gift
for organization. Within a few hours, he had trigger men, bananas,
moll-buzzers, slashers, rippers, defrocked clergymen, and even
those aristocrats of the underworld, the cecil pushers, lugging
water in pails from the railroad tank and sloshing it into sheep
troughs as if they had been at it all their lives.

The terrified sheep were reloaded, and while the revels in
Glendive were at their height, the long train of stock cars, filled
with baaing stinkers, the noisiest of which were clubbed into
insensibility by their gangster escorts, crept unnoticed through
Glendive, was switched on the branch line to Circle, from which

point they were driven to corrals concealed in the Big Dry Creek foothills and given a chance to recuperate.

Coincidently, a courier was entering Northern Wyoming and holding a powwow with Tall-Horse-in-Flytime, Chief of the outlaw Shoshone band, and Noisy Snake, his lieutenant. Both Shoshones and their followers had grown restive again on Uncle Sam's preserves and were ready once more to follow Gilligan's banner, on which was a device more potent than "Excelsior," namely: "Stop at nothing." By night, so stealthily that any Arabs in the vicinity would have sounded like moose in dead underbrush, the Shoshone band stole off the reservation at a dogtrot, in single file, war paint glistening, eagle feathers flapping, and soft moccasins feeling the way as surely as cat's feet on a familiar lawn.

Meanwhile, at Gilligan's ranch, each gangster, as a reward for good behavior, was permitted to kill his own sheep in any style he saw fit, after which each man skun the unfortunate animal of his choice and hung the pelt up to dry.

On the flat, just within earshot of the Glendive red-light district, Tumbleweed O'Flaherty was standing guard over the *Honi Soit* and its furious pilot, Cash-and-Carry Corkery, whose instant dislike for Homer Evans had increased momently throughout the endless day since first they had met in the badlands. O'Flaherty, who was no mean psychologist, inflamed the flier's vile temper by turning on the *Honi's* radio whenever there were hymns on the air. That, in the great open country, is practically always.

In the Hotel Jordan, the Fish, well-oiled with ceremonial Old Crow, were changing from jimswingers into golfing outfits, both having been promised by Evans and Hjalmar that they could take part in the battle, if any, along the Redwater. The elder Fish, it developed, while at Harvard had developed some aptitude as an amateur ventriloquist and was able not only to throw his voice, but to change its quality and scatter it in all directions. That gift might easily prove useful in trench warfare, Evans believed. And he was also glad that the younger attorney was adept with a jew's-harp, which might help keep the troops amused if long periods of inaction occurred.

To the westward, just across the Great Divide, the lizards and birds of the former town of Red Dog were flickering and twittering in astonishment, for, after having been left tranquil years on end, they suddenly were being disturbed by the sound of trucks jolting over the roads, the tapping of hammers and the singing of saws, the diapason of dynamite as blasts were set off, and the tramping of feet as miners and Chinamen trekked back to the hills their fathers had left in disgust, and without even a grubstake. For gold was being found aplenty in the Old Glory mine. That it had been brought there in trucks from Nevada did not trouble the carefree itinerant workers to any noticeable extent, except a brace of real oldtime prospectors, who promptly went raving mad.

This brings the reader to the zigzag line of trenches which had been dug all the way from the western extremity of Mountain Sheep Bluffs to the head of Redwater Creek. In commodious dugouts, that had been blasted out of the sandstone of the bluffs, were housed a valiant company, including: Hugo Weiss, whose mysterious disappearance, the sixteenth in his brilliant career, was shaking the financial world and causing huge fortunes to be lost; Unreal Bear and her sister, Tinted Cloud, of royal Blackfeet blood; Trout-tail III, the medicine man, who shared a two-man dugout with Dr. Hyacinthe Toudoux, with whom the Indian was making plans for first-aid and hospital services for the combatants; Stenka, who had done a full share of the heavy work, shoulder to shoulder with the men. Besides, she had found time to scoop out a dainty little shelter for her beloved mistress, Miriam, and to deck it with the flowers of the prairie: the prairie artichoke, button snakeroot, bird's-foot trefoil; the rose-colored evening primrose, sacred to Luna; the purple prairie smoke; the symbolic poppy, easily the peer of those on Flanders fields; the lilac-hued sabbatia, and the pink chaparral pea. The warm-hearted Serbian giantess seemed to know what resting soldiers needed most, and without thought of herself or possible consequences, had dished it out to them without stint or complaint, to the point that the cattlemen's forces on the eve of the hurly-burly were an exceptionally self-satisfied and optimistic lot, and not the prey of nervous fears and premonitions, as is the case so often with troops about to go under fire.

Among the forces there entrenched, must be mentioned also: Chief Shot-on-Both-Sides, with a far-away look in his eyes; the sergeants Schlumberger and Bonnet, both of whom had been made supremely happy by a whispered "Yes" from the lips of their fond Nono and Bébé; Rain-No-More, who had arrived about midnight, accompanied by Moritz the dog; the Professor; Tom Jackson, the reporter, for whom the press dugout had been reserved; Galilee Zach, who because of the lightness of his fingers had been detailed in the hospital squad; Frémont, chief of the Paris detectives, who was chief engineering officer in charge of the trenches and refuges, machine-gun nests, pill boxes and gopher-hole entanglements.

But in the struggle that was imminent, for once in modern warfare, the noble ancient branch of the service known as cavalry was about to enjoy a renaissance, and at the head of the cattlemen's forces, despite the skill of the buckaroos, were deservedly placed in order of rank, Colonel Lvov Kvek and Captain Grigori Lidin, both of whom were wild with joy. That did not interfere with their efficiency, however. Corrals had been built at strategic points, a patrol established, all up and down the deadlines; and a system of signals, using heliograph if by day and lanterns if by night, had been instituted and was in smooth operation.

"Should the blackest of despair descend upon us and our unhappy land forever and a day, could it be said that we have lived in vain?" asked Lvov Kvek, embracing his junior officer and reaching for the vodka with his free hand.

"Ah, fate! I blow you a thousand kisses!" roared Lidin, detaching himself in order to swing his saber right and left, but principally up and down. "Darling enemies, sent by God on high to a peace-famished soldier, I shall split you from skull to crotch, or vice versa, as the case may be, not in anger but in the spirit known only to true fighting men. Not one of you, should I spare you, would live forever; so in advance, forgive me for shortening your days on earth, as I forgive you freely for the possible stain of sin on my soul."

Back at the sheep ranch on Big Dry Creek, where he had quartered his gangsters in lofts and bunkhouses as best he could, Larkspur Gilligan was poring over a Government map of the Yellowstone-Missouri watershed. But as he pored, sipping whiskey the while, the saturnine face of Homer Evans kept coming between Larkspur and the sheet of paper on which the creeks, coulees, buttes, mesas and foothills had been drawn in plan, with contours to indicate elevations and depressions.

"God durn 'im," muttered Gilligan. "Now what did he want to come a-hornin' into Dawson County for? I'll give him one durn good lickin' then make him Senator whether he wants the job or not, or my name ain't Gilligan."

The longer Larkspur looked at the map, the surer he was that the way to get his sheep on the cattle range was through the pass between the Redwater and Mountain Sheep Bluffs. The sheepman also was certain that Homer Evans would anticipate the maneuver and concentrate his forces in that area. Suddenly Gilligan rose and began a sort of buck and wing, and seeing the cat taking refuge on top of a stuffed bear, called out reassuringly.

"We've got 'em, puss," Larkspur cackled. "We've sure got 'em where the hair is short."

For Gilligan, staring at the map, had had an inspiration worthy of Napoleon. The cattle range had four corners, being shaped something like a postage stamp two hundred miles deep by one hundred and fifty miles wide. Evans would place his troops in the southwest corner, near the bluffs; Glendive, filled with prying eyes, was on the southeast corner. At the northeast corner were camped the Blackfeet braves with ten thousand shorthorns ready for shipment. That left the northwest corner, across from the unguarded lodge of Shot-on-Both-Sides, wide open to attack. And it was not impossible to get there with the cream of his gangster mob and fifteen thousand sheep. He had only to re-route the remainder of his woollies to the Great Northern and transport them in the night through Mondak, past Muddy Creek where stood the special train, and onto the Blackfeet reservation. The sheep train could be halted across from the mouth of the Redwater, driven a few miles to the banks of the Missouri . . . Ah, there was the rub. The Missouri, wide and raging, and no bridge within sixty miles.

Gilligan retrieved the indignant cat and poured out a full double can of condensed milk for her. "We must think. God durn it. That young goof, Evans, if only I had him here! I'm goin' to fan Baldy Santo with a pick handle, for lettin' him get away," he said. But he settled down to a bout of cerebration, chewing furiously on a long black cigar, twitching and filliping his handlebar moustaches, belching, unbuttoning his vest and otherwise giving evidence of the fierce concentration of which he was capable. Six minutes passed, then eight.

"Holy mackinaw," he said. "Why not pinch the bridge near Bison Creek, haul it up river with an eighteen-horse team, then sling it across where we want it? Sheep can pass a given point, single file, at the rate of 3,600 an hour. In one night we can have our whole herd, and men to protect 'em, on the northwestern corner of the range. By that time the Shoshones will be on deck to fight off the Blackfeet and stampede the cattle again. My boys from Chicago will outnumber the cattlemen more than two to one. We can drive the herd south and strip the range of fodder as clean as if it had been shaved. I've got papers from Washington, to boot."

A moment later, Gilligan was riding hard toward Glendive, where secret orders flashed over the telegraph to Idaho and points along the line. Not only were fifteen thousand woollies sent bumping over the rails toward the junction of the N.P. branch with the Great Northern, but eighteen strong draft horses, two skinners, a crew of riggers and a supply of extra cable and tools were loaded on the same long train. The Bison Creek footbridge could be cut from its mooring towers, hauled to the Great Northern tracks, loaded on flat cars, and within two hours could be unloaded on the reservation, with only a few squaws to protest. The eighteen horses would haul it back to the Missouri, riggers could ford the river, carrying ropes with which to pull over the heavier cables, and by midnight, if all went well, sheep would be pouring on Jim Leonard's range, well inside the deadline, at the rate of 3,600 per hour. Larkspur felt so spry, after getting his campaign in motion, that when Sheriff Hockaday complained to him of the treatment the sheriff had received at the hands of Hjalmar, Larkspur blacked both of his eyes. The furniture in Judge Patterson's former home, however, the sheepman left in place, intending to offer the whole shebang to Miriam Leonard, as an inducement to marry his son and take command of the social life of Dawson County in place of the deposed Myra.

Unsuspectingly, the pro-cattle forces at the head of the Red-water were making final preparations to resist an onslaught, and Gilligan, his head clearing as the plan of attack took shape, decided to send the fifteen thousand sheep he had near Circle, and the less promising of his gangsters, to make the expected offensive there, as a feinting maneuver. If both sallies succeeded, so much to the good for him.

At eleven o'clock that evening, Evans walked briskly from the Hotel Jordan to the sagebrush flat where he had left the *Honi Soit* and its disgruntled pilot, under guard of Tumbleweed O'Flaherty.

"Start up the engines," Homer ordered, and sulkily the flier obeyed. His moment would come, of that Cash-and-Carry was sure, or at least, hopeful. He did not notice that Homer, his alert mind at its keenest, was observing every move he made, every turn of a screw, each squirt of the oil can, the levers, indicators and controls. For Homer, quick to sense hostility, was aware that the airman was not fond of him and had resolved to learn what he could of aviation before the bust-up occurred.

The flight to Mountain Sheep Bluffs was a short one and the landing presented no difficulties. Diluvio was chosen to guard the plane, and Evans went straight to the headquarters dugout that had been prepared for him and got to work. First Frémont reported the progress of trench construction and infantry organization. Colonel Kvek gave a masterful summary of the cavalry disposition and the system of patrols. Moritz the dog took his place just outside the doorway, to add his prestige to that of the sentry on guard. Hjalmar had taken great pains with the camouflage and had turned in a tiptop job, for the plentiful sagebrush lent itself well to the purpose, and all trenches, machine-gun emplacements and entrances to dugouts were hidden from the buzzards and coyotes, in fact, were all but invisible. In the daylight hours, the members of the defending units had kept carefully out of sight. So that while Evans knew nothing of the flanking operation planned by Gilligan, the sheepman had no idea of what was in store for his second-string army and the fifteen thousand stinkers among which the gangsters were to be hidden in sheeps' clothing.

Shot-on-Both-Sides and Rain-No-More assured the commander that the Blackfeet were willing and ready. But after the interviews were over and Evans was about to snatch a wink of sleep, the orderly announced that the doctors, Trout-tail III and Hyacinthe Toudoux, wished to have a word with him.

"By all means," said Homer, advancing to greet the smiling pair.

At the suggestion of Trout-tail, the sentry was asked to remove himself twenty paces, just out of earshot, and to leave the task of guarding the inner portal to Moritz, the thinking dog.

"First of all, I have a plan for salvaging the meat of the sheep who will be slain," said the medicine man. "Our tribe has a secret method of curing deermeat and the flesh of mountain goats. It would be equally applicable to domestic sheep. Therefore, with the commander's permission, I will have a squad of squaws in readiness to gather up the carcasses, clean and skin them and sling them into packsaddles to be transported to the tribal smokery."

"An excellent idea," said Evans. But Dr. Hyacinthe Toudoux, usually reserved and decorous, burst into riotous laughter. The medical examiner, tears rolling down his cheeks, held tightly to his sides while mirth had its will with him and he rolled to the ground, exhausted. Trout-tail III, the personification of dignity, held out as long as he could, but his colleague's hilarity was so infectious that the medicine man had to let himself go, and joined his pleasing baritone to the voice of Toudoux with such abandon that first Evans, then Moritz the dog, could not remain solemn. Homer smiled, then laughed aloud and the Boxer leaped and cavorted, rolling playfully beside the medical examiner and making gentle passes with his paws.

"Haw, haw, haw. Ho! Ho! I shall die. Kek kek kek kek. Waaa-
aaah. Ho haw," roared Dr. Toudoux, pointing toward Trout-tail III
and doubling up again.

"I trust you gentlemen will enlighten me in due time as to what
amuses you so," said Evans.

The response was peals, gales, roars, ripples, gasps, burbles,
and gusts of laughter, until Trout-tail III and Dr. Toudoux were
sitting on the ground, face to face, pointing, each to the other and
gasping to catch their breath. The Indian turned the color of a well-
smoked Meerschaum, while the Frenchman took on a wistaria hue.

Eventually Toudoux, still pointing to Trout-tail as if to disclaim
all credit himself, was able to stand erect and whisper into Evans'
ear, at which the impassive Homer let out such a volley of guffaws
that Miriam, in her distant dugout, heard the sound and came
running. Never had she heard the man of her choice give vent to
such uncontrolled hilarity before. The sentry, whose sides were
splitting, was helpless and let her pass.

"Why, Homer! What is the matter?" she asked, her hands poised
in their characteristic interrogatory and expectant way.

He stepped to her side and whispered into her shell-like ear,
touching ever so lightly with his lips a wisp of fragrant hair (Forvil's
Les Yeux Noirs).

Like the daintiest of rockets paraboling skyward, the silver of
her laughter rose and fell. "Oh, Homer. Could I tell Father? He's
been so taciturn, so troubled . . ."

"By all means, call him," said Evans, and soon the rancher and
his daughter appeared in the dugout entrance, arm in arm.
Succinctly Trout-tail outlined his secret plan, and Miriam wept with
joy at the sight of her undemonstrative father, doubled up and in
convulsions, alternately roaring and gasping, "Now ain't that a
humdinger?" or "Jesus to Jesus, and eight hands round."

The company was sworn to secrecy and into the night, on the
fastest pintos, rode Trout-tail III and Dr. Hyacinthe Toudoux, the
backs of their saddles bulging with empty gunny-sacks. Polaris,
beacon of wanderers by land and sea, kept up its distant five-star
merry-go-round, of the north the monarch of silent mysteries.

And may the reader, in his journey across this most comical and tragic of all possible worlds, find ever a guide as beneficent and sure.

32
The Battle of the Redwater: Phase One

ONE OF OUR MINOR-LEAGUE POETS, who was given to somewhat rash but musical statements, has handed down the line, "He travels the fastest who travels alone." Perhaps that may be granted, but the weakness of all heroes, past and present, who played lone hands, is this: when they need faithful lieutenants, known in underworld parlance as "airedales," they find themselves behind the eight ball. Thus Larkspur Gilligan, obliged to make the roundabout journey to the Blackfeet Reservation to command his main body of sheep and gangsters, had to leave Sheriff Hockaday to direct the movements of the troops and animals who were to crash the cattle range on the Redwater side. The sheepman cursed as he thought of Terence, his son, far away and in captivity, and was even more blasphemous when reminded of the absent Baldy Santo and his precocious heir.

Nevertheless, with a force of forty gangsters, all equipped with rods, choppers, saps, pineapples, scatter guns, brass knuckles, sheep skins to which the wool still clung, and other weapons and implements, some new to the prairies, Sheriff Hockaday set out from Circle just at dusk. The sheep, moving steadily and in a fairly compact mass, were kept in order by eight herders whose fear of Gilligan was a jot or tittle stronger than their dread of death. Each herder had a pair of well-trained dogs who, feeling the tenseness in the atmosphere, were on their mettle, dashing here and there. In the capacious pockets of the sheriff were documents from Washington authorizing all sheepmen whom they might concern to graze their sheep, goats or other ruminant mammals in the area bounded on the north by the Missouri, on the east by the Yellowstone, on the south by the N.P. tracks and the west by Redwater Creek.

Hugo Weiss, not to be outdone, had procured for Jim Leonard a temporary injunction to estop, prevent and otherwise prohibit the grazing of sheep, goats or other ruminants on the area just described. Since the two sets of papers had been issued by separate authorities, neither of which had had its powers clearly defined, and each of which claimed to outrank the other, legally the two opposed camps were horse and horse.

The storekeeper at Circle, Johnny O'Brien, long a friend of Jim Leonard but obliged for business reasons to pretend to favor Gilligan, saw the grim preparations and, stealing away, unobserved, he mounted a broncho and set out on the gallop for Three Buttes. Luckily, he chose the shortest trail which led him right to the trenches, where he reported that the sheep were on the move, escorted by forty gangsters and young Hockaday.

"What is Hockaday wearing?" asked Miriam, before she took her place in the sharpshooter's nest which had been cut into the face of the highest bluff overlooking the approach to the trenches. She was determined to pick off the sheriff first of all, if he came within range of her forty-forty, on which the front sight had been filed to the finest needle point.

The perfect order with which Evans' small army got into position for defensive action was a tribute to the zeal and skill of his assistants, and as he passed through trenches and inspected the pill boxes and other emplacements he was generous with his praise, although his men seemed to need no encouragement. On the contrary, they were so anxious for contact with the enemy that Homer had to dissuade Hjalmar, Kvek, Diluvio and some of the more impetuous of his subordinates from abandoning their fortifications and tearing across country to meet the gangsters half way.

Evans, however, issued curt instructions of quite another order.

"Withhold your fire and remain in concealment until the sheep are within easy range. I will then give the signal. If the enemy reaches our front-line trenches in any sort of order, in the face of

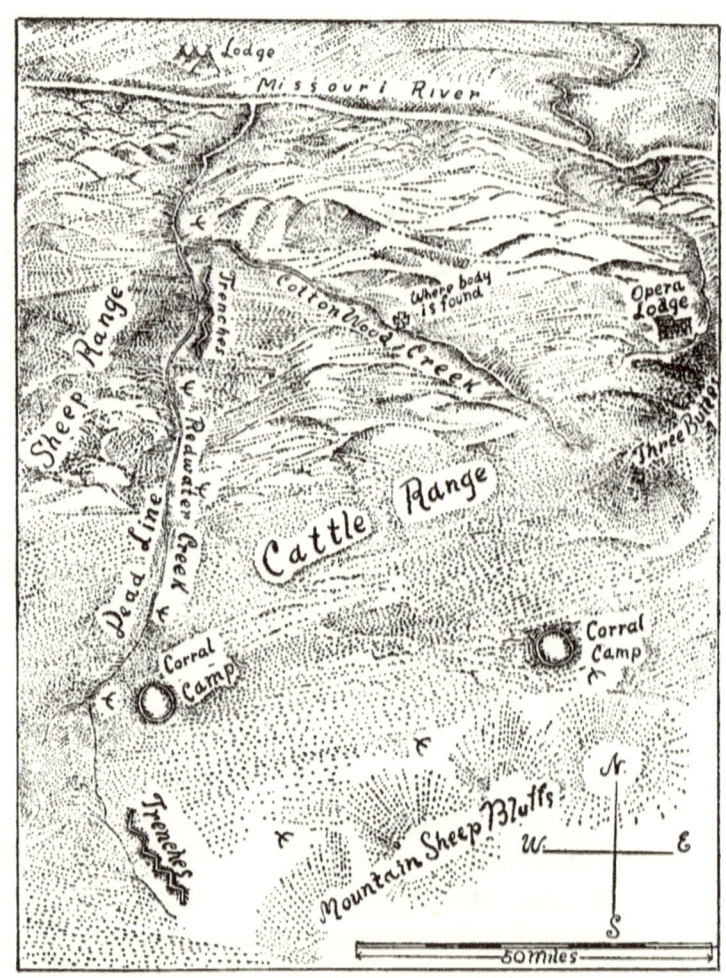

THE BATTLE OF THE REDWATER

our machine guns, retire to the second line defenses to give our gunners a chance to get in some enfilading fire. Do not hesitate to kill plenty of sheep, since the meat will not be wasted and the dead animals will afford us cover if the enemy is obliged to fall back. We are outnumbered two to one, and while we have shelter, it must be remembered that the enemy has a moving screen behind which he may operate.

"To those of you who have had military experience, I wish to say a word in particular. When one is fighting for one's country, it is considered traitorous to pause in advance or retreat to give aid to wounded comrades. With us, and Mr. Leonard is in perfect agreement with me, the conservation of the lives of our comrades takes first place in the order of the day. We want no honored dead, if we can help it.

"In conclusion, I wish to announce that we are about to try out a new weapon, hitherto unknown in warfare, and to that end I must caution you all to obey orders strictly, on no account to overrun your objectives and by no means, however bizarre the situation, to depart from the letter of my commands."

"Ha ha! Ho ho! Damme! Damme! I shall bust," roared Jim Leonard, to the astonishment of the company, while Miriam giggled like a schoolgirl and even Homer could not repress a smile.

Since it would require several hours to drive the grazing sheep from Circle to the battlefield, Evans ordered his companions to turn in for some much-needed sleep, leaving only a skeleton guard. Moritz, however, did not follow his usual practice of sleeping across the threshhold of Miriam's quarters. For one thing, several of the flowers with which Stenka had bedecked the dugout had a deadening effect on the Boxer's keen sense of smell. Foremost among those were the prairie false boneset and the green-white blossoms of the spurge. But the principal factor in the dog's decision was the feeling that he was to be useful to his friends, in some special way. So along the picket line, and stealthily in front of the parapets and pill boxes, stepped the faun-colored Boxer, black nose sniffing eagerly the air, paws placed carefully. After startling two sentries into discharging their rifles in the air, the dog sat down to think things over and a conclusion he had drawn several weeks before was confirmed in his mind, namely: that his human friends, and also enemies, had practically no sense of smell; and that, in approaching them, a dog should or should not give warning, as the case might be. After that he resumed his vigil and when nearing a sentry he coughed discreetly, then waited before stalking into view.

However, at midnight, after Moritz had inspected the concealed detachment of cavalry on the protected slope of the western butte, in crossing what would be no man's land the dog was assailed by a whiff of something so unpleasant that he wished for a moment he was as impervious to odors as human beings seemed to be. To the reader who has not smelled fifteen thousand sheep in a bunch, and it is to be hoped that most readers have been spared, this incident will lose somewhat of its force.

Moritz, the hair bristling at the back of his thick sturdy neck, sought out the officer of the day, who chanced to be Frémont. The Boxer scratched on the entrance of the dugout, waited for a response, and entered.

"Welcome, beast from Boston," Frémont said. "You had better move away from that entrance, since there is a terrible draft . . ."

The Boxer wrinkled his forehead, motioned with his head in the direction from which the sheep were coming and, as a last resort, put his paw on Frémont's knee. The Chief of Detectives, touched by the demonstration, shook hands cordially, but let it go at that.

"In spite of the time it wastes for humans, and the way in which it appears to substitute itself for thought, speech would be convenient under many circumstances," said Moritz to himself. Then he made another stab at warning the genial officer. The wind had veered slightly so that the scent of the woollies was so strong, from Moritz's point of smell, that he even hoped Frémont would detect it himself.

Now Frémont had worked on cases with Moritz in Paris and respected the animal, as was his due. He concluded, when the Boxer actually took hold of his trousers leg and gently tugged him to the doorway, that the thinking dog had something important on his mind.

"The devil," said Frémont. "How many times one wishes one had been brought up on a farm, or in a zoo. Monsieur Evans, that phenomenon, can talk with beasts as if they were information bureaux. I, son of the pavements, have no such power."

So reluctantly Frémont decided to wake Evans and see what the latter could make of Moritz's strange behavior. On the way to headquarters, however, the Frenchman reflected that Homer had been hours without sleep and would have to direct the combat on the morrow.

"I have it," said Frémont, at last, to Moritz. "There are among our forces two of your countrymen, the Fish, *pére et fils*. They also are men of education, having graduated from what is equivalent to our Sorbonne, or l'Ecole Superieure Normale, I believe. Let us consult with them first."

The Fish, sleeping comfortably in their blankets, were aroused and, blinking into the starlight, tried to pull themselves together. Frémont, in French, explained that a Boston dog was trying to communicate something. Since the messieurs were from that city . . .

"Oh, quite," said Fitz-Henry, Sr., who had narrowly missed being an M.F.H.

The State Street attorney felt the Boxer over carefully and pronounced him, not only sound, but the finest specimen of that little-known race he had ever had the pleasure of feeling. Moritz, flattered as he was by the cultured Bostonian's approval, was by no means satisfied.

"Perhaps he's spotted an Alpinist in distress," said young Fitz-Henry, who had always preferred poker, or practically anything else, to a gallop behind the hounds.

Moritz, by that time, had given up hope of getting cooperation from those present, but, like Evans, the Boxer always seized on anything unusual in a situation. The dog had assumed that Evans would be fetched. Evans had not been called. There must be some reason, although Moritz could not fathom it. Miriam was barricaded behind bouquets and sprigs of flowers among which Moritz could not risk his nose. There remained the large Serbian girl who had proved herself amenable to all kinds of suggestion. At present,

Moritz knew, Stenka was helping Hjalmar on his crowning job of camouflage, the hiding of the *Honi Soit* by means of a sagebrush screen. So he left Frémont with the Fish and dashed through the doorway.

"Ah, darling," said Stenka, laughing, as she caught up the Boxer in her strong shapely arms and lifted him clear of the ground.

Moritz beckoned with his head and trotted away, as soon as he was on his feet again, and Stenka followed, asking Hjalmar also to come along. With her quaint Slavic accent and a mixture of several languages she pronounced a phrase she knew Hjalmar used frequently, in the hope that it would be applicable. "It gives roof-stoof, maybe," she said.

"Rough stuff? Where?" asked Hjalmar eagerly, emerging from the sagebrush like a bear.

On the crest of a low hill, out in front of the trenches, Moritz stood still and rigid, sniffing.

"He smells the sheep. They are coming that way," said Stenka, and pointed in the direction from which the wind was blowing. Hjalmar had an inner struggle, right then and there. Evans had ordered him to wait, all his own instincts prompted him to go out looking for Sheriff Hockaday. That Hjalmar had knocked only three teeth at one swipe from the mouth of that zealous official had been the cause of some bantering comment on the parts of Lvov and Grigori, both of whom had claimed that they could have bettered the score. In the end, the big Norwegian painter's loyalty to Evans won the day and, sighing, he went back to his camouflage.

The sentries, however, were all warned and Colonel Kvek, the only one who knew the battle plans in detail, made a final round of inspection. Not a buckle nor strap, not one six-shooter or gleaming saber evaded his watchful eye.

"Embrace me, Grigori Hippolitovich," he said to Captain Lidin. "Then note carefully my orders. The enemy will approach from a southwesterly direction at the rate of three miles the hour. That is a severe test of the nerves of our horses. Every effort will be made to keep the animals calm until the moment for the charge, the moment, Grigori, old friend and companion in arms, for which we have waited, eating the bitter bread of sorrow and humiliation, these many months and years.

"The enemy, forgive my tears, will creep upon the line of trenches, the existence of which, let us hope, is unknown to him. Hidden among the innumerable sheep will be sharpshooters of scurvy character but skill to be respected. When our commander, Evans, says 'Fire' the machine gunners will mow down the front ranks, and it is probable that the men concealed by sheepskins will either lie down flat among the fleeing sheep or stand erect and try to run. The gangsters have worked singly, or in pairs, and know nothing of battle.

"Our moment will have come, when the infantry starts firing. Your detachment, with Hank second in command, will ride at a moderate canter until the enemy is outflanked at least two hundred yards, at which time you will wheel, charge and cleave like lobsters any sheep that show peculiarities of appearance or behavior. The moment you wheel, the infantry and machine gunners will cease firing, to give you full play. With the other half of the cavalry, I will ride the longer distance necessary to outflank the sheepmen on the other side, with our horses at a gallop. Unless I have miscalculated, we shall wheel and charge at the same moment, or very nearly."

The constellations glowed and shifted, the winking cigarettes of the sentries were carefully concealed. In dugouts slept soundly Sergeants Bonnet and Schlumberger and their fiancées, Unreal Bear and Tinted Cloud; Corrigan, Galilee Zach, Hank the foreman, old Tumbleweed O'Flaherty, the Professor, Chief Shot-on-Both-Sides and Hugo Weiss, the shares of stock in whose corporations had dropped another dozen points that day.

Among those who slept fitfully, if at all, were: Cromwell and Washington, the waiters, both of whom had been with the engineers in the Argonne and had had several shovels shot out of their hands. War, to them, meant spade work, and while, to date, the conflict in which they were engaged seemed to be an exception, they were skeptical by nature. Tom Jackson was notoriously unlucky. At one time, when ten thousand people had been standing outside Braves Field in Boston, waiting to buy tickets for the world's series, a pop fly had come over the grandstand and landed squarely on Tom. But that was not the worst. Myra Patterson, with no husband to guide her, had really let herself go. She had thrown to the winds her political ambitions and had decided that she and Tom would form a writing team and go right to the front rank in American letters, hand in hand. All in all, the reporter was beginning to fear for the fine sense of freedom he had so carefully preserved through his years abroad and in these states.

But generally speaking, night silence, starlight and philosophic expectancy prevailed at the headwaters of Redwater Creek and in the jagged shelter of Mountain Sheep Bluffs.

NOT SO IN OTHER QUARTERS of the Lower Yellowstone. For advancing steadily, in spite of the difficulties presented by the badland trail, the outlaw Shoshones were trotting on in single file. Their Chief, Tall-Horse-in-Flytime, had divided his force in two. One detachment, commanded by Noisy Snake, had hit northward, and its leader was intending to cross the Yellowstone above Leonard Creek, while the other detachment took an oblique trail which would lead them nearer the delta of the Yellowstone and the Missouri. The Shoshones had been instructed by Gilligan to stampede Leonard's cattle, drive them away from the loading corrals outside of Mondak, and massacre as many Blackfeet as possible.

The long trek led by Tall-Horse-in-Flytime was comparatively uneventful, as journeys through uninhabited volcanic wastelands are likely to be, ruling out snakes, lizards, scorpions and thorny plants of various kinds. On the other hand, Noisy Snake's surreptitious crew, lithe and tireless, suddenly halted as one man in a particularly vile stretch of disintegrated sandstone and sharp quartz. For to their ears, each and severally, had come the faint strains of an out-of-tune piano.

"That music," said Noisy Snake, who had been west to Sacramento and east as far as Omaha, "is sacred to the paleface utility squaws, or I'm a lousy Ute."

At the prospect of finding unprotected paleface squaws, or squaws of any color whatsoever, the Shoshones were so elated that had there been room on the perilous narrow trail they would have performed the tribal elation dance.

Like a long many-colored serpent the file of braves in their war paint and feathers wound its way swiftly toward the hideout in which was imprisoned Baldy Santo, in solitary; Terence Gilligan and Antonio Santo, in the bitterest of enmity; seven gangsters, Mona Mason, the piano player and the three girls, Violet, Rose and Lil.

It must be confessed that the Blackfeet braves who were guarding the strange assortment of captives had got a bit careless, what with the inaccessibility of the badlands and the pleasant forms of entertainment available. Also, the noise of the piano, on which the old reprobate was thumping out "Frankie and Johnnie" covered the approach of the attacking party. In less time than it takes to tell it, the Blackfeet were overpowered, bound and rolled into a steep ravine. Baldy Santo, his son and the son of Larkspur Gilligan, all known to Noisy Snake, were released at once. So were the rank-and-file gangsters. The professor at the piano continued playing furiously, believing that if he paused for breath he might be scalped.

The author, being prudish almost to a fault, will omit from the text what happened to Mona and the girls, especially Violet and Lil, who chanced to be blondes.

Just before dawn, a long train of stock cars filled with sheep, some box cars carrying eighteen horses, and several flats with rigging equipment slid through Muddy Creek, where all was tranquil in the deserted special train. Up ahead, the passenger coaches contained Larkspur Gilligan, his skinners, riggers, herders and forty Class A gangsters from the Santo mob. Machine guns, grenades, rifles and small arms of all descriptions, with plenty of ammunition, were stacked in the caboose.

Just across the line of the Blackfeet Reservation, on the eastern boundary near the lodge of Trout-tail III, the freight train came to a halt, Gilligan and his riggers hurried riverward and it was a short task to cut the swinging footbridge from its moorings and drag it ashore. Deftly it was loaded on wagons and the whips of the skinners cracked as the eighteen horses threw their weight against their breast bands and started back to the railroad tracks with their load. The freight started westward again, steamed thirty miles, then stopped again and all hands fell to and unloaded it clean. The horses were hitched up and dragged the bridge to the Missouri again. A rigger forded the stream with a rope in his hand. Cables were hauled over to the south bank, and towers were erected. Gilligan, thumbs in vest, was striding to and fro, offering huge bonuses. Glancing to the south, in the direction of the distant Mountain Sheep Bluffs, the sheepman laughed aloud and slapped his thigh.

"The range cleared of cattle, for a handsome price; that Leonard gal to marry Terry and make a man of him; Jim Leonard not to leave Californy, except by written permission; and that smart young fella Evans for the Senate. Them's my terms, and nobody can say I'm unreasonable."

Thus Gilligan was speaking as Aurora, who has to be awakened before her act goes on, stretched her long pink legs and was forced to call it a night.

"Fair and warmer, with cirrus clouds," her handmaiden reported, as soon as she dared.

"That means extra work for me, but this day may be worth it," the goddess said, with a peep through the curtains at the vast Lower Yellowstone.

33
The Fierce and Memorable Battle of the
Redwater: Phase One (continued)

HAS THE READER CHANCED AT DAWN to witness the barely perceptible advance of an immense flock of sheep, creeping forward in the dim light of the awakening east? If not, and the author can convey a fraction of that poignant sensation, the latter will have atoned in part for the exorbitant price of this unworthy book.

"The desert groweth," Zarathustra said. And he added: "Woe to him who containeth deserts."

Mantled with massed and nibbling sheep in thousands, the prairie seems to crawl. The dun and slate of the sage and grasses give way to the rusty gray of wool. The tempo is slower than masters of music have dared employ in terms of sound. At a distance, the chorus of nagging baas is muffled and acceptable. The odors are purified in the tang of sage. The busy dogs, and dogs are thrilled by useful employment, regard their task as mentors and protectors of their less-gifted charges with appropriate seriousness. Even the sheepherders, cleansed by merciful distance, take on an almost Biblical significance.

"Miriam, my dear," said Homer, as he watched the oncoming and ill-fated flocks. "We are about, with heavy hands, to tear a miracle, to fall upon beauty in the raw."

"It's Hockaday I'm after," she said, dusting off her sights with a dainty forefinger.

"And the meat, I understand, will be conserved," Frémont said. "Not that of the unsympathetic sheriff, but of the ewes and little lambs. Ah, Americans!"

And softly the hardened officer began to hum a song of his childhood:

C'etait une bergere,
(Petit patapon, petit patapon.)
C'etait une bergere,
Qui gardait ses moutons.

Already have been touched upon the emotions of the veterans of the several wars, some vanquished, some victorious; of the stirring of strong silent plainsmen and others, who yearned to combine manly exercise with the righting of modern and ancient wrongs; of the women who, unlike their sisters of old who were forced to await trembling and swooning in bowers and cloisters the news of battle, were privileged to stand side by side with their men. But none of these at dawn that day had a thrill comparable to that experienced by Moritz the dog.

A dog, reader, is left out of so many of the pleasures and activities of his master that often he would exchange his dogship for a mess of Cream of Wheat. Imagine, then, the joy of Moritz when he saw that in the ranks of the enemy advancing in battle array were members of his own species, if not the exact breed, at least good sound ones. They were, of course, for him. And the fact that he was outnumbered eight to one did not cause the slightest flutter of his staunch courageous heart. The Boxer strained his eyes in the waxing light, sniffed avidly, and got right down to some solid ratiocination.

Item A. The enemy dogs were not unlike police dogs, with whom he was familiar. Ergo, they were quick but not tenacious, and copied in an oversubservient manner the antics of men.

Q. Were they friendly enough to each other to gang
   up on him?
A. Most probably.
Q. What tactics would be most efficacious?
A. To crush a foreleg with one clamping of his jaws,
   then tackle another.

If he could disorganize the canine escort, the sheep would run every which way, Moritz believed. So the greater the odds under which he fought, the more he would accomplish for his side.

In the trenches grim activity was afoot. Every man (and that term, being generic, includes combatant women) was at his station, with weapons and equipment in order. He understood that he was to wait in concealment until Evans gave the word to fire. The Russians and the buckaroos were trying to calm the tense nerves of their horses, to whom the smell of sheep was strange and disturbing.

Glancing over the sage-cloaked parapet in the front-line observation post, Evans glanced at his watch.

"Another hour," he said, and Hjalmar groaned. Hugo Weiss, beside him, smiled.

"If the members of the Stock Exchange could see me now the market would sink still lower," said the financier.

THE DAWN FOUND YOUNG GILLIGAN and his companion, Tony, in conference with Baldy Santo and Noisy Snake, the latter of whom was giving the former prisoners the news as best he could. The two young men, who had been anxious to get at each other's throats while trussed up in the cave, found that all was to forgive and forget the moment their bonds were loosened. They were bosom pals again. The Blackfeet, lying helpless in the ravine exposed to sun, hunger, reptiles and insects, were left to die a lingering death, it was decided. Mona and the girls, with the professor and the piano, it was agreed, should be removed to another hideout, and held for ransom. The citizens of Mondak would pay handsomely for their return, Baldy Santo believed.

"It is true. There is not another piano nearer than Fargo," Noisy Snake said hopefully.

It was Terence Gilligan's idea that the ranch house at Three Buttes, which would be left unprotected because of the shorthorns near Mondak and the attack on another corner of the range, should be destroyed. Noisy Snake, knowing there would be stores of liquor, asked nothing better. Baldy Santo beamed with pleasure at

the prospect of getting even, in part, with Homer Evans. The rank-
and-file Shoshones, in the best of spirits, were ready for anything
at all.

So WHILE THE SHEEP on the Redwater were inching forward to their
doom, and the gangsters concealed among them were complaining in hoarse whispers about their aching backs, the Santos, young
Gilligan and the outlaw Shoshones were streaking across country
toward Opera Lodge. The fair Beatrice Diluvio was on guard at the
springs on the western butte; Eugénie Toudoux, true to her war-
time habits, was knitting socks for the troops; Hydrangea was in
her gym clothes practicing a lively dance routine; while Laramee
Bob watched the prisoners glumly.

In the front observation post on the Redwater, Homer Evans
glanced at his watch again, and then turned toward the north, scan-
ning carefully the foothills with his powerful field glasses.

"I don't understand. They should be here," he said to Frémont
at his side.

"You mean the doctors? Ah, well. We shall not need them for
an hour," Frémont said, glancing proudly up and down the
trenches.

"Their errand was not a medical one," Evans said.

"Damme. Damme. Haw. Haw. Bless my gizzards," moaned Jim
Leonard, trying hard not to let his laughter erupt and warn the
approaching enemy.

Hjalmar, in order to hold himself in check, started counting
sheep, and in the act succeeded in spotting several he thought
might be Hockaday. Miriam, from the sharpshooter's parapet, was
also looking for the sheriff, being careful, however, not to strain
her eyes.

On came the enormous herd, still compact and moving slowly.
The herders were keeping well to the rear, depending on their dogs
to preserve the formation. The rays of the rising sun gilded areas
of fleece while the morning breeze bore to the defenders of the gap
the odor that had earned the sheep the epithet "stinkers." The

sounds they made, some sharp, others quavering, with no rhythm or regard for pitch, began to rasp the nerves of the waiting cattle-men and their allies. Still no sight of Trout-tail III or Dr. Hyacinthe Toudoux.

"I shall have to get on without them," Evans said, disappointed. In five minutes more, he would give the word to fire and the battle would be on.

Fifty yards down the line, in a section of a zigzag trench allot-ted to the stretcher bearers, Galilee Zach was trying to peer through a periscope and keep his teeth from chattering. At last, in despera-tion, he left his post to seek out Stenka, whose machine gun was set up near by.

"You won't let me run. Now promise," Zach said, white with terror.

"There, there," said Stenka, comfortingly and smoothed his forehead with her horny hand.

Two minutes to the zero hour.

And then the mishap occurred.

It chanced that one of the sheep dogs, in advance of the herd, caught the scent of the defenders, growled, bristled and advanced cautiously toward the very trench in which Moritz was poised for action. The temptation was too great, since the plan of battle had not been made clear to him. Like a faun-colored black-tipped pro-jectile the Boxer shot out of his trench and was running so fast that when the shepherd dog saw what was coming and tried to brace himself, the impact knocked him clean off his pins.

"Front leg. Pass up the throat," said Moritz to himself, and crunched his powerful jaws around the ankle of the hapless collie. Two more sheep dogs were coming, on the run. Moritz was up and at 'em, fighting with ferocious coolness, feeling nothing but stimu-lation as the sharp teeth of the sheep dogs tore his hide and flesh. Crunch! One was out of commission, still trying, but helpless on three legs. Crunch. The other went down. Herders were yelling. Three more dogs, far distant, were approaching on the run. Then Moritz, with a breathing space, had a sickening thought. From the

trenches behind him, not a bullet had sped, although the front
ranks of sheep were dangerously near. It was he who had gummed
up the battle, by running into the line of fire.

Evans, pale and, for once, hesitant, could not utter the word
that would mean death to the dog. Miriam, in her crow's nest, was
half-blinded with tears. Kvek, awaiting the volley, was sizzling and
fuming like a peanut whistle.

Then from the line of trenches rose a gasp that in a moment
swelled into a cheer. For Moritz, front paws flying, hind legs kicking away loose dirt, was digging in. One inch, two inches, finally,
just as three shepherd dogs whizzed over him, he was safe in his
shallow dugout. Evans gave the signal, machine guns stuttered and
rattled all along the line, the sharpshooters picked off with rifles
sheep that looked like men in disguise, but avoided killing the innocent herders who soon got out of range.

The carnage among the front ranks of the sheep was shocking
to behold, for the oncoming woollies, never bright and decidedly
not at their best in warfare, came stumbling on, piling up dead
bodies until they could no longer climb over.

On the left flank, Grigori Lidin, Hank, Hjalmar Jansen, Old
Tumbleweed O'Flaherty, Diluvio, Long-time Pipe and Unreal Bear
were carrying out the flanking movement at a perfect canter, while
their leader roared a Caucasian battle song about wild grape blossoms and fate. Behind the first line of trenches, Lvov Kvek, Rain-
No-More, Shot-on-Both-Sides, Bonnet, Tinted Cloud, Jim Leonard
and the Professor galloped wildly around the right flank.

But although young Hockaday, the sheriff, was not covering
himself with glory, or anything but sheep, the ex-witness for the
State against Jim Leonard, known variously as Diocanne, Mike
Flato or Alky the Jerk, proved the man of the hour for the sheepmen. Seeing that his fellow gangsters were about to be outflanked
on two sides, the wily Italian ordered the Chicago contingent to turn
their choppers on the sheep behind and around them, and in no time
at all had improvised a sort of fort, or block house, the bloody walls
of which could not be pierced by enemy projectiles. And through
the chinks between dead and dying woollies, the gangsters set up

a murderous and accurate fire. They were cornered, fighting for their lives, and rose to the occasion in an astonishing way.

Lvov Kvek, seeing how the situation had changed, gave the signal to Grigori not to charge the fortress. Instead, he employed the cavalry forces in scattering and driving back westward the terrified sheep, without herders or dogs to guide them, until a full ten thousand were running in all directions, bereft of what intelligence they had in calmer times. If any of the woollies turned and tried to pass the deadline, Frémont's infantry sharpshooters picked them off singly and wasted few bullets in so doing.

So within a half hour of the opening of the first phase of the battle of the Redwater, the sheepmen's forces were trapped in a hollow square of dead sheep, with their chuck wagons and an ample supply of water, ammunition and arms and thirty remaining trigger men who could stand off cavalry or infantry without exposing themselves.

Evans, relieved that his casualties had included no deaths, but only superficial wounds, glanced anxiously northward again and sighed. He went up and down the line, cautioning the defenders not to expose themselves, for the moment a cap appeared above the parapet, some gangster took a shot at it and seldom missed. Frémont was concerned about the mutton. Would or would it not be possible to conserve it, if it lay long hours in the sun?

ONE HUNDRED AND TWENTY MILES AWAY, at the mouth of Redwater Creek, where it empties into the Missouri, the sheepmen's main army, under Larkspur Gilligan, was having an unopposed success. The footbridge had been set up across the ford and over it, at the rate of 3,600 the hour, were pouring sheep and gangsters, at a point not more than fifty miles from Opera Lodge. By the time the upper Redwater skirmish had reached a temporary stalemate, the other half of the herd, numbering fifteen thousand, were already on the cattle range and were working their way across the best grazing land at three miles per hour.

Furthermore, the outlaw Shoshones, with the Santos and Terry Gilligan, were crossing the Yellowstone just south of Leonard

Creek, Tall-Horse-in-Flytime and Noisy Snake having joined forces. They would reach Three Buttes by nightfall.

To give a proper understanding of Evans' anxiety and his reasons for allowing the battle to remain at a standstill on the upper Redwater, it is necessary to follow the movements of Trout-tail III and Dr. Hyacinthe Toudoux, who, it will be recalled, left the cattlemen's encampment on the eve of the battle, headed north and with empty gunny sacks tied on their saddles.

By riding relays of tough pintos, eating and sleeping in the saddle, and straining every nerve, the two scientists forded the Missouri at the only available point before the same ford was reached and appropriated by Larkspur Gilligan. But on returning from their mission on the northern stretches of the reservation, traveling more slowly because of the long pack train of laden mules driven by Blackfeet squaws and children that followed them, the doctors were dismayed to find the sheepmen in possession of the ford, with a bridge erected, and to watch helplessly, from a hidden point of vantage, vast herds of sheep pouring over the cattle range.

"We are lamentably unstuck," said Dr. Hyacinthe Toudoux.

"*Ki ma ka pi u*" (And how), added Trout-tail III.

"What shall we do?" asked the medical examiner.

Trout-tail smoked a pipe and stared into space about fifteen minutes, while 900 sheep got over the bridge. Then he spoke slowly and thoughtfully.

"The nearest bridge or ford, aside from the one which the enemy holds and cavalierly moved from place to place, is at Mondak, one hundred and fifty miles to the west. Our pack train could not reach it in six suns. That is bad," the medicine man said.

"Simply awful," agreed Hyacinthe Toudoux.

"Mr. Evans' strategy will be upset, his forces may be overpowered. That would be terrible."

"Catastrophic," groaned Toudoux.

"The sheep you see before you will, if permitted to graze many days, ruin the cattle range. Woe. Woe."

"Ghastly," Toudoux murmured and bowed his head.

"On the other hand," Trout-tail said, "Mr. Evans is an intelligent man, almost unique, in fact."

His companion perked up a little.

"When our swift advance courier does not appear, as agreed, Evans will understand we are in trouble. He has an airplane at his disposal. He will investigate. If not, you may call me a Ute," the medicine man said.

"I hope you are right," said Toudoux. "When I think of all those sheep and ruffians between me and my helpless Eugénie . . ."

"There are moments when thinking is disturbing," Trout- tail said, and passed the pipe. In a few seconds he was sound asleep.

Trout-tail III, medicine man of the Blackfeet, was not destined to be called a Ute, for Evans at just that moment was strapping on his parachute and ordering Cash-and-Carry Corkery to tune up the *Honi Soit*. He had recalled Kvek and Lidin, who had left a few riders to prevent the gangsters escaping to the westward, arranged a supplementary system of signal fires and heliograph signals and soon was in the air, glancing downward over the Redwater as the plane followed the course of the creek to the Missouri. Within an hour, he saw the sheep, the gangsters and the footbridge, to his dismay, which changed to laughter when he caught sight of the signal mound set up by Trout-tail's tireless squaws at the medicine man's command.

Gilligan, who had seen the plane approaching, was not alarmed. His sheep and his men were safely on the cattle range; so what could a single airplane do? Even if the sheep were stampeded, they could not cross the river or the creek, and would devastate the grazing land more rapidly if driven helter-skelter. Consequently, the gangsters gathered around the chuck wagons for a victory meal of deer meat and mutton, washed down with gallons of whiskey and wine, now and then waving defiance at the *Honi Soit* which circled aloft, then descended some distance across the Missouri.

Had they known what was in store for them, their blood would have turned to water, which they despised one and all, and their victory baked meats to ashes in their mouths. For Evans, the moment he was on *terra firma*, was shown the concealed pack train and began to throw back his head and laugh, as did Trout-tail III, Dr. Hyacinthe Toudoux, the squaws and children and even Cash-and-Carry Corkery.

"I didn't make you at first, cap, but blast me if you're not a card," the flier roared, holding his sides and choking with heart-felt mirth.

"Can you fly as low as fifty feet? We can't drop them too far, or they'll be stunned," asked Evans.

"I can skim off tall hats," said Cash-and-Carry, vaulting eagerly back into the plane, into the cockpit of which were loaded with great care a number of gunnysacks containing a mysterious and ever-shifting load. Evans tried the draw string that closed the top.

"O.K.," he said. "Dr. Toudoux. You and Trout-tail, with what squaws you have, will advance and cut the rope cables of the foot-bridge. They have left it unprotected on this side. This new ad-mirer of mine and I will do the rest, but to you gentlemen will go full credit."

The propeller spun, the motor roared, the *Honi Soit* taxied, took off, banked, then soared.

"The damn fools are coming over," said a gangster to Gilligan, who was munching a smoked deer's hindquarter with relish, and opening a bottle of High Life beer.

"Let 'em come. We can take a few pot shots at 'em, even if it doesn't do no good," Larkspur said.

The gangsters were seated in a compact group, half drunk and very gay, and the herd of sheep was already a half mile distant, in charge of the herders and shepherd dogs.

"Pass over them as low as you can, then turn sharply and fly over them again. After that, we'll chase the stragglers, one by one. There's nowhere they can hide," Homer said.

The *Honi Soit* did a series of jumps like a car on a roller coaster, so shaken was the pilot with merriment.

"You're all right, buddy. I'm for you. Understand. I didn't make you at first. . . . Haw, haw, haw. Kek, kek. Ho, ho," was the pilot's contribution, aside from a masterful handling of the plane.

With the greatest care, his hands protected with heavy leather gauntlets, Evans reached for one of the sacks of prairie rattlers and calmly examined the draw strings once again.

"You may descend when ready, Corkery," he said.

What follows defies description, but here goes:

Losing altitude steadily, the *Honi Soit* headed straight for the gangsters' feasting grounds, while the desperate crew on land simply reached for rods or choppers without troubling to rise. Evans moved the sack to the edge of the cockpit, released the draw string and as the plane passed over, he upended the sack and on the gangsters rained writhing snakes, their rattles vibrating angrily, their blunt wedge-shaped heads striking this way and that.

The *Honi Soit* had ascended, wheeled and was diving again. Another load of snakes was dumped on the fleeing gangsters.

Some of the mobsters tried to make the bridge, and found it had been cut on the northern side. Others dived into the water and tried to swim. Of the forty effectives, twenty were bitten and lay screaming on the flat, begging for mercy and for medical aid. One of the cooks carried his frying pan all the way to Cottonwood Creek, twenty odd miles away, before he remembered to drop it. The draft horses stampeded, riggers and skinners swore and waved white dish rags and fragments of underwear as the *Honi Soit* swept back and forth.

"Follow Gilligan. I want him," Evans said, chalking a message on a piece of board. In a moment they were over the frantic Larkspur, who lay flat on the ground. Homer dropped the message, Gilligan crawled over to where it lay, then stood up ludicrously and stretched his arms to heaven. He was in the same position when Homer, descending from the *Honi Soit*, approached him, automatic in hand, bound him, and slung him into the cockpit.

It was a short hop across the river, where the sheepman was handed over to the Blackfeet squaws for safekeeping. Toudoux, always the humanitarian, asked permission to ford the river and do what he could for the gangsters who had been bitten, and was accompanied by Trout-tail III. Evans, however, had other fish to fry. First he sent word to the sheepherders that they were to keep the herd grazing due west, toward the deadline and not to encroach another foot on the cattle range. Then, taking on a full load of rattlesnakes, he ordered Corkery, who now responded willingly to his slightest request, to get going again.

34
The Bloody and Ruthless Affray on Redwater
Creek and Elsewhere: Second and Final Phase

ONCE IN THE AIR, Evans was aware of a disturbing premonition that all was not well at Three Buttes, so he asked the willing Corkery to change their course and twenty minutes brought him over Opera Lodge where the watchful Laramee Bob signaled "O.K." Homer still was not satisfied, and directed the pilot to take the *Honi Soit* to the northeastern corner of the range, where the Blackfeet braves were holding the herd of shorthorns for shipment. To the astonishment of the Indians below, Cash-and-Carry, at Evans' suggestion, wrote *sup po ot tse sit* (content?) across the sky and the reply, in the form of tiny twinkling fires on the prairie was "*a*," or "yes."

From the delta, the flier followed the stage road southward, however, and Evans spied the furtive band of Shoshones, who in their haste to reach Three Buttes had thrown aside caution and were traveling in broad daylight. With his strong telescope, Homer was able to distinguish among the Indians, Baldy Santo, Tony Santo and young Terry Gilligan. Alarmed for the Blackfeet who had been guarding the prisoners in the badlands, Homer again changed his course and soon was over the hideout, where an emergency landing was made. Quickly he found the suffering tribesmen, bound and gasping with thirst in the bleak ravine, cut their bonds, left food and water for them, and hurried back to the head of the Redwater.

There, in the gap, he found the situation unchanged. The gangsters, and Sheriff Hockaday, were still holding their improvised blockhouse, which could not be attacked without risking the lives of many men.

Tersely Evans reported to Jim Leonard and Miriam what had taken place at the mouth of the creek, one hundred and twenty miles northward, and also what was threatening the garrison at Opera Lodge. Kvek and Lidin were called in from the cavalry patrol and within five minutes an eager detachment was headed for the ranch house on the gallop. Its membership comprised, besides the daring Russians, Chief Shot-on-Both-Sides, Rain-No-More, Hjalmar Jansen, Anton Diluvio, Hank and the Professor, and Hugo Weiss, to bring up the rear.

The remaining forces responded to mess call and were served by Corrigan and the colored waiters with mutton stew. Then, while Jim Leonard gazed at the bulging sacks of rattlesnakes and held his sides to contain his laughter, Evans ripped the cover from a case of dynamite and with carpenter's chalk wrote a message addressed to the leader of the besieged gangsters, whom he had identified as Alky the Jerk, who had pinch hit for Gilligan as the supposed father of Donniker Louey. Homer, who had talked with the District Attorney in Chicago, had promised not to bring back too many gangsters, since the office was snowed under with work, but only the one or ones guilty of killing the Englishman, Montmorency Lewson-Phipps. So his ultimatum to Alky the Jerk was a generous one.

"Disarm Sheriff Hockaday and surrender him to us. Afterward the rest of you may cut across the range to the railroad, on condition that you leave the State today."

The error Homer made was a psychological one. The terms were so generous that the gangster lieutenant could not believe in them. So after the board had been dropped into the fort from the *Honi Soit*, the trapped gangsters renewed their fire.

"I'll give them one more chance," Evans said, reluctant to slaughter his foes in cold blood. He asked Corkery to tune up the motor, and after the pilot had stepped into the cockpit, Homer took his place at his side.

Frémont, his eyes bulging, saw that the contents of the gunny-sacks were moving. "What have you there?" the Frenchman asked, and, when told, he sighed and, taking his voluminous report from his pocket, he tore it into bits.

"No use," he said. "In France it would not be believed."

"Don't let the snakes get Hockaday. I want to finish him off myself," said Miriam.

"This time the snakes will be rendered harmless. The prairie rattler, *crotalus confluentus*, is stunned if not permanently disabled by a drop of seventy-five feet. I shall pass over the fort at an elevation of thirty yards and release my first load. That will give them an idea of what is in store for them if they do not surrender," Evans said.

"Haw, haw. Ho, ho," roared Jim Leonard, and in his hearty laughter was joined by Frémont, Stenka and the Fish, both senior and junior.

"We must take home a sack or two, *pater*, to liven up the Union Club," Fitz-Henry, Jr., said.

An orderly came running. "Quick," he said. "They got the nance."

The take-off was postponed while Evans hurried to the section of trench in which lay Galilee Zach, who, bored by hours of awaiting the worst in hand-to-hand combat had carelessly exposed his head and shoulders above the parapet.

Homer made a rapid examination of the wounded boy and shook his head sadly. "Take him to the rear, with the utmost care," he said, and the expression on his face was grim indeed as he climbed into the *Honi Soit*. In the weeks since the crowd had left Chicago, everyone had grown fond of the game little pickpocket who was utterly without malice, and frank about his likes and dislikes, however bizarre.

The plane taxied briskly, then rose, as the gangsters behind the stacked carcasses of sheep took futile shots at the occupants.

"One hundred feet, if you please," asked Evans.

"As you say, cap," replied the pilot, but he shaved the elevation to seventy-five when Homer turned to place his sack of snakes in the alert position.

Now Evans had experimented carefully with rattlesnakes and knew what they could survive. Not so Alky the Jerk, the Great Lakes

Palefaces, or even Sheriff Hockaday, who was quaking in a mass of defunct woollies and begging the gangsters not to give him up. The *Honi Soit* passed over, Homer loosened the draw string, and a stream of writhing snakes descended into the gory blockhouse. The result was beyond anything Homer or the cattle range defenders had anticipated. For the fortress seemed to waver and the walls, like those of Jericho, went tumbling down, as gangsters, like startled quail, larruped every which way, forgetting even to fire. Some of them ran straight into the cattlemen's trenches, where they were clubbed into submission and tied up for future reference. Others ran out on the flat, to be ridden down by the remainder of the cavalry patrol. Alky the Jerk alone had the presence of mind to grab a couple of dead sheep as a shield for his head and shoulders, but old Tumbleweed O'Flaherty roped the fleeing ex-witness, sheep and all, and dragged him into camp.

In the ruins of the blockhouse was left only Sheriff Hockaday, demoralized and cringing. He was crouching in a corner, stained with blood and sweat, babbling and shrieking, and had not noticed that the rattlers strewn about him were limp and motionless. His eyes were protruding from their sockets, his hands clenched and unclenched spasmodically.

"Take 'em off. Take 'em off," he yelled.

There was one old rattler, not of the prairie breed but of the mountain variety, *crotalus atrox*, and he proved to be tougher than his fellows. Aroused by the frantic screams and motions of the sheriff, the old snake looked himself all over, coiled experimentally, and then set out across the hollow square to get even with somebody, and only Hockaday was available.

Meanwhile Miriam, still determined to settle accounts with the unscrupulous politician who had been willing enough to send her father to disgrace and death, risked snakes and bullets in a dash from the front-line trenches across no man's land.

"Look out. He'll shoot," yelled Homer and her father simultaneously, but the warning was too late. The girl, automatic in hand, rushed through a breech in the stacks of inanimate sheep just at the split second when the old vindictive rattlesnake, with a motion quicker than the human eye can follow, transformed himself from a tightly wound coil to a stiff projectile, straight as a ramrod, striking the gibbering Hockaday just below his glittering badge.

For a moment Miriam hesitated and was about to turn away, but quickly her gentler instincts got the upper hand and, after looking the fear-crazed Hockaday straight in the eyes and receiving what she took to be a glance of recognition, she fired from the hip and the merciful bullet went precisely through the heart. And in after years, whenever some association of ideas recalled the scene to mind, she was glad she had spared him the indescribable suffering that was in store for him. A snake bite on an arm or leg may be treated, sometimes successfully. That is not the case when a full-grown rattler sinks his fangs in the body and empties, by constriction of his powerful muscles, the poison glands.

So the sun on its westward journey beheld that afternoon the cattlemen's forces in triumph, completing their mopping up operations all along the Redwater.

The situation at Opera Lodge, however, was not so enviable, for Baldy Santo and his raiders, under Tall-Horse-in-Flytime and Noisy Snake, had upset all calculations in the following way: The reader will recall that while snow was still on the ground, Jim Leonard and his buckaroos had been obliged to turn loose a bunch of saddle horses on the Yellowstone. Unluckily the outlaw Shoshones came upon the bronchos grazing in a coulee near the stage road, just after Evans had passed by.

Beatrice Diluvio, at her post on the western butte, was therefore alarmed to see approaching on the dead run a band of strangers, most of whom were Indians whose war paint betrayed that they were not of the Blackfeet. Kindling a signal fire to give the alarm, the fair Bostonienne legged it to the lodge, discharging her rifle as she fled.

Laramee Bob, near the prisoners' corral, drew his Smith & Wesson. "Get up, every one of you," he said. "Stick up your hands and march to the lodge, or I'll drill you all right here."

The prisoners, all except Bat-ear McClosky, the mechanician, obeyed. The Smith & Wesson spoke twice, and each bullet shattered a bone in Bat-ear's right arm and right leg, respectively. The cow-boy had barely closed the door of the lodge when the first of the outlaw Shoshones rode tearing across the porch, yelling like maniacs. Young Terry Gilligan followed.

To defend the ranch only the cowpuncher just mentioned, Beatrice Diluvio, Eugénie Toudoux, Hydrangea and Wing Lee were available. But all of them, in their separate ways, rose to their sudden responsibility in a way the best among men and women, whatever their race or background, are likely to do.

"Wing Lee shoot plenty bum. Me watchee plisnas b'long one-piece blutcha knife," the Chinese cook said, and suiting the action to the word he took up the long butcher knife in one hand and a cleaver in the other and prodded the prisoners over near the bed in which Slipnoose Pete was sitting up, a six-gun in each hand.

Meanwhile Eugénie Toudoux, with a wry little moue, was trying to set up a machine gun and somehow she succeeded, so that when the second file of Indians rode yelling across the porch, she got at least half of them and put four bronchos out of commission. The attacking party, not knowing how few the defenders were, and that most of them were women who had led somewhat sheltered lives, grew cautious and wary. On the butte two Shoshones were stamping out the signal fire, but already it had been spied by a Blackfeet scout who was riding full speed to summon his tribesmen thirty miles away.

Slipnoose Pete, against the doctor's orders, tried to get out of bed, and fell flat on the floor. Wing Lee had the presence of mind not to take his eyes off the prisoners, however, and the convalescent cowpuncher finally dragged himself to a chair near enough the open window so that he could shoot whenever a gangster or an Indian rode that way. Thus he was able to pick off two of the Chicago palefaces who had taken part in the Muddy Creek raid, and send Baldy Santo's derby flying into the air.

"Let's smoke 'em out," said Terry Gilligan, with a wisp of dry hay in his hand. "Why wait?"

Noisy Snake at once vetoed that barbarous idea, not from humanitarian motives, but in order to preserve the hootch supply from possible ruin. In fact, the Shoshone lieutenant was stealthily creeping from one outbuilding to another in search of firewater and to his joy came on a keg of rye whiskey in the root cellar. Oblivious to the pleading of Baldy Santo, who blustered and threatened until Noisy Snake walked over and pulled the mutilated derby down over Baldy's face, the outlaw Shoshones forgot all else for the time and started drinking greedily.

Within five minutes, Bunkhouse No. 1, which had been appropriated by the Indians as a shelter, was a bedlam. Enraged by the Shoshones' insubordination, young Gilligan ignited his wisp of alfalfa and set the bunkhouse afire. Soon the building was in flames and the Shoshones, drunk and reckless, danced around it, clubs and rifles in hand.

Beatrice Baxter then had an inspiration. She pulled the rocking chair containing Slipnoose Pete, who was a dead shot, to the window facing the burning bunkhouse and as the Shoshones danced around clockwise, the injured cowpuncher potted them one after another until only Noisy Snake, who seemed to bear a charmed life, remained. Hydrangea, who had never fired a gun, took the rifles from the hands of the others and reloaded them. Wing Sam, who had escaped death so narrowly in the recent stampede, lit some joss sticks on his bed table and recited his version of *Rock of Ages* in a singsong voice:

> *Velly old Lock, plenty busted*
> *Maybe Wing Sam 'e hide bottomside.*

Just then, Tall-Horse-in-Flytime and his band of Shoshones reined their bronchos at the crest of the butte and charged down into the yard. The Shoshone Chief, being sober, ordered the half-empty keg of whiskey to be rolled away from the burning bunkhouse and guarded until the occupants of the lodge had been massacred or captured. Reluctantly Noisy Snake obeyed. Baldy Santo and the newly arrived chieftain went into a huddle and emerged with a plan of campaign. Behind Opera Lodge, which faced due north, the ground sloped rather steeply from the western butte.

An old Studebaker wagon was hauled up the slope, loaded with rocks and dynamite, and a fuse was attached to one of the sticks of nitroglycerine just as the vehicle was started rolling down the hill, headed straight for the rear of the ranch house. The defenders were aware of a roar and a frightful concussion and all of them, including the prisoners, were thrown flat on the floor.

When the smoke cleared away, it was discovered that a hole ten feet square had been blasted in the wall.

While Wing Lee got the prisoners back in order, after carving a Chinese character on the Paperhanger, as an example, Eugénie Toudoux dragged her machine gun to the breech and fired on the gangsters and Shoshones, wounding three, among them Tony Santo.

It became evident to Beatrice Baxter, who had calmly done her best to co-ordinate the efforts of her companions, that the danger was not from the invaders but the fire. With the weapons at hand they might be able to stand off the attack until help could arrive, but the flames had crept over the flat and a rising breeze was fanning them and causing them to spread toward the porch of the ranch house. Hydrangea, meanwhile, found a short length of hose in the kitchen, which she attached to the pump, and by working frantically the ex-Blackbird soaked the porch boards and the exposed walls of the lodge as best she could, until the hose was shot from her hand and riddled by the gangsters' bullets. Another wagon was being prepared to be rolled against the rear wall, filled with high explosives.

EVANS, MEANWHILE, HAD FLOWN to the reservation across the Missouri, where Larkspur Gilligan, still unable to believe his clever scheming had gone so definitely wrong, was trying to intimidate the Blackfeet squaws who had him in durance. Their only response had been to sit on him, shaking with laughter, and cut off the ends of his handlebar moustaches for use as charms. Both Trout-tail III and Dr. Hyacinthe Toudoux were still busy with the snake-bite cases, eight of which had proven fatal, and a dozen had a chance of recovery. To calm the inflamed nerves of the sufferers, the

Blackfeet boys had been given the tribal drums and were making the best of their rare opportunity.

Frémont, sitting in the headquarters dugout at the head of Redwater Creek, was trying to piece together the fragments of his torn report, to which he added:

"To sum up: I find that American police are less bound by precedent and tradition than we are in Europe, if indeed it can be said that Americans are bound at all. I have witnessed, in the course of the enforcement of a single injunction, the ingenious use of a hardy shrub called sagebrush; hordes of domestic animals, the meat of which was afterward smoked according to a formula I shall obtain for use in France; and innumerable live rattlesnakes which apparently can be rented or purchased in sacks containing at least seventy kilos by weight. Needless to say, in crowded cities this method of subduing criminals would be unfeasible, because of danger to bystanders, risk of the serpents escaping and causing panic, etc., etc. Aside from that would arise the problem of supply.

"I do not wish to convey the idea that Americans are more, or less, lawless than the citizens of older nations. That is a misapprehension fostered by our sensational press. The willingness of North Americans to take part in violent action of practically any kind, and at all times of day or night, arises, I am forced to believe, not from contempt of the law, but a sense of personal responsibility for its enforcement.

"There is in the United States a Federal Bureau corresponding very loosely to our *Sûreté Genérale*, but for reasons I have been unable to fathom, the agents of this national detective force confine their activities to the surveillance, one is tempted almost to say persecution, of women of the demi-monde and are indifferent to threats against the public safety, generally. Occasionally the attention of these federal officers is diverted to members of left-wing parties, but this is only in times, I understand, of political stress. Thus the citizenry is obliged to interest itself in the preservation or disruption of public order, assisted by local police officers who are under a system of neighborhood control which requires them to think first of popularity with minor political lieutenants called variously 'ward heelers' or in rural districts, 'leading citizens.'

"I cannot urge too strongly the abandonment of any attempt on the part of France to copy or adapt American police methods, and if French methods were imported here, one of the picturesque spectacles of our century, in fact, of the Christian era, would be marred if not obliterated."

BACK AT OPERA LODGE, Eugénie Toudoux and Beatrice Baxter were in desperate straits, but no one would have suspected their plight, so calmly and considerately did they comport themselves. Out of earshot of Hydrangea and Wing Lee, who were making heroic efforts to subdue their excitable natures and keep up the defense, Madame Toudoux said to her Boston friend serenely:

"If the wagon of dynamite now being prepared is rolled down the hill and enters the breech in our wall, the explosion will wreck the house, *n'est ce pas?*"

"*Probablement, madame,*" agreed Beatrice Baxter, pushing back a wisp of honey-colored hair from her shapely forehead.

"Still, of course, one cannot surrender," said the scion of the Faubourg St. Germain.

Beacon Street's entry came up to scratch in a way that would have stirred any true American's heart, had there been disinterested spectators to the harrowing scene.

"I quite agree. Were the Indians less drunk, one might buy them off, but I fear they are beyond any mercenary appeal," Beatrice said.

"Too bad," murmured Eugenie.

"Let us comfort the others," said Beatrice, and approaching Hydrangea she placed a warm hand on the ex-Blackbird's shoulder.

"Things are going rather badly, my dear," she said soothingly.

Hydrangea glanced toward the hilltop, where the second Studebaker, bright blue against the sage, was being loaded.

"We've got to do something," said the girl from Harlem.

"It will be over in a moment. *Bon courage,*" said Eugenie Toudoux.

The prisoners set up a howl of protest, causing Wing Lee to hop around them like a cricket, brandishing his knife and cleaver.

"You ought to let us go. It's in the articles of war," said Bird's-eye Cohen, who had served in the A.E.F., but mostly in the guard house.

"We'll put in a good word for you with Baldy, the big shot. So help me, we will," added the Paperhanger.

On the hill, Noisy Snake was igniting the time fuse.

Suddenly Hydrangea had an idea. As part of her training as a dancer, she had played indoor baseball with a mean underhand delivery. In desperation she grabbed up a pineapple hand grenade and as the death wagon rumbled down the slope, cheered on by the gangsters and outlaw Shoshones, the ex-Blackbird fumbled with the pin, loosed it, and counted: "One . . . two . . . three." Then carefully she took aim at the moving Studebaker, and her excellent sense of timing came to her aid as she tossed the grenade a full twenty yards. The pineapple described in the air a tantalizing parabola, fell square on the load of rocks, and a deafening crash shook the lodge to its foundations, but the explosion took place outside and the building remained secure.

"Well tossed," said Beatrice.

"Ingenious," added Eugénie, kissing the fainting Hydrangea on both cheeks.

It was just that moment that over the crest rode, neck and neck, four reckless riders who had outstripped the others of the rescue party. Ahead in the lead was Rain-No-More, and a triple tie for place would have been revealed by the fastest lens as Shot-on-Both-Sides, his blood stirred by memories of ancient wars on the Shoshones, and the wild Russians, Lvov Kvek and Grigori Lidin, tore into the group on the hillside, and took the enemy unaware. The Blackfeet wielded tribal war clubs grotesquely knobbed and knotted; the sabers of the Russians flashed. Shoshones and gangsters went down, weltering in their own blood, and those who escaped the first onslaught ran straight into the pathway of the rear guard of the rescuers.

"There's Anton. Oh, darling. Get him. Cut that other one in two. Oh, be careful. There's another," cried Beatrice, as the bow arm of her husband beat a merciless tattoo on the heads and shoulders of the fleeing Indians.

Hjalmar Jansen, whose weight had caused his horse to fall slightly behind, spotted Terry Gilligan and Young Santo making for the twin springs as fast as they could run. Urging on his panting broncho, Hjalmar caught up with the young bandits and dismounted. Terry tried to shoot, but too late. He was lifted in the air by a haymaker and had not landed flat on his back, out for the count, before Hjalmar had caught him by the feet and, using him as a club, bowled over Tony Santo. The Professor, meanwhile, had roped Baldy and was dragging him down the hill to the lodge. When the cowpuncher slid off his broncho, the gang chief was still alive, but was bruised almost beyond recognition. And while the hunt for stray Shoshones was still in progress, the main body of Blackfeet came streaming in from the east, clinging closely to their swift pintos and uttering as of old the tribal yell.

Lvov Kvek was drinking from the unfinished keg of whiskey, handling it as though it were a liqueur glass. Then gallantly he passed it over to Hjalmar and Grigori, who had spotted the Colonel from afar and believed themselves entitled also to refreshment. Beatrice was clasped in Anton's fond arms, Hydrangea and Eugénie Toudoux were consoling each other. Slipnoose Pete, in defiance of medical advice, was crawling toward the keg, clad in a nightshirt, on his hands and knees. Wing Lee was lugging water and wet blankets to put out the remnants of the grass fire.

"You ride well, my son," said Shot-on-Both-Sides, who was passing the Blackfeet in review. And his son who was soon to succeed him returned the old Chief's gaze with frank admiration.

"I had the better horse," said Rain-No-More.

The Chief gazed wistfully to where the Russians, Hjalmar and the buckaroos were tapping a second keg.

"Go and drink like a man," said Shot-on-Both-Sides. "For me and for your tribe."

35
Asbestos

IN THE COURSE OF THE GEOLOGIC ERAS through which it had passed, the cattle country of the Lower Yellowstone had furnished the setting for strange and wonderful things. But nothing in the long unwritten history of that remote land could have exceeded in verve and variety the ten-day feast around Opera Lodge, held in celebration of the cattlemen's victory and the sheepmen's rout.

Trenches were dug in which were barbecued, under the direction of Cromwell and Washington, prime steers, elk, deer, domestic swine, and mountain goats. There was roast meat in plenty, but no mutton on the bill of fare, the entire supply resulting from the battle having been smoked and sold in bulk to the Swedes in Minneapolis. The Blackfeet cooks prepared rods of the famous tribal sausage, resembling the Balearic *sobresada*. Wing Lee, with the help of the prisoners who took turns at K.P., served fresh mounds of fried potatoes, and baked innumerable pies. Beer and whiskey were rushed in wagons and by pack train from Mondak and Glendive, and flowed as copiously as the springs on the hillside.

The occasions for celebration were so numerous that special days were set aside, one for the Blackfeet to pay tribute to the sun and to perform the sacred tobacco rites, and at twilight on that day, Shot-on-Both-Sides called the tribe together, which then included the entire company of white allies, and solemnly pronounced his farewell.

"I am old," he said, "but not too old to see Paris."

Two skins of the sacred white buffalo were spread on the ground, and the tribesmen filed past, bearing in one hand a strip of bark on which had been burned the sign of their choice for a new chief. At the request of Shot-on-Both-Sides, the election was presided over by Hugo Weiss, who was introduced as a paleface champion counter of tokens. The multimillionaire had never had a simpler assignment, for every vote cast was for Rain-No-More, whose speech of acceptance was translated on the spot into six languages.

The nuptial ceremonies of Tinted Cloud and Sergeant Schlumberger were performed in Indian fashion, and later were confirmed by a priest. So, to even up matters, Unreal Bear and Sergeant Bonnet were married first by the priest, and later by Trout-tail III, the medicine man.

Huge tables had been built out of doors, and one of these was reserved for the prisoners, who were to be judged and sentenced on the next to the last day. Gilligan, intact except for his moustaches, was chained at the head, and Baldy Santo, dented derby on his head, was tied securely in his place at the foot.

Jim Leonard played the genial host, and years seemed to have dropped from his shoulders as he surveyed his friends, victorious. The charge of murder was never even mentioned again in the new Dawson County court house, which was built of concrete with Ionian pillars from Montgomery Ward. Evans, however, consented to give a public elucidation of moot points in the case and by means of amplifiers rigged up by the friendly juryman who was also an electrician, Homer's voice was carried to all corners of the ranch.

"The task of identifying the corpse Mr. Gilligan endeavored to pass off as Donniker Louey was simple, indeed. First of all, I noticed that several members of the Santo gang wore the same style of Oxfords as did the corpse and, through the agency of the junior counsel for the defense, I learned that in the course of a raid on an enemy saloon, Santo's gang had broken into a shoe store adjacent and helped themselves. Now the measurements of nearly all the gangsters were on record in Chicago, and only one wore the size shoe found in the grave. He was called Bangtail Charley, who was taken for a ride as a disciplinary measure, on orders of Baldy Santo, later was shipped to Gilligan on ice, along with several salmon, and buried on Cottonwood Creek by the sheepherders Stumpbroke and Jill. Am I right, Mr. Gilligan?"

"Don't rub it in," the sheepman said.

"Now as to that flower of evil nurtured by teeming Illinois, who was known as Donniker Louey . . ."

The Blackfeet leaders, Shot-on-Both-Sides and Rain-No-More, betrayed their keen interest by turning on a demi-shade more of the tribal inscrutability.

"Donniker Louey," continued Evans suavely, "has joined that one and half of one-tenth of one per cent of our citizenry which, according to Dr. Louis Dublin of the Metropolitan Insurance Company, disappears without trace each year in this republic. Mr. Weiss has been generous enough to offer, at my suggestion, a handsome reward for any information concerning the missing man."

"But what about my Remington 40-40 and the hole in the corpse, whoever you say he was?" asked Jim Leonard.

"I should have brought that out in court, if necessary. The path of the 40-40 bullet, and Dr. Hyacinthe Toudoux will bear me out, shows definitely that it passed through the body of Bangtail Charley some weeks after the said Bangtail was defunct and dead. In passing, it obliterated the trace of the bullet that actually killed Charley, in so far as could be observed on the surface. A few inches inside, of course, the second bullet was deflected by a rib and cut a swath all its own.

"Someone in the Gilligan entourage simply borrowed your rifle, Mr. Leonard, from the nails above the doorway, and substituted another of the same make and caliber. Later the guns were transposed again. That was before we had our faithful Moritz on the job."

The Boxer, who had been catching up with some neglected eating, looked up and wagged his tail, left-right, left-right.

"I have extradition papers and authority from Cook County to take back to Chicago any or all members of the Santo mob, but I shall not burden Illinois with an excessive number of criminals. Antonio Santo was one of two men who shot Montmorency Lewson-Phipps, and that young man will be shipped East for trial." (Laughter from young Gilligan.) "Santo the elder, I am turning over to the North Dakota authorities to answer for having murdered in cold blood the station agent at Mondak.

"Already I have arranged with Tumbleweed O'Flaherty for his campaign for the office of sheriff of Dawson County, now vacant, and his election is assured. Those of us who know the candidate are convinced that his regime will mark some much-needed reforms."

Larkspur Gilligan groaned.

"Now, as for Mr. Gilligan. He was indiscreet enough to outline his terms on which he would accept our surrender, at a time when he fatuously supposed he had the upper hand. He was about to drive Mr. Leonard from the range, send him in exile to California, and make me his candidate for State Senator, as a part of his political machine. I shall be no more exigent. Mr. Gilligan will clear the eastern range of larkspur and other noxious weeds, drive what sheep he still has down into Idaho and cede his rights to the Yellowstone Valley grazing lands. He will then construct a model bungalow in Monterey, California, and give his parole to remain there except at times when he has written permission from Mr. Leonard to leave that paradise of artists and intellectuals for the purpose of clearing his excellent mind. His son will quit the State of Montana and will not return until he has completed a full course as an aesthetic dancer with the Diaghileff ballet." (Uproarious laughter on the part of young Santo.)

"Mr. Jackson, proprietor of the Glendive X-Ray, I regret to say, cannot be with us, having chartered a plane to undertake a commission for Mr. Weiss in Siberia, but in the meantime, his assistant, Mrs. Myra Patterson, will carry on as editor, at Mr. Jackson's urgent request."

The privilege of returning Mona Mason and her three staunch hookers, with the professor and the piano, free of charge, to the citizens of Mondak was extended to Rain-No-More, who thereby gained much good will for his tribesmen.

Hugo Weiss, on the third day of the feast, let it be known in New York that he was safe and sound, and on the fourth day Jim Leonard's profits on the stock transactions amounted to four million dollars. The bewildered rancher had barely recovered from the shock of sudden wealth when Fitz-Henry Fish, Sr., acting for the former Miss Baxter, announced that gold had been struck in the Old Glory mine, a rich vein having been discovered when foundations were dug for a saloon and chop suey restaurant in Red Dog. So not only the ore lugged in from Nevada but the genuine lode boosted the mining stock to fabulous prices and started a gold rush that brought prosperity to all Montana.

So on the fourth day of the feast, following an exchange of telegrams, Weiss's large staff of accountants, after working forty-eight hours and wearing out sixteen adding machines, computed the Leonard fortune at seven hundred and fifty millions, at the most conservative estimate. Beatrice Diluvio's holdings had doubled, and Hugo Weiss's pile had almost tripled, which was the only gloomy note in the festivities. But, in order not to spoil the party, the genial billionaire took his immense gains in good part and sighed philosophically.

"Another coup like that, and bang goes the capitalist system," he said. "Perhaps I shall attempt it, who knows?"

Throughout the days of carouse and merriment, Larkspur Gilligan sat wrapped in studied impassivity, but late in the afternoon of the fifth day, just after a bucking contest, the defeated sheepman asked leave of Homer to say a few words.

"Brothers and sisters," began Larkspur, "I can take my medicine as well as the next man, without turning a hair. Only one thing I want to say, and then I'm off for Monterey.

"I lost this fight, not because Jim Leonard's square-shootin' is good policy, but due to under-ratin' my opponent. So I want to warn you not to draw any foolish moral conclusions, like a bunch of psalm singers, but to catch on to yourselves now you've got a big stake and play fast and loose like me. You'll thank me for this, before you get through.

"That's all, and damn your eyes."

Glossary

Airedale	A faithful lieutenant; a yes-man.
Algonquian	An American Indian nation or language group in the northwest of what is now the United States.
Andouilletes de Vire	Famous Norman sausage.
Au point	Exactly ready.
Appleknocker	A rustic or hick.
Baptism	Dilution of liquor.
Bat	Whore.
Beetles	Girls.
Beetlebuzzer	Ladies' man, Rudolph, riot with the skirts, etc.
To bell	To complain (Pidgin English).
Bird's-eye	Weak shot of dope.
To blow one's top	To go crazy; lose one's mind.
Boilerplate	Syndicated news, with or without pictures.
Bokis	Box, container, airplane (Pidgin English).
Borscht	Beet soup.
Bottomside	Below, downstairs, under, lower, etc. (Pidgin English).
Bridgeport	Any city or town except New York or Chicago.
Broad	Girl.
Bronc	Broncho, imperfectly broken horse.

Buckaroo	Cowboy (from Spanish, *vaquero*).
Bullhorrors	Fear of police.
Bump off	To kill.
Butte	Flat-topped hill.
Button	Chin or solar plexus.
Caboose	Car used on freight trains for the crew.
Can	Posterior, safe, privy or toilet, receptacle for beer.
Can-can	Sprightly French 19th-century music-hall dance.
Canot	Lifeboat (French).
Canshooter	Safe blower.
Cathouse	Disorderly house, lupanar.
Catoot	Epithet, equivalent to "damn."
Cayuse	Horse or pony, not thoroughbred.
Cecil pusher	Drug peddler.
Chi	Chicago.
Chopper	Machine gun.
Clink	Jail, hoosegow, can, cooler, etc.
Coot	Water bird which behaves unpredictably and makes weird sounds. "Crazy as a coot." "Drunk as a coot."
Corny	With an obvious or vulgar appeal, old-fashioned.
Corpus delicti	The body of the crime. Sometimes used to denote the dead body itself.
Coulee	Creek, dry most of the year
Coup stick	Indian wand notched to record achievements officially acknowledged.
Crow Water Society	Honorary society among Blackfeet braves.
Deadline	Line separating sheep and cattle ranges.
Dick	Detective.
Dip	Pickpocket.
Dogie	Range cow.
Donniker	Pot, chamber pot.

Dry farmer	Farmer whose land is unirrigated and who must depend on rainfall.
Dudelsack	German bagpipe.
Dusted	Fled, left, departed.
Eight-ball	Negro.
Behind the eight-ball	Out of luck.
Fire strip	Plowed area around ranch buildings, to protect them from fire.
Flat	Table land; freight car without sides; pancake.
Flok	Fork (Pidgin English).
Four bits	Fifty cents.
Fourflusher	Braggart or boastard, pretentious fellow, bluffer.
Frame-up	Conspiracy to incriminate.
Frigola	Thyme.
Frisk	To search.
Fudge	The establishment of a mediant point.
Gaboon	Cuspidor.
Gon	Gonif, thief.
Gondola	Freight car with no top and low sides.
Gonk	To strike on the head.
Hearse rap	Life sentence.
Heebie-Jeebies	Nervous agitation.
Heeled	Armed or flush.
Highball	To proceed (railroad term).
Hooker	Whore, prostitute, loose woman.
Hookshop	Whore house.
Hooley-ann	To ride a wild horse.
Horse Opera	Western movie.
Jackpot	Scrape or predicament.
Jim-swinger	A frock coat.
John	Backhouse or toilet, Rhett and Scarlett.
Kettle 'em	Thump 'em with your heels.
Killpecker shift	From midnight to breakfast.
Knockers	Testicles.

Legaler	Lawyer.
Lemming	Rodent.
Loco weed	Marijuana, or *Cannabis Indica*.
Lunch hooks	Hands.
Marc de Bourgogne	Liquor distilled from apples after cider has been pressed out.
Mesa	Flat land, literally "table."
M.F.H.	Master of Fox Hounds.
Mobster	Gangster.
Mollbuzzer	Robber of women, gallant.
Monniker	Name.
Mulled	Drunk.
Nipper	Child, infant (Strictly, "unweaned").
One piece	One, a, or the (Pidgin English).
One-piece Mary	A white woman (Pidgin English).
Onion	Head.
Palooka	Strong and well-meaning, but inadequate party. A failure, for lack of natural equipment.
Paperhanger	Writer of bad checks.
Pepperoni	Medium spiced Italian sausage.
Piegan	Tribe of Northwestern American Indian.
Pineapple	Hand grenade with long handle and corrugated bomb.
Pinto	Parti-colored horse.
Plaires	Prayers (Pidgin English).
Police	Verb, to clean up (Army usage).
Pour in leather	To beat with quirt.
Powwow	Conference.
Prickly Heated Throne	Electric chair.
Pulling leather	Grabbing the saddle horn.
Punk	Young man physically loose and mentally unprepossessing.
Puss	Face.
Reefer	Cigarette impregnated with marijuana.
Rod	Automatic pistol.

Sachem	Chief.
Schnozzle	Nose.
Scissorbill	Non-union-minded itinerant laborer.
Sent	Elated or inspired.
Sibley stove	Flared stove-pipe with large end resting in sand, with door and damper.
Skinbeater	A talented drummer.
Skinner	A driver of horses or mules.
Slicker	Oilskin raincoat.
Slough	A wide and shallow creek.
Sobresada	Balearic sausage flavored with saffron.
Sorrel	Very light brown.
Spondoolix	Money.
Squat	To live on government land before filing papers. To be electrocuted (Hot squat).
Squirrel Meadows	Grass plots of the genus *hordeum* with bushy spikelets.
Steer	Castrated bull.
Stiff	A corpse.
Stinkers	Sheep.
Talk box	Telephone (Pidgin English).
Tarp	Tarpaulin.
Tea	Marijuana.
Tepee	Indian tent.
Tinhorn	A gambler; a cheap or unreliable person.
Tommygun	Sub-machine gun.
Topside	Above stairs, the sky, upstairs, up, high
Trigger man	Gunman.
Ts'ow E'e fly	African insect with annoying habits.
Twist 'em	Rein him.
Typewriter	Machine gun.
Untouchable	A man who cannot be bribed.
Whack	An eccentric or mildly crazy person.
Woollies	Sheep.
Wrongo	An outsider, or unsympathetic person.
Zipper Mug	Shut up.

Coachwhip Publications
CoachwhipBooks.com

The Mysterious Mickey Finn
Elliot Paul

The Mysterious Mickey Finn
ISBN 1-61646-293-0

COACHWHIP PUBLICATIONS

COACHWHIPBOOKS.COM

Hugger Mugger in the Louvre
Elliot Paul

Hugger Mugger in the Louvre
ISBN 1-61646-294-9

COACHWHIP PUBLICATIONS

ALSO AVAILABLE

Mayhem in B-Flat
Elliot Paul

Mayhem in B-Flat
ISBN 1-61646-295-7

COACHWHIP PUBLICATIONS
COACHWHIPBOOKS.COM

THE QUINNY HITE
MYSTERIES

CHINESE RED · HERE LIES THE BODY

RICHARD BURKE

Quinny Hite Mysteries
ISBN 1-61646-247-7

THE QUINNY HITE
MYSTERIES

THE FOURTH STAR · SINISTER STREET

RICHARD BURKE

Quinny Hite Mysteries
ISBN 1-61646-248-5